The Global View

The Global View

The Goldman Trilogy Book 1

W.L. Liberman

1

Toronto, 1995

My father, Ephraim Goldman, was considered a great man by reputation, by aura and through a highly visible public identity. Who considered him great, you may well ask? Well, he hobnobbed with Prime Ministers, advised Presidents and was on intimate terms with royalty; albeit in his words, 'ersatz aristocrats'. He knew Berenson, Bertrand Russell and Marc Chagall. In his office, behind his desk, there is a photograph of him shaking hands with a shy, rumpled Albert Einstein. Einstein, the man who put absolute destruction within man's reach and with his halo of white hair looked so harmless, like a kind uncle.

Once, he shared a private plane with Armand Hammer of Occidental Petroleum. They played chess together and my father remembered it as 'fun'. Mr. Hammer named his chess pieces after famous works of art, so it was even more painful for him to lose. "My, my," he muttered as my father swept a bishop, "there goes 'Guernica'." Hammer chewed his purplish lips in pain as my father snatched Van Gogh's self-portrait. After Hammer lost the match, he advised my father to invest in drilling futures.

"I don't know why such people would pay attention to me," Dad used to say. "After all," he'd continue, "I'm just a modest history teacher who thinks about politics and world affairs, that's all. Nothing special about that."

But there was, of course. My father wrote a book, 'The Global View', that was published by William Dent & Sons in 1955. His editors thought the book far too academic, but went ahead anyway. They'd had a bad year and hoped to crack the college market. It sold 100,000 copies in hard cover and that made it a publishing phenomenon. And now, some forty-five years later, it continues to sell 75,000 copies every year without fail. The book has been a miniature gold mine.

The Global View has been through six printings, revised twice and issued in paperback. It has been translated into fifteen languages and sold in sixty-five countries worldwide. The BBC, CBC and PBS have all filmed documentary specials about my father. He has become a TV star, although it is a medium he cares little about, but he acknowledges that it plays a vital role in global communications and reflects many of our cultural values. That's an intellectual's way of saying it's bullshit.

He has written other books, of course, but none of them were as well-received as the first. And what a success it was. It brought both academic and popular acclaim. He has been a visiting professor at Harvard, Oxford, the Sorbonne and Salzberg. Editors snapped up every article he wrote. Prestigious magazines like Harpers, Fortune, the Atlantic Monthly and the New Yorker published his essays. Both Time and Newsweek featured stories on him, and all of his books have been reviewed, usually favorably, by the New York Times Review of Books. His career has been long and fulfilling, especially so for a humble teacher of history.

Apart from being his son, how do I know these things? As it turns out, I am writing my father's biography. Writing his biography while he's still alive has advantages and disadvantages. He intimidates me, to be blunt about it, but mainly it has forced me to examine our relationship, which has been remarkably lousy.

"Don't worry about objectivity," my publisher, Julian De Groot said. "Just write from the heart. Readers aren't interested in a clinical analysis. They want to know the man. And who is better qualified, I ask you?" Then he smiled, leaned back in his leather chair, and lit a cigarette. He ran long, slim fingers through his sleek white hair.

De Groot stared at me impassively, his thin lips slightly pursed, fishing for an angle. "Do you know", he asked lazily, "whether your father was always faithful to your mother?"

His words sank in slowly. It was a question I had asked myself many times but wouldn't admit it to the likes of De Groot. The truth was; my father was very much a stranger to me. We had never really talked in the way I would have liked. In the way other fathers and sons, who shared things together, talked. Baseball. Stamps. Fishing. Girls. Music. These were a few of the things we never shared. We had never gone out and got loaded together. Never goofed off together. I had no idea what sort of inner life he lived. He'd always been thrifty with his feelings, saving all his excess energy for work.

"After all, he traveled a great deal on his own, didn't he?" De Groot reasoned and slid one fine transparent eyebrow up to his hairline, giving his long face a lopsided appearance, like a disproportionate mask.

"Yes, he traveled quite a bit," I replied. "But that doesn't mean anything, you know."

"Have you seen his correspondence?" De Groot countered, glancing at a mass of disheveled papers heaped on his desk, then flicked his eyes up at me.

"No, I haven't," I admitted. "But I don't intend to pursue this line in the book, De Groot. This is not a book for supermarket check-outs."

De Groot smiled again and pointed a nicotine-stained forefinger at me. It looked like the finger of death, long and knobby.

" There's nothing wrong with supermarkets," he sniffed. " They sell a lot of books. I've even bought some there myself. Just remember," he warned me, "we want the man, Bernard. All of him, the warts, hidden thoughts, nestled secrets."

"I'll do what I think is best," I said.

"You have illusions about him?"

"Probably," I snapped

"You may have to shatter some, you know, to get what you want. Press him until he's uncomfortable and tells you the truth. Some of it may come as a shock to you but ultimately, it will be very revealing. You will gain from this," he assured me, pulling at his thin nostrils, "It will be worth the pain."

"Jesus, he's not dead, you know. He's my father and I have to deal with him. And the rest of my family. I have to think about that too." I saw myself ostracized, but De Groot wasn't listening to me. He was hearing the coins drop into the till, his head ringing with the music of silver.

De Groot looked at his wristwatch, a Concord, then rose smoothly. He eased me out of the office, smiling like an undertaker, sizing me up for the coffin. "I just want you to be productive, Bernard, and write a book that will build on your reputation and also..." here he paused and looked down at me fixedly, crooning in a low mellifluous tone, "...sell as well as can be expected." He took my hand in his. It was very dry, like smooth, light paper. The palm was curved and quite plump.

"Keep me posted on your progress. I want to see a draft by October first. Make it brilliant."

How did I get myself into this? I thought.

To my shame, a $20,000 advance had been a very powerful persuader. So, I felt guilty about the money and guilty about the subject. What if my father had been a philanderer? Or worse? It would make a juicier story on the surface. If people wanted to divine his thoughts, they could read his books... that seemed reasonable. But his books were cerebral, full of cogent analysis and layered anecdotes set out in logical sequence. My father's writing left himself, the blood, the heart and the guts, very much out of it. His intelligent vista curtained the background, fashioning a 'spiritual form' for the dialogue in which he enjoined the reader. I pictured that phrase – spiritual form – liberally sprinkled throughout his text. He'd popularized it. His thoughts were so painstakingly shaped that admiration might be the only genuine reaction upon realizing, as a reader, the intricate body he'd constructed. Very impressive, indeed and appealed to every bloodless, sterile sensibility imaginable. He wrote like a soulless, mirthless automaton, albeit one with sophisticated circuitry. I'd read ten words and drop from boredom... and frustration.

No matter how clever, it was still just a construction, like the shell of a skyscraper – clean and flawless and built like a pragmatic machine. A literary Volkswagen that gets you where you want to go. Up, in this case. De Groot slavered after a portrait of Eph Goldman which let it all hang out. He wanted to give the mundane reading public something to drool over. Did I want to write a tell-all book for the tabloid-obsessed masses? I think I did. I really think I did. Jesus.

My nuts were in the squisher. An interesting dilemma. And the only person who could help me solve the dilemma was the elusive subject himself.

Daddy-O.

2

I located him by the glowing tip of a medium-sized Rheas which brightened then lessened in intensity, like an uneven pulse. He was seated on the flagstone patio watching the blinking lights flicker across Georgian Bay. We were staying at the summerhouse for the weekend. Just he and I. It was a chance to try out our new roles because of this new 'connection' between us. I was now his official biographer and that changed things. He was acting as if everything he did or said would be recorded for the book. As if he expected me to follow him into the john with a microphone, asking what it's like to pee and think simultaneously. I could imagine his response: "Hard to say, but my right leg is wet."

The cigar end drew a short arc in the air as my father waved at a mosquito buzzing near his face. The night was pleasant and light and full of smells. Pungent smoke, damp grass, the sweet musk of roses and the luxuriousness of buttercups. The humidity wafting up from Georgian Bay rotted everything. Especially wood. That's why Eph decreed that the deck should be cast in stone, the summerhouse built of brick and the furniture forged of wrought iron. Nothing would ever give way or crumble beneath us. There were no let-downs from the physical world. We would never be disappointed by a chair, the stone picnic table, or the plastic laundry stand. "Brick is more permanent," my father often said, "wood is a natural disintegrater."

De Groot didn't know my father well and imagined a self-effacing academic with a lot of secrets. A man who held his chin in hand and thought deeply about everything, but did not put himself above normal feelings and temptations. Someone he suspected of being a closet hedonist with at least two pregnant coeds hidden away in some secluded dorm. De Groot always suspected something more.

The tip of the cigar brightened again as he held it close to his face, exhaling smoke. I made out his profile, the still-thick white hair, curling in the back around his neck, the broad nose and pointed jaw. The high forehead, breastplate for a brain of rare ability, many would say. It was a sensual face, full and fleshy, except for his eyes which were too small and a limpid blue. They were a bit chilling, I thought, revealing a crunchy layer of perma frost piled deep within. I'd felt it many times when I'd made him angry, just playing about the house, making noise, knocking over things – as kids do. He'd stalk out of his study, teeth clenched, fists balled, eyes hardened like ice crystals. Growl like a bear, bellow like a pig caller. I was the one who always got into trouble. When not fighting with me, my brother, Harry was really a very good child and quite placid. But I liked to act things out and whoop and holler in the throes of make-believe. Things seemed far more real if they were vocalized but my father didn't seem to understand the needs of the imagination because he didn't have any. And imagination demanded noise. So, he wasn't at all appreciative. I realize now I was just trying to attract his attention, attention that was glued to the books and notes in that gloomy room. Any sort of attention was better than none at all.

"Come on out and sit down," he said gruffly. "Would you like a cigar?"

"No thanks."

"They keep the mosquitoes away."

"I know," I replied. "But they're not too bad tonight."

"Why are you doing this book thing?" he asked suddenly, although he continued to gaze at the water. The bay wasn't visible but we could hear the sound of water lapping faintly on the shore. A ghost sound. My throat tightened.

"I'm not really sure, to be honest," I said hoarsely, then made a guttural noise deep down in my chest. I snorted. "I was given an advance."

"Do you think writing about me will make you famous? Is that it? Do you want to expose me?" He sounded like a political columnist now, pressing a sensitive point.

I laughed. "Expose you how? What is there to expose?"

"Isn't that what De Groot wants, Bernie? An exposé?"

"I think he wants a good book, Dad. That's all. People are interested in you. Biographies are very popular these days."

"I see," he answered in a non-committal, dead tone. "Bernie?" The voice came hard like pressed cement.

"Yes?" I stuttered.

"I'll make you a deal…"

"What kind of deal?" I asked, clearing my throat.

"A fair deal. You know I don't like De Groot. He has a low mind and thinks only of exploiting people to make money. I know this project could mean a lot to you. Don't forget that before I wrote The Global View, I hungered for an audience. I wanted to reach out, to influence people with my thoughts and aspirations. So, I can understand that impulse, son, better than you think."

"Okay," I said. "What's the deal?" In past situations, where we had made deals, I had come out on the short end. Consequently, I was wary of deals. There was a pair of skis, I recall, that I never owned, a trip to France on which I was never sent and a loan that never materialized. "And it better be good," I warned him.

I thought I saw him smile. "Okay, tough guy. Here it is. If you're so determined to write this thing, then I challenge you to write a book as popular as The Global View." He stopped to let me consider, but just for a second.

"Am I missing something, or where is the deal part?" I asked, puzzled now.

"I'm coming to that."

"Well, let's not rush or anything."

"The deal is this… I will step out of it, the whole thing. I will graciously fade away and cede my spot to you. In fact, I will actively work toward making that happen," he said.

"Some deal," I retorted. Short-changed again. But then I thought a moment further. "Is there something you're not telling me? You almost sound… fatalistic."

"Maybe, I am." he shrugged. "But that's nothing new."

He dropped the cigar onto the pavement and watched it slowly die out. "Now then. What about our deal? Are you in?"

"For what it's worth?" I said, which was probably nothing, "sure, I'm in." Humor him, I told myself.

He grunted. "Good. That's good." And made a smacking sound with his lips. "Why don't you get us a drink. I'll have some of that brandy we keep under the sink… for medicinal purposes," he said wryly.

"Okay."

"Will you join me?"

"Why not?"

I moved off, slid the screen door open quickly, then shut, not wanting to let any mosquitoes inside the house. The evening had taken on a timbre that seemed quite strange. I had a feeling of anticipation, a queasiness in my stomach. I experienced a kind of dreaded excitement as I wondered what he would say. Part of being a parent was keeping secrets, I knew that. Children never really knew their parents or much of their lives before becoming parents, withholding from us a vital part of the puzzle masking who Mommy and Daddy were. And maybe they were entitled to them. Maybe we should never know. We couldn't figure our parents out and perhaps that was one reason we failed miserably to understand them. Or were too afraid to admit how much like them we were.

I returned to the deck carrying two tumblers of brandy. My father's mood had turned from pensive to somber now and he accepted the drink immediately. He held the crude glass in his gnarled fingers, the knuckles swollen with arthritis, the joints splayed at different angles. Perhaps he was having second thoughts about lifting the veil of fatherhood? We were just people now, two adults, and I could see the idea of it worried him. *He cared about what I thought of him.* A surge of emotion welled up in me from nowhere, some cavity, something I had suppressed for years; tenderness... compassion... I wasn't sure, but I almost felt sorry for him. His life was nearly done and now he was on the verge of baring some pain. I just knew it. I had desperately wanted that, to feel something back from him for as long as I could remember. Feelings were doled out like a prized liqueur, drop by drop, just enough to sting the tip of your tongue, leaving you wanting more.

"You think you know me," he said, sipping the brandy. I grunted at the irony of it. His lips glistened from the liquid and his mouth was set almost in a smirk, the blue eyes knowing, quizzical. But there was no laughter, no happiness in that deserted grin.

"Maybe," I shrugged.

"I felt the same way about my father, you know. I've come to the conclusion that every son thinks he knows more in the end. But I've come full circle..."

"We actually know less...?" I interjected.

"Less?" He laughed, then drank some more and waggled a bowed forefinger at me. "We know nothing. Nothing!" he spat emphatically, underlining it in the cooling night air.

"And what is it we're supposed to know about?" I asked.

My father looked at me and I could only see his age. The drawn cheeks, the whitish stubble pebbling his long chin, the lace-netted wrinkles gently etched in the creases of his reddened eyes. The deep grooves pressed into the broad forehead whose widening expanse built the fortification protecting that cogent mind. All masking the bones and tissue of a naked white structure beneath. The physical part of him had grown old and so had the spirit. I heard a new lament of fatigue in his voice that drooped, then faded when he tried to speak at length. His sentences trailed away now whereas, when he was younger, each phrase carried upward cutting through a packed lecture hall with force and vigor. His words bravely reverberated with tone and tenor and drama, a force that commandeered the audience's attention. Listen to me, it used to say. And they did. With rapt seriousness. *Perhaps this is it,* I thought, rather melodramatically, *the last hurrah.* Then cringed, as I thought it.

"Why, everything," he exclaimed. "Love, sex, feelings… the whole shebang. It. It being whatever you want because it doesn't matter. You know, I was an arrogant son of a bitch when I wrote The Global View. Really thought I had the answers. And you know what? A lot of people thought so too. But they were as ignorant as I was. It was all very much an elaborate lie. The whole thing."

"Don't you think you're being too hard on yourself? You believed it at the time. That's what really mattered."

"What the hell do you know?" he growled, then pulled himself back. "I mean, that's a very charitable view, Bernie. But damn it, I can't abide charity. Maybe I've grown more arrogant over these last forty-odd years. Smug. Thought I was smarter than everyone. But when you grow old it doesn't matter. Dying wipes it all away."

I was puzzled. "What are you so bitter about? You've had it pretty much your own way. You always have." I tried, without success, to keep the bitterness out of my own voice but it went right by him.

He raised his glass and examined it, searching out the answer in the amber depths of the sloshing liquor. After a long pause, he said, "It didn't matter because you always think of yourself as different. And no matter what you've achieved, it's never enough. You're never satisfied. Which is why…" he continued, looking through me now, "it's easy to be such a bastard at times. Nothing else matters but you. There are those moments when you absolutely loathe yourself…"

"But it's that restlessness that keeps you looking for new answers, drives you forward."

"Maybe. I used to think so, but now I'm not so sure."

"And this has something to do with your challenge to me? To surpass The Global View?" This was a peculiar kind of test and I was feeling uncomfortable, nauseous almost.

"That's only part of it…"

My father continued to stare at the ground between his feet, shoulders sagging. He rubbed the back of his neck again before he finally nodded. "I'm a fool and a fake," he said, his voice infused with anger. I saw the rigid set of his jaw as he shook his head in disgust. "I'm afraid of dying… Bernie, I'm afraid of becoming pointless… meaningless." His voice broke, his lips trembled with rage. "Of not being… remembered."

"May I quote you on that?" I asked lightly. If my levity was offensive, he gave no sign he'd heard me but continued with mounting passion. There was an intensity about him that was new to me. Clearly, something had broken.

"I wanted so much to be a success. To be more and have more than everyone I knew. A new car. A nice home. And most importantly, freedom to do as I liked. I wanted your mother to be proud of me and after that first success, I strutted around like a vain peacock, feeding on the attention. Thriving on it like it was a seductive drug or a lusty woman. I felt such intense pleasure in those days. It was like a smooth caress that made your body tingle from head to toe. Thinking about my good fortune then actually gave me goose bumps. And it all came from here," he said, tapping his forehead. "That was the best part of it. It wasn't looks or athletic prowess or connections, but intellect. My God, I loved it. I had become famous because of it. And it made me feel absolutely exquisite. It was a kind of luxuriousness. Like the feeling of fine fur or pure satin, or simply of the earth, as if to just touch the ground itself every single moment was pure joy. Don't you see, Bernie? I spoke with Einstein. He asked me to visit him. We shared thoughts and ideas. Think of it. A young man, barely thirty-five years old speaking to Einstein as an equal. Can you possibly imagine what that was like? I felt as if I was in the forefront of a new movement of thought, a new wave… it was so intense, so exciting."

And then his voice dropped to a hoarse, sad whisper. "At the same time, Bernie, I was ruined. The Global View hadn't made a difference. It had not changed the world, or even touched peoples' lives in any fundamental way.

A way that made any difference at all. The realization of this came on like a hurricane, like some evil howling wind.

I remember lecturing at Columbia in the fall of 1962, in front of two hundred social scientists. And it struck like a hammer blow. My mouth dried, I lost my place in my notes, my thoughts became scrambled. The sea of faces in front of me merged into a bilious mass as I suddenly… just… *lost* it. What I was about to say seemed totally and utterly irrelevant. I was irrelevant," he said, with a short dry laugh. My father looked at me hollow-eyed. "At that precise moment, I knew I was only mediocre." He stopped for a moment and I could almost feel his thoughts burn.

I realized now that he looked at me and saw someone else. I finally understood him and knew too, here was my opportunity to do my best work. The time to take my place in the literary sun, a moment for which I had hungered. Yes. He had been ridiculed by the ironic nature of history. I could see now how maddening that must have been.

I stood apart and listened to him curse his luck. Curse his empty heart and soul. He did touch me. Oh yes, on my honor, he did. And as he sat there wrenched with despair, my mind raced as I thought not how but where this episode would fit into the book. Oh, my father. I will mold you into a ruined God. De Groot would love it.

3

I felt like a thief in my father's house – I had no right to be there. The room, which had been my mother's sewing room on the third floor stood abandoned. He never came up here. This room housed memories. And mementos. That's why I'd 'broken in' to the house without telling my father, ransacking her old tin trunk, an immigrant's trunk which shrieked 'steerage'.

I pawed through the layers of ribbons, material, buttons, and needles; all of my report cards and Harry's too; my high school graduation diploma and my university degree. He'd be home anytime soon. My fingertips brushed a wad of tightly-bound paper envelopes. I freed them from the heap of cherished refuse. A photograph spilled out of the bundle and fluttered to the floor. I picked it up.

It came as a shock, a sharp jolt of recognition and dismay. The hair was long and disheveled, giving him a wild, mad Alice Cooper look. The face I saw was my face but it had mysteriously sprouted a full moustache. Instinctively, I touched my smooth upper lip. I noticed a rakish glint in the dark eyes. I glimpsed an air of devilry about him.

Whoever he was, he wore a dark suit jacket that was too tight across the shoulders and short in the sleeves. Why was this person's photograph in my mother's old tin trunk?

I turned the photo over gingerly, the edges brittle and cracked. The image had traveled over a great distance, passed from hand-to-hand, creased and bent a little more after each stage in its lengthy journey until it arrived in Canada. Luckily, it had been bandaged in a letter. On the back, I saw my mother's rounded, fluid hand: *Isaac, 1928*. My mother knew him and presumably my father, so why didn't I?

I picked up the packet of letters and fumbled with the string. The knot had become brittle with age and I snapped and tugged at it impatiently. Each letter had been preserved in its original envelope. The ink had faded, but I could make out my grandmother's name and part of an address. Inside, the paper crackled. I spread the first letter on the table and looked it over. Apart from the date, I couldn't read a word. It looked as if it had been written in code and the handwriting, though uniform and neat, slanted sharply backward. I flipped the pages over. He'd signed it off all right. There was the name... Isaac. At least I now knew what this unreadable code was... it was Yiddish. But it left me with a grave dilemma. How to read the damn things?

For some reason I couldn't really explain, I didn't want my father to know I'd found the letters. I suspected I'd come across something secret and hidden and didn't want to share it. When I heard the door slam two floors below and knew my father had returned, I piled the letters into my leather satchel. I made no secret about being there – he would have seen my car anyway – and trod noisily down the stairs, not minding the creaks and groans. He was in the study, sitting at his desk writing already, even though he'd only just come in.

"Thought I heard you," he said, without turning around. "Want a cup of tea or something?"

I shook my head to his back. "I was just going."

"Find anything useful?" he asked, which made me start for a moment and forced me to try to sound more casual than I felt.

"No, not really." Then he looked up and eyed me solemnly. I could never fool him or lie convincingly and he knew it.

"How's the book coming?" he asked, knowing that I dreaded the question.

I shrugged. "Haven't really started it yet. Uh, still doing the research." He nodded at that, understanding how foolish it was, but didn't let on.

"Well let me know when you need to talk about something. Do I get to check the technical details at least? Prevent any glaring inaccuracies that may arise unknowingly?" He was prodding me now, mocking me, once again.

I wanted to yell at him but I didn't. "I don't know. I guess so. Um, I'll talk to De Groot about it."

He nodded again, that of dismissal. "You do that." And before I could turn to leave, he spoke up. "Everything okay at home? Sharon and the kids?"

"Yeah, fine. I mean, Sean had a bout with the stomach flu again. Nathan never seems to get touched by it."

"How are they doing at school? What about their school work?"

You'd know if you came around more often, I thought. And it reminded me of the lack of interest he'd exhibited toward Harry and me. "Great, they're doing great. I'm really pleased, Dad, really. I'm very happy with the program." The boys nattered in French all day and now, in grade four, they chatted away effortlessly. I couldn't say as much for their writing, but that would come in time.

I had to go and prepare supper. They'd be waiting for me. "I've gotta go Dad. It's supper time."

He turned back to his work. "Right," he said.

And that was that. I could have thrown a brick at his head, but I didn't. I realized I had to let him live, at least until the book was finished.

As I drove home, I thought the thought that had been in the back of my mind for twelve years—I didn't know why Sharon agreed to marry me. Why have we stayed together?

4

I lived in a 4500 square foot teardown in the suburbs – mid-town. That was Sharon's choice and since she'd paid for it, I didn't have much say in the matter. I'm not complaining; it's a beautiful house.

Sharon and I had made our deal but I couldn't help feeling it had been a mistake. Sharon was Irish born and emigrated when she was five. Ten years later, her parents split up. There was still a trace of an accent which came out when she was angry or drunk. That evil thought... why did she marry me?

Sharon is impulsive and emotional. She and her three brothers and mother fight like rabid wolves; then after they've got it all out, tearfully kiss and make up. If you cross her, or break a confidence, Sharon will carry it to her grave. Talk about carrying a grudge – my god, the McCarthys cast the mold when it came to unforgiveness. They took the concept of vendetta and carried it to new heights. Once that sacred trust was lost, it was lost forever.

It wasn't her father's infidelity that split up Sharon's parents, although you'd think that'd be enough. No, it was the fact that Sharon's father broke a confidence in public, something personal her mother held close to her heart. I never did find out what it was. Couldn't be trusted because I'd married into the family and was and always will be, an outsider. One evening, when friends were visiting and he had more than a few beers in him, Rory spilled his guts, whatever it was he said, and laughed, encouraging hoots and hollers all around. The audacity of him. Well, that finished it for Felicity, never mind the screwing around. His coffin was nailed, bolted, and hermetically sealed. When Rory awoke the next morning, his clothes were packed and sitting on the doorstep.

"You dark-eyed bastard", she screamed at him, "you ruined my life!" And with that, she threw him out and never regretted it for a second, she said. That was sixteen years ago. Rory's since taken up with a girl about Sharon's age and is playing in a country bar band.

Here was the deal: Sharon would have the high-powered career and I would look after the domestic things; cooking, cleaning, shopping, and all of the minutiae to do with the kids–doctors, dentists, swimming, piano, hockey, daycare, car pool and so on. At the time, at the ripe old age of twenty-two, it seemed pretty good to me. A beautiful, full-blooded, intelligent woman on the verge of great success – we both knew it and accepted the fact – had propositioned me. She'd thought it all through carefully –she was a planner, no question about that – and long before I came along, she'd worked it all out.

I'd known her for about a month when she told me about it. In fact, I don't even think we'd slept together yet, or maybe just once. This is what she said:

"I want to get married, have a wonderful career and a perfect family, are you interested?" Laying it on with the musicality of the Irish in her voice, lifting the words at the end as if performing a lyrical ballad.

All I could think to say was, "Go on." As she talked, I realized that she'd sized me up perfectly, or at least, unlike most women I'd dated, listened to what I had said. I talked about wanting children, not wanting a conventional job, not climbing the corporate ladder, about writing and working from home. It didn't hurt that I was obsessed with her and if she'd told me to live in a wet dungeon and pee in a bowl, I probably would have.

Her three brothers were brawny, strapping young men, fair-haired, snub-nosed, and blue-eyed – rarely seen without a beer in hand. When they gathered together, her relatives talked at once over and above and across each other, seven different conversations going non-stop, all the babble seeming to make sense to them. I was baffled and couldn't understand a word. Once I followed a thread, I'd get lost, pick up another one and follow that for a bit, then lose it until I gave up. It was simply hopeless. Now and again, I'd catch her watching me. She'd give me a quick look or glance and smile at my confusion. Her brothers were all older and sounded as if they'd just arrived fresh from Donegal that day. Instead of conversation, I heard notes and tones climbing and wailing up and down different vocal scales. The two eldest, Kevin and Patrick, were pipefitters and staunch unionists. They were solid, family men who went out to work each day at seven and came back promptly at four-thirty to wash up and eat their dinner. It was as if they'd carried on the life of earlier generations. Instead of crawling around inside the bowels of massive ships down by the dockyards, they worked on the automated assembly lines of Ford. "We're learnin' about computers," they said, in the knowledge that if they didn't, like as not they'd be replaced by a blinkin' machine.

The youngest of the brothers, Egan, was a painter. Felicity said that giving birth to Egan caused her so much pain that she was in agony and that's how he came by his name. I believe her worst agony was yet to come where Egan was concerned. He was sheer motorized energy and raw nerves, darker of mien than his brothers, a bit of a brooder, a puzzler of meanings, unpredictable, volatile, and completely untrustworthy. I loved him immediately. He was funny and kind, and in my untutored opinion, enormously talented. But he drank prodigiously and snorted a wide variety of chemical substances. But whenever he came to himself, this young, blond giant was a sweet, sensitive soul who never got over the desertion of his father. He expunged the pain through his art and to some unfathomable degree, his relationships. His art. Enormous canvases breathing color, filled with caustic images of martyrs, crucifixes, doom and destruction, worlds exploding, lives colliding, souls screaming but all done with that touch of impishness, that bit of what I loved so well, irony, which made his work both moving and amusing and powerful.

On one of those puzzling and confusing evenings, I found myself drinking beer with Egan on the back step of his mother's house. After Rory left her, Felicity decided she wanted to get out more and see the city. So she got a cabbie's license and drove a hack for ten years. The cab company recognized that she had rather intimidating organizational abilities and promoted her to dispatcher. And now, she's the head dispatcher for the largest cab company, Ruby Cabs, in the metropolitan Toronto area. She worked hard and saved her money and bought herself a "wee house" in Cabbagetown, before the prices for renovated brownstones skyrocketed.

My father found the McCarthys amusing and enjoyed their company as if he were attending an entertainment. Felicity's salty talk and vivacity tickled him and he treated her with the greatest respect and amiability. Once she got to know me a bit better, Felicity never refrained from giving me motherly advice that I accepted with a shrug and rarely took even when she was right, which was most of the time. She had a hard knowledge of people and behavior and didn't refrain from voicing her opinions, even if it meant she had to be cruel to be kind, according to her way of thinking.

"Are you riding her?" Egan asked me.

"I beg your pardon?"

"Are you riding my sister?" he asked again casually, more naturally curious than menacing but you could never be too sure with Egan.

"Are you asking if we're sleeping together?" I replied.

"Right, man. Have you never heard that expression before?"

"No, but I get the gist and the answer is yes."

He nodded. "I figured. I'd do the same in your place, man. She's beautiful right enough. Are ya gettin married? No reason to just because you're riding her, you know. Though Ma'd have a different opinion, you can be sure, but she's from another era, a bit more of the prim and proper, that's her all right." This was typical of our conversations, as if he just needed an ear to talk to, someone willing to be his audience for a time. And of course, there were those surprising twists and turns in his chatter and questions which seemed to come from the ether, that told me Egan was no fool and a savage intelligence lurked behind the wild man brow.

"What's it like being a Jew, Bernie? Did ya get the shit beaten outta ya in school? Did the other kids bully ya an' all? Did they throw money at yer feet?" And before I could answer he'd go on.

"We had one Jewish kid on our block at home, Barry Greenberg was his name. God, what a character, wasn't he? He was a tall kid and reedy like and very clever, by god. Clever in school, I mean but he wasn't afraid, neither. His folks came after the war and Barry was born there. The father was a kid when they come over and an amateur boxer. He and the granda opened a gym, as a kind of sideline, like, to their regular business which was runnin' the book-ies, ya know, and taught sporting skills, boxing chiefly, to the kids in the area. They'd a good roster an' all and a few of 'em made it to the Olympics. You ever hear o' Billy McInerny? Christ, hands like flies, a blur they were, you couldn't even see 'em comin' at ya and then before ye'd blink, yer on the canvas."

The more Egan drank, the thicker his accent became and the words began to slide together as I struggled to make sense of them, to decode what he was say-ing. "Anyway," he went on after polishing off his third beer since we'd moved out on the step, and while I was nursing my first, "one day a kid by the name o' Devlin Shaughnessy stopped Barry on Derry Street, near our house, you know? I was sitting on the stoop just passing the time. I'd be about eight or nine and Barry was maybe twelve. Devlin was just one of a group of local bullies who liked to pick on those who were weaker, but he wasn't from the block, you know? He didn't know Barry at all, just that he was a Jew. Devlin was a bagger, you know what I mean? Stocky, thick in the body and the head. One of his pals knew Barry was a topper, you know? A polished pugilist, you might say, but he fought with a kind of incendiary fury, like a white-hot flame burned in his heart but he never let it get out of control – but the heat, the flame of it inside was intense.

He always knew who he was, did Barry, and was sensitive like. So Devlin, who was a couple a years older, by the way, calls out to Barry. He says, "There goes that dirty Christ killer, that dirty jew Greenberg." Barry stopped in the street and he was wearing, like, this sort of pea jacket I guess you'd call 'em, and he kept his hands in his pockets. He was half a head taller than Devlin but skinny and weak looking, not the sort who'd give ya a thrashin' anyway, but Devlin didn't look at Barry's expression, the heat in his eyes, he just kinda bored in, in his stupid way, you know? And Barry stood there with that look, a look of anticipated enjoyment almost as Devlin moved in on him with his pals behind him, eggin' him on."

"Come on, Greenberg, you dirty jew bastard, fight me if you can!" And Devlin turned to look over his shoulder and give his pals the thumbs up, like he's got Barry quakin' in his boots, you know? But that was all Barry needed, just that bit of an openin' and as Devlin turned around, Barry's hands were all over 'im in the quickest flurry you'd ever see, swarmin' like and in about a second and a half, Devlin had blood comin' out of his nose, a swollen lip and he hit the pavement flat on his back before he could take even a bit of a swing. And when he went down, he stared up at Barry like a wounded animal beyond the reach of knowledge or understandin', like how could this a happened to 'im in front o' his pals on the street, in front o' everybody like that – wasn't possible, was it?

And then that fire, that white-hot fire in Barry's expression burned down a bit, you could see that the heat o' it was gone, you know and he reached a hand down to help Devlin up but Devlin was still dazed and shook him off preferring to lie there, I guess – I don't know really, doesn't matter. And Barry said, "I hope I didn't hurt you too much," and said it with feelin' like he meant it, no smilin' or anything like, he did it because it was expected but it wasn't really somethin' he enjoyed, you know? And then Barry looked around him and nodded, kind of casual and sauntered off about his business." And then Egan turned and gave me a penetrating look. "It was then that I learned to respect the Jews," he said. "So if yer goin' to be my brother-in-law, that'd be fine, but ya know if any harm comes to Sharon I'll beat the shit outta ya meself, assumin o' course that ya don't come from a long line o' boxers, Bernie. Okay?"

I nodded and grinned. "Fair enough," I said. How could you not love someone for that? He'd won me over just like he expected to and we'd been allies ever since, even though we're as different as beagles and banjos. Then seeing our heads together, Sharon popped out the back door and gave us a look of feigned disapproval.

"Hey, what are you two on about? You look guilty as sin."

"Nothing," I said. "Just talking."

Egan raised his beer and grinned at her. "That's right, luv. Just talking, no harm is there?"

That evening, during the car ride home, I asked Sharon to marry me. And wouldn't you know, she actually said yes. We were twenty-two years old.

5

I knew I was late and I arrived home anxious and excited and curious about the booty I'd smuggled out of my father's house. Sharon was propped on a stool with her elbows on the island in the kitchen, an island in the storm I thought, safe haven amidst the chaos of family life, a glass of white wine by her elbow. A Garth Brooks CD blared from the stereo. She was still in her work clothes, an Anne Klein II tailored, cream-colored suit and matching shoes. Her hair gleamed burnished gold in the glare of the kitchen lights. She looked a bit melancholy but with Sharon I never knew whether it was just her Irish nature or something that happened at work. She glanced up as I blew in the door.

"You're late," she said.

"I know. Sorry. I'll go get the kids." It was my job too, to pick them up from daycare by six o'clock. It was now five minutes to and we'd be charged an extra twenty bucks for every ten minutes after the hour. Fortunately, the Merryvale childcare center was less than three blocks away in the school the boys attended. I could be there in forty seconds flat. I know, I'd done it before.

"Don't bother. I've got them already. They're downstairs, futzing on the computer."

"Ah."

"What were you doin'?" she asked, knowing that I knew this contravened the deal, that it was a transgression in our contract being late, but tonight her voice sounded weary, as if she didn't care one way or the other.

"I was at my dad's, poking around, that's all."

"Find anything? Anything useful, I mean?"

"I don't know. Maybe. Listen, I'm sorry about being late. I'll get some supper organized quick as I can."

She took a sip of the wine. "Don't worry about it, luv. I've ordered in, anyway. Have a drink. How's Eph? How's he doing?"

"Ordered what?"

"Ach, just a pizza, that's all. Don't sweat it, okay?"

"He's fine. Just the same. Busy with work. I only saw him for a moment. He came in later on, just as I was leaving."

She smiled then. "Ah, so you were nosing around on your own, were you? Peeking in drawers, checking out the closets and underwear? What's in the fridge?"

"Now why would I do that? It's my father's house, after all, not some…"

"Stranger's?" she finished it up for me. "You know what I think?" I didn't answer because it wouldn't have done any good anyway. She'd tell me whether I wanted to hear it or not. Sharon was a lot like Felicity in that way. She turned to face me more directly, wriggling her hips on the stool. "I think you're writing this book for yourself. It's an attempt to figure him out, maybe even take him on in a way, best him if you like. I mean, the parallels, Bernie, are striking."

"That sounds like another human asset course talking," I said, knowing that Sharon loved going on these seminars that delved into the human psychology of employer-employee relations and thinking it gave her keen insight into the everyman's mentality.

"Don't knock it. Those courses have done all right by me and us, haven't they?" and she raised her hands to indicate all the riches about her. She was right about that, in fact, she was always right about it and it sawed on my nerves more and more.

"Pizza here?" screamed Sean, as he raced down the hall and slid into the kitchen with Nathan, grinning as he stomped up the stairs hitching up his pants behind him like he always did. "Hi Dad," Sean said as he slid up to my ankles and stopped. "Cool slide."

"Hey Bub. You know I've told you not to do that. This isn't a baseball diamond, much as you'd like to think it is. Hey Nathan. You guys have a good day today?"

Nathan, swarthy and sleek-looking, his short, dark hair cut like a seal's pelt, nodded. Looked more like an Inuit every day, wide dark eyes staring at you unabashedly. "I took him out in Marathon, again. When's the pizza coming?" he asked.

"Oh shut up," Sean yelled and jumped at Nathan and instantly they were tumbling on the floor.

"Hey, you two heathens, knock it off. Somebody's going to get hurt. Sean. Nathan. I mean it," Sharon said her voice cracking with strain as they were a whirlwind now, all motion with no beginning or ending, and then inevitably turned to me, like she always did, as if she were just a bystander. "Do something, will ya?" She was saying, 'this is your responsibility, so take care of it'. I lent myself wearily to the task without enthusiasm.

I clapped my hands. "Okay guys. Your mother's going to hit the roof in a second. Get up now or it's an early night for the two of you. Come on now, let's go." No reaction. "Let's go. One more time." Still, no reaction. "Okay, here we go." And in my sergeant-major drill instructor voice bellowed out. "Counting down... one... two..."

They always timed it perfectly, sensing the margin of safety before I hit three, the danger zone, the point of no return, where they knew I'd have to do something, take away a privilege or punish them somehow depending how much anger I'd built up or how Sharon reacted. They played me for a sap and I knew it but it was part of the game in our family life that abided by its own mysterious rules and boundaries. Most of the time, everyone stayed in bounds.

The two of them lay panting and laughing at our feet, not really caring but just tired from the exertion of it. No one ended up crying. This time. "Get up now," I said sharply. Nathan pulled himself up and made a big show of dusting himself off.

"When's the pizza coming?" he asked again.

Sharon looked at her watch. "In two minutes or it's free. Come on you two, go and wash your hands while I set the table. Off with you now."

Before Nathan could make a beeline for the bathroom, Sean had tugged his pants down below his hips and scampered off laughing like a crazed elf. "You asshole!" shouted Nathan, taking off after him.

"Christ," Sharon said. "Don't they ever bloody well stop? It makes me crazy when they're so hyper."

I put my arm around her shoulder and leaned in to her. "Nice to see you," I whispered. "Did you have a good day?" She put her face out to be kissed and I obliged.

"Ach," she replied, in that husky way she had about her. "The usual crap. But I took care of it."

"Like you always do."

"That's right. I do, don't I?"

She left the question hanging as the doorbell rang for the pizza deliveryman. Sharon looked at her watch. "Thirty seconds to spare," she said, sliding off the stool. I watched her go and felt yet again that tingling, even after all this time she was still a mystery to me. I didn't know what she wanted and was always too embarrassed to ask but I did know that she excited me like no one else. During the day when I indulged in idling moments and allowed my thoughts to drift, inevitably, I strayed back to her. In my sleep, even during erotic dreams and fantasies, it was always Sharon I saw, no one else. Perhaps that's why they always seemed so real.

6

"What are you thinkin' about?" Sharon asked, tipping her glasses down her nose, dropping the financial reports into her lap.

"Yiddish."

"Yiddish? What about it?"

"That I can't read it and never bothered to learn."

"So what? Are you thinking of taking lessons?" She seemed amused, a smile playing upon her full lips.

I told her about the letters I'd found but not about the photograph. I don't know why exactly but I wanted it to be my secret for now.

"So, why do you think these letters, in Yiddish, are important?"

"I don't know. I just do."

"What are you going to do about them? Can you get them translated?"

"Yes, I suppose so. That'd be the best thing."

All logical and making sense, and that seemed to satisfy her, that a plan of action had been decided and she went back to reading the reports, thick wads of computer printouts, pushing the glasses back up her nose to focus properly. But as I was thinking about it, not just any translator would do. It would need someone I knew, someone I considered trustworthy and who wouldn't blab to my father, who was too well known in the community and beyond. Someone a little bit out of touch. I lay back in bed, as I always did, staring at the ceiling, hands folded behind my head.

After some minutes, Sharon sighed, removed her glasses, reached over and shut off the lamp and rolled on to her side away from me. I moved in behind her. Sharon had been spending longer hours at work, coming home later, pushing us into the background of her working life.

"What's that?" she said.

"Nothing."

"It's a helluva lot of nothing," she retorted reaching behind her, then laughed. I felt her probing fingers. "Come on then or I'll be dead in the morning."

Afterward, I lay awake and I thought about those Sunday mornings I'd dreaded with old Mr. Bernstein, the Hebrew teacher. From ten until noon, I sat in the study of his old house that smelled of milk of magnesia, pickles, and mothballs while he droned away in my ear, relentlessly drilling me in preparation for my bar mitzvah, the big day. He wasn't a bad old guy really, just slightly deaf with an incredibly loud voice.

I never said anything to him, never offered comment unless I was asked and I think he did his best to make me cry, to break me down but he never succeeded. I guess that was just his way, carrying on some tradition that had been drilled into him at the yeshiva in Poland all those years ago.

The chairs were hard and uncomfortable, the house smelly and stale, the glasses sticky but my god I learned that bloody portion of the Torah and my god I learned how to sing with feeling, with power, with depth without even being aware of it. So I had the old man to thank for that.

In the intervening years, I'd lost track of old man Bernstein but do remember that every New Year, my father dropped off a bottle of whiskey and usually took me with him, and made me deliver it while he waited in the car. I always felt guilty because I figured the old man wanted me to continue on, but he never said anything, I just knew.

Over the three years, we'd established a kind of trust and understanding so that by the end it wasn't such an ordeal and we actually talked and he let me ask him questions about his life and background and explained as best he could about the Torah and interpreted the Hebrew for me since there wasn't actually time to teach me to read it.

In the end, I grew to like and respect him and realized that he had been taking my measure. When Harry was going, sometimes I'd drop him off and pick him up since I was old enough to drive and Bernstein always said the same thing. "Your brother, he always cries. You," he said pointing at me, "you never cried. But him, that's a different story, yeah?" I smiled and said little in return but we understood each other and I was grateful that he got me through it the way he did.

7

Later that morning, I found myself standing in front of old man Bernstein's house with a bottle of Johnny Walker Red in a brown paper bag. I rang the bell. After a moment, I heard sounds and then someone tugged at the door, trying several times as if it were a tremendous weight before it flew back with a crash. A tiny woman with frizzled hair and thick glasses, wearing a patterned housecoat stood on the threshold.

"Yes?" she said in a querulous tone. "What is it?"

"Hi, Mrs. Bernstein. How are you? You remember me? Bernie. Bernie Goldman? I studied with your husband for my bar mitzvah?"

She sized me up and down. "Many boys studied with him," she said. "What did you say your name was?"

"Bernie. Bernie Goldman. And my brother Harry studied too."

"Ach, what's the difference?" She eyed the package in my arms suspiciously. "You selling something? You're a salesman? I'm not buying." And waggled a bony finger under my nose.

I smiled indulgently. "No. It's a present for Mr. Bernstein. A bottle of whiskey. I know he likes to take a drink now and then."

She lifted her head and moved her mouth around into what may have passed for a smile. "Well, Bernie, you'd better come in." I followed behind her and closed the door. I expected it to be a journey into the past but got quite a shock. The living room had been changed completely. There was new wallpaper, a vivacious yellow with sunflowers, the furniture had been redone in earth tones and the carpet was new too. The only thing I recognized was the old mahogany sideboard. It was exactly the same and in the very same spot. "Sit!" she commanded. I sat obediently. "So tell me, what am I going to do with another bottle of whiskey?" she asked me accusingly. She went to the sideboard, threw open the cupboard door and revealed at least a dozen bottles, unopened, the seals intact. "You think I'm an alcoholic, young man, that I could drink so much?"

"No, of course not," I stammered. "It's for Mr. Bernstein like I said." My powers of perception were not attuned at the best of times and it really should have dawned on me why there were so many bottles crammed into the cupboard.

"Nudnik, listen. My husband died five years ago last December. I thought maybe I'd give them as gifts but it's enough already!" She plunked herself down in a chair opposite me. I put the bottle of whiskey down on the coffee table.

"I'm terribly sorry. This is so embarrassing, Mrs. Bernstein but really, I didn't know. Really. I hope I didn't upset you," I said in a feeble, stuttery way.

"No darling, don't worry. It's a shock for you I can see. Me? I'm used to it. Why shouldn't I be? Fifty-five years we had and that was plenty, believe me. You want a cup of tea?"

I nodded. "Sure."

"You take lemon?"

"Please."

Mrs. Bernstein hauled her tiny carcass out of the chair and trundled off to the kitchen where I heard the clinking of cups and the latch of the refrigerator opening and closing several times. She muttered to herself all along. The kettle whistled and I heard her pour the water out. There was the rustling of paper and then she emerged carrying a small tray. I sprang up.

"Let me help you." She shooed me away.

"Sit. Sit. I'm not an invalid." She set the tray down. "I put out a few cookies. Try them, they're good. I get them at the supermarket. You like chocolate?"

"Thanks." She poured out the tea and handed me a cup. I helped myself to a slice of lemon. I took my tea very weak, like pee.

"So, what did you want with Mr. Bernstein?" she asked quite pointedly.

I explained to her about the letters, that I needed them translated. That I was writing a book, a kind of family history and just wanted to know what the letters said in case there was anything important that I should know. She gave me a shrewd look.

"Your father doesn't speak Yiddish?" she asked. "The great perfesser himself?"

The old bird had almost got me there. I'd better watch myself. "Uh, he understands it to speak a little but not enough to translate," I replied.

"Hiding something from him, Bernie, hmm?" she asked me.

I gave an embarrassed chuckle. "Well, now that you mention it, Mrs. Bernstein, this book I'm writing, it's kind of a surprise you know? I want to surprise him with it as a kind of present, you might say."

"A present?"" she repeated skeptically.

I nodded. "That's right. A present."

"Okay," she said. "I do it for you."

Suddenly, I was confused. "Sorry? Do what?"

"You need the translation, no? Why else are you here, yeah? I'll do it," she pronounced and sat back with her arms folded.

"You?"

She gave me another stabbing look. "And why not? You think that Mr. Bernstein was the only educated person in this house? I went to university too, you know. I graduated before the War. He just played the big shot all the time but believe me I helped him plenty. You think I'm kidding?""

"No, of course not."

"What about the terms?" she asked me.

Now I was completely bewildered.

"Terms?"

"Of course, terms. You think I do this out of the goodness of my heart? I'm a widow on a pension. I don't do this for my health you know. So, what are the terms?" she asked again.

"Uh, I don't know. What's reasonable? What do you think is fair?"

"A hundred dollars a letter, that's what I think."

"A hundred dollars? Now, Mrs. Bernstein, that's a little bit steep…"

"Ninety-five dollars."

"How about fifty?"

"Fifty? That's an insult to me, young man. Fifty? Bah!"

Eventually, we settled on seventy-five dollars a letter. I'd take it out of my precious advance from De Groot. I still had the feeling I'd been mauled, however. Blind-sided by this old biddy who sat opposite me with a carrion expression, smugly satisfied.

"You got a tape recorder?" Mrs. Bernstein asked me.

"Yeah. I've got a tape recorder," I replied, puzzled.

"Good. You bring it here and show me how it works. And I read the letters into the machine. Then you play them back. Okay?"

"Well. Okay. If you think that's easier for you."

"Don't worry. It'll be okay," she said. And then our business transaction being concluded, I found myself hustled out into the street.

"Bye Mrs. Bernstein."

"Bring the tape," she commanded, then slammed the door.

The next morning, I went out and dropped the tape recorder, one that was voice activated, ten one-hour tapes and the packet of letters off to Mrs. Bernstein. I showed her how to use it and told her to call if she had any problems. And I gave her a cheque for four hundred dollars, something we'd also agreed on. I was anxious to get the translations back, eager to find out what my great uncle Isaac had written from a land and time far away.

8

We lived in a hybrid, fragmented neighborhood and our house was on the cusp of it, our property the demarcation against which different cultures and traditions were set. To the east and south of us was an ultra-orthodox Jewish enclave, an isolated, distinct community that kept entirely to itself. To the west and north were the Italian, Greek and Portuguese households, boisterous and outgoing, denoted by crisp lawns and luxurious gardens overflowing with flowers, vegetables, and a wide variety of fruits.

The orthodox area had its own stores, schools, synagogues and shops and the families, which seemed enormous in size with ten kids and more, had taken over the park a block away from our house. They were omnipresent, these Jews, strolling in groups up and down the walk, the men in front and the women behind. Sometimes a horde of twenty or more young men drove a wedge through the strollers as they emerged from prayer, walking briskly en masse as if on parade in their box hats and white leggings and long, dark coats.

They drove around in huge, old station wagons with more rust than metal showing, driving recklessly, back ends swaying on wilted springs as they careened around corners, jammed to the ceiling with their families. By god, they were the worst bloody drivers.

At the park, gangs of children played, again with the sexes separated as the girls congregated by the swings, jungle gym and sandbox while the boys played ferocious games of baseball where calls were hotly contested and the play animated. Insults flew every which way in English, Yiddish and Hebrew. The parents weren't often about, flaked out at home more than likely, as the children looked after the next youngest in order right down to the babies. Sometimes, a young girl of nine or ten would take charge of five or six youngsters on her own. And they always kept to themselves. An invisible wall separated us. When I took the boys to the park and we played baseball, the orthodox kids edged away when the ball rolled near them, ignoring it, having been warned, severely, I guess, against any contact with the Others. Us.

So you can imagine my shock when, on a steaming hot Sunday in July, we were approached by two young boys, their sidecurls flapping in the searing blasts that stood in for a breeze and asked us if they could join the game. Their names were Zvi and Schmuel, they said and they loved to play baseball and the older boys in their own crowd wouldn't let them play. The two boys, who were eight and nine, spoke in that middle European way which gave their English an accent meaning that mostly, they spoke Yiddish or Hebrew at home. This kid, Zvi, was a character and a bit of a smartass, I could see. The other boy, Schmuel, didn't seem too sure about this gambit but had been egged on by his pal.

"I'm a great player," Zvi cracked. "Best in my class."

"Oh yeah?" I said. "We'll see." The kid was cocky all right, a puffed up little bantam punter in a skullcap.

This is the way the game worked. I was the pitcher and played defense for both sides. That meant I pitched everyone the same way and ran as little as possible since chasing down balls was getting harder and harder to do with each passing year. It was Sean and Nathan against the other two. Each batter got four pitches to swing at or was out. And since there were only two players a side, it was two outs to the half inning.

Nathan was an enthusiastic and aggressive player but Sean was not. Although agile and coordinated, if he didn't get a good result immediately, Sean had a tendency to give up. He could be a bit of a spoilsport, but I knew it was lack of confidence mainly. And anyway, it was only a game. We established the boundaries. Two bare spots and a maple tree formed the bases and I stood back about twenty feet from what was designated as home plate. I did the coin toss and Zvi called it right. Sean and Nathan took the field. Zvi picked up the bat and stepped up. He took a few swings.

"Down the middle," he called. "Right down the middle."

I served him up the first one. It was high and he watched it go by with disgust. Schmuel was catching, just to keep the play going. The second pitch was more to his liking and he belted it. The ball took off like a rocket, well over Nathan's head, who gave me a look of disgust as he vainly tried to run it down.

"Home run," yelled Zvi triumphantly and with self-assurance trotted around the bases.

"All right Zvi!" screamed Schmuel. "Whatta hit!" And as Zvi jogged home, they slapped hands. I covered home plate as Nathan threw it in and made it a closer play than it might have been.

"Not bad," I said to him. "I'll have to pitch you a little differently next time."

It was clear that Schmuel was not Zvi's equal. I struck him out on three pitches. The boy was reckless and swung at everything.

"Take your time," I said.

"Dad," Sean protested. "You don't have to help them."

"I'm not, anymore than I'd help you," I replied. "Okay. Next batter." Zvi swaggered up again. I decided to pitch him harder, and low and inside. He took the first pitch and Schmuel had to chase it back to the fence. Zvi gave me a knowing look that said I know what you're trying to do buster and it won't work. The next one went high and outside. Zvi tagged it and tagged it well. It soared farther than the first. Nathan threw up his arms in anger and ran back after it. I covered home but it wasn't even close.

"Good hit," said Sean with grudging admiration, as Nathan's throw trickled in.

Once again, Schmuel went down on three pitches. They changed sides. Two nothing for the other side. Sean was up first. He was a good hitter but always hit every ball to left field. I had tried to get him to change his stance a little and swing earlier, but old habits die hard. As a result, Sean hit a lot of foul balls. The pattern stayed even as Sean fouled off the first two pitches to the left. The kid, Zvi, was pretty sharp all right. He must have noticed something and crept over from centre field. As Sean tagged the third pitch and tagged it well to left field, naturally, Zvi was there right on the mark and took it in without moving an inch. He threw it back in with a smirk. Sean threw the bat down in disgust and then gave it a kick for good measure.

Nathan, ever the sportsman, patted him on the back and said he'd do better next time. Nathan stepped up and tapped the plate with the bat and took a single, measured swing, then went into his stance. He had it down all right, I thought. I fed him one that was up around the shoulders only because his crouch was so low and being small for his age, his strike zone was the size of a postage stamp. He swung and missed, then smacked himself on the forehead with his palm.

"Come on, Dad, a good one this time."

I put a lot more velocity on the second pitch but it was right down the middle and belt high. Nathan tattooed it, a cannon shot to dead-away center. I followed the ball's trajectory over my shoulder and then, to my amazement, saw the kid, Zvi, streaking back, arms outstretched, legs pumping and then he launched into a dive flat out and parallel to the ground. I saw a plume of dust when he hit and his body jerked up and down as he slid along his chest through the scrub and brush in the outfield. After a moment, though, he jumped up triumphantly, arms in the air and to my astonishment, I saw the ball settled neatly in the webbing of his glove.

"Wow!" I said. "Great catch." Is it possible that Jackie Robinson had come back in the form of a little orthodox Jew?

Nathan pulled up at second and stared. "How did he do that?" he asked, stunned. "How did he do that?" Zvi trotted in and as he passed by, flipped me the ball. He wore a cocky grin all right and the front of his striped T-shirt was powdered with dirt and dust. The fringes sticking out underneath were just as grimy. The kid'll probably get a good tongue-lashing coming home so dirty. The score was still two-zip. Sean and Nathan took the field.

Zvi came up. I decided to stick to the corners as best I could and down low. The first pitch was outside and he watched it go by. The second pitch nipped in on the inside and Zvi, taking a fluid swing, pasted it low and hard–a skidding line drive that caught me square on the left kneecap before I could get my glove hand down. The ball hit with such velocity that my leg buckled and I went down as the ball ricocheted into foul territory. I could see that Zvi smirked at my discomfort. Angered, I got up and chased the ball down as he turned away from me and sauntered around the bases. I thought, however, I'd surprise him. I used to be a pretty good sprinter not that long ago. I got to the ball pretty quickly and then turned it on, making a beeline for his back to make the tag.

Zvi sensed that I was coming up and glanced over his shoulder. He hurried his pace, starting to pick it up as I came up behind him racing like a madman. We were on a collision course for second base. I could see the expression on his face change from cockiness to fear to determination as I drew within inches, stretching the ball out to tag him from behind and charging like a bull out of control. The kid put a hand on his flapping skullcap, lowered his head and dove for the base. I would have hit him about belt high and square on if I hadn't thought to avoid him and more by instinct than anything else, went into a somersault over Zvi's streaking body. I saw him somewhere down around my ankles as I went up and over and felt the impact of the ground coming up and the slamming of my back against the hard turf, the breath bursting out of me.

"Jesus. Oh sweet Jesus."

I lay there for a moment huffing. As I turned my head, I noticed that little daredevil, Zvi had scrambled up and scampered home to score. I didn't care. I'd done myself a serious injury. Sean and Nathan came racing over.

"Are you okay, Dad? Are you hurt?" they yelled in unison. Feeling came back into my limbs slowly and I nodded as I rolled over on my side, stifling the moans and groans. I was more embarrassed than anything. Slowly, I dragged myself to my feet.

"You okay mister?" Zvi called out. I nodded.

"Let's play," I croaked, even though I had a sneaking suspicion that the kid had nailed me in the kneecap on purpose but I had no way of proving it. We played another five innings and then I'd had enough. The heat had climbed and I must have dropped ten pounds in water. As the game came to an end, we shook hands all around. The score was eight to six for Zvi and Schmuel.

"You play well, kid," I said to Zvi. "Next time, I'll pitch you overhand."

"Sure," he grinned back. "I like hardball a lot."

"We'll see you around then," I said. "See you Schmuel. Next time."

The two orthodox, Jewish boys went off arm-in-arm, as grubby as dirt farmers and just as happy about it. We never saw them at the park again.

"Boy," said Sean, "he was good."

"He was okay," Nathan conceded.

"I'd say he was pretty good," I said.

"Better than me, Dad?" Nathan asked.

"I'd say so. Although it's pretty close," I replied.

"You gave them better pitches," Nathan accused me.

"No, I didn't."

"Looked like it."

"He just hit everything I threw, that's all."

"How come we never play with any of the other kids?" Sean asked, as we took turns slurping at the water fountain. This was a perplexing and complicated question, as most of their questions were these days.

"They just stick to themselves, Sean, that's all," I said.

"But why?" he insisted.

"That's just the way they are," I replied. "Good ball players though." Still, I envied them their unblinking sense of identity. They knew exactly who they were and where they came from.

I was clearing the dishes when the phone rang. Sharon.

"How's your day going?"

"Fine," I said. "Working away, you know."

"Making progress, are you?" she asked in an arch tone of voice.

"We try my love, we can only try."

"Look, I've got to dash, I've got a meeting starting in a minute. I was thinkin' though luv, why don't you invite your dad over for supper tomorrow night?"

"My dad? Why?"

"Do you have to have a reason, for god sake? He's your dad and he's on his own isn't he?"

"Are you trying to fix him up again, Sharon? After the last time, are you mad? Have you lost your senses?"

"All right, that was a mistake, I admit it but this will be different, I promise. This woman's very bright, energetic, vivacious and well-educated too."

"Sharon, I don't know about this..."

"Got to go luv. Give him a call, all right, but don't say anything else, mind. Bye." And she hung up before I could get out a reply.

"By God, she tests me so she does," I said to no one in particular.

9

Mrs. Bernstein must have used a full roll of adhesive on the package I received in the mail as it seemed impenetrable, layer upon layer all stuck together, and the deeper in, the more impenetrable it became. Finally, after slashing frantically away with a box cutter, then flailing at it, the pieces came apart and the first tiny tape fell out onto the surface of my desk. With trepidation and heart jumping erratically, I slipped the tape into the machine and pressed play. The eerie silence of static ground on for what seemed an eon. But then I was startled to hear Mrs. Bernstein blowing into the microphone. She blew several times and finally began to speak. Her voice and delivery were disconcerting, to say the least.

"First of all, Bernie, let me say that this Isaac, whoever he is or was, is a nogoodnik, I tell you. I am ashamed for you that you should be related to such a person but who am I tell you such things? What a story, I shouldn't believe if you ask me. I think he's pulling the wool over the sheep's eyes. You must decide yourself if you believe this nogoodnik and what he has to say, but I can tell you if he were my son, his backside would be plenty sore that's for sure. He'd be sitting in a zitz from morning to night soaking his bum from the spankings he'd get.

"And believe me you got a bargain. Seventy-five dollars? Bah, what a deal you got. The writing is lousy, so hard for me even with my glasses on double strength, like Egyptians write and the language? Not just Yiddish that's for sure, some Polish and Hungarian too, all mixed up, so vermischt, who needs it, I ask you? But a deal's a deal and I keep my word. I don't back out of a deal once I make it but you got a real bargain, so I hope you're happy." There was a pause on the tape. I was beginning to think she'd used up the first side just moaning and complaining, but then, she cleared her throat and I heard the tinkle of a cup on a saucer, a noisy swallow and she began again.

"July, 1926. My Dearest Sister Fanny. It is two days now since I have left home and I am writing you this letter. I miss you terribly and thinking of you helps me when I feel lonely. By now you know that on the day I left, I went in to Mama and Papa's room and dug up the money tin from the corner and stole half the gelt from there. I didn't take it all, you see, but some 300 zlotys to see me through. I didn't know where I was going or what I was going to do. I can just imagine the geschrei when he found out, I wasn't too careful when I put the tin back, there was a mess, some schmutz on the floor and on me too.

"If I'd been a real goniff I would have taken it all, but I didn't out of respect for Papa and Mama and of course you, my dear sister. How, I miss you, not Papa mind, and Mama a little bit although she always took Papa's side against me. But you stood by me, dear Fanny and what did you get for your trouble? A smack in the puss from Papa and for me that was it, the end. I knew then I had to get out or I would die a thousand tiny deaths.

"Maybe you wonder what has happened? What I've been doing? Where I've been? So, nu, I will tell you. Naturally, I had a plan, don't you know? To make my way to Budapest to see Uncle Herman and stay with him, maybe. How I was to get there, well, that's a different story. Did I even know how far it was or how long it might take? If I had wings and could fly, maybe a day or two. Using my two own feet or travelling by cart if I should be so lucky, in God's hands, I would be delivered before winter comes and that would suffice me.

"First, I went to Zelig the tailor and gave him all my clothes and in return we did an exchange. I dressed like a Polish peasant −wool trousers and vest, open-necked cotton shirt, hobnailed boots, a seaman's cap and jacket. I paid him five zlotys to cut my hair and shave my new beard. No more peyos. He didn't want to do it but the money shut him up. He said God would curse him so I had to give him another five zlotys for his trouble. When I looked in the mirror I couldn't believe my eyes, dear Fanny; I was no longer a shtetl Jew but a young Polack with red hair and blue eyes and freckles. I made Zelig promise not to tell anyone and said nothing about my plans and that meant I had an hour or two before everyone knew about me and what I had done. Zelig's wife packed me some food and I gave her another ten zlotys so Zelig didn't do so bad from me after all, but I didn't know the value of money and what it could or couldn't buy. But I am learning fast.

"I walked quickly away, down the road and felt like a heavy weight had dropped off my shoulders. I was free! Goodbye Muzhik my home. No regrets did I have as I set off as fast as my new boots would carry me. I wanted to get away so badly, my dear Fanny and set off toward my future.

"I will write again soon, my dearest sister, even if I am only talking to myself, I am talking to you in my heart and mind. One day, we will be together again. I beg you not to marry Raffi the butcher. He is ugly and fat and when he farts, the world dies around him. When I get to Budapest, I will send for you. Love, Your brother, Isaac."

Then Mrs. Bernstein's scratchy voice broke in again with some additional commentary. "So, Bernie, what do you think of that? A boy who steals from his family? Who hides who he is? Who insults people? A disgrace, I say. But wait there's plenty where that comes from I can tell you. Talk about moral character? Feh! This Isaac is empty as the Central Bank of Warsaw in 1939."

Again, there was a clearing of the throat and the tinkle of cup against saucer and light gargling – all recorded for posterity and at my expense. I thought about the young boy some sixty or sixty-five years earlier who went against his family, breaking away to seek his fortune, running to the unknown and the mixture of bravado and misguided romanticism that propelled him. Although Mrs. Bernstein's rendition, her delivery, was disjointed, I fell into the rhythm of her cadences and gradually, the voice beneath emerged and Isaac came out clearer and clearer, speaking more confidently through his querulous medium.

"August, 1926. My dearest Fanny. It has been some two weeks and I bet you are dying to know what has become of me. For two days I walked. I didn't know where I was going, did they teach us such things in the yeshiva? How to find Budapest at the other end of the world? 'Nonsense', Rabbi Blecher would roar, to the text, to the text, slapping his dirty palm down on the pages. Ach, I'm so happy to be far, far away from all that. The world is much greater than the yeshiva, much wider than the shtetl, more exciting than the lives within our families where every day is carved in stone and just as dull, just as every other day, all so routine, so boring.

"I had been walking on the Gorodny Road pointing in the direction I took to be south. Wasn't I smart, to know the sun rose in the east and set in the west and in between was north and south, this much I knew at least? I had little food and after dark, I would seek out peasant farms and sneak into the henhouse, steal an egg or two, or pick blackberries in the woods and buy what I could, bread and cheese, for a few zlotys from the merchants in the villages I passed through on my way.

"The days were hot, the road dusty and my clothes were heavy and warm. I tied my coat into a bundle and carried it on my back with my other possessions, few and humble as they were. I found some work here and there, helping a farmer bundle hay for a few days. He let me sleep in his barn with the animals but fed me well enough. To everyone, I told the same story, going to Budapest to live with my uncle. Naturally, they didn't have to know I was a Jew and at first, I forced myself to eat trafe thinking it would turn to ashes in my mouth but it really wasn't at all bad, quite good and when your belly is empty, why argue when food is handed to you? God will forgive.

"When I repeated this story, they usually shook their heads and said, Budapest? Isn't Warsaw good enough for you? And it wasn't long before they, these farmers and peasants, said something bad about the Jews; wait long enough and it would come out. Of course, I said nothing in reply, sometimes just nodded to let them know I was listening and if they thought I agreed, so much the better, the fools. Yes, we were comrades of sorts, they thought. And I began to think about ways to take back from them, what they have taken from us, my dear sister. And I found something to take as you will see.

"And as I travelled from farm to farm, I realized that during the harvest time, there was work to be had, decent food and more besides. Many of these farmers raised healthy families, daughters included. I noticed that among the goyim the men and women worked together, side by side, even if they were not yet married. The girls did not cover their bodies from head to toe, hiding who and what they were. When you looked at them, they did not turn away, at least not right away, some even returned the look you gave them boldly. Indeed, this was a new world.

"This was how I met Malka, a young farm girl. She was not very pretty but had fair skin and her hair was very blond and fine. She was sturdily built with good shoulders and a full bosom. The second day after I started working for her father, Piotr and his wife Maria, I caught sight of her by the family well and hid behind the barn watching her wash her feet and legs. Using a bar of lard in a bucket, she soaped her feet and drew the cloth up pulling her skirt back above the knee. I had never seen such fair, smooth skin, never seen it revealed like this so openly as if it was always done and not a sin. Her skin shone in the sunlight and I could see the faint wisps of soft down. I watched as she drew the cloth higher and higher and thought for a moment I might pass out on the spot, such feelings and urges did I have. I knew what they were of course, we'd talked about them among ourselves back in the shtetl, the other yeshiva buchers and me. But I know we were talking out of our kipas, who knew really? Not Aaron or Tsimmy or Herschel, you can count on it.

"Then Piotr missed me and called out and I turned. I must have made a noise or loosed a stone. Malka heard too and looked up and at that instant, our eyes met across the yard and there was a moment, a quick flame between us, the kind that happens between a man and a woman, you just know it. I could do nothing, just stand and stare frozen to my spot. Then she smiled, such a small, sly smile and playfully dropped her skirt, tossed her blonde hair, picked up her bucket and returned to the house. I was in a high state of excitement I can tell you, dear Fanny, perhaps you understand these things but I do not. She smiled you see. I just knew that Malka wasn't upset with me but seemed to enjoy it, enjoyed when I watched her. I returned to the fields in a daze. Piotr looked at me strangely but said nothing, thinking perhaps it was just the heat that affected me so.

"I was not completely surprised then, when after settling in for the night in my straw bed, did I hear Malka softly call my name. She came into the barn, moonlight flooding in behind her as she cautiously opened the door, then quickly shut it behind her. I could see she was in her nightdress.

"'I brought you some milk and a few biscuits,' she said to me, and again there was the smile. She held them out to me.

"'Thank you,' I replied. 'Please sit down, Malka.' She sat beside me in the straw and hugged her knees to her breasts with her sturdy arms. We sat without saying anything for a moment or two, then she turned her face up to me with her eyes closed and I kissed her.

"'We must be very quiet,' she murmured. 'Papa must not hear, he is a light sleeper.' And she lay back in the straw bed. And it came to me then that this is how I could take my revenge and even steal some pleasure out of this miserable life.

"Ah, my dear Fanny, that was my first experience..." My concentration was interrupted when the phone rang. I was annoyed. I didn't want to keep a phone in my office but Sharon had been adamant. Before the phone, I'd be running from room to room to pick it up, never getting there on time or just hadn't bothered to answer and she'd put her foot down, asserting that when she needed to reach me, it was important to get me right away. So, now I have a phone in the sanctuary where the mundane world intervened. Reluctantly, I shut off the tape and answered it. *How do you like that,* I thought, *that devil Isaac was schtupping Polish farm girls as a perverse form of revenge.* This wasn't what I'd expected. No wonder Mrs. Bernstein was incensed. Good Jewish boy acting this way? No such thing.

"Hello Sharon," I said.

"Psychic now, are we?" she lilted.

"What do you want?"

"Shirty too," she added.

"Sorry. I was busy, you know."

"Mooning away were you, as usual?"

"Something like that."

"I just wanted to make sure everything was arranged, with supper tonight, I mean," she said and I could hear that anxious edge in her voice, the hostess tone, where she thought her character and reputation were at risk if everything didn't go exactly as planned – which with kids about, was practically a certainty.

"You know I'll look after everything, I always do. Don't sweat it."

"Thank god you can cook, Bernie. We'd all be dead, or worse, tubs of lard rollin' in the street. Have you fixed the menu yet?"

"Yeah."

"Is it a secret then?"

"Okay. Garlic bread. Caesar Salad. Steamed mussels. Pasta e fagioli. Glazed chicken and wild rice. Schnitz pie and French vanilla ice cream for dessert. Coffee and/or tea."

"Sounds good," she admitted, still sounding a wee bit unsure. "What about the wine?"

"I've got a new Chilean Chardonnay white and a good husky red Italian Valpolicella just in case. My dad doesn't drink, you know, since that trouble with his prostate."

"No, but I do and you… and Katherine does for sure."

"Not a lush, is she?"

"Of course, not, don't be silly."

"And just who is this Katherine person?"

"Just a colleague."

"From the office?"

"No, I met her at the Executive Society luncheon. We got to chatting and hit it off and had a few lunches and get-togethers since, that's all. Don't make it all sound so bloody conniving and sinister, Bernie, for god's sake. I think you've got a bloody suspicious mind, I do."

"How old is she?"

I heard her smack her palm down on her desk. "There you go, you see?" She stopped to gather herself. "You're doing this on purpose, to upset me," she hissed.

I sighed heavily into the phone, then paused. "How old, Sharon."

"What bloody difference does it make?" she snapped going into her feigned anger routine.

"Isn't this the point where you ring off?" I said. "But before you do and if you want to come home to a clean house and a properly cooked dinner, just answer the question, will you? Or I'll have Sean and Nathan buck naked, wearing their filthy underwear on their heads, waiting at the door to greet our guests, howling like wild animals." They were capable of it and Sharon knew it.

Sharon swallowed heavily. "Katherine is forty-two," she said in a smaller voice.

"Forty-two? My father is seventy-four years old Sharon. That's a thirty-two year difference."

"I can count, Bernie. I'm an accountant, after all. But your father's a young seventy-four and..."

"What's wrong with her?" I asked.

"Nothing. Nothing's wrong with her," Sharon retorted.

"Sharon, my father is old enough to be her father, so what's the problem? Is she ugly, fat, has a walleye or what?"

"Don't get smarmy now. Katherine's very attractive. Very attractive, indeed. She's lonely, that's all. She's been through a difficult divorce and is finding it hard to meet intelligent men. Don't you know, Bernie, that men like your father are as rare as bloody plutonium? They don't just grow on trees, you know. Katherine's been through dating hell."

"Oh great, so now we're running a dating service for the geriatric set. Wonderful."

"Just do your bit okay, hon? They're adults. If they hit it off, great. If not, then no one loses anything, all right? There's no obligation."

"Well, it's just awkward, Sharon, you know. I want my dad to know I had nothing to do with this. He's doing fine on his own."

"That's just what you want to believe. He's lonely and don't tell me he isn't. You just don't or won't see it. And you can't stand the thought of anyone replacing your mother, saint that she was. Anyway, look, I've got to go, someone's calling me. I know you'll do a great job. You always do. I'll see you around 5:30 okay? And I'll get the boys, so you won't have to run out. Bye love." And she hung up.

Now, I was so agitated that the only thing left for me to do was clean the house before doing the shopping, just to calm me down a bit. Nothing like swabbing toilets, of which we had four, to work off some aggressive, pent up feelings.

I longed to stay in the past, to listen to Isaac's letters or bury myself in my father's papers, which were remarkably varied. When he was writing The Global View, he made notes on bits of envelopes, itty notepads, lined notebooks partly filled and re-filled, scraps and wisps, anything with a writing surface that was handy when an idea or notion seized him. He kept them in chronological sequence but beyond that, there is no order, no organization to them at all. They are memory bits, flashes of insight into his state of mind at a point in time and are infuriating and tedious to sift through. I'm eager for information, eager to know who and what he was before I was born, mirroring me at the same age, fashioning and shaping his masterpiece, his Sistine Chapel.

10

The doorbell rang. I've got Sean and Nathan in clean shirts and twill pants. They've had showers and their hair is neatly combed – not their souls mind, but that's asking a lot of anyone, especially nine-year olds. Sharon is upstairs getting dressed. I'm wearing a crew neck rowing shirt over jeans and the usual apron and topsiders, no socks.

The table is set, the wine is chilling and the bouquet of smells from the soup and chicken fill the house. That's one of the good things about cooking. The aroma permeates every elbow and crack of the place, it's almost magical. Coming in from outside, you step into the instantaneous warmth that signifies family. It is a connection to my childhood. My mother would do the same, cooking up dishes that enraptured the guests and kept Harry and me begging for a sip or a lick as she worked away. No wonder I'm confused about my life, I'm trying to be my mother and father at the same time.

As I pull open the door, I notice Sean lying in wait under the dining room table like a cat about to pounce. He is watching Nathan, anticipating the perfect moment, then will leap out seemingly from nowhere and scare the bejeesus out of him and like as not, pull down half the china and glasses with him.

"Ah, you must be Katharine," I said briskly to the well-turned-out brunette before me. Before she can open her mouth to reply, I grab her arm and yank her in. "Do come in." She practically falls through the door on her high heels and I back quickly away from her to the dining room and slide a rubber toe up to Sean's face and hiss downward. "Come out carefully or you'll never see your Game Gear again." Katherine seemed confused and not quite sure what to do but before she collapsed into total uncertainty, I slid back up to her and saw

Sean slink away. His clean clothes were askew, small clouds of dust clinging to his white shirt.

"May I take your jacket? It is warm tonight, isn't it?"

She gave me a fearful look like I may not bring it back but slipped it off and held it out guardedly. "Yes. Thank you." I hung it in the hall closet.

"Sharon's getting changed. She'll be down in a minute. Sean. Nathan. Come say hello to our guest." The two of them peeled up like cartoon characters stopping on a dime in their sneakers. I pointed to each in turn. "Nathan. Sean."

"Hello," they echoed.

"Well, aren't you both handsome and so different looking? Are you sure you're brothers?" They looked at each other and nodded.

"Yes," they said. "We're sure." They've got the twins act down to a tee, knowing it's what adults expect, so they've practiced talking in unison and then go off to titter about it afterwards.

"Okay, you two, off you go. Be ready when I call and no fooling around. You need to stay clean." They shot off just as quickly and I could imagine the muffled peals and squeals slipping out.

"They're adorable," said Katherine, "but a handful I'll bet."

"They have their moments," I replied. "Why don't you come into the kitchen while I putter. Perhaps you'd care for some wine?"

She nodded and I noticed her make-up was applied a little too carefully and intended to cover a few sins. "That'd be nice." I could see she was nervous, feeling on display in an unfamiliar household. "This is a lovely house," she said, following behind me.

"I can't take any credit for it," I replied and noticing her surprise added, "I mean for the way it looks. That was all Sharon's doing. I'm just the hewer of water and chopper of wood."

Katherine looked around. "I love this kitchen. You could do your own cooking show in here."

"Sometimes I feel like I do," I said.

She smiled and for the first time, relaxed a bit. "I'll bet you do."

Her smile was quite disarming and I found that on further inspection she was quite an attractive woman; middle-aged, but looked after herself and watched her figure. She was wearing a dark Chanel suit, not inexpensive and matching shoes. Of medium height but trim and had good legs, something I always noticed, starting with the ankles first. "Do you have children, Katherine?" I asked while checking the soup, stirring the salad dressing and then basting the chicken. She was leaning up against the counter opposite.

"Yes. A girl who is eighteen and a boy who's turning sixteen next month."

"And how do you find dealing with all those raging hormones?"

"It's bloody awful, to tell the truth. One minute my son's shaving his head and the next, my daughter's adding another ring to her nose."

"Well it could be a cheek or an eyebrow," I added helpfully.

"We've been through that and finally, I put my foot down."

"And they actually listened?" I asked.

Katherine nodded. "Surprised the hell out of me too. I guess they were testing the limits. They're good kids really, they just want to be accepted by their friends, be cool, you know. God forbid that anyone should think they're nerds. That's a fate worse than death. When I was their age, it was bell bottoms, tie-dye and beads. Now it's pierced body parts and tattoos. Things that are harder to undo and sure cost a hell of a lot more."

"What about their father? Is he in the picture at all?"

She gave me a look with some steel in it. The question was forward and personal and that was precisely why I'd asked it. "If you want to know, Bernie," she said acidly, "he left me for a younger woman five years ago. She was twenty-four and he was forty at the time. Mid-life crisis, most would say. But we probably married too young and just grew apart. Do I hate him for it? At the time I did, and I still call her his bimbo, after the kids come back from their obligatory visits once a month. He does the bare minimum and that's it. Besides, the bimbo is expecting a baby. Maybe he thinks he'll be a better father the second time around, after he's made all his mistakes the first time. They've been his guinea pigs, his great experiment."

"I thought that was what they said about grandparents. More wine?" I asked and reached for the bottle. She nodded.

"You're a bit of a Nosey Parker, aren't you?" she said with a tinge of malice.

"I am."

"I'm not going to jump your father at the dinner table, you know, and rape him in his seat."

"I'm not suggesting you will, Katherine but who knows? He might actually enjoy that."

"I'll keep that in mind," she said, taking a sip of the second glass of wine with a flourish.

"Enjoy what?" Sharon asked, bursting into the kitchen.

"The wine, my dear," I said. "If he could drink it I mean, with his wonky prostate and all."

Sharon gave me a dirty look. "Hallo Katherine," she said and gave her a hug. "You look smashing. That's a lovely suit."

"Thanks, it's new. First time out."

"Well, we're honored then," I said, and I believe Sharon was about to belt me when the doorbell went.

"That'll be Dad," Sharon said. "I'll go."

After she'd left, Katherine gave me a self-satisfied look. "Well, Bernie, that was pretty smooth. Prostate? I know men as young as forty five who've had prostate trouble and if you're dad's been stricken, then you'd better watch out yourself." And pointed downward knowingly.

I raised my wine glass. "Touché."

"Look," Katherine said. "I just want to have a pleasant evening and enjoy what I know will be your marvelous dinner."

"All right. Perhaps I'm a wee bit over-protective," I conceded. "I just find that matchmaking has a habit of blowing up in your face when you try to please everyone and no one ends up happy and then we're in the middle of it taking the blame when it doesn't work out. Besides, Sharon just sprang this on me without any warning or discussion, so really, it's nothing to do with you personally, you see."

"I do," Katherine said as we heard my father's voice in the living room, calling out for his grandsons. "But try to have a little faith." Then she patted my arm, put down the glass, tugged at her suit, turned, wiggled her bottom provocatively for my benefit and marched out.

So far, the evening had been a smash. I heard Sharon make the introductions and the upswing in my father's voice. He doesn't like surprises, but who knows, he might not even suspect that he's being set up by his daughter-in-law.

We made it through the first three courses and I began to relax. Nathan spilled his juice once and Sean dropped his fork three times with a clatter as it hit the ceramic tile floor, splattering whatever was on it at the time. They were behaving themselves, which made me suspect that Sharon had put a bribe in place, like extra allowance or something else they may have wanted to keep them in line. In the kitchen, I cornered her and forced it out.

"Okay, how much?" I demanded.

"How much what?" Sharon asked, feigning innocence.

"Money, Sharon. Don't kid me, I'm on to you, smarty. You slipped them something, didn't you?"

Her eyes opened wide with indignation. "Well, I never… Bernie. Would I do somethin' like that? Me?"

"Damn right you would. It's only a matter of how much, that's all."

She slid her hands down between my legs and moved in closer. "My, aren't we the suspicious one? Maybe you could slip me a little something later?"

I nodded, trying to ignore her. "I'm guessing five bucks. Am I right?"

"Mmm. I'll let you know. We'll discuss it in private, okay?" I felt the pressure increase and it was a good thing I was wearing an apron. She gave me that look, the one I knew so well and I raised my eyebrows in acquiescence, the signal that I was in. She'd had a bit more wine than I thought. She turned and rubbed her buttocks against me and then glanced provocatively over her shoulder, and went to join the guests while I dredged up more chicken.

Upon my return, Katharine was peppering my dad with questions, hanging on his every word. He was Spinoza himself, grinding philosophy instead of lenses, the Montefiori of Metro, the Aristotle of now. I am the blind son, listening to every sound, every whisper, every auditory sign to find my way as I fumble along the tattered trail. I barged in offering more chicken and Katherine gave me an annoyed look, refusing curtly. My father accepted a breast, white meat. And as I sat and watched how Katherine wove a cocoon around him, pulled him into her to the exclusion of the rest of us, the boys disappeared somewhere, declaring themselves full and waiting for dessert. Sharon was split, looking on approvingly as my father nodded his greying head, eyes alight and then turned her gaze on me full of what I can only call happiness. I thought to myself, that perhaps I was really the bitter son instead.

I contemplated the drone of his voice and saw Katherine react, nodding seriously, laughing quickly, putting out a hand lightly to touch his gnarled, brown forearm and I knew she was captivated by his reputation, by his cerebral celebrity and that is what she saw at first. It is what they all see at first and my father accepted this graciously, and enjoyed it. *After all,* I thought, *this may be all he has left.* I was now the cruel son and perhaps Sharon was right, also the jealous son, full of envy and longing, hurting in the search for that microscopic sign of approval. That gracious acknowledgement of accepting me as I am, as an adult taking his place in the world, as an equal among equals. The doorbell jolted me out of this melancholic debauch. Everyone turned at once.

"Who on earth can that be?" Sharon asked. "Are you expecting anyone, Bernie?" She was thinking that, since she sprung something on me, perhaps I'd return the kindness but alas, I am not that quick or vindictive.

"Probably someone selling something," I said getting up to answer the door. Sean and Nathan shot in ahead of me, having heard the bell and were fighting to answer it first. "I'll get it. Leave the door, you hoodlums," I shouted and grabbed their shirts stopping them in their tracks.

"Aw Dad," wailed Sean. "We had a bet."

"And you lost," hollered Nathan.

"We tied."

"No we didn't, I won."

The inevitable scuffle began and I knew that Nathan would get the worst of it. He always did. And when he came to us crying because Sean had hurt him, a large bruise on his head or laceration down his back, Sean would proclaim his innocence, that it was an accident and that Nathan had started it. And when that didn't work with me, he'd accuse me of blaming him for everything, every catastrophe in the western hemisphere was suddenly his fault.

"Knock it off you two. And I'm going to answer the door."

"Good God!" I exclaimed. "Egan. What are you doing here?"

He had made an attempt at civility. A tweed jacket hung on him, bunched at the shoulders and sleeves. An elegant red and white striped tie with some sort of crest stuck on it had come askew and his shirt, pale yellow, had but one or two stains and billowed out of his grey flannel trousers. He'd slicked his hair back and I noticed the tips of his ears were a fiery red. He held something.

"I've brought champagne and I mean to drink all of it," he said. Sean and Nathan targeted him like a pair of bird dogs.

"Uncle Egan!" And they were in orbit. Before I could blink Egan was sprawled on his back on the porch. They were practically licking his face.

"Spare the bottles boys," he cried, holding up one bottle in each hand, full of fright.

I shook my head. What was it about Egan that invited such contact? He's made for it, I think. "Sean. Nathan. Get off your uncle. You could have hurt him. Boys, get up now." And I felt like a referee picking through a scrum and pulling bodies out of the pile. The boys were entirely disheveled now and giggling uncontrollably. I sent them off. "Go wash your hands and get cleaned up. Hurry up now before your mother sees."

As Egan was picking himself off the cement, I noticed that he wasn't alone. A young woman had been standing behind him blocked from view.

"Hello," I said tentatively.

"Hello," she replied, then put out her hand across Egan, who was struggling to regain his feet. "I'm Bernadette."

I accepted her hand and gave it a shake. "Not Devlin? Or Song of?"

"Ha Ha," groused Egan.

She shook her head full of spiked hair, something I thought had gone out of style ten years ago. "O'Rourke," she replied. "I'm a friend of Egan's. I hope you don't mind our barging in like this?"

I could see that I'd been handed, by some divine providence, a reprieve, and that the commotion at the doorway brought Sharon scrambling to the door.

"Oh God, no," she cried, looking down at Egan.

"Evenin' Sharon," he said. "How are ya?" I put my hand down to help him up. "Ta," he said gratefully and attempted to brush himself off which was awkward while holding the two bottles.

Bernadette looked a throw-back to some bleak period relating to earlier popular culture. She was exceedingly skinny, almost emaciated, and wore a micro-mini patent leather skirt, fishnet pantyhose, wedge-shaped black shoes with enormous heels that accentuated the reediness of her legs, a white satin blouse and short, black velvet bolero jacket. Her hair, which may not make it under the doorframe, shrieked purple, shot through with green streaks. As Bernadette stood behind Egan smiling, I also saw that she had an extreme overbite. There were two rivets in her nose and an earring through her right eyebrow. Sharon looked at Bernadette and appeared to gag.

"I've brought champagne," Egan said to her.

Sharon looked at the two of them rather blankly. Gently, I moved Sharon aside. I could see she was seething and for some reason, I drew perverse pleasure out of it.

"Egan. Bernadette. Do come in." I ushered them inside and felt Sharon's nails rake my forearm but sailed forward anyway. She let go. I knew I'd pay for this later.

All the while, Katherine and my father hadn't budged, sitting at the table with their heads together in rapt conversation. As we all trooped in, my father looked around.

"Egan," he said in surprise. He got up from the table and came around to him. "How nice to see you. Who's your friend?"

Bernadette stepped up and appeared to curtsey. "Bernadette O'Rourke," she announced.

"Nice to meet you, Bernadette. I'm Eph Goldman, Bernie's father. And let me introduce you and Egan to Katherine Edgerton." Katherine ventured over to shake hands.

"My son wears his hair like that," she said to Bernadette.

"Good for him," Bernadette said with spirit and pumped her arm. Egan stood in the center of the room, teetering slightly. After the formalities, silence fell.

"I've got news," he said solemnly. "And I want to drink this champagne. And I want everyone to have a drink with me." His tone was slightly menacing, as if by refusing, it would inflict a great insult. Sharon had shrunk into the background, wanting as little to do with this as possible. With Egan, good news was rare enough.

"Why don't I get us some glasses?" I offered and disappeared into the kitchen to let the scene evolve on its own. I was afraid Sharon might follow me and wanted to avoid that at all costs.

I returned with the glasses on a tray. I took the two bottles from Egan and popped them both. Each cork shot off like a bullet. The champagne had been aroused from all the jostling Egan had taken since his arrival. I poured the glasses full and handed them all around. We stood quietly waiting for Egan to make his announcement. Even the boys were silent. They'd crept in and sat demurely on the couch. I'd given them each a small glass to drink.

Egan drank it off in a single toss and held the flute out to be refilled. I obliged. He took a deep swallow of the second, gritted his teeth and wiped his lips on the sleeve of his jacket. He was listing badly.

But he pulled himself together, straightened up and spoke. "I'm going to have a show," he said solemnly. "At an art gallery," he added, as if we thought it might be in a prison or a shopping mall. He swept his right hand aside in a broad gesture. "And I have Bernadette to thank for it."

Bernadette blushed. "It was nothing. If he didn't have the talent, it wouldn't have happened in the first place."

My father was the first to respond. "Well, Egan. Congratulations. You must be thrilled," he said and shook his hand. Some of the champagne slopped on to the floor and I noticed that Sharon hadn't missed that.

"Yes," Katherine piped in. "That's wonderful news." *She was not missing a trick,* I thought.

"Fantastic Egan," I said. "You're the Irish Picasso."

Sharon broke her frozen stance and went up and pecked her brother on the cheek. "That's terrific, luv. All the best, really."

"Details, man," I said. "Details. Where. What. How. When. Whatever." Not to be denied, Sean and Nathan, realizing something special was taking place, each grabbed a leg and gave it a hug.

"Whoa," Egan said waving his arms to stay upright. I sent the boys in to the kitchen for popsicles.

Bernadette had slipped her arm through Egan's. He began. "Well, as I was saying, it was all Bernadette's doing really. She's a teacher at the art college and happens to know Robert Levinsky, who's pretty influential in the art world and got him to take a look at my stuff. He liked it and there it is. I'm having a show at Levinsky's gallery," he said and paused blowing through his lips. "There is a wee problem though."

"What's the problem?" I asked.

"Well, it's one of the paintings," he replied.

"What about it?"

"You see, I'd run out of money for supplies." He shook his head slowly. "No more canvases. So I used the wall of my flat. Levinsky wants that piece in the show, so I took the wall right out. The landlord happened by and was seriously pissed, wasn't he? After all, the wall had disappeared, hadn't it? Now he wants me out of the flat."

"Couldn't you put it back?"

Egan nodded. He was in slow motion now. "Ya, I offered to but he would have none of it. But I invited him to the show, you know, as a gesture. Anyway, I'm having a show." And with that, his eyes rolled up into his head and he toppled face down on the throw rug and commenced to snore. By instinct, I imagine, he'd held his hand with the champagne flute out from his body and saved the glass and its now meagre contents. Carefully, I removed the glass from his hand.

"Quite an exit," said Katherine.

Sharon stood over Egan's body and looked down at him shaking her head. "Just leave him there," she said. "He's comfortable enough. I'll get a blanket." And went off to find one.

"Ah Bernadette," I said. "Can I call you a taxi?"

She nodded without a beat. "Sure. That'd be grand," she replied. "Lovely to meet you all."

11

A remote-controlled racecar butted Egan in the nose. To the grand amusement of Nathan and Sean, he snored lustily through it all. They'd also erected an intricate network of pillows around and above him. If he moved, even slightly, they'd tumble down burying the poor, helpless bastard. I stood and admired their clever handiwork. The boys were hiding upstairs, peeking from around a corner overlooking the living room. It was Saturday and no one was disposed to rush anywhere. The car backed up for another run at him. Egan looked quite content in his makeshift bed. A rumpling of clothes and tufts of hair. To save him more humiliation, unconscious though it might be, I tossed a pillow in the car's path. The boys rammed the pillow and the car flipped over. I heard distant cries of frustration and stood waiting at the bottom of the stairs. They came skidding around the corner, then stopped.

I looked up at them sternly. "Leave your uncle alone or I'll take the car and chuck it in the trash."

"Aw dad," Sean protested. "We were just having some fun."

"It wasn't hurting him," added Nathan.

"No, but you're taking advantage of him. Just let him be. Believe me, when he wakes up, your uncle will be in a great deal of pain."

"Why?" asked Sean. "Did he hurt himself when he fell?"

"No, stupid," Nathan retorted. "His head will hurt from all the wine he drank; right dad? He'll be bung over, right?" he asked anxiously, concerned about being right.

"Yeah, something like that. Don't bother him now. I like the tent though. Very architectural."

"Thanks," grinned Sean. "I made it. Nathan helped a little. It's good, right? The best you've ever seen?"

"The absolute best," I agreed. "Now go get dressed, make your beds and come have breakfast." I knew that would keep them occupied for at least half an hour and they'd resurface when they were hungry.

I was right about Sharon's anger. After Egan had crashed and we'd packed everybody else off, she went into a rage.

"Why does he have to spoil everything?" she fumed.

"Listen. At least it was good news for once. He's going to have a show. He is talented, you know."

"But he's self-destructive, Bernie. It'll come to no good. Somehow, he'll destroy it. He always does. Egan can never leave well enough alone. He'll screw it up. I love my brother but I want him out of my life, do you hear?"

I was sitting in bed watching Sharon march back and forward in varying stages of undress, pulling her blouse off over her head and dropping it on the floor, kicking off her shoes, unhooking her bra and tossing it on the dresser top, shimmying out of her pantyhose and slipping off her panties, until she stood stark naked and entirely unconscious of it. Still spouting and ranting. Stopped suddenly by my look.

"What?" she demanded.

I smiled. "Nothing." But I was admiring, no question. There was still a lot to admire.

She put her balled fists on her hips. "Christ. Don't you ever think of anything else?"

I shook my head. "Not when you're parading up and down in front of me like *that.*"

She regarded me for a moment, not saying anything. I could feel her mind working. "All right then," she said looking down at her painted toes, then up at me. "Come and rescue me from my predicament."

I couldn't sleep that night. Even the warm afterglow of love-making settling into my bones couldn't lull my mind enough. I closed my eyes but saw bright lights popping and flashing. The house was noisier than usual. Each house had its own set of sounds. Snaps. Cracks. Groans. Moans. The settling of the foundation, the shifting of bones. The sounds were very distinct, like voices calling. The walls conversing. I wondered if the house had been built on top of a landfilled swamp and one morning, we'd find ourselves submerged. Sliding out the front door, slithering out windows to safety.

I could feel my life pressing in on my chest. It was painful. I got up out of bed and went to my office. The past beckoned.

12

"November, 1926. My dearest Fanny. I am worlds away from you, mama and papa. I have travelled so far, so quickly. I'm sorry dear sister that you have not been part of my thoughts for such a long time. I am Isaac no longer. Vlasic is now my name. I make my living as a conniver and a thief. I engage in criminal activities. I and my companions elude the Russian army and the police with ease. We know how to disappear, to become invisible. I shall tell you how this came to be.

"You remember Malka? She was simple and affectionate. I was supposed to stay but a few days on Piotr's farm but Malka found more things for me to do. She conjured up tasks like a magician and Piotr, although a peasant and a brute, wasn't stupid. He must have sensed, he and his wife Maria also, that something was taking place. I stayed a month. Then two months. Then three. The harvest was long done and Piotr and his son could easily take care of the farm. It was time I left. Malka didn't want me to go. But there was no more work. No more reasons to stay. Winter was coming. One evening as I prepared for bed, I heard an argument coming from the farmhouse. The voices were harsh and shrill. I could tell Piotr by the guttural sounds he made, like a grunting animal. Malka wailed and shrieked and the mother wailed and shrieked even higher, louder.

"I listened for a moment or two but couldn't contain myself, dear Fanny. I knew then that Piotr had discovered our secret and was punishing poor Malka. I felt no true attachment to her but she had been kind to me. I resolved to defend her somehow. I put on my clothes and prepared my things for leaving. In the darkness, I strode across the farmyard toward the house, coming closer to the tumult of voices. Piotr angry and yelling, Malka frightened and whimpering.

I pushed open the door. Piotr was standing over a weeping Malka huddled on the floor, moaning into herself. There was blood on her face. I stepped inside.

"'You!' Piotr roared. 'You have broken my home. You have stolen my daughter's virtue. You have gotten her with child.'

"As you can imagine, dear Fanny, this was news to me and I was dazed by the suddenness of it. Piotr was not a tall man but broad, with sloping shoulders and long, muscled arms. While I was trying to get over the shock of what he said, Piotr sprang at me. In an instant his powerful hands were around my throat. Believe me, Fanny, when I say I thought it was the end for me. That God was laughing at me and I was being paid in full for my betrayals. I tried to loosen his grip but the Polack was as powerful as an ox. He squeezed harder, tightening the noose made by his fingers and the room started to twirl. I thought that my eyes would pop out of my head. My tongue was the size of mama's overcooked flanken. I had no breath. No life. The volcano roared in my ears.

"I heard a crash and Piotr tilted back. His hands went slack, his knees buckled and he slid away from me. Stupid with horror, Malka stood clutching the remains of the water jug which had shattered into many fragments. She'd split Piotr's head open and blood poured from the wound onto the wooden floor. Maria screamed and fainted. Malka seemed like she was in a trance. I remained bent over, heaving, wheezing, gasping, trying to find my breath. Malka then shook her head and blinked. She looked at me.

"'Get out of here,' she said. 'Get out of here now, you devil. Get away while you can,' she cried, then fell to her knees weeping hysterically.

"I needed no further urging from her. I ran out of the room, gathered my things and left. I flew along for miles, following the road by moonlight until I could move no more and lay down to rest for a moment.

"When I awoke, it was daylight. Thinking about what happened, I was convinced that Malka had killed Piotr. There had been a great deal of blood. I also knew that soldiers would come and she would tell them about me. How did I know? I just knew. In truth, I couldn't blame her. I decided to get as far away from there as I could and continue my journey to Budapest and Uncle Herman.

"I had been on the road for not more than an hour when I heard the rumble of hooves. Men riding quickly on horseback. The road curved behind me. I hid. Lay flat to the ground behind a thicket and waited. It took only a moment. Half a dozen Russian soldiers, rifles slung over their backs, bandoliers adorning their jackets, riding with speed and concentration. Their tense bodies leaned into the wind and the horses' necks were stretched forward as they pressed on and on urgently. They passed me by. It was me they wanted. And it wouldn't be long before they realized I couldn't be that far ahead. They would circle back and search.

"We'd all heard stories about the Russians, dear Fanny and what they would do. How brutish and cruel they could be. I'd be shot. Or tortured, then shot. Or perhaps, gutted, then shot. No matter. I backed away from the road and ran wildly into the woods, not thinking clearly. Not knowing where I was going or what I would do. I was blinded. Lashed by fear.

"I ran for a long time, afraid to stop. The sun was now high and I fell to the ground exhausted. Ahead was a small stream. I crawled to it and drank deeply. Then I rolled over and looked up at the sky, panting like a crippled beast. A cloud had passed overhead, casting a shadow. It was not a cloud I saw but the shadow of a man..."

The tape had come to an end and I put my head down and fell asleep. When I awoke, it was not yet light. The house was still. No mischief was yet afoot. I crept into the bedroom, removed my pajamas, pulled out fresh clothes and stole into the bathroom to shower and shave. In the mirror, I saw the crease of the desk organizer etched along my forehead and down my right cheek. Scarface. Let's scare the neighbors.

After I was done and feeling more alert, I went down to the kitchen and made a pot of coffee. I carried the pot upstairs to the office to resume listening to the tale of my great uncle Isaac. I turned over the tape and began again. Mrs. Bernstein seemed to have come to terms with Isaac and his story. Perhaps she was getting caught up in it. No more preambles. No more sharp opinions. Just the accented, nasal voice; her counterpoint, reliving Isaac's early life.

"You must understand, dearest Fanny, I was tired, cold and hungry. I was on the verge of hysteria. The sun blinded me and I thought I was looking into the face of a monster. Sharp, cold steel pressed in against my throat. I dared not breathe. When I swallowed, I felt a thin trickle of blood roll down my neck. I was to be murdered and robbed. My body would be forgotten and desecrated. I would dwell far from home where no one knew me. No one in this peasant land would say kaddish for me. My soul would wander the earth forever, restless and unyielding... As you can tell, sister, I was approaching madness itself.

"The man holding the knife looked down at me calmly. He didn't say any-thing, just looked at me with dark, fierce eyes. He squatted on his haunches. I saw the tops of leather boots that came up to his knees. His moustaches flowed out from his face, curling down his cheeks to a stubbled chin. He wore a broad-brimmed hat held by a string knotted at his throat, pulled low on his forehead. His coat or cloak, fashioned from some coarse cloth came over his head and lay open at the sides. I'd never seen the likes of him before. Then the man licked his lips and smiled an evil smile. His teeth were rotten, blackened and broken in his mouth. He spat then said something.

"I shook my head. I didn't understand. The man glanced up behind me. I knew then he wasn't alone. He said something else. There was a low reply from the other one.

"'What are you doing here, boy? What is your business?' he said in Russian.

"Fortunately, dear Fanny, we had parents who spoke Polish, Yiddish and Russian to us and I understood this barbarian.

"'I am lost sir,' I stammered. The knifepoint withdrew slightly and I rubbed where it had pricked me.

"'You're lying,' he hissed. 'We heard horses. We saw Russian horses and Russian soldiers on them.'

"'What horses would those be?'

"'And you speak Russian,' he added, ignoring my question. 'Why are those Cossacks chasing you boy? What have you done? Answer me now.'

"I didn't know what to say. If I continued to lie, I feared that I would tangle myself up even more. 'They think I've stolen something,' I said.

"The man shifted his weight. I heard a slight rustle as the other came up behind me. "What did you steal, then?" he said.

"'They thought I took money, but I didn't. I didn't take anything. But the farmer reported me.'

"'Why would he do such a thing?' Moustaches asked in mock surprise, shrugging his shoulders as if the notion was ridiculous. Why indeed?

"I decided to take a chance, dear Fanny. These were men, after all and crude at that. 'It was the daughter. She, uh… that is… we, uh…' and I couldn't finish what I was saying.

"Moustaches sat on his rump, threw his head back and roared. The other joined him. That I was miserable seemed to make it funnier to them. The more they looked at me, the more they laughed. 'The daughter… ah yes… the daughter…' Moustaches wheezed, tears squeezing out of his eyes. Finally, he stopped. He slid the knife into a leather sheath attached to his belt. The blade was the length of my forearm, Fanny, I swear it. He stopped abruptly and stuck his forefinger against my nose.

"'This is a good story, boy. But if you are lying, I will cut out your guts and feed them to the wolves. Now, we go. It is good for you that we hate Russians, as much as they hate us. You come with us,' he ordered and lifted me to my feet. The other man was dressed like Moustaches, but taller. Both wore their hair down over their collar and were unkempt. They were not like any I had seen before. More animals than men. Untamed and cruel. They held me between them Fanny, and strode quickly into the woods, propping me with their shoulders, directing me like they would a dog or horse by using their bodies, not words. Deeper and deeper, we travelled.

"I learned their names were Markos and Zeus and they were brothers. They were taking me to an encampment far into the forest, away from prying eyes and ears. They thought the Russians might be after them and had been watching the road carefully, just in case. They had been plying their trade in the area. Whatever that was, I did not know then. I discovered too, they were gypsies or Magyars as Markos called themselves. It didn't matter to me, Fanny. I was relieved they were not going to kill me, that they didn't like Russians and for the moment my life had been spared. Perhaps God had come back from vacation and watched over me after all? Perhaps it is the sinners he likes best, yes?

"After some quarter of an hour of walking, the two gypsy brothers were practically carrying me between them. I could barely hold my head up. My limbs felt like wet logs, heavy and dense. I couldn't tell where we were. Each tree, bush, leaf looked the same as the last but the gypsies pulled up and I sunk to my knees. They crouched low and peered around. Markos made a gesture. Zeus slipped away and quietly circled around to our left. Meanwhile, Markos remained low and alert. After a moment, came a whistle that I took to be the call of some foolish bird. Markos tugged my arm and indicated we must go.

"Luckily, dear Fanny, some twenty-five meters ahead we came to a rutted path that may have been used by peasants and farmers many years ago. But now it was overgrown, barely passable. We followed this path and very quickly it opened into a clearing. In the center of the clearing was an encampment, three contained wagons formed an arc around an open fire. Half a dozen horses, pitiful, mangy-looking beasts, were tethered off to the side. I spotted another man, three women and running in the pasture behind, young children playing a game.

"Zeus appeared from the far side and approached the other man. They put their heads close together and whispered among themselves. Markos and I excited some curiosity. The children ran up to him immediately, two young girls and a boy. They stopped short when they saw me. Markos beckoned.

"'Come', he said to them. 'He won't harm you, little ones.' Then he turned to me. 'How are you called?' he asked.

"I hesitated not wanting to give them my real name. If they knew me as Isaac, they would know I was a Jew and turn me in or kill me. 'I am Vlasic,' I replied, thinking of one of the Polacks from the village near the shtetl. 'My name is Vlasic.'

"'You see?' Markos said, turning back to the children. 'He is Vlasic. With a name like that, he won't hurt anyone.' The children giggled and came forward. They touched me shyly, then became bolder and put their hands all over me, feeling my body up and down, searching like kittens for milk. Then they went back to their father. And suddenly, he laughed uproariously.

"'Good, my pets. Very good.' Then he turned to me and held up something in his hand. It was my money pouch! But how did he get it? He tossed it to me. The children giggled and ran away.

"'They have learned well,' he said as I stared at the pouch in my hand in astonishment. 'You made it easy for them, Vlasic. Don't make that mistake again.'

"'Yes, of course,' I replied. 'I won't.' And naturally, I felt like a fool letting myself be robbed by little children so easily. But I began to get an idea of what these Magyars were about and it was no wonder they were wary of the Russian soldiers.

"Markos clapped his hands on my shoulders and held me fast in front of him. 'Come,' he said. 'You must be hungry and thirsty. You will eat and drink. Then, we shall see what we can do together, eh?'

"I had no choice, Fanny. It was true that I was starving and my throat was dry. But I also knew that Markos was keeping me close for a reason and I remembered the long knife under his cloak. He did not seem the type of person to do a kindness for its own sake. Perhaps he needed a boy to do some work? Or if I was caught by the Russian soldiers, they may be snared also? I felt wary but at the same time grateful..."

I was beginning to think that Mrs. Bernstein was earning her keep. That seventy-five dollars wasn't a bad price, after all. The thought cheered me up. I heard Sharon in the shower and went down to fix some breakfast.

Why did I think that my father was connected to Isaac and his extraordinary tale? I didn't know how or why, but felt it. Yet they were separated by more than time and distance, by personal history. Isaac was a peasant. My father was an urbanized intellectual. But I had the strangest sense of it. It unsettled me. The natural solution was simple: ask him. Again, I hesitated. Perhaps it had something to do with my mother and rekindling those memories that stopped me. Or maybe Isaac's story was just something I wanted to keep to myself. Like a small boy, perhaps I feared that my father would take it away from me.

Most Saturday mornings I made pancakes. It had now assumed the status of a ritual. It was simply expected. And so, I was flipping them with great concentration when Sharon appeared in the kitchen, walking carefully as if the floor might dissolve beneath her. She was dressed in sweat gear, upscale fleece, and came over for a hug. I was flipping the 'cakes when she put her arms around my waist from behind and rested her head on my shoulders. I waggled my arms free. Sharon was not a morning person and cherished her sleep. She resented having to get up early at any time and only did so for work. Otherwise, the world could be in flames and she'd sleep through it.

"They'll burn," I said.

"And a good morning to you too," she retorted and punched me between the shoulder blades.

I turned around and kissed her. "Sorry. Didn't mean to be grumpy. But they will burn if I don't pay attention," I said, turning back to the stovetop. "That's the key in cooking, Sharon. Vigilance. Without it, you might as well boil boots or fry shingles, because that's what they'll taste like if they're overdone."

She laughed. Despite Egan snoring away on our living room floor and the disruption of her plans the night before, she seemed in a decent enough mood. She punched me in the back again, playfully this time.

"Ow!"

"I happen to like boiled boots," she said.

I flipped enough pancakes. "Boys!" I yelled up into the ceiling.

There weren't many times we shared meals together as a family. Sharon was often late coming home from work. Sean and Nathan were starving the minute they walked in the door and required feeding on the spot. Like most families, we were often out of sync, slaves to the daily routine; swimming lessons, ball hockey in the winter, baseball and soccer in the summer, sports camps, work and Sharon's travel schedule. She had a trip coming up soon where she'd be out west for the better part of a week, 'terrorizing the branch offices' as she called it. Knowing her as I do, I had no doubt about it.

The boys lapped up the pancakes. Nathan managed to leave a trail of syrup from his seat to the sink as he cleared his plate. Well, at least he cleared his plate. The two of them took off to resume their rumpus in the basement. It involved winging tennis balls at each other. A vicious form of dodge ball. Sharon watched me scrub the floor clean. The irony of it wasn't lost on me. But if I didn't do it, we'd be stepping in it all day. She sat at the counter, quietly sipping her tea.

"You don't have to do that, you know."

"Yes, I do," I said. She didn't argue it but looked out the doorway through to the living room.

"Look at the big lunk, snoring away like an elephant. He's like a big kid barely able to look after himself. He needs a guardian, someone to take care of him," she said wistfully.

"He's got to take responsibility for himself, Sharon. You treat him like a kid, he'll continue to act like one. We've let him know how we feel and that's all you can do," I said. "Besides, maybe his career is going to take off with this show. You never know."

"Maybe. You're so rational, Bernie. It's maddening sometimes, you know?"

"I know," I admitted. "I'm everyone's conscience, Sharon. And it can be a heavy burden at times." And then I sensed a wave of sadness had come over her and she got up from the counter and put her arms around me tightly and buried her face in my shoulder. I felt her tears wet my T-shirt.

"I know it can," she whispered. "I love you for it."

We held each other closely in the kitchen while I heard the tennis balls ricocheting off the walls below and Egan's ragged snores in the next room.

13

"...I didn't know it then, my dear Fanny, but the most important event of my young life was about to take place. Something I could never have imagined. Markos walked me into the camp and pointed to each person, calling out their names. The children were Mara, Georg and Basha. Markos' wife was called Tamara and the other man, Horst. Then Markos put his hands on his hips and whistled. A young girl emerged from the lead wagon. She was about my age, I believe. Her hair was black and very long and it covered her face. Like a growing, moving mask.

"Holding out his hand, Markos said, 'And this is my other daughter, Dagmar.' "I nodded curtly. 'How do you do, miss?' I said to her.

She parted her hair and peered at me coldly. 'He looks a fool, papa. He will not be any use to us.'

"Markos shrugged. 'Don't worry, my pretty. Leave it to me, yes?'

"She came up to me and looked me up and down like a farmer would examine a pig or goat. She squeezed my bicep, then a calf. 'He's very skinny. And clumsy looking.'

"Markos found himself defending me, which I think went against his natural instincts, but he couldn't let his daughter see he'd made a mistake. And a mistake about what, I had no idea. But I also knew, dear Fanny, whatever it was, it meant that my life depended on performing well. This I knew.

"My face grew hot. 'I am strong,' I said and picked up this Dagmar, this annoying girl, hoisting her high above my head, then set her down again. Her hair flew every which way. 'You felt as light as a feather,' I said, teasing her.

"Her hand flashed out, ready to strike me but I caught her by the wrist. Markos and the others looked on silently. I did not wish to hurt her, but held

66

her hand steady. Then she kicked out with her feet. I stepped back and in doing so, released her. In an instant, a knife appeared in her hand and she came at me. I tripped over a fallen branch and fell backward to the ground. She pounced on me, attempting to strike. God in heaven, dear sister, I thought I'd been attacked by a demon. She tossed the hair out of her eyes with a flip of her head. Our faces were close together and I stared into eyes that were green as emeralds, dear Fanny. Captivating as only jewels can mesmerize the greedy. She stared back at me and something happened. Her eyes widened, then grew narrow. I felt her strength slacken. I held the knife away, even as she pressed in hard with her weight. Then I managed to twist her wrist until she screamed in pain and dropped it. I pushed her off me and picked up the knife.

"'This belongs to you?' I said. Before I could move, she lashed out and raked her nails down my face. I felt the sting and pain of the torn skin. I knew that the others were watching closely and instead of cringing from the hurt, which I would do under most circumstances, I threw the knife at her feet and spat with contempt. She made to spring at me again but Markos seized her from behind.

"'All right, daughter. That is enough,' he commanded sternly. 'This Vlasic will do. He has shown me that he is man enough.'

"Dagmar's green eyes flashed. 'He's still too skinny.' Then she stormed off and disappeared into the wagon.

"Zeus appeared at my side. 'Pity the man who beds that one,' he said in a low voice. 'She'll tear him to shreds.'

Markos clapped me on the shoulder. 'Well done, Vlasic. Dagmar likes you.'

"I was amazed. 'Like me? But… but… you saw! She tried to kill me.'

"Markos laughed softly. 'If she wanted to kill you, boy, believe me you would be dead on the ground with the blade in your chest. No one is better with a knife than Dagmar. Come,' he said. 'We must dress your wound and then we eat. Tonight, we rest. Tomorrow we travel. And you must stay in the wagon. We don't want to have trouble with the Russian soldiers, yes?'

"'But where are we going?' I asked.

"Markos looked at me coldly. 'Does it matter to you, Vlasic, if that is your name? We leave here and go elsewhere. And Dagmar will be disappointed if you try to leave,' he chuckled.

"And that was that, dear Fanny. I was now a Jewish criminal called Vlasic, living and travelling with a band of Magyars, and hated by a dangerous young woman called Dagmar.

"We ate with our fingers out of wooden bowls. It was some kind of stew, lamb I think, and we drank from wineskins. No prayers or blessings, not even goyishe ones. No implements for eating. We did not wash before and after. The men wiped their greasy fingers on the backs of their pants and the children wiped themselves on whatever was handy. The men and women did their business in the woods and used leaves to clean themselves. That was it. I thought of Mama and Papa and what they would say of this. They would curse their luck and pray to take away the horror. Better they not know anything. I told myself not to think of the future, dear sister or what was to be. I should accept what had happened and be thankful my life had been spared. For what purpose? I did not know.

"I learned that Markos had been a soldier in the German Army during the Great War and that he fought in the trenches in France. He could read and write. He had a fondness for the French, even though he fought them as the enemy. He liked French food. His life was saved by a Jewish surgeon, an officer. Markos had taken a bayonet in the thigh. The surgeon asked him if he wanted to go back in the trenches. Markos shook his head. Then, the surgeon had said, *I will write in my report that you should be sent home. Your wound is too serious for active duty.* Markos thanked the surgeon. He asked him why he had helped him. The surgeon replied that he believed all life was sacred. Markos was amazed. He looked at the carnage around him in the tent hospital. The wounded cried out in anguish. Some were missing limbs, had eyes shot out, heads exploded, bodies shattered. The surgeon's smock was covered in blood. *Here,* Markos cried, *you believe life is sacred? Especially here,* replied the surgeon. *Next week, you shall be sent home. Good luck to you my friend.* The surgeon nodded, then left to attend to his duties.

"Markos never spoke to him again. He saw him from his bed, talking to the wounded, fixing bandages, and verifying the dead. The following week, Markos was sent home. He was given a wooden crutch to help with the leg, but the wound wasn't that bad. Markos took the train back to his family. He was thirty-seven years old. The year was 1917 and the War would continue for another year. He still has his uniform, rifle, boots, and helmet from the German Army.

"Markos told me all this, dear Fanny, as I crouched behind him inside the wagon while he sat up front holding the reins. In between, he spoke softly to the horse, then flicked the reins lightly across its back. It was twilight and we followed a track out of the woods to the main road. I had a feeling that he told me this story for a reason. The part about the Jewish surgeon, he gave special meaning and paused. I may have been wrong, Fanny, so I said nothing. I did not wish to give anything away. I was fearful of the outside world still. Every other was a potential enemy, waiting to do me harm. It is a terrible shame, Fanny dear, that we do not learn to trust, no? But then, we can see what too much trust can do. After a short while, I fell asleep to the rhythm of the wagon bumping along the road…"

I shut off the tape to contemplate Isaac's life and the surprising twists he'd experienced so early on. I had ambiguous feelings toward him. At once, he was both despicable and appealing. There was something that I couldn't help but admire a little bit. That he was content to go forward into the unknown, no matter the uncertainty or danger. But I did not think of him as a person with high moral character. Only my grandmother, Fanny, was singled out for his affection. It was not too long afterward, when she left the Old Country and emigrated to Canada. There, she met and married my grandfather. She was eighteen and my grandfather twenty-seven when they courted. They married a year later.

The phone rang.

"Ah, Bernard, my dear boy. How are you?"

"Hello, De Groot. I'm fine, thank you. And you?"

I heard him draw breath, then exhale. Dragging on a cigarillo, undoubtedly. "Anxious, Bernard. I'm always anxious and I'm anxious about you. You haven't called me. I never hear from you," he oozed.

"Ah, I didn't know you cared. I'm touched, really."

"And the book, Bernard? How is the book? Is it palpable? Is it newsworthy? Is it finished?"

"The book is fine. No, it's not finished. I still have four months. It's not due until October, you said." Haven't even started it, really, but I wasn't going to tell him that.

"Yes," he replied with a note of sadness. "I know that's what I said but I'm afraid I've got some bad news for you. I need it for September, dear boy. We're moving it up."

I was incredulous. "What? But why, for God's sake?"

De Groot made much of a sigh, breathing heavily into the receiver. "Well, I suppose it's the vagaries of publishing, Bernard. We've had a crapper, you see. If you must know, someone bailed out and we're a book short for the Fall list.

Ergo, your brilliant biography must step in and fill the void. You understand, don't you?"

"For Christ sake... no, I don't... I won't... I'm not..."

But it was too late as always. De Groot slid away.

"I know you're upset and I know I can count on you, Bernard. Make it wonderful. Let's see it in twelve weeks, my boy. Bye. Bye." And he was gone. I stared at the phone, then dropped it into its place with a clatter.

"Shit!" was the best I could muster. That sneaky bastard. No one wanted to do de Groot's bidding. But it came with the contract and the advance.

14

My father had requested that I submit questions to him in writing rather than get involved in a taped question and answer type interview. Too sloppy, he said. He preferred to respond in kind. That way, the purity of his thoughts would be rigorously maintained. The clarity and conciseness delivered as he had intended. After all, it was reasonable to interpret these qualities as essential to his character. Bloody boring though. How the hell to make this interesting reading? How to get it done by September when it was already May? How to stop my heart from cannoning around my chest cavity?

I went to work on the first set of questions. I'd left it until now, procrastinating, in fact. I was a highly accomplished procrastinator. But given de Groot's recent dictum, I couldn't avoid these issues. I had to get on with it. And quickly.

Research Questions for Eph Goldman
From His Son, Bernard

1. **How did you come to write The Global View?** (Open-ended, I liked that)

2. **What impact did your upbringing have on your career path and in turn, writing The Global View?**

3. **How influential was your spouse when it came to researching and writing The Global View?**

4. **Do you have a philosophy of life? What is it?**

5. **What about your own family? Did your children have an impact on your chosen career? Did they play any role in determining how**

you would conduct your personal and/or professional life? (This would be interesting, since, as a child, I was never privy to this nor would I have dared ask)

6. **Compare your life before and after The Global View was published. Did anything change essentially? If so, why?**

7. **How would you describe your life since The Global View has been published. Can you compare it to your other books and writings?**

8. **Do you think you've left a legacy to the world? If so, what is it? In turn, do you think you've left a legacy to your family? Is it different from the former? If so, describe it in detail.**

9. **What gives you the most pleasure?**

10. **What yields the most pain?**

11. **If you were to write your own epitaph, what would it say? And why?** (Touchy subject that, but I had no time now to broach such things tactfully)

I could almost sense his reaction to what I'd asked. The whole thing was absurd really. I asked myself, why can't I answer these questions? To be fair, I probably could but my answers would differ. To pay my father his due, I had to hear from him what he thought. I hoped he would contemplate these things deeply. I hoped he would take them seriously. I hoped he'd respond quickly.

I sealed the questions in an envelope and called a messenger to deliver them to his office at the university. I knew he'd be there about now. In any event, his secretary would keep them for him. At home, there was always the chance he'd misplace the questions I'd asked him. Now, I must await his response.

15

"You're serious about this?" my father asked me.

"No, I'm kidding. Let's forget the whole thing," I replied testily.

"All right, all right," he muttered through his corned beef on rye. "Keep your shirt on." Then took a swallow of coffee. He held the cup up, indicating to Trudy, our waitress, that he wanted a refill. We were sitting in Zak's Delicatessen having lunch. It was located conveniently near my father's office and house, almost equidistant, in fact. It was only out of the way for me.

Upon receiving the list of questions I'd sent, then having reviewed them, his response was to invite me out for lunch.

"When can I have them back?" I asked.

My father looked amused. "I'll get to it, don't worry."

"Hey, Eph. Time is marching on here. The world is stamping its foot impatiently, eager to read all about you."

"That's it," he said. "Encourage me." Trudy came by finally and refilled his coffee cup, and mine too. He nodded his thanks. Trudy tipped her orange-dyed head. She and my father went way back and had a non-verbal understanding. They communicated with gestures, expressions and who knows? Maybe Bliss symbols too. Then he held up his forefinger to me just like he used to do when I was a child. It could mean, you're in trouble. Or perhaps, wait, something momentous is about to happen.

"I've got something for you." He reached into the briefcase at his feet and pulled out an envelope, the type that had space on the front to write names. It was fastened with a string wrapped around a paper disk in the center. Many names had been written and crossed out. Departmental recycling.

"What is it?" I asked as he handed it over.

"Correspondence," he replied.

"With who?"

"Read the list," he said.

I opened the envelope and removed the top sheet. I scanned the names.

"Let's see. There's Einstein, Russell, Alan Turing, Coco Chanel?"

My father nodded. "She read the book and liked it very much."

I continued. "Okay. Galbraith. Chagall?"

"A very learned and well-read individual," said Eph.

"Hmm. Too bad you couldn't swap a signed copy for an original print."

"Wise guy," my father said.

"Oh, come on," I exclaimed. "John Lennon?"

My father smiled. "Why not? He was no dummy, you know. He thought I was very hip."

"Say, listen. These aren't originals, are they?" I said, indicating the envelope.

"Bernie, Bernie," my father, shook his head. "You think I am a numbskull? Photocopies only. The originals are in a safety deposit box. I'll probably donate them to the university archives after I go."

"Let's not be too hasty," I said, and returned to the list. "R.D. Laing, hmm." The famous Scottish psychoanalyst who committed suicide. "Reading your book didn't push him over the edge, did it?"

"Ha. Ha," my father retorted.

"Oh, come on, now," I exclaimed. "Woody Allen? Have you even seen one of his films? Are you a fan?"

"That doesn't matter. He wrote me a very nice letter saying that The Global View summed up his feelings of hopelessness concerning the future of western civilization and that, in the few thousands of years left, accelerated debauchery was the only sane alternative."

"Sounds reasonable. I understand he practices what he preaches," I replied. I was growing tired of this, however. "You've never shown me these letters before. Why now?"

"It's for the book, of course."

That stopped me momentarily. "You couldn't have predicted that I'd be writing a book about you a year ago, two years ago…"

He nodded in agreement. "True. But I thought someone would eventually."

"You expected your biography to be published?"

"Well, I thought someone would write it, yes. I didn't expect it to be you, Bernie."

"And the letters?" I asked.

"Saved for my own version."

"Your version?"

"Of course. You don't think I'd let my life be mangled by some stranger, some hack writer, do you? But now, I don't have to worry," he said and permitted himself a shrewd grin.

"Because I'll mangle it instead?"

He patted my hand. "Don't be silly. You'll do a great job. I have faith in you."

"Well, that is gratifying." I got up to go.

He slurped more coffee. "You're upset."

I put on my jean jacket. "No, I'm not upset."

"Bernie. I've known you for a while now. I can tell when you're upset. You can't con me like you can Sharon."

"I don't con her either. She pretends not to notice."

"Whatever," my father said. "You've got the letters. Use them."

And for a moment, I was confused. Which letters did he mean? The ones I held in my hand? The celebrity accolades? Or the ones I'd found in his house? The Isaac letters.

"What's the matter?" he asked me.

"Uh, nothing. Just forgot about something that's all." I looked down at his grizzled head. He wore a turtleneck. In May. My mother would cringe. "How did you like Katherine?"

He looked up at me. "A nice girl, very bright."

"A little young though, don't you think?"

Eph laughed. "You think I'm in the market, is that it? She might be, or maybe not. I'm having coffee with her tomorrow night."

"You are?"

"Sure. Why not?"

"I thought you said she was young."

"No, Bernie. That's what you said. I liked her, that's all. We'll just talk a bit. Listen, when you were married for as long as I was to your mother, and then she's no longer there, it's a difficult adjustment. You bury yourself in work but you know what? At my age, there isn't as much work as before or it just doesn't seem as important. There are times, Bernie, when I feel the need for some company," he said.

I sat back down. "So, what does that mean? That you're looking for a little action?"

He looked right back at me, blue eyes boring in. "Maybe I am," he replied. "What of it?"

"She's half your age."

"Right," he said with a tight-lipped smile. "More power to me."

"I thought that this prostate thing, uh, you know, uh, well, made certain things... difficult."

"Are you asking me if I'm impotent?"

I cringed. This was awkward territory here. "Uh, sort of."

"Not any more. I take pills. That's all over," he said with more satisfaction than I would have liked. "You know, I exercise every day. I play squash for an hour and I run. I'm in pretty good shape."

"I'm glad to hear it," I replied.

Then he put on a certain look. "Why are you asking me this? Not that my personal affairs are anybody's business, including yours."

In a way, I wanted to laugh. I was only writing his biography, after all. I hesitated though, not wanting to break a long and deeply held confidence. "Mom told me," I said. "She said that you... that you and her... that you slept in separate beds..."

Eph touched the tips of his fingers together and pressed, up, then down. It reminded me of that joke about the spider doing push-ups on a mirror. Yet, the skin had tightened around his eyes, the jaw line tense. "I'll tell you something about your mother, Bernie, something you may not wish to know..."

"I don't want to know," I said.

He didn't hear me or pretended not to. "Your mother had very a rigid attitude when it came to sex. When we got older, after you and Harry left home, she lost interest. I was still willing. Her reluctance may have started with the prostate trouble but to tell you the truth, I think she was relieved. Relieved that she didn't have to deal with it. Put up with it," he said.

I felt slightly ill. More than slightly. "Sorry I asked." Then hesitated. "Maybe there was a reason she lost interest."

"Yes," he said. "She was a prude. She never liked sex. You can decide whether you want to include that in the book," he said angrily. Then he bent down and replaced the folder in his briefcase, snatched it from my hands.

I got up to go again. For real this time. I had to get out of the enclosed space of the restaurant, away from the smell of hot oil and fried food. He'd shown me another side that made me question everything. I tried to sound casual. To my ears, I was asking for the death penalty in a court of law. "So, when will you have the answers for me?"

"Give me a couple of days," he said briskly. The forefinger went up again. The Prussian headmaster reappeared. "And don't let de Groot dictate to you. It's your book. Don't rush it, if it doesn't feel right."

I gulped, then nodded curtly. "So long."

I ran out of the deli. Trudy swooped in to clear my things. In one hand she gripped the coffee pot, already refilling my father's cup. He bent low over some papers he'd taken out of his briefcase. Looking back through the window from the street, I could see him muttering to himself. Pouring curses on me, likely.

16

I returned to the tapes.

"...January, 1927. My dearest Fanny. I have not written you in a long while. I ask your forgiveness. It is difficult for me to write you now as I must be careful that I am not discovered. And what I write is not discovered. Markos can read and even though I do not think he can read Yiddish, God knows, he may recognize the script. And then my secret would be revealed. I must be extremely careful.

"We have travelled south to the Mediterranean for the winter months. There are many tourists and people on vacation in the resort towns along the coast. We stay in one for several days, then move along to the next one plying our trade. We must camp outside the town limits. The local gendarmes, the police, won't let us bring our wagons into the centers. It is simpler to camp outside.

"On our way south, we passed through Budapest. I managed to steal away for a few hours and see Uncle Herman. His merchandising business is doing well and he has prospered. He asked me to stay but I wanted to get away from the old life, Fanny. He told me of your plans to leave for Canada soon. I think this is a good thing. The old ways are leading nowhere. There is no progress, no hope of getting ahead. Mama and papa are stuck in the hard earth and they can't move. They will die poor and broken. This is cruel to say but I believe it will come to be.

"But I have seen, my dear sister, that the world is changing quickly. I see people with money. I see motorcars choking the roads where once only carts and horses went. I see big houses, like hotels, where single families dwell. Houses that are matched in space by half our shtetl at least. It is difficult to imagine such palaces. Yes, there is movement everywhere except at home. Someday, I would like to join you in Canada. When the time is right to build a brand-new life. Uncle Herman will keep us in touch and when you are settled, I can send my letters to you directly. Some day, my dearest Fanny, we will be together again.

"Uncle Herman was kind enough to make me a loan of some money, which I have promised to repay. It was unfortunate, but I had to leave Budapest rather quickly. We were plying our trade on the streets and I am still learning. My hand found itself in the pocket of a gentleman walking to his office. He was strong and held me tightly while a policeman was summoned. I spent the night in a prison cell. Uncle Herman was good enough to pay the fine and get me released. Markos said that it was time to move on. He was angry. The Magyars normally spend many weeks in the city plying their trade. There is much opportunity to be had. Much money and goods to be taken. It is a life of excitement.

"I would have been abandoned by the Magyars, if it hadn't been for Dagmar. Yes, the very same who raked my face with her nails. The very same who thought I would be useless to them. It is odd, my dear sister, but I thought she hated me. I know that I am young still but the girlish mind is like a fog to me. I can't see into it. And yet she argued with Markos on my behalf. I could not understand what they said. They spoke Hungarian and I have only picked up bits and pieces of it.

"We left Budapest. Markos was sullen and angry. He did not speak to me but held the reins tightly and lashed at the poor horse in fits of cruelty. Until then, I felt I had been useful. I'd learned the art of distraction, so the little children could run their clever hands through pockets and purses. I learned deception, not to give anything away through gestures or the expression on my face. The children would pass me in the street and without stopping, transfer the goods. I, in turn, would do the same, passing the goods to Markos or Zeus. If the children were chased and caught, nothing was in their possession.

"Passing the goods to a second and third person caused confusion to the victims and the police. By the time it was sorted out, we were gone. We had performed this countless times, even in the few short monthsI had been with the Magyars. Markos kept all the money and other items in a lockbox in his wagon. Only he had the key. But there was a great deal of money there. I offered to count it for him as I was always good at sums, but he refused. He was suspicious and guarded his treasure closely. Once, I asked him what he would do with the money. I thought perhaps he would not answer me, but he did.

"'I wish to buy a vineyard,' he said.

"I didn't know what he was talking about. 'A vineyard?'"

"He nodded, then smoothed his long moustaches with the back of his hand. 'It has always been my dream. To be a maker of good wines. To grow healthy grapes. To own much land. Here,' he said. 'I've made a study of it.'"

"And he reached up to a high shelf and brought down a book covered in dust. He blew the dust away and held it out to me. I looked inside. There were pictures of fields and different types of grapes and all sorts of barrels, jugs, and bottles. There were pictures of tubes sticking out of glass vessels. But I couldn't read the script.

"'It's in French,' Markos said. 'I wish to go back to France and purchase the land I need.'"

"'How much will this cost?' I asked.

"'Many thousands of francs,' he replied.

"'And what is the value of a franc?' I inquired.

"Markos looked at me and I could see suspicion cross his face.

"'I have said enough for now,' he said. And he replaced the book on the shelf. 'In two years, I will have enough. See to the horses,' he instructed abruptly.

"'Of course,' I replied. And went off to do his bidding. Naturally, my dear sister, I was curious. Every person had a dream. I didn't know what mine was to be but I began to think about what Markos had said. I also thought about his lockbox and what was inside. I also thought that learning the language of France would be very useful..."

Isaac had a transparent mind. He had made the transition from shtetl life to the outside very quickly.

"...It was not until some days later, my dear sister, when I found myself alone with Dagmar. I had not spoken to her about Budapest and the help she had offered me. I was up early one morning. Brushing the coats of the horses was part of my duties and I liked to do this in the morning. I found sleeping in the wagons cramped and the air stale. I liked the fresh air and on this particular morning, the sun was out. The ground was hard but the clear sky meant a warmer day. Dagmar came out of her wagon to stoke the fire for the morning meal. The rest were still asleep. The Magyars were not too particular about rising early. Often, they stayed up late into the night, drinking spirits and talking.

"We were awkward with each other. She merely nodded to me and went directly to the fire. I continued to brush the horses. I didn't know how to begin with her. I watched her work for a moment. Her hands were strong and quick.

Her long, dark hair shone in the light from the sun. Dagmar kept herself well, better than the others. She rubbed her teeth with a cloth morning and night and rinsed her mouth with balsam and mint to sweeten her breath. I'd learned from her and did the same.

"'I wish to thank you,' I said to her.

"She looked up from the pot she was stirring. 'Thank me. But why?'

"I shrugged. 'You defended me with your father. He was not happy with me. He wanted to leave me behind.'

"'You were careless and it caused much trouble,' she said.

"'But I paid Markos the money from my uncle, yes?'

"'This is true,' she admitted. 'My father was disappointed. He expected to make much more than this.'

"'To buy his vineyard?'

"She looked up sharply. 'He told you of this?' I nodded and she continued. 'Then he is a fool, I think. What do we know of wines and winemaking? We drink only, we don't make the wine.'

"'But it is his dream,' I said.

"She continued to stir the pot. 'Yes,' she said. 'And you Vlasic, what is your dream?'

"'I don't know. Not yet. What about you Dagmar? Do you have a dream?'

"She wiped her hands on her apron, then stood up and stretched in the sunlight. It was a moment, dear Fanny, of some magic. This young girl was having an effect on me. She came over to me and spoke quietly.

"'My dream, Vlasic, is to be rich. To leave this filthy life. To have a house and servants. That is my dream.'

"I paused from the brushing and looked at her. 'Perhaps that is my dream also,' I said, cringing inside at my foolishness. Dagmar would laugh at me or worse, tell Markos. But no, Fanny, she smiled. And her teeth were even and white.

"'Then perhaps, Vlasic, you will be of some use to me, yes?'

"Our faces were quite close together. 'I would welcome it,' I said. I smelled the mint on her breath and the rose of attar she dabbed on her neck. We stood there not saying anything, not touching but locked in a powerful embrace. Then we heard the others stirring. Our eyes met and there was a message. I felt it. She nodded slightly.

" 'We will speak of this another time,' she whispered, then turned back to her work. I continued to brush the horse's coat as I had been taught. But I felt terribly excited. Excited in a way that I had never felt before, dear sister. That for the first time, I had found a true companion…"

That night I hoped to sleep well and tackle my work first thing in the morning. I was in bed when Sharon came home. She was incapable of moving about quietly. She and her mother both had leaden feet. And the clackety-clack of her high heels sounded like a snare drum in a jazz band. She opened and closed drawers. She ran the water. She flushed the toilet. She sorted through her closet, moving hangers back and forth. Metal grated on metal.

"You up?" she finally asked.

"Cripes, who wouldn't be?" I replied. I checked the clock. It was eleven-thirty. "What took you?"

She shrugged. "Just working on the financials, you know. Year-end is coming up. God, I'm buggered," she said and yawned deeply. "How're the boys?"

"They're sleeping like babies and look like angels. Rather deceiving, isn't it?" I said.

"Anything happen?" she asked, finally climbing into bed.

"They got into it a little bit at school," I said.

"What do you mean?"

"Oh, a bunch of them were playing tag. Sean was It. He slipped and fell into a puddle and got himself soaked. They all laughed, including Nathan. So, Sean took it badly and went into a major huff. You know, the usual."

"But you sorted it out?" she asked.

"Didn't you get my message? That I called?"

"I think I did. To tell the truth, I don't remember. I get so many of them. There's no bloody time to answer them all."

"Not even from your husband?"

"Well, I figured we could work it out at home, if anything came up," she said and smiled in her dazzling way. "But the boys are all right now, are they not?" Her expression told me she wanted me to say yes.

"Yeah," I said. "It's fine now. They're right as rain. I let them watch Batman as a treat. That seemed to mollify the situation."

Sharon arched an eyebrow. "Mollify? Lovely word that, isn't it?"

"Yeah, mollify. Something wrong with mollify?"

She leaned in. "Nothing. Nothing's wrong with it," she said. Then arched a pale eyebrow. "Why don't you think about mollifying me then?"

Sharon knew I wasn't completely awake. "My, you're awfully frisky," I said. Then I thought for a second and looked at her quizzically. "That's unusual, especially at this hour," I said, suddenly coming alert.

"I know, so you'd better take advantage of it when you can, hadn't you? It doesn't happen often. Come on then," she said, "show me your mollifier."

I didn't tell Sharon about the verbal duel I'd fought with my father. More terror under the surface. I knew it would blow a hole in the earth's crust some day. The pressure was building up. Nor did I mention that her friend seemed to have caught Eph's fancy. More than just a little. I didn't want to give her the satisfaction.

I was back at it early the next morning, as soon as everyone was out the door. I carried coffee up the stairs and settled behind my desk. The pressure was making its presence felt. Like the Force, de Groot seemed to be with me. Mrs. Bernstein had kept a steady supply of tapes coming. The last came with a note. It read: *Only one more tape, I think*. She signed it, *Mrs. B.*

"...March, 1927. My Dearest Fanny. Dagmar and I have drawn closer together. She whispers things to me now. Sometimes, we manage to slip away and meet together, just to talk. She talks and I listen. We are the same age but she has seen much more than I. This life is so different from the shtetl, Fanny. Constantly moving, never staying still. When I think of our little town and Mama and Papa, it seems to me that time never moved at all. We did everything in the same way, never changing, never learning. It was like being smothered with a pillow, that kind of life. I'm happy to leave it behind.

"Dagmar speaks of what her life will be like once she leaves her family and goes off on her own. I ask her where will she go and how will she live? But she never answers directly, only smiles back at me. *You leave that to me*, she always says. Once, our conversation became serious and a bit strange, dear sister.

"'Do you like me, Vlasic?' Dagmar asked.

"I touched my hand to my cheek, remembering the tearing of her nails. 'Yes, I think so,' I replied.

"She smiled broadly. Her lips were painted, I noticed. 'Do you know what I mean when I ask if you like me?' And she stepped closer. I smelled the mint on her breath.

"This made me nervous, dear sister. We were in the woods, away from the camp but I was afraid we'd be seen. I glanced around.

"'I know what you mean, Dagmar,' I said.

"Dagmar swayed slowly on her feet. 'Good,' she replied. 'Then you must kiss me to prove it.'

"And dear Fanny, this I did. And more besides. It was very confusing for me. I was feeling things toward her that were new to me. She knew a great deal more than I. But I knew too that I was clever and learned quickly of things. Over the coming months, Dagmar drew me to her more and more. Finally, we were inseparable. We tried to keep it a secret and I was very much afraid of Markos and what he would think. That he might kill me when he found out. I did not know at the time, that my closeness with Dagmar was not of concern to him. The Magyars were very open about such things, but I did not know this. No, my dear, it was what we did afterward that sparked Markos' hatred and bitterness toward me. But then, I move too quickly and before I am ready…"

17

I'd had a call from Egan. The opening of his show at the Levinsky Gallery was but two days away. Ads had been run in the Arts sections of all the local papers touting Egan as a 'dazzling new talent'. Levinsky had arranged some advance notices from local art critics and the reviews were positive, if not glowing. The reviewers all remarked on Egan's flamboyant personality and his unconventional lifestyle. He was compared to Pollock. Heady stuff, indeed. One critic had hailed him as the painterly equivalent to Yeats. Egan was flush with excitement. I was pleased for him.

"You've got to pinch me, Bernie. Is it really happening?" he asked.

"Looks like it," I said.

"You mean I'm not going to wake up and find it's all a dream?" he said, much like a young child asking his dad.

I laughed. "We're all asleep then. How's your mum feel about it?"

"Ach, she's marvelous, she is, just marvelous. Those other two, now," he said, referring to his brothers, "they keep telling me they've saved a spot for me at the factory, just in case."

"Superstitious, are they?" I asked, since I often felt that way myself.

"Ah no. Just stupid, I think Bernie. They don't understand this stuff. They don't understand why someone'd bother, you know? Why take time off to look at paintings when you could watch football on the telly? Ignoramuses, the pair of them. Still, they're family and they said they'd come. For a while anyway," he said.

"You told them about the free beer?" I said.

"Right," Egan replied and then laughed. "You've a dirty mind, Bernie. Are you Irish, by the way?"

I laughed back at him. "Not yet, but it's wearing on me."

"Listen, I've got to ring off now, okay? We're still hanging the show and Levinsky wants me down there to supervise. So, I'll see you there, right?" he asked and I sensed his nervousness and his need for the support of familiar faces.

"We'll be there," I assured him. "Without fail."

"Right," he replied. "I'm off then. Ta." And he hung up.

I should have known that when Egan was involved, nothing was simple or straightforward. Mundane events became a spectacle. Why should this be any different?

I turned my attention back to the tapes. I found that I liked Mrs. Bernstein's renditions now. She should consider narrating a Talking Books series; Modern Shtetl Stories perhaps, or Sholom Aleichem–the Abridged Version. Who knows, she might develop a serious cult following.

"...May, 1927. My Dearest Fanny. Do you remember that it was my birthday, just yesterday? I feel as if many years have passed by. And so quickly. I think of the sponge cake mama always baked and how she would set the table with her best things. She would bring out the linen tablecloth she was given for her wedding. She would polish the silverware and we would have a wonderful meal. Even papa was quiet and respectful, not tiresome as he is normally. You may ask, do I miss this? How is this possible since the life I now lead is so wonderful? So exciting? I quarreled with papa from sunrise to sunset and he slapped my face too. His slapping me became a regular occurrence, part of the day. Like putting on tefillin. Like davening. Like keeping kosher.

"And yet, there was the good and the bad. So, there is something to miss. But you are in Canada now, my dear sister, and things would never be the same again at home. I have heard that Canada is a cold and forbidding place. I know that Jews live there but in what circumstances? Are there shtetls? Can Jews own property and operate businesses? Do they fear the police? Ach, I am writing nonsense, I think. Do not mind me.

"I write to you like this because my circumstances are quite different now. It is all upside down and I'm not even sure how or why this has happened. Once again, some force has pulled me forward and I feel weak and powerless.

"It began some weeks ago. Dagmar called me to her because she wanted to show me something. We slipped inside her wagon and she told me to seat myself. Then she showed me two urns. One was bright and shiny. It looked as if the forge had just finished with it. The other was ancient looking, as if it had just been unearthed from a cave or deep pit. I did not know what I was to look for. Dagmar held each up in turn.

"'Which do you think is more valuable?' she asked me.

"I shrugged, before pointing to the shiny urn. Dagmar laughed at me.

"'I thought you'd say so. You are foolish,' she said.

"I became angry. 'If you knew the answer, then why ask me?'

"She stroked my face. 'You are too quick to anger, Vlasic. Look now,' and she held up the shiny urn. 'This will fetch five francs only. Now this,' and she pointed to the other, dingy urn, 'will fetch 100 francs,' she said.

"'But it is old and dirty,' I cried. 'Who would want it?'

"'That is why, silly, because it is old. The older the better. And the more some fool will pay for it,' she said.

"This made no sense to me, Fanny dear. All of our things at home looked like the old urn and I knew they had no value to anyone. They were worthless. 'I don't believe you,' I said.

Dagmar ignored me. 'Do you know, Vlasic, that these two urns were made by the same man on the same day?'

"I was incredulous. 'This is not possible,' I replied. 'The other is clearly old and badly used.'

"Dagmar shook her head. 'But it is the truth and I shall prove it. Look!' She turned each urn over and on the bottom was the imprinted date.

'But how?' I asked her.

"'Don't you see, silly? I have learned how to do this trick with many different objects. Make them look old and people will pay many francs for ordinary things. This, you see, dear Vlasic, is my plan,' she said.

"'To make everything look older?' I asked foolishly and grinned.

"She slapped my face. 'Do not mock me, Vlasic.'

"I grabbed her wrist and we were back to the beginning. 'And do not slap me, ever,' I cried. I held her hard and finally, she nodded. 'Now tell me of this plan,' I said.

"Dagmar had collected many things that she kept in her wagon. And she had been practicing this art of aging. She told me she had perfected it and was ready to begin on her own. That Markos had sold many of these objects for a great deal of money. Money that belonged to her. Money that was in the lockbox. Dagmar wanted me to help her steal the money from Markos, then she and I would leave. We would run away to Paris and become dealers in these objects. We would use the money, her money, to get us started.

"I sensed terrible danger in her plan. I feared Markos and what he would do. I knew he had plans to start a vineyard and the money was for that purpose. To steal it would smash his dream. A man wouldn't let go of that easily, even for his own daughter. He would not forgive – he would follow us and he would kill me. This I felt, as sure as trees sprout leaves.

"I told her it was too dangerous, but she wouldn't listen. I told her Markos would kill me, and her too. She scoffed. Dagmar is very strong-willed and stubborn, Fanny, and I could not break her will. And then she told me something that made me give in to her. She told me she was carrying my child. And if Markos found this out, which he would soon, he'd kill me anyway. So, you see dear Fanny, there was little choice. I called on God to watch over me, sinner that I am and we made our plans.

"Over the coming weeks, my dear sister, we talked of how it would be. I kept thinking about this and felt deep in my heart that I would be cursed. That evil would come of it. Like the old women in the shtetl, I took to spitting at every little thing and saying blessings to myself. To protect me from this evil. I was afraid, Fanny, of what would happen. What if it all went wrong? I pleaded with Dagmar to change her mind but she wouldn't listen. Her heart was hard; do you understand, Fanny? She had hardened her heart against her own family.

"She told me that we needn't take all of Markos' money. He would have plenty left. We'd only take what was hers. How much could this be, I asked myself? And how could I argue, Fanny, when I had done the same to my own mama and papa not even a year ago? I understood her desire to do this since I'd done the same. But still, I hesitated.

"We were walking in the woods, hand in hand when I told her of my doubts. She reminded me of the child and that her body was beginning to change. And then she said something that nearly chased my soul.

"'And what do you think would happen to a Jewish baby?' Dagmar asked.

"I stopped still. I could feel my heart thumping, Fanny. 'What do you mean, Dagmar? You confuse me.'

"Dagmar put her hands on her hips. It was true they were more rounded now, and her bosom had grown fuller. 'You think I am a fool, Vlasic?'

"'Of course not. You, my pretty Dagmar, are not a fool,' I replied. It was hot and I was sweating profusely. My mouth was parched.

"'I have seen your writings. Your letters,' she said. 'I cannot read them, but I have seen such script before. We pass them by, those people, in the little towns and villages. I see them with their long coats and funny hats and thick beards. Everyone hates them. Do you want our child to be hated?' she asked matter-of-factly.

"I stammered. I stuttered. 'You… you… looked at my letters? Without my knowing?'

"She waved at a fly. 'Yes. But it didn't matter, my dear. I suspected anyway. For a woman, it isn't difficult to tell,' she said.

"Again, she confused me, Fanny. This mind, it is always a mystery, a puzzle. No way in or out. 'And what does being a woman have to do with it?' I said arrogantly. And she laughed and laughed, Fanny, until I thought she would faint.

"'You are such a boy, Vlasic. Shall I still call you Vlasic? Yes, I think I shall. I like this name for you. And it is safer too,' she said.

"I seized her wrists. 'Answer me!' I roared. 'How do you know?'

"She didn't say anything, but glanced down at me. I looked at her. She glanced down at me again. I must admit, dear sister, I was as thick as an ox. Then, finally, she touched me and I understood.

"I became suspicious then. 'Have you been with others, Dagmar? Don't torture me. Tell me the truth. Have there been others?'

"She wanted to laugh, I could see it, but she shook her head. She knew the thought of it caused me pain. 'No, don't be silly, Vlasic.'

"'Then, how…?'

'I have a little brother, don't I? And an uncle and a father too? In the summer time, we often bathe out of doors or swim in rivers and lakes we pass by. Do you think we put on bathing costumes like aristocrats? Silly boy, that's how I know,' she said. 'Papa wouldn't let the child live, Vlasic. Do you hear? If he knew, I mean. You have been very clever until now. I won't take that chance with my child, Vlasic, do you hear? I won't. And we will need money,' she said.

"Of course, my dear Fanny, Dagmar was right. So, I set my fears aside. We made our plans. Markos kept the key to the lockbox on a chain around his neck. To slip it off would be difficult. Dagmar could read and write only a little but she knew of many things. She told me of her grandmother and her skills with potions and curses. Dagmar learned from her how to put people into a sweet, dreamless sleep. Then, they would wake up, no harm done and remember nothing. What of the children? I asked her. The children would receive half the amount, she said. I was suspicious of her and her potions. We agreed to a test. She slipped a potion into the cup of Zeus one evening as he drank wine. We watched, as, within a few minutes only, he slipped into a deep sleep. He did not awaken the next day until nearly midday, his wits dulled. Zeus reasoned that the drink was very powerful to make him feel this way. Finally, I was convinced. We were ready..."

18

In the summer of 1950, my father had occasion to spend time in Italy. He had become interested in the exploits of early Italian explorers and received a small grant from the government of Italy and the Italian-Canadian Benevolent Society to carry out his research. In early July of that year, some five years before I was born, he boarded an Air Canada flight to Rome which lasted some twelve and a half hours, then stayed overnight in a small hotel near the airport. The next morning, he rented a car and drove to the beautiful city of Florence where he planned to spend the next six weeks pursuing research in a small, obscure library housed in a building named after Arturo Toscanini. The Medici library was relegated to the basement of the Toscanini building, itself quite grand, practically palatial in size and bearing. The basement was ill-lit and damp.

My father was delighted to discover, however, that the library was exceptionally well organized and scrupulously maintained. The orderliness that Eph witnessed there was entirely due to the head librarian, a man named Francesco Barzini. Barzini was well-suited to the role of librarian, he had a labyrinthine mind that housed a googolplex of disparate facts he was able to connect and weave together. Barzini was a computer on legs before the world could ever have fully conceived of such a thing. And unlike many librarians of my father's acquaintance, and many others I suspect, the fellow had a raucous sense of humor and rarely spoke in hushed tones.

"Why should I keep my voice down?" he'd say. "There's never anyone here." That is, until Ephraim Goldman arrived on a blazing July day circumspect from his journey while having felt the scorn, firsthand, of Italian drivers who thought they were competing in the latest Grand Prix at Monaco. Barzini kept an office in the library, but he preferred to sit at a badly scarred desk near the entrance.

This way, he could keep tabs on the comings and goings of the few academics who used his services and more importantly, monitor the status of his precious books. And precious they were, some in fact, dating back to the tenth and eleventh centuries. Books that had been penned by Franciscan monks, who labored by waxy taper, meticulously scribing in Latin, Italian and classical Greek.

My father, of course, was eager and bursting to do something. He was young and full of energy. Barzini recognized this immediately. "Aha," Barzini exclaimed as my father stepped boldly through the library door, "here is a man of great intellect, bristling with curiosity."

"Thank you," my father said. "But how would you know?"

"I can see it clearly," Barzini replied. "Besides, so few come down here to do research that it is only those who are exceptional who show up, you see." My father would come to celebrate and exult in the moment that he met Barzini for as we shall see, it set him on his course with destiny.

What Eph saw before him was a rotund man, tufts of black hair shooting off his scalp at all angles, victim of a mischievous child. Barzini had a pair of liquid brown eyes and a small, delicate mouth. His nose was almost snubbed and appeared even smaller within the contours of his round face. Eph was surprised to see that Barzini was as tall, if not taller than himself. He stood some six feet at least and his slumped shoulders were broad and powerful, although he appeared bow-legged and dipped when he walked. Barzini represented a presence, a fully dimensional character who breathed fire into his place in the world, stoking up an active persona when engaged.

Barzini beckoned as my father stood there transfixed. "Come professor, enter my humble domain. How may I serve you?"

"I am not a professor yet, merely doing some research."

"You have your degree, do you not?" Barzini murmured.

"Yes."

"Then you are a *dottore*, signor. It is simple, no?" Eph shrugged, then stepped forward. You have to realize that this was a different sort of Eph Goldman, a man who, unlike Barzini, hadn't found his place in the world. Not shy or hesitant about his intellect or his basic inherent qualities, he was at this point in his life a bit directionless. He hadn't yet found his niche. I found this Eph quite appealing because he seemed more like myself. The best thing in Eph's life up until that point, apart from earning his doctorate in almost record time, was being married to my mother.

"What are you seeking, young dottore? Where may I direct you?"

"Italian explorers," my father mumbled.

Barzini's eyes widened, his round face lit up. "That is wonderful, marvelous! You, signor, have come to the right place."

"Thank you."

My father had come prepared to research. His battered briefcase was stuffed with paper and pens, a Latin and an Italian dictionary, ruler, magnifying glass and no less than fourteen erasers. But he didn't set hands on a single tome that day, eager as he was to begin. Barzini took over and bade him to set down opposite.

"Now what is it about Italian explorers, exactly signor?"

"Umm, the obscure ones. The ones who travelled widely and made important discoveries but haven't been given the recognition they deserve."

Barzini craned forward in his seat, which squeaked loudly. He seemed excited and licked his lips in anticipation. "Yes? Go on."

My father hesitated. This was a competitive business and he didn't know this Italian fellow. What if he gave away his research by happenstance? But again, something about Barzini's eagerness, his animated round face reassured him. Eph felt he was in the presence of a scholar and a man who loved knowledge and learning for its own sake. Why else would he sit in this dungeon, so comfortably, yet so far away from the pulse of the university?

"Matamoro," my father muttered.

Barzini slammed his hand down on his desk, sending up a fine cloud of dust as he hit the jacket of a well-thumbed book. "It is God's will," he pronounced and looked heavenward. "I knew you would come." And Barzini jumped up out of his chair and began pumping my father's hand. "I have been praying for this day."

My father was bewildered. "But..." He attempted to remove his hand from the other's plump grasp and with a strong tug finally did manage to pull himself free. "I don't understand."

"Matamoro. Matamoro," Barzini repeated. "An ill-understood man who achieved greatness, signor, not by design, yes? But by a force of nature that propelled him to a subdued glory."

"You know Matamoro?" Eph was incredulous. He thought that he was the only one who had latched on to Matamoro. How could this be? "How? Where?"

Barzini clapped his hands and rubbed his plump palms together. "I have translated the diaries of Diego Matamoro," he announced triumphantly.

My father didn't know whether to rejoice or throw up. He chose to drop his briefcase and slump into a chair.

"I didn't know Matamoro left a diary," he said miserably.

"Oh yes. And a fantastic document, signor."

"You translated it into what, exactly?"

"Italian from the original Latin." Barzini reached into his trouser pocket and pulled out an ancient, dented pocket watch. He flipped the lid and scrutinized it carefully. "It is lunch time nearly. Come, I shall close up and we shall have lunch in the piazza. There is a marvelous little café there. We can sit outside but it is nicely shaded and there is a cooling breeze. Come. Come. And I shall tell you what I know of Matamoro. This is a stroke of good fortune, don't you agree?"

My father wasn't sure, his competitive hackles were on the rise but he was willing to compromise. "Yes, of course," he replied primly.

Barzini removed his cardigan and hung it over the back of his chair. He rolled up his shirtsleeves to reveal a pair of meaty arms and from his shirt pocket took out a pair of dark glasses that he set on his narrow little nose. Barzini locked the door behind them and rattled it vigorously until the glass pane shook.

"There are thieves everywhere," he cried.

Satisfied, he took my father by the arm and steered him down a series of corridors, then up three sets of stairs before they emerged into the sunshine. Before them lay a beautiful little square with shops and cafés full of strolling people chatting and laughing in the sunshine. Eph was disarmed. The effect of the bright sun and the good humor of students linked arm-in-arm was charming. He marveled at the small cars and the motor scooters the Italians used for transport. He had difficulty negotiating the narrow roads in the small Fiat he'd rented and had trouble folding himself inside.

Barzini led him to a sidewalk café where the waiters wore spotless white aprons over black trousers. Their white shirts sparkled in the sunlight. Barzini called out to one of the waiters, whose name was Paulo. He acquired a table situated just as he had described, one which afforded a perfect view of the street scene yet was set back just far enough to give perspective and a feeling of distance.

"I told you, eh? This is my table. They hold it for me every day."

"You eat here every day?"

"But of course. It connects me to the world. Otherwise, I am in the dungeon from morning to night. That is not good for any man, let alone an Italian who loves life, signor. And now, of course, we must introduce. I am Barzini, Francesco Barzini."

"Eph Goldman." And they shook hands.

"Eph? I have never heard of such a name."

"It means Phil or Phillip."

Barzini raised his large head. "Ah, I see. Phillip." The waiter bustled over and Barzini ordered rapidly in Italian. Eph, who spoke passable Italian, couldn't pick up a word of it. When he had finished, Barzini turned to my father and said, "So, you are a scholar, Phillip?"

"Yes."

"Then you must come to dinner at my villa this evening. I am always happy to entertain a scholar at my house."

"But that's not necessary, really."

"I insist. So, it is decided. Ah, here is the vino." Barzini ate and drank prodigiously talking all the while. In comparison, my father was taciturn, a quiet and reluctant companion, all of which seemed to spur the gregarious Italian on even more. This fellow, this Canadian was so serious, so dour.

"The wine is very good."

"I know this," Barzini said importantly. "And I am glad you remarked on it, signor. This wine comes from the grapes that my family have been growing for many generations. This is Barzini wine and it is famous throughout this region."

They tucked into the pasta with relish. Although the day was hot, Barzini's table was perfectly situated, in the shade with a good view of the streetscape and attended by a mild breeze that Eph found refreshing. Four courses later, however, after having finished the pasta, then the veal, the salad and finally, the dessert with coffee, Eph found himself reeling and infused with torpor. He wasn't sure he could push himself away from the table and stand up, let alone do any work. Barzini, however, took it all in stride.

"Now," he said. "We begin with Matamoro but it is a beginning only, no?"

"Of course." Eph sipped the strong coffee, the espresso. The hairs on the backs of his hands felt like they were standing on end. Barzini settled back in his chair and began to speak.

"And here is the beginning of the story. Diego Matamoro was born in 1483 in Genoa, Italy. He came from a family whose life had been consumed by the sea. His fathers and brothers were fishermen. When he was young, Matamoro worked on the boats hauling nets, sorting the fish. But there was a tradition where the youngest of the family – there were eight children – was sent into the priesthood. Matamoro's mother had prepared him from a young age. He was the only one of the children who went to school regularly. He was taught to read and write by the Jesuits and in the evenings after school and after the boats were moored and the nets set out to dry, Matamoro practiced his letters in a small, neat hand. Ink and paper were precious commodities, so Matamoro learned how to use every space on the paper. He learned how to scribe in tight rows and pursued his lessons by candlelight, writing out his Latin and Italian in teeny-tiny little letters. One interesting thing about Matamoro was that his given name was not Diego but Donato. Years later, he was to change it for reasons he thought made sense at the time. From the age of six, Matamoro attended the priests in the local church, and by the age of nine, was a full-fledged altar boy. He also sang in the choir and had a lovely light tenor voice. Matamoro did not question his path in life. It was God's will. Besides, it was expected of him and he couldn't disappoint his parents, who took great pride in having a priest in the family. It gave them a measure of respect in the community. Although, Matamoro did not question his parents or his role, it was true that he was restless. In the evenings, when he lay in his cot at night, he thought of the sea. At any time during the day, he would turn toward the sea, he would think of the smell of the brine and look for the swirl of the current, the force of the tide, imagine the feel of the swell beneath his feet on the boat. The relentless routine that began at 4 a.m. with morning prayers and ended at dusk with evening prayers did not enliven Matamoro's soul; it deadened it.

"The church had always been able to provide for its own. Although the food was plain, it was plentiful. There was much work to do as Genoa was a lively place even in 1498, when Matamoro was in his sixteenth year and about to begin his studies in earnest. Ships from all over Italy and indeed the known world; Spain, Portugal, France and England, stopped in Genoa and the city was known for its commerce and as a center for trade. Matamoro knew this meant that on every tide, ships went out to sea seeking adventures of the type that only inflamed his mind. One of Donato Matamoro's daily tasks was to dump the refuse from the previous day. According to the custom of the times, the waste was hauled in a cart and dumped a short distance away from the back of the church. If there was convenient hill or stream, the garbage would have been deposited there, but in Genoa, there was no such convenience. The poor and the destitute of the community waited for Donato Matamoro. Usually, he was accompanied by a tall, sturdy prelate whose name was Father Finzi. Father Finzi carried a cudgel that he used to beat off the overeager of the destitute and poor who came to scavenge among the garbage.

"One of these poor souls – at least, that's the way Matamoro thought of them – was a young girl close to him in age. Her hair was long and dank and her face was covered in dirt. Her clothes were threadbare and scarcely covered what Matamoro noticed was a fulsome bosom. She wore no shoes. The girl knew that the young priest-to-be had noticed her and they exchanged glances. Afterward, Matamoro made certain he dumped the garbage closest to the girl, so she might have the first pick. She looked at him gratefully, even smiled shyly. This girl, as girls in her social class often were, was well-acquainted with the coarser aspects of life, including having been used by the men in her family for crude purposes. Their attentions repulsed her but she had come to accept it, having realized there wasn't much she could do. She tried talking to a priest once but he had accused her of being wanton and deliberately trying to be provocative and made her do much in the way of penance. But she dreamed of a different life and the look of the innocent young priest-in-training charmed her. He was to her, the ideal man, kind and caring and attentive. The girl had no illusions but still, she dreamed. But she realized that there was more to these glances and looks than mere innocence could provide. She knew how to recognize lust and she saw it clearly in the brightly scrubbed face of Donato Matamoro, whose beard had scarcely begun to grow.

"It was not long before Luciana, for that was her name, found the means to cross paths with Matamoro. The young man was not hidden away in the church all day, every day. There were other duties to perform, those of the more mundane kind, such as helping load and unload provisions, going with some of the older priests who were called to the homes of the parishioners to preside at the bedsides of the ill or otherwise stricken. Luciana had decided she wished to experience love or at least her understanding of it and she had fixated on this young man whose clean persona appealed to her. We have heard many stories over the years of things that had gone on behind the walls of churches and abbeys and indeed, in the late 1400s, these rumors circulated from time to time. Stories of orgies between priests and nuns, or other pagan rituals where young girls and boys had been snatched off the streets and forced to participate in heinous acts. According to Matamoro and his diary, no evidence of such acts was displayed. However, it was known that even a priest was a human being and there were occasions when some of them had a special relationship with some of the parishioners. The hulking priest with the cudgel, Father Finzi, was just such an example. Matamoro had accompanied Father Finzi on some of his visits outside the walls of the church. There was a widow, a Signora Delvecchio who Father Finzi visited regularly. On these occasions, Matamoro was left to wait in the kitchen of the Signora's large house. One time, Matamoro waited in the kitchen with only the cook, an ugly woman with warts all over her face. Just looking at her made Matamoro cross himself repeatedly. After half an hour or more – Matamoro wasn't sure since he had no way of actually telling time – he became restless and left the kitchen to find Father Finzi. The cook called to him, imploring him to return, that she would give him a bowl of broth but Matamoro turned a deaf ear. He wandered through the halls and in and out of rooms. So many rooms for a house with only one person living in it, he thought. There was a sitting room which had a pianoforte and a room filled with books and another room where Matamoro saw only baskets for sewing. This Signora Delvecchio must do a great deal of sewing to devote an entire room to its practice, he thought. And finally, he found a stairway and slowly climbed the stairs, careful not to make too much noise. At the top of the stairs, Matamoro could turn right or left. He turned left and immediately spotted Father Finzi's cudgel propped up against the wall, for Father Finzi never went anywhere without his cudgel. So this was very curious indeed. Matamoro picked it up, feeling the heft of it in his hands. A formidable weapon indeed. He leaned against the nearest door and was surprised to find it gave way. Matamoro started back but the door opened enough for him to see inside. And what he saw astonished him. The first thing he saw were the buttocks of Father Finzi and they were moving up and down in a pumping action. Matamoro realized there was another pair of legs and that the widow Signora Delvecchio was lying beneath Father Finzi, her knees pointed upward and the two of them were making quite extraordinary sounds. For some reason, Matamoro found himself both confused and excited. Just over the good Father's shoulder, he could see the signora's face flushed with a pained expression. In fact, she seemed to be in great pain if the depth of her moans was any indication at all. She seemed transported in fact, and for a moment Matamoro toyed with the fact that Father Finzi was administering a new form of benediction but his rational being rejected that as he felt himself get an erection. Then he knew that benediction had nothing to do with it. Matamoro was lost in these personal revelations until the good signora, having gasped her last and greatest explosion of pleasure, raked the good father's back with her nails, allowed her head to loll back on the pillow. Glancing up through half-opened and blurry eyes, she spotted the young priest-to-be standing on the threshold staring at her wide-eyed and mouth unhinged. Thus, her last moan of pleasure was followed with a shriek of fright such that even Father Finzi was immediately roused from his state of exhaustion and rolled over to take a look. When Matamoro saw the furious expression on Father Finzi's face, he stepped backward and as a reflex picked up the cudgel. Father Finzi roared in anger and gathering his strength and wits – not necessarily in that order – sprang at the young man, letting out a bellow of rage. As the specter of Father Finzi, all naked and sweating and bellowing came at Matamoro, he jumped back and the unfortunate Father tripped and tumbled out of control, legs and arms flying in all directions down the stairs where he was rendered either dead or unconscious. Having pulled a light wrapper around herself, one that didn't conceal all of her womanly charms, the good signora flew to her lover's side crying and shrieking hysterically. Matamoro descended the stairs on shaky legs, the cudgel still in his hand, dragging it as he stepped down.

"She continued to cry and weep over the prostrate form of the good Father. "Is he dead, signora?". Matamoro felt around the priest's neck and face, then with a great effort managed to roll him over and placed his hand over his mouth and then over his heart. "He lives still. Perhaps we should get him upstairs and then summon the physician?" Matamoro was exhibiting quite a calm presence of mind given the situation. The signora looked at him dully and nodded her agreement without speaking. She ran to the kitchen where she summoned the ugly cook. Together, the three of them managed to half-carry, half-drag the unfortunate Father Finzi to the bedroom and settle him as comfortably as possible in the bed, her bed. "I shall tell the Bishop he has had an accident, signora."

"Yes, do that. Now go quickly and get help."

"Young Matamoro ran as quickly as he could, although encumbered by the cassock and sandals that he wore. Poor Father Finzi was never the same afterward. He had crushed part of his skull and had become a drooling idiot. No more would he carry the cudgel that sparked terror in the rabble around the church. He required care for the rest of his days. And certainly, young Matamoro, being impressionable, could not rid from his mind the images that haunted him, those of the good but unfortunate father and the signora in bed together. The look on her face as the father pressed against her seemed full of bliss and the sounds she made were those of pleasure not pain. Matamoro wondered about this and it wasn't long before he was summoned to the house of the signora.

"Sit by me," Signora Delvecchio said to him and she patted the finely brocaded pillow. Timidly, he did as she bade him. After he had sat himself down, he could feel the closeness of her, could smell the sweet scent that she wore and see the space between her breasts where a dazzling pendant hung very low. She placed a hand on his knee and he jumped. "My, you are nervous. Don't be." Then she sighed deeply and Matamoro watched the pendant rise and fall with each breath. "I have been so lonely since Father Finzi had his unfortunate accident. Will you be so good as to keep me company just as Father Finzi did?" And the signora, who was very beautiful looked deep into his eyes. Donato Matamoro could barely speak, his words had dried in his throat. He felt the stirring between his legs and shyly, he nodded without saying a word. The signora kissed his hands. "Then I know that I am being blessed by God. Come." She pulled him to his feet and led him upstairs to her bedroom. She sat him on the bed and slowly undressed, allowing him to watch her. "I am a great benefactress to the church, you know," she said standing naked before him except for her pendant, her pumps, and a fan. She sat beside him and kissed his cheek, then reached under his robe. "Oh my," she exclaimed. "I believe I shall become the beneficiary of the church's natural gifts and riches. She pulled the robe over his head and dropped it on the floor. She lay back in her luxurious bed and pulled him to her. It was not long before the signora was expressing her pleasure with the church and God's holy rites. This was the beginning of Matamoro's break with the church – that and the girl, Luciana.

"As his visits with the signora progressed, Matamoro's demeanor changed and he looked for the girl. Now he carried the cudgel of Father Finzi, but he never used it. And he made sure that the girl got first pick at the leavings. He saved things for her that he kept under his cassock or in a sack that he tossed to her. As the weeks went by, they became increasingly aware of each other. Matamoro's visits with the signora continued, but he contrived to meet with Luciana and finally, he succeeded in speaking with her. One evening, they met in a laneway behind the church and Luciana took him into the loft of a stable where, for the first time, they lay together. As a result of his visits with the signora, Matamoro knew what to do with a woman and his time with Luciana pleased her greatly. They would lie in each other's arms until four o'clock, when Matamoro was required back at the church to carry out his duties. All went well until one evening, when Luciana seemed unusually quiet.

"What is it?"

"I am with child, Donato." And she looked at him tentatively, not certain of his feelings or reaction concerning the news.

"I see." But his thoughts were in turmoil. He decided to go to the signora and ask her advice. This turned out to be a poor decision on Matamoro's part, as it never occurred to him that the signora might be jealous or angry. She was startled at the news but was careful not to let it show. Rather, she showed sympathy and a willingness to help him.

"Such things can be easily fixed, Donato." In his happiness, Matamoro, didn't think to question her or ask more pointedly about what could be fixed exactly.

"At the appointed day and hour, Matamoro brought Luciana to the signora who welcomed her with a fixed smile on her face. Luciana was terrified. She didn't want Matamoro to leave her alone with this aristocratic lady but the signora insisted and Matamoro trusted her. He remembered the wild look of fear in Luciana's eyes and the trembling of her lips, and that would be his last memory of the girl. When he returned to fetch Luciana later that day, the signora admitted him to her house and she was dressed in black from head to toe. Matamoro dropped to his knees and clasped his hands heavenward.

"For the love of God, what has happened?"

"The signora shook her head and lifted the dark veil from her face. "It did not go well. She bled a great deal. It could not be stopped and the poor child perished."

"It was then that Matamoro had a revelation, that it was as if a light now illuminated the signora and her intentions. "This is you. This is your doing. Luciana would now be alive if not for you."

"The signora smiled grimly. "I understand you are grieving, Donato. It is a tragic loss. She was so young. You came to me for help and I gave it to the best of my ability. It was God's will."

"Matamoro shook his head. "No signora. I see it all clearly now. An older woman, jealous of the younger, plotting, scheming to be rid of her. This is about possession, not God's will. God would not condone such a thing. You and only you are responsible. You have killed her."

"Don't be a fool. You must keep calm. Do you want this to come out? Think of your position. You will be expelled from the church and ex-communicated."

"I care not. My greatest sin was coming to you and putting her under your care. You are a monster and I shall denounce you."

"You do so at your own peril," she hissed. "I have influential friends and you are but a boy, a friendless boy. You have no allies, only enemies." She stretched out her hand to him. "Come. I am prepared to forgive you. I know you are distraught."

"Matamoro was young and impulsive. He spat at her hand and shrank back from her as if to touch her flesh would burn him. "Never," he shrieked and began to back out of the room as the signora advanced toward him. She advanced more swiftly, until they were very close together.

"Donato, I implore you."

"He felt her breath on his face and it was sweet and tempting, but the image of poor Luciana rose before him. "No," he bellowed and seized her bodice in the front and tore it away from her body. The signora stood exposed and naked, her magnificent breasts ripe as melons. She squealed and attempted to cover herself. Matamoro removed the crucifix from around his neck and flung it at her. "Evil bitch." Then he ran from the room.

"Matamoro did not go back to the church. He waited until darkness fell and stole back to his home. He crept inside, not wishing to wake anyone. No doubt they would hear of his shame, soon enough. He packed some of his things in a sack and changed his clothes. Silently, he bade goodbye to his family who snored lustily away, fast asleep until early in the morning when they would be up for the early tide. Although it was late, Matamoro found his way to a waterfront tavern. There, he knew, were captains of vessels who could use sea-soned seamen and would take a man on, no questions asked. Seated at a table by himself was a hearty fellow drinking ale. He had long fair hair and beard. His eyes were blue and a long scar which travelled from the corner of his left eye to the edge of his mouth pulled his face down on that side. Matamoro approached him. "Excuse me sir, are you looking for seamen?"

"The man looked up at him. "I might be, boy. Have a seat and tell me who you are and what you have to offer."

"Matamoro explained that he had been on the sea all his life working in the fishing boats, and that he missed it terribly. His parents forced him to go into the church and now he was running away. He did not mention Luciana and his troubles with the signora.

"The fellow, who called himself Captain Montoya, sympathized. "This church. It is bad business. I did lose a few men on this last trip. The pay is not much but I share with the men when we deliver the cargo. I sail on the morning tide. The name of the ship is Conquistador and a fine ship she is. Not much to look at, but she rides the waves like a champion. Be there as the sun rises and I will take you on. Your name?"

"Diego."

"Very well, Diego."

"Thank you, Captain."

"Montoya stood up a bit shakily and clapped the young man on the shoulder. "Say goodbye to your loved ones, eh? It will be a long time before you see them again."

"Matamoro looked down, red-faced. "There is no one."

"Montoya looked at him. "Then I will see you as the sun rises." And he tottered out of the tavern.

"And that," Barzini said, "is how Matamoro ended up going to sea."

"That's a great story," said Eph sipping his expresso.

"Ah, but it gets better dottore, I assure you." Barzini examined his wristwatch. "I shall be back at the library at three o'clock, signor. Now, I go to my wife for a short visit. The children, they are still in school." And Barzini grinned, enormously pleased with himself.

"Fine. I'll see you there at three. How late does the library stay open?"

"Until six-o'clock. Then it is closed until ten o'clock in the morning."

Eph had over an hour to kill and decided to go back to his hotel and write some letters. He and Barzini parted and Eph felt sluggish in the heat and from the large meal he'd eaten. At home, he'd have a bacon, lettuce and tomato sandwich and a cup of tea with lemon, then get on with his work. Here, in Florence, he felt it difficult to take a single step. Nonetheless, he made it back to his room and sat down at the desk to write. He spent the first half hour writing up notes from his conversation, or to put it more accurately, lecture from Barzini. He had read about Matamoro, of course. There had been references to him in some seminal works; *Voyages of the Italians by Giuseppe Verduci* and *Early Italian Seamen by Ross Montgomery*, an historian out of Ohio State who he'd found quite good. But there hadn't been much detail and Matamoro had remained very much an intriguing figure to Eph. He suspected that Matamoro had put his fingers into many things – one of those shady, background characters who hadn't been given much substance or form by modern day historians, but whose influence may have been significant. Certainly, Eph hadn't twigged yet to the illumination that Matamoro would have a great deal of influence on him. The hunt was just beginning but there'd been a promising start.

Eph sauntered back to the library, only to find the doors still locked. He checked his watch and saw that it was ten past three. A chair had been provided outside the door, as if this was a known and familiar practice. Eph sank into it, placing his briefcase on his knees and waited, drumming his fingers on the leather exterior. He was thinking of a poem he'd been composing to Madeleine. Actually, he was thinking of two that he'd written during their courtship. Matamoro's tale of ill-fated love made him think of it. The first was called:

A Saturated Poem

Breathes there a man with soul so dead
Who never to his wife has said
Darling, dearest one
Can anything be done
To make the sun shine
For lovers on St. Valentine?

And the other:

Bridge of Love

The world and I
Are about to build
A bridge,
A brave, new bridge
Wide enough to hold
The
Strong and weak
Bold and meek
And *us.*
Burn the old,
Run up the new.

19

People had told him he looked like a young Arthur Miller and this had pleased him. With his high forehead, dark, curling hair and black-rimmed glasses, all he needed was the pipe sending poetic clouds of smoke to the heavens. But Eph didn't smoke: too expensive and wasteful a habit. But when he had written those poems, something had seized him, something akin to romanticism. He knew he'd wanted Maddy enough to make the effort, wanted to impress her and appeal to her emotionally. He wasn't just in love with her, she pleased him, the look and touch of her. She was intelligent and warm and witty, exactly what he needed in a life companion, someone who would understand his angst and sympathize without clinging, someone who knew instinctively what to do and when. And he'd been right. And that was why he missed her now, while he sat in the dank corridor in the basement of the Toscanini building and cooled his heels waiting for Barzini to return from a tryst with his wife. At least, Eph assumed he'd gone to see his wife but who knew? The Italians were a different breed altogether.

I must confess that when I found those poems of my father's, I was surprised at their sentimentality. It was so out of keeping with what I knew, or thought I knew to be my father's character. They too, had been hidden in the same room with the letters and the old photograph. I had only found the two and that made me think Eph's romantic output was scarce, but I was also surprised to discover that I liked the poems quite a lot. It made me wonder why he didn't write more of them. I remember looking at photographs of my father from that period and I thought that he looked very cool. Dressed in narrow black suits and turtlenecks, or charcoal grey izod sweaters and dark sunglasses. Those shots gave him a detached air of mystery and intrigue. I found myself wanting to know my father back then, but of course, that was impossible. As impossible as it was now.

Twenty minutes of drumming later, Barzini showed up, whistling under his breath, a self-satisfied smile creasing his broad face. His eyes lit up when he spotted Eph sitting stiffly in the chair, the picture of impatience.

"Ah, my good friend, you look so American sitting there."

"I am Canadian."

Barzini chuckled. "Quite so. Forgive me for being late but I will compensate, yes, by keeping the library open later. We shall close at six-twenty this evening. I am fair, I think?"

Eph was mildly mollified but couldn't help but smile back at the fellow; he was so incongruous looking, so eager to please. "Of course. That's fair enough."

Barzini slapped him on the back, then brought out a cluster of jangling keys that he sorted through very quickly before unlocking the door and turning on the lights. Then he bowed Eph into the room. "Sit. Sit. I shall get us some coffee, eh? And then we shall talk about Matamoro a little more." Eph shed his jacket. It was a relief to slip it over the back of the chair and loosen the knot in his tie. Barzini returned carrying two steaming cups that he set down on the surface of his desk, checkered by many previous cups that had been wet on the bottom. Eph sat opposite the desk and reached for one. Barzini settled himself. "You went back to your hotel?" he inquired politely.

"I wrote a letter to my wife."

"Ah, you miss her, do you not?"

"Yes."

"Have you been married long?"

"Only a year."

"Children?"

"Not yet."

"I have six children. The youngest is two and the eldest is eleven. I have been married for twelve years, signor, and they have been a sheer joy, each moment. I am the luckiest of men. My wife, Juliana, is very beautiful. I charmed her with the brain, not the body."

"How so?"

"I was witty with her and very attentive. Women appreciate such things. Every evening, I bring to her the flowers. If I do not bring the flowers, then my foot should not cross the door. I bring her little gifts to show that she is in my affection; a book, a pair of earrings or some perfume. I write her poetry and send her notes and cards."

My father was astounded. "Still? After twelve years?"

"Oh yes, signor. It is the key to a good marriage. Especially when one partner is not the equal of the other." Eph wondered about that and wasn't sure which qualities were being measured; the physical or the intellectual. And then he thought of himself and Madeleine and his mind drifted. Glancing back quickly at Barzini, he wondered if the stocky librarian had guessed what he'd been thinking. Barzini cleared his throat. "Your wife, she is beautiful?"

"Yes, very beautiful and very smart."

'Then you too are the luckiest of men. Once you have children you will be more than lucky, signor, you will be blessed."

"I hope so."

"Trust me, signor." Barzini rubbed his hands together and smiled. "Where were we…? Ah yes, so poor unfortunate Donato who had changed his name to Diego to sound as if he were indeed a Spaniard, set sail on The Conquistador on the tide that morning. He left behind the beautiful but scornful signora, his beloved Luciana, his family, the church, and all that he'd known in Genoa. But he thought to himself too, signor, that I, Matamoro am Genovese and we belong on the sea. At first, he was employed by Montoya as a simple deck hand, but he proved himself to be very able and skilled having worked on the fishing boats all his life. Plus, Montoya found him to be a trustworthy young fellow, and obedient. The Conquistador was owned by a Spanish trading cartel which dealt in a number of commodities; shipments of spices from the east, linens and cloth from France, England and Germany, even spirits and guns were part of the cargo. The cartel had obtained a charter from the King of Spain and that meant that The Conquistador was essentially a privateer, empowered to seize goods from other ships running under the flags of hostile nations, that for the most part, were either English or French."

Barzini managed to spin out his tale, for that is what it might have been, for the better part of a week. That evening, my father did indeed dine with the Barzinis and was astonished to discover that the energetic librarian had been telling the truth. Signora Barzini, was indeed as beautiful as described. Juliana Barzini was tall, taller than her husband and sleek, with long legs, a tucked waist and an Italian bosom. Eph was astonished that she seemed so calm, so capable amongst the various pitches of the voices of their children, who made the household not just noisy but positively cacophonic. Through it all, the Barzinis beamed at each other and shouted over the din. Eph could scarcely hear himself talk but fell into the pattern of shouting like his hosts and soon, with ample pasta, veal, salad and the homemade vino, became comfortable with it. He even removed his jacket, as had Barzini as soon as he arrived home and rolled up his sleeves. Although the children were animated and busy, when Barzini clapped his hands for silence, they obeyed at once.

Barzini lifted his glass. "To our new friend and colleague, Signor Goldman." They all drank, even the children, who were given miniature glasses filled with wine. Eph was sober enough to see that this was a drunken household, not from alcohol but from love and it made an impression on him. It caused him to reflect on his own growing up and the coldness permeated by the Depression and the constant scrabbling for money, for putting food on the table. "To the signor," they all shouted at once and Eph, perhaps for the first time in his life, blushed in embarrassment at the fuss being made over him. He'd never been welcomed anywhere like this before. A young scholar, he'd received his PhD at the age of twenty-four, but it had been bestowed upon him with a grudging sense of acknowledgement by his elderly professors, none of whom had come close to equaling that achievement in their careers. Most of them had passed the orals well into their thirties. So, there was no celebration, just a cursory slap on the back and a handshake with a chorus of 'Well done', murmured by his mainly English professors who'd resented a native Canadian doing so well, and not to mention, a Jew at that. He'd been given a teaching position and a research stipend and was expected to bend to the will of the old guard, who set the course for the history department at the University of Toronto in those days. The young were not to be heard from for at least ten or fifteen years, until they had earned their spurs, in the words of the old codgers. And that's the way it was. To say then, that my father was overcome, even astonished at the way he was being received by the Barzinis would have been an understatement. He gave a counter-toast. He surged to his feet so awkwardly that the chair fell over backwards. The children tittered and pointed.

"My Italian friends. I am so honored to be here. I only wish that my darling wife, Madeleine, could be here to share this wonderful moment with me. I can't thank you enough for your warmth and generosity. You have made me feel at home in a strange place. Thank you, from the bottom of my heart." Then he sat down, forgetting that he'd knocked the chair over and landed between the chair legs where he got stuck. The children screamed with laughter as their father had just finished translating the toast Eph had given. Juliana Barzini helped Eph up while wiping tears of laughter and happiness from her eyes, moved by what my father had said. Not the words exactly but the fervor he'd exuded. Barzini took his other arm and when Eph looked into his face, Barzini nodded and gave him a look of what my father would call one of the most important things in the world, something he'd sought all of his life and was to find finally after publishing The Global View; that of acceptance.

20

The next day, Barzini continued the story: "Matamoro sailed with Captain Montoya and The Conquistador for seven years. During that time, he grew up and became a man. He was now twenty-three years old and a veteran seaman. He could clamber up to the crow's nest in a matter of seconds. He understood winds and currents, could navigate by the stars, and knew how to steer the ship away from reefs, barriers and killer storms. He had experienced battle and tasted the shedding of blood. The year was now 1506 and Christopher Columbus had returned from his voyage to the New World and all the sea, and all the ships and men on her were abuzz with such news. For truly, it took quite some time for news to travel. The Conquistador was rounding the Horn of Africa when a terrible storm came up behind her and drove the small, sturdy ship northward. The crew was terrified as the vessel seemed to leap out of the water like a dolphin. The captain had heard of such winds but never experienced such a thing before. The ship hurtled through the water, its flanks groaning from the pressure of the wind and the current and the waves; so much so, that Matamoro feared the good ship would blow apart, blasted by god into smithereens. During those tense days and nights, Matamoro thought of his days in the church and wondered if this was God's punishment for him. Everything on deck had to be lashed down and below as well. Men were tied into their bunks, although too terrified to sleep. Even the Captain, who had been through many storms and rough seas had never seen such power, such fury and crossed himself frequently. And the height of the waves – simply monstrous. Standing walls of water had crashed over the side, sweeping anything in their path overboard. Matamoro had been drenched in just such a blast of water, one which caught him unawares. He'd been struggling with the wheel trying to keep the ship upright when an unbearable weight fell in on him and he felt himself leaving his feet and sliding effortlessly along the deck. Against the Captain's orders, he hadn't lashed himself to the wheel, so intent had he been on ensuring the ship stayed upright. Most of the sails had been taken down lest they be ripped to pieces. Matamoro did then utter a prayer. As he was dragged to the edge of the ship, he managed to grab an oar from one of the lifeboats. Holding the oar in front of him somehow, and with the evil current dragging him down, he was pulled to the very edge where the oar he gripped with talons of fear wedged itself between two wooden spars of the railing and stopped him from going over, but left him dangling over the side. It was no use calling for help, as the roar of the water and the wind howled all about him. He prayed for some inner strength to pull himself up to safety. He couldn't last much longer. Matamoro was drenched to the bone and losing his grip quickly. His fingers were beginning to loosen on the oar. He needed a slight break in the wind, a narrow trough of calm to beat back the angel of death. Just as he'd given up all hope, and begun to pray for his mortal soul in earnest, a hand reached down and grabbed him by the scruff of the neck and roughly pulled him back onto the deck, where he lay panting and spitting water. It was the Captain. "I could feel that the wheel had spun free and I knew something had happened to you," he shouted.

"Thank God," Matamoro replied.

"No, just me, Diego. You are a lucky one." And with that, Captain Montoya hauled Matamoro to his feet and together they staggered back to the wheel and secured it. There, braced against each other, they took turns lashing themselves to the helm. The storm lasted another fifty-six hours and by this time, most of the ship's sails had been shredded and the main mast had toppled. The Conquistador had been blown north up along the west coast of Africa. By the end of the third day, the ship sailed into calmer waters, the clouds dissipated, and the sun came out strong and clear. Both Matamoro and Captain Montoya were exhausted, as were the rest of the crew. They'd had little to eat or drink, and very little sleep. The little ship had been badly battered, pieces of sail and strips of rope were stuck to the deck, which itself had sustained a number of cracks and smashed boards. In all, it was a miracle the ship had survived and only two crew were lost, both swept overboard. Matamoro might have been the third if it hadn't been for the Captain."

During this recitation, I can imagine that Eph may have felt just a little bit like a small kid at bedtime, hoping the story would continue so he could stay up later. It was obvious that Barzini was a colorful and dramatic narrator.

"The Conquistador put in to a small, protected bay to make its repairs and generally recuperate from the ordeal of the great storm. Matamoro had heard stories of such storms, but indeed this was the first time he'd experienced one of such terrifying force. Montoya had been through two such storms in his years at sea and in one of them, his ship had been lost. He hadn't been the Captain of that one, but a senior officer. If they hadn't been in warmer waters and he had not found some floating debris to which to cling, he too may have perished. Eight days later, he was picked up by a passing galleon destined to rendezvous with the unfortunate ship. Montoya and ten others survived that ordeal. He took the hand of god Who, he believed, saved him.

"Matamoro felt grateful for the calm weather and the warm breeze. He appreciated the time they were taking, to rest and gather their spirits before they resumed their journey up the coast of Africa on the way back to Spain. He sincerely thought his life had been spared for a reason and he wondered when that reason might be revealed. It didn't take long. Several days later, after The Conquistador's crew had made their repairs and re-stepped the mast, her sails were hoisted, and they left the harbor of safety. This turned out to be a fatal error. No sooner had they gained the open sea and were making good speed, than The Conquistador had its mast shot out by an English privateer that boasted sixty guns and some 200 crew. The Conquistador was no match at a mere twenty guns and some fifty crew. Her advantage was speed but with the main mast lying in pieces, it was impossible to outrun the English barbarians. Nor did Montoya wish to lose his crew in a lopsided battle that he knew they couldn't win. He was loath to give up his cargo, however and just as the English boarded, the good Captain blew up the ship and himself with it. The rest of the crew had crept away in the lifeboats, hoping the element of surprise might give them enough time to get away. No such luck, however. The Captain of the English ship was so enraged at Montoya's trickery that he followed the lifeboats and blasted each and every one of them out of the water. Once again, Matamoro clung to some oars and debris he'd managed to lash together. He drifted on the ocean tide, no sign of his companions, no sound but the lapping water. The days were hot, and the sun soared and without any water to drink, Matamoro soon fell into a sailor's delirium in which he dreamed all manner of people, places and things."

Barzini went to fetch some more coffee. My father shuffled his feet uncomfortably, yet still wanted to hear more. He had been taking notes and Barzini said he would arrange to have the diary mimeographed for him. There came a rattle of cups as Barzini lumbered back from the office where he'd plugged in the electric percolator. Carefully, he placed the cups down on the desk, then settled back in his chair, which groaned under his weight. Barzini righted himself then continued. "This was a very serious situation for Matamoro but of course, in his condition, he didn't know whether he was alive or dead. He dreamed that he was touched by mermaids, who ran their hands all over him. He dreamed that many strong hands lifted him high into the sky and he heard from a far-away place a kind of chanting that came from another world. Matamoro didn't know if he actually heard anything or not but gradually, the sounds of the sea, the lapping of the water, the whistling of the wind, faded in his consciousness. But the chanting could have come from the devil or angels, and that was all he knew. It was there and somehow, he heard it. For many days, Matamoro remained barely conscious. Again, and again, pairs of hands touched him but he did not really feel. He was fed a warm broth which was spooned into him and again, he heard the mysterious chanting that seemed to come from the earth itself. He seemed to exist in an eternal twilight where there was no real light or deep darkness but something in between. Finally, after many days, it appeared that Matamoro was coming to his senses. He moaned and groaned and moved his head and limbs. A cry went up and one of those attending him fetched the boss man. A voice, rich and low, spoke to him in Spanish. Having spent seven years on The Conquistador, Matamoro had learned the language from Montoya and the other crewmen until he was fluent in that tongue. "Madre mio," Matamoro breathed and opened his eyes. He lay in some kind of inner chamber that was quite dark and somber looking. There were torches set into the ground and they flared and danced. Matamoro stared at the man whose voice he'd heard. The man's beard sprouted fully, and his hair tumbled and fell about his shoulders. Matamoro was struck by the intensity of the man's blue eyes. He seemed to be dressed in the habit of the day, wearing a robe that had seen better days and a skullcap on his head. Surrounding the bearded stranger were tall, powerful-looking men with very dark skin and kinky hair. Most of them were virtually bare-skinned, except for a loincloth and leather bands which knotted up each arm. The dark men with kinky hair stared down at him with both curiosity and sympathy, he thought.

"Who are you?" he croaked.

The bearded man turned and spoke rapidly in a language that Matamoro didn't comprehend. A moment later, the man was handed a wooden bowl which he brought to Matamoro's lips. "Drink."

Matamoro drank greedily, spilling some of the water down his chest.

"Not too quickly, my friend."

Matamoro wiped his lips. "Who are you?" He tried to rise and the man pushed him back with his fingertips.

"Easy, you must rest yet. I am Schmuel Mendelsohn, from Granada."

"And what place is this?"

"This is Bazuland on the west coast of Africa."

"Africa?" Matamoro thought for a moment. "Yes, of course. We were not too far when my ship was attacked by English privateers." And then he had a thought. "Did you...?

Mendelsohn shook his head. "There was no one else."

Matamoro lifted his head and looked at the dark men before him. "I have seen such black men before but only as slaves."

"Here they are free. This is their land, their country. We are guests here."

"But are they not savages? Do they not eat mortal flesh?"

"They do not, but perhaps some of their brethren might. I do not know. The Bazu are hunters and farmers both. The women and children cultivate the land while the men form hunting parties and search for meat." Schmuel Mendelsohn made a gesture. He held a bowl to Matamoro's lips and bade him drink which he did. The liquid was hot and tasty.

"What is this?"

"It is broth made from the flesh of poultry." Matamoro drank some more and kept drinking until all the broth had been finished.

"What manner of man are you?"

"How do you mean? I told you that I am from Granada."

"Yes, and whose god do you follow?"

"I am a Jew."

"And what is a Jew doing in Africa?" Matamoro glanced at the black men who stood about, watching him curiously. These men were tall and fine-limbed and well-proportioned.

"My story is not that much different from yours, Diego Matamoro, although I do not think you are Spanish but Italian, perhaps."

Matamoro shrugged. "Perhaps."

"You have heard of the Inquisition?"

"Yes."

"My family was persecuted like many others. I was brought before the Inquisition and tortured. I had a wife and two children. They were put to death because I refused to submit. The others in my family converted and are now practicing Catholics. They go to mass every Sunday. They seek holy communion. They confess their sins to the priest. My brother had his daughter baptized in the Church. For some reason, and I don't know why, I was freed. Perhaps, they realized there was nothing more they could take from me, except my life and that was deemed too insignificant. There is still a community, you see, although they do not reveal themselves. From them, I secured the money to buy passage on a ship that was to go to England but before we had been to sea more than a matter of days, a Portuguese vessel attacked us. The cargo and passengers were seized. Our ship was overrun and then taken over. The crew were taken prisoner to be ransomed. Instead of turning north, this vessel turned south. I had no value to them so with the other passengers – there were three of us – we were pushed overboard. Of the three, I was the only one who could swim, and I made it to the shore exhausted, spitting water but alive. The Portuguese captain had been kind enough to put us in view of land before we were sent on our way. I fell asleep more dead than alive on the beach and awoke to discover these people all around me, looking at me curiously. I don't know how many white men they have seen, perhaps just one or two. They nursed me back to health and I have been here over a year now. I knew that one day another ship would come this way and I was right."

Matamoro stared at the Jew as he took in the details of this tale. *To be abandoned here for over a year,* he thought, *how intolerable to live among these savages.* Yet, what was his fate? He had now joined this Jew in his misery. Over the next few days, Matamoro was nursed back to health. Within a week, he was up and walking about. He was also an object of curiosity. The children, in particular, would follow him about the village and titter into their hands when he looked at them. But it was as if he had a permanent shadow. He didn't think there was much to the village life with the women planting and tending their crops, looking after children and animals while the men were off hunting, often for weeks at a time. He did notice though, that some of the women, the younger ones, all of whom went topless, were shapely and attractive with long limbs and brilliant white teeth. One or two would smile at him shyly. Mendelsohn was rarely to be seen, however. Matamoro might see him first thing in the morning and then again, when they took their evening meal, usually some sort of stew served in a hand-carved wooden bowl. The villagers ate with their fingers or used implements made of bone or the tusks of elephants. Matamoro was not fond of being idle, this was something he'd learned from the church and from being at sea for so long. He was still a young man, while he considered Mendelsohn to be quite old, perhaps thirty-five or forty years. The man's beard was peppered with grey and there were deep creases around his eyes and across his forehead. Matamoro, whose hair had grown long, found that the children of the village liked to stroke his hair. It was so different from their own. One evening, he asked Mendelsohn what he did all day.

Schmuel set down his bowl of food, then wiped his lips. "Come, I will show you." He led Matamoro away from the fire that was fuelled from the dried dung of animals. Wood was considered too precious a commodity and not to be wasted on burning. They proceeded through the village and beyond.

"Isn't this dangerous? Are there not animals on the prowl?"

"It is not too far." Mendelsohn walked calmly in front. Further into the bush, they came upon a clearing. Within the clearing was a hut but much larger than the others in the village and it appeared newly built.

"What is this?"

"You shall see." Mendelsohn pulled back a flap and beckoned him inside. Matamoro hesitated, then went in. He could not see until Mendelsohn followed with the small torch he carried, which he slid into a holder on the center pole of the hut. As he looked about, Matamoro was surprised to see a large wooden contraption, a machine, sitting in the middle of the hut.

"What manner of machine is this?"

"It is called a loom."

"And what does it do?"

"It is for making cloth."

"Cloth?"

"Yes."

"And where did this machine come from?"

And here, Mendelsohn grinned broadly. "I constructed it, with their help, of course."

"You?"

"Yes."

Matamoro shook his head in disbelief. "And what do you want with this cloth-making machine here?"

"That, my friend, is the best part. We make clothes for the villagers and they wear these clothes. Others will see them and want the same thing. So we make clothes for them, but this time at a price."

"What others?"

"From the other tribes."

"There are more of them?"

Mendelsohn pulled at his beard and laughed. "Oh yes, many more. Thousands and thousands. Africa is a very big place, Diego, with many people."

"And how shall they pay for these things that you are thinking of making?"

Mendelsohn wagged a forefinger and nodded his shaggy head sagely. "My family has been in the textile business for hundreds of years. We sell our cloths all over Europe, England, France, Italy, many places in Spain and Portugal." Then he tossed something to Matamoro who caught it by reflex, fumbling with the object in his hands. "What do you think that is?"

"It looks like gold."

Mendelsohn tossed something else. "And this?"

"A precious stone."

"Diamonds. They have rubies and emeralds as well."

"But...?"

"Dug out of the hills. The Bazus and others wear them for ornamentation, but to them there is no other value."

Matamoro examined the jewel, turning it around in his fingers, marveling at how large it was. Then he laughed snorting derisively. "And what good will these do for us here?"

"One day, Diego, a ship will come and on that day, we shall leave this place wealthy men. And then you can do anything you wish, have anything you wish. You will be as rich as the emperors of Rome were rich, two thousand years ago. You may have your own empire, if that is your desire."

"And you?"

"I wish to return to Europe and establish a good house with servants, spawn children and live out my life in comfort. Nothing more."

"How can I help you?" Matamoro asked almost accusingly. "I do not know how to work this machine. I do not know anything about cloth. I am a sailor."

Schmuel continued to stroke his beard. "You will learn. It is simple. There is not much else for you to do, no?"

Just then, Matamoro heard a rustling in the corner recesses of the hut. A woman stepped out of the shadows. She was of the tribe, tall, lean-limbed, and dignified. She held a child in her arms. On the child's head was a small skullcap. Matamoro gaped.

Schmuel laughed again. "And I shall leave a little something of myself behind." He spoke to the woman in a tongue full of clucking and clicking sounds. She responded to him in kind. "This is Tuwara and the little one, I am calling, Adam, for the first born of this new tribe of Israel." The child sucked on one of its tiny toes. Its skin was caramel and its tiny round face yielded dark, liquid eyes and slim lips. "We Jews wander the earth, Diego, and we leave our seed behind. It shall grow and prosper. I shall teach him Torah and he shall teach his children and his children's children." Schmuel spoke to the woman again. She nodded and withdrew, the burbling child in her arms.

"I think you are mad." But already, Matamoro was beginning to wonder.

"Perhaps, but what else have you got to do?"

Schmuel Mendelsohn taught Diego Matamoro the ways of the loom. Within a few months, they managed to build another one and the women worked in shifts, leaving time to tend to their crops and their children while the men, seemingly oblivious to the women's work, continued to hunt. Schmuel found red and purple berries. He stripped the bark off trees. He dug in the earth until he found red clay and mixed the varieties of herbs that grew in the jungle. By mashing the berries and the bark and the herbs, then boiling them in water and straining the various noxious brews through banana leaves pricked with holes, Schmuel concocted different types of dyes for his cloth. Thus, the villagers could weave and produce materials of many different colors and patterns which Schmuel taught them to fashion in becoming ways. Word of this new activity spread through the jungle and around the countryside. It was not long before they had visitors. Most were the sworn enemy of the Bazu, yet the rumors were so enticing, that despite their historical enmity, the others could not stay away. They sent runners on ahead after the beating of drums over many days warned of the approach. Thus, the Bazus were well aware of the interest that had been stirred up.

Mendelsohn had taken under his wing a fellow by the name of B'kela who acted as interpreter between the white men and the visitors. B'kela was not tall and lean-limbed like his brethren, but small and spindly yet he was not a young man. There were flecks of gray in his hair and beard. He told Schmuel that something had happened when he was born. His mother had been frightened by a lion and she went into her labors early, before the baby, B'kela, was ready to come. The birth was a long and difficult one with much blood spilling out of B'kela's mother, who tragically died, giving him life. She was with the spirits, he said. He was raised by the women of the village collectively, each taking turns looking after him. In this way, he had many mothers and felt the most fortunate of men. On the other side, he had been a sickly child and never grown as he should. He was never allowed to go on the hunt because his spindly legs wouldn't carry him for weeks on end, as the hunters often ran ten or twelve hours a day searching for game. Consequently, he was a helper to the women, the lowest status given to a male in Bazu society. Schmuel found that B'kela was quick-witted and learned quickly, an able candidate to act as a sort of foreman overseeing the women as they worked. It was B'kela who made certain the women did not spend too much time gossiping or drinking too much of the bark tea that made them slow and drowsy, not to mention having to rise and leave the hut to relieve themselves outside. He scolded and clucked and tapped them on the shoulder sharply with a bamboo switch if there was a lag in the production of the cloth. As some of the women worked the loom, others turned the liquid in the dye pots working with paddles fashioned out of bamboo. They also used broad banana leaves which had been dried and hardened with a type of clay heated over the fire until it had the consistency of stone, but was much lighter. Even still, the thick, glutinous dyes were difficult to turn in the large wooden bowls Schmuel had asked B'kela to carve. The production of the colorful cloth went well. Stoppages occurred only when the Bazu had to pray or make an acknowledgement to their gods, of whom, there were many. There was the earth god, the stone god, god of the trees, the sky, wind, various bird and animal gods, god of the water and the most important, god of fertility. Without fertility, the Bazu would disappear and it was the duty of every girl when she turned thirteen and every male to produce children. The more children, the greater the prosperity, the Bazus believed. In this frame of mind, Tuwara was again pregnant with Mendelsohn's child. Matamoro too, had succumbed to the charms of the Bazu women but hadn't settled on one in particular, and the Bazu seemed indifferent to the concept of monogamy. The hunters had many wives and after a particularly good hunt, and depending upon who did what, the men might share their wives among themselves as an act of good will or generosity. It was difficult to tell then, who was the father of who exactly, but since the Bazu considered themselves all one family and addressed each other in the familiar which meant brother or sister, it didn't seem to matter to them. They tolerated the two white men and the intrusion into their lives because prestige was brought to their family by the weaving machine. They liked to see their women finely dressed and liked the attention and compliments other tribes paid to them. Still, it was a distraction only. It did not mean that the Bazu men, with the exception of B'kela, should remove their attention from the most important activity and that was hunting. Without hunting, the men reasoned, there would be no meat and without meat, the community would starve, and the children would not grow tall and strong.

The Bazu, however, were not without their enemies. Principally, a tribe that lived to the south, known as the Arakai; a jungle race of lighter skin and broader stature, who did not get on with the Bazu. This new-found attention and prosperity excited the jealousy of the Arakai. They were a tree people who built elaborate huts in the great trees of the jungle and lived above ground. They were foragers and hunters only. They did not keep animals apart from a few dogs, for pleasure, and they did not cultivate crops, nor did they participate in any forms of commerce. The Arakai preferred to raid the encampments of their enemies, this is what gave them pleasure and courage. Sometimes, they might steal some animals or kidnap a child, but such occurrences were rare as the Arakai were also a careless people and had enough to do raising their own children. Taking others seemed nonsensical to them. Why ask for more trouble? Being impishly cruel by nature, and harassing their neighbors was also a form of recreation for the Arakai. It gave them something to do.

Hearing of this, Matamoro decided that the Bazu must be able to defend themselves and drive away the troublesome Arakai for good. When he examined the Bazu, Matamoro saw a people still mired in ancient times and certainly if they could work looms, then using more modern weaponry shouldn't be all that difficult. As he had travelled widely and been involved in many skirmishes, Matamoro had seen how others defended themselves. He knew he could not manufacture swords or knives as there was no forge and no obvious source of metal with which to make steel, but the Bazu and the Arakai still carried stone-tipped spears as their principal weapons. The fact that each side had the same thing meant that there had been no shift in the balance of power. Each encounter between the Bazu and the Arakai resulted in a stalemate with neither side gaining any advantage and that left the Arakai free to continue to harass the Bazu. The ideal weapon, in Matamoro's mind, was the long bow – something he had seen on English ships and they'd been well employed in a battle he'd witnessed some years before. They were not difficult to construct and there was plenty of wood to make the bows and arrows while animal guts would form the bowstrings. The forest was crowded with docile birds, cockatoos and all manner of cackling macaws and parrots from which to pluck the necessary feathers. Matamoro set about making his long bow, selecting the wood, carving it carefully using the stone and shale implements that the Bazu possessed. They had never seen metals before and had no means of, or idea about the construction of weapons made of metals. Unfortunately, Matamoro had lost everything in the sea; his cutlass, his dagger and the bronzed medallion he wore around his neck. Once the bow had been constructed to his satisfaction and the gut for the string selected and tested for the proper tension, he set to work on the arrows. He discovered that stone tips were too heavy and disrupted the symmetry and balance. B'kela was captivated by Matamoro and followed him about, watching in fascination. Matamoro had picked up just enough of the language to explain to B'kela, in rudimentary terms, what he was doing. That he must measure the arrow's shaft and make it as true as possible. That the tip must be both light and sharp and the feathers must be a uniform distance apart and of the same, proper height for the arrow to fly properly. Just outside the village, where he wouldn't be bothered or hit anyone by accident, Matamoro set up a target range for practice. He also fashioned a sheath out of the skin of a hyena and a strap so that the cache of arrows could be slung across his back as he had seen the English, who were among the world's most skillful archers, do. Matamoro tested his arrows at varying distances until he could stand and fire an arrow from far away and still hit the target. Meanwhile, B'kela had made his own smaller version of the bow and arrow, more ably suited to his reduced frame. The set made by Matamoro was suitable for the fully-grown hunters who could pull back on a bow that was easily the height of a man while the tension on the string was no challenge. It wasn't long before Matamoro saw that B'kela's version was also effective and useful.

Mendelsohn wasn't interested in weapons but in commerce. He knew the ways of man, however, and recognized that superior weaponry did help commerce flourish in different parts of the world, so why should it be any different in Bazuland? He encouraged the men, when they were around to take an interest in Matamoro's craftmanship. It was decided to have a general demonstration. On the appointed day, Matamoro and Mendelsohn led about a hundred of the Bazu hunters to the clearing while the women and children trailed behind at a respectable distance. Before they could begin, certain prayers and incantations were made to the various deities. A pig sacrifice to the forest god, the spilling of ornamental blood for the wind god and so on. The group had sat on its haunches for the better part of an hour before anything of significance took place. And finally, it was Matamoro's turn. He strode up to the spot he had marked in the clearing, drew an arrow, notched it carefully and let it fly toward the target where it sunk in with a resonant thunk. The Bazu yielded a collective gasp, then applauded. This was a delightful entertainment for them. It was when Matamoro shot a jungle pigeon out of the sky that the Bazu were amazed and astounded. The men began jabbering at once while the women keened in admiration…"

21

My father returned to his room in the small hotel, his head swimming with details, ideas, and questions. He had turned down Barzini's generous offer of dinner but had agreed to drop by for coffee later. He wanted to sort out his notes and organize his thoughts.

Rather than take dinner in his room, he ate in the small dining room. There were perhaps, fifteen or sixteen tables. The waiter seated Eph near the front window so he could look out on to the street, if he wished. He carried his briefcase and took out a sheaf of papers upon sitting down. He ordered a carafe of the house wine and some cold melon soup to start. From time to time, he would make a notation, a point to remember or some clarification. Each sheet was carefully annotated, numbered and dated. He made certain to fill in the context of a line lest it appear to come out of nowhere. He had just set down the soup spoon with a louder clatter than he'd intended and was dabbing his lips when a lilting voice rang out.

"May I sit by the window, please, near to that gentleman?" Eph heard julep and honeysuckle emanating out of a lovely white throat. The waiter ushered over a pretty blonde woman in her late twenties, who wore a fitted cream-colored suit with hat and shoes to match and a small strand of pearls augmented an elegantly long neck. After she was seated, she leaned over and said, "Are you a fish out of water too?"

Eph smiled. "I suppose you might say that."

"Are you a tourist, sir?"

"Actually, I'm doing research at the university for a few weeks."

The young woman leaned forward with interest. Her pale hair was prettily bobbed. "I wish I could say that I was doing something so worthwhile. Instead,

I am here to escape a bad marriage. I'm to keep my head down until it all blows over. At least, that's what mother said. I didn't know where to go but it had to be somewhere far away from Mobile – that's in Alabama…"

"I know where it is."

"Of course you do. So silly of me. I guess I'm a bit nervous and when I'm nervous I do prattle on. You see, I haven't really spoken to anyone for a couple of days. I don't speak any Italian and I assumed you were American."

"Canadian actually."

"Oh. Canada. The great white north, or so I hear."

Eph smiled politely. "It's not all like that. We actually have cities too. And houses with roofs on them. Some of us have running water and electricity."

The young woman sat back and chewed on her lip. "I guess I deserved that. Playing the ignorant American and all."

"I didn't mean to be rude." Eph hesitated. "Look. Since you're on your own, perhaps you'd care to join me?"

"Well, I don't know. Mother said to watch out for strangers."

"We'll just be eating dinner."

The lip-chewing continued. "Well, all right then. There's no harm, I suppose." Eph signaled the waiter, who bustled over and helped the young woman change her seat. He set a place in front of her.

"That's better. I guess we should introduce ourselves… Eph Goldman."

"Eph? What an unusual name. I like it. I'm Henrietta Sparshot, but all my friends call me Henny." And she extended a white hand with long, tapered fingers. Eph took it in his and squeezed it reassuringly. "My, it is warm in here. I guess it's too much to expect air conditioning over on the continent. Do you mind if I remove my jacket?"

"Not at all."

Henny Sparshot shrugged out of the short jacket and before she could turn around, the waiter was by her side helping her. "My, they are attentive here."

"Yes. I suppose they are, Henny." She displayed a pair of surprising square shoulders as her blouse was both sleeveless and rather low cut. Eph tried not to look at the swell of her creamy bosom.

"What are you drinking there, Eph?"

"Just some red wine. Would you care for some?"

"That would be lovely, thank you." Eph signaled the waiter for another glass, which again, was promptly delivered. The waiters couldn't take their eyes off Henny Sparshot.

"You've got some admirers there, Henny."

She pouted, but in a pretty way. "Oh, I know but it's so silly. Waiters are forever falling in love with me."

"Not just waiters, I'll bet."

"Oh sir, you're being gallant."

"Nope. Just honest. It surprises me that you're here to escape a marriage. I would imagine that any man would do his utmost to keep you."

She smiled widely. Naturally, her teeth were perfect. "You're turning my head and I hardly know you but Hunter, that's my husband, preferred women of a different sort. Unfortunately, I didn't find this out until after our wedding day. It was a gala affair in Mobile, one of the highlights of the social season. At least that's what The Register said."

"How long have you been married?"

"Four years. We got engaged in college. I was Homecoming Queen and Hunter starred on the football team. It's all too typical, isn't it? Everybody envied us, always saying we were the perfect couple. But, uh… I don't know why I'm telling you this, Mr. Goldman…"

"Eph. And it's fine."

"Well. Hunter had, has… a drinking problem. He crashed the car three times. He works in his daddy's law office but spends most of his time in bars, drinking it up with his buddies. He doesn't do any work really. And because he drinks so much," and her voice dropped to a low whisper, "I think it affects his performance, you know, in the bedroom." And she blushed, down her cheeks into her neck. Eph was charmed by this southern creature, utterly charmed. They ordered their meals and chatted away through dinner, finishing not one but two bottles of wine. Henny was very flushed by the time desert came around. Eph's head was spinning. He was aware that he seemed to have a very large grin on his face.

"Oh, I couldn't eat another bite. I'll bust my girdle for sure."

"How about coffee then?"

"Why certainly."

The coffee brought his senses back and he became more aware of his surroundings, outside the aura of Henny Sparshot.

"It's been very good of you, Eph, to listen to all my problems. I feel very comfortable talking with you. I mean, I find it difficult to talk about my marriage with my girlfriends, even my mother. She knows something is terribly wrong, but she doesn't want to know the details. And my daddy still thinks I'm his little girl and need his protection. I'd like to do something with my life, really do something."

"What did you study in college?"

"Psychology. But it was just something to do really, I wasn't serious about it. I just figured I was putting in some time until I got married and had babies. Isn't that the silliest thing?"

"No, it isn't. You do have choices, Henny. You could go back to school. What sort of work would interest you?"

She took a sip of her coffee. "Do you mind if I smoke?"

"Not at all."

She reached into her purse and took out a gold cigarette case. She held it out to him, but he shook his head. She lit up with a gold lighter. "Engagement presents." She laughed. "You may think this is foolish, but I've always wanted to be a teacher. I like children and I do think I'd be a good mother. But teaching is not what my Daddy wants for me. I'd like to give it a try, though."

"I can't think of a reason why you shouldn't, can you?"

She shook her head and the tight curls bobbed around her face. "No, I can't."

"I hope you will forgive me for saying this, but I think you've always done what other people wanted you to do. Lived up, in a way, to their expectations, not your own. Don't you think, Henny, that it's time you lived your own life? You're an intelligent and beautiful woman, and charming, I might add."

She blushed again. "Oh, go on, you're turning my head, Mr. Goldman. I believe you are. And thank you for saying that, it's like a tonic to me right now. I was blaming myself for everything. For Hunter's behavior. My Daddy's disappointment. Momma's disapproval. After all, there's never been a failed marriage in the family before. Why did I have to be the first? The shame and embarrassment of it all. She tells all her friends and our relatives that I'm just taking a vacation with a girlfriend and that Hunter's far too busy at the office to leave right now. Course, nobody believes that because half the town sees him careening down the street on any given day, drunk as a dawg in a biscuit factory. You know what? I just might do it. I can get my teaching certificate in a year. I mean, I can start back at school this fall, I have a little money of my own. I can get a small apartment... it will be perfect."

Eph was feeling the heat of the meal settling inside of him and the heat of her now that she'd convinced herself she had a plan. The restaurant was feeling stuffy and claustrophobic. He called for the bill. "Shall we get some air?"

"Let's," she said emphatically.

As he paid the bill, she reached into her purse.

"You must let me pay my half, please. I insist. Daddy's paying anyway, and I so enjoyed your company. I won't take no for an answer."

Rather than put up an argument, my father, who wasn't the most generous of men with his money, relented. "Well, if you insist."

"I do. This was just a lucky encounter and I would have paid for my own dinner anyway. But thank you for the thought."

"You're welcome." As they rose to go, Eph thought he saw the waiter give one of the others a nudge and a knowing smile. Anger flared up in him momentarily, but he realized that was the male attitude the world over. Who was he to change it even if it was wrong-headed?

They strolled along the quiet streets, dodging the lights of the occasional small car as it sped past. "I've been invited to a friend's home for coffee. Would you care to come along?" Eph asked.

Henny slipped her arm through his. "Why not? I don't have any other plans."

"Well then. It's not far from here."

The heels of their shoes clacked on the stone walkway. Once again, Eph could feel the warmth of her, the womanliness of her as she moved against him easily and naturally. "Tell me about your research. What are you studying?"

She was quite tall and in her high heels, just a little shorter than he and when he turned his head, he gazed down slightly into her very bright blue eyes. "Your husband is a fool," he murmured.

"Eph. I thought we were talkin' about your research?"

"Right. It's something to do with Italian explorers and their travels. Not very exciting, I'm afraid. I mean, it's not nuclear physics or anything like that."

"I'd love to hear about it. I think the Italians are very romantic, don't you?"

And so, he recapped the tale of Matamoro and how he left the bustling port of Genoa to spend his life at sea, only to be cast away and beached off the west coast of Africa. How he met the most extraordinary man who lived with a native tribe and the things they set out to accomplish. Soon, they were at Barzini's door, dropping the knocker. Juliana Barzini came to the door and beamed.

"Ah, dottore, it is a pleasure to see you again. And who is this beautiful lady?" Before he could introduce them, Barzini himself appeared. The high-pitched squeals and screams of their children could be heard emanating from the back of the house.

"The children, they are playing a card game. Ah, signora, it is a pleasure to meet you."

"I haven't introduced you yet," Eph laughed.

"Come in. Come in. We'll have coffee, eh? And a... a... what? Brandy? Cognac? I have some English sherry. What is your pleasure tonight?" Barzini beamed, delighted to have company.

"It's not too late?" Henny asked demurely.

Barzini laughed as his wife went off to the kitchen. "You make me laugh, signora. We live for company. It makes our dull lives brighter. It is how we keep in touch with the news and the other delights that make our lives worth living, eh?" He slammed the door behind them. "Come out to the garden. It is very pleasant there now."

"What's that I'm smelling. Is it honeysuckle? I do believe I smell honeysuckle."

Barzini roared with delight. "You are right. Yes, by the gods of Italy, you are right. It is Juliana, she planted in the commencement of the summer. She loved the idea of it and the smell, yes, it is divine. It is especially fragrant tonight. As are you, signora."

Henny slapped his wrist lightly. "Oh, go on with you. You Italian men are always full of compliments, always wooing a lady."

"But of course. You only realize this now? That is the main role for the Italian man. I ask you, what else is he good for? That's it. Ah, here is Juliana."

Juliana bustled out with a tray full of coffee and cakes and small liqueur glasses and a variety of bottles. Quickly, she emptied the tray and then sat down. "This is almond cake, I make it myself. You must try some."

"Thank you," said Eph. Juliana cut slices efficiently and handed around the plates.

Henny took a small forkful. "It's delightful," she pronounced.

"Thank you," Julian replied, beaming. "You are on vacation?"

Henny glanced quickly at Eph. "Yes. I've never been to Italy before and I've always wanted to come here. I'm going back to school you see, and I wanted to travel a little first. I've decided to get my teaching degree. There's such a need for teachers where I come from."

"Ah, but that is wonderful!" Juliana exclaimed. "What better occupation is there than a teacher? We thank god for the teachers and the work they do. Eh, Francesco?"

Barzini shrugged. "If you say so, my dear." Then he pulled a face.

"Why do you make that face, Francesco?" his wife asked him.

"Well, my darling, I just think back to when I was a child in school and the priests, they were severe disciplinarians and…"

"And you think the nuns were any better?" exclaimed Juliana. "Besides, we are talking about America, not Italy. America is a liberal country, is it not?" And she turned to her guests. Eph shrugged. Henny smiled.

"In some ways, I suppose it is," she said demurely.

"Ah, but you don't have the Pope. You don't have the Church that tells us what to do, how to feel, where women do not have a say in their lives…"

"But my darling…" Barzini protested. "You have a say in everything that we do."

"You are such a child. Who stays home with the children? Is it you? I love my children, but you must appreciate that I too have a mind. I am not just a pair of hands that cleans the house, makes the food, does the shopping and comforts all of you when there is a tragedy," she said heatedly, then she stopped suddenly and looked at the astonished faces of her guests and burst out laughing. After a moment, Barzini joined in with his rather endearing guffaw. Henny started to giggle and Eph, not known as a full-blown laugher, nearly spat out the coffee which was in his mouth. It took some moments for them to settle down. "And now, that I have got this out of my mind, may I please offer you liqueur?" Juliana asked.

Barzini leapt up. "I'll get it, my darling." He left the room, forgetting the liqueurs were still on the tray she'd brought in.

"I frighten him," Juliana whispered. "But it is good for our marriage, no? He should not think that things will always be the same. It is good for some variety. Do you think so?"

"Yes, I do," Henny answered sincerely. "I wish I had some variety in my marriage. It was always the same. My husband would come home late, dinner would be burnt or dried out and he'd be drunk. By eight o'clock, he'd have passed out on the sofa and I would go to my room to read. Most nights, I cried my eyes out."

Juliana put her arm around Henny. "Ah, my poor dear. That must have been terrible for you. Such a man is not worth the likes of you. I would have thrown him out on his head and thank Jesus he has gone."

"Who has gone?" asked Barzini, returning red-faced, although he carried a bottle of something, despite having realized the liqueurs had been brought out by Juliana.

"This poor Henny's husband. He is a drunkard. I say, throw him out of the house."

"Yes, that is the ticket," agreed Barzini, then held up the bottle. "A special cognac. May I interest anyone? Very old. Very good."

"Sure," said Eph, who wasn't known as a drinking man and had exceeded his limit by quite some margin. But he was in a foreign country. It was a beautiful night, he was in the company of an alluring woman not his wife, and charmed by the warmth of his hosts. Eph was seduced. He loved the intimacy of Italy, the vibrancy of the people and the life in the streets, the beauty of the art and architecture, and the resounding appeal of the nation's food and drink.

As if reading his thoughts, Henny said, "How does anyone ever stay slim here? There is so much food. So much to drink. It would be so easy to let yourself go."

Barzini took a sip of the liqueur. "One must be a moderate, signora. That is all. Don't go crazy. It is not going to disappear. It will be there tomorrow."

"Look who's talking, eh? You need to lose thirty pounds at least," brayed Juliana. "He loves my cooking," she added to her guests.

"Of course, my darling, I love your cooking. But if I was truly a glutton, then I would need to lose sixty pounds not just thirty. I could lose thirty like that." And he snapped his fingers.

"Ah, you think so?"

"I know so."

"You are a stubborn fool."

"Perhaps, but I can do it."

"Then you will. Right now, you go on the diet." And Juliana snatched away the piece of cake he was about to fork into his mouth. She took the liqueur glass out of his hand and drained it herself. "There, no more of that for you until the thirty pounds has vanished."

"But, but, really, my darling! I can start tomorrow."

"No. You start now."

Barzini's broad shoulders slumped. He hung his head and even his eyelids and eyebrows drooped. He looked up at the heavens, as if to ask 'why is such a curse being called down upon my head?'. Henny stifled a titter behind her hands, then feigned a yawn. Eph slurped the rest of his coffee and polished off the piece of almond cake with a bit of a flourish. He was agonizingly thin. His clothes hung on him to such an extent that his body rattled around in them somewhere. Barzini looked at him sorrowfully. "You, dottore, are a lucky man, eh? You are skin and bones. You may eat and drink what you wish. But me? I look at gelato and my belly expands. Ah, this will be a real fight, I can see."

Eph looked at Henny and could see that she was ready to go. He stood up.

"I wish to thank you for your hospitality Francesco, and you Juliana, for the same and the wonderful conversation. You have made me, uh, us, feel very welcome here."

Barzini clasped his hand. "It is our pleasure, Ephraim. You are always welcome in our home. One day, I hope you will come with your wife and your children."

Eph swallowed hard. "I'd like that. Thank you."

"So nice to meet you," Henny said as she rose, and she put out her hand. Barzini shook it formally, while Juliana kissed her on both cheeks.

"Remember, get rid of that husband," she said, waggling her finger.

Henny grinned painfully. "I will. Thank you all again."

Barzini walked them to the door and then to the outskirts of the garden. As they turned up the walk, he waved. Juliana was framed in the doorway, her hair aglow from the hall light. Barzini shrugged at her, as if he didn't know what to make of the American woman and the Canadian man.

Henny and Eph walked along in silence for quite awhile.

"That was very nice. Thank you for taking me there. They are lovely people."

"Yes, they are. Very warm and hospitable. Their home reminds me of my own growing up. We didn't have much, but it was a place where family and friends would gather in the evenings to talk, play cards, drink tea, have a slice of cake. It was a good place to be." Though Eph knew there wasn't the warmth or the spontaneity, the expression of emotion that resounded in the Barzini household. He thought of that with some regret, some ache for what he had missed in the past.

They drew up at the entrance to the hotel and hesitated. Suddenly, they both felt awkward. Eph jammed his hands in his pockets and stared at the points of his shoes. Henny hugged herself.

"Thank you so much, Eph, for talking to me and letting me have such a wonderful evening. I'm— I'm leaving Florence tomorrow for Rome and then I fly back to the States. I just want you to know that this was a special night." And then she leaned up to him and without knowing how or why, Henny was suddenly in his arms and he could feel the firmness of her body against him and their lips were together. Henny pressed against him and he read the message loud and clear.

"I've been so lonely, Eph," she whispered into his ear. "I need to be with someone…" She left the rest hanging. Eph was clearly confused and muddle-headed by the drink, the food and Henny's aura. "Shall I go up first?"

"Yes. Yes, that's a good idea."

She stepped away from him, then turned. "You'll follow in a minute?"

He nodded. "Of course, Henny. Of course I will." She looked at him warmly, her face breaking into a smile, then she turned and walked into the lobby of the hotel. Eph watched her slim back disappear into the glass and wood of the hotel. He was gripped by fear and indecision. A bolder man than my father wouldn't have hesitated. As it was, he spent a full fifteen minutes walking up and down before he made up his mind, then he strode into the hotel.

22

By the time Eph woke up the next morning, Henny had checked out of the hotel. It was late for him. Normally an early riser, he glanced at his watch and saw that it was after ten o'clock. He didn't want to get out of bed. He felt groggy and thick-headed, his tongue a rubber mat stuck in the cavity of his mouth. He dragged himself into the bathroom, filled the sink with cold water and doused his head in it. It worked. He was shocked into consciousness. Last night seemed like a dream. He could still smell her, feel the pressure of her lips on his. He remembered the contours of her body as they embraced. But my father was a realist and as he shook his head clear and dried his face, he pushed her out of his memory. Henny had disappeared, perhaps forever.

When he showed up at the Medici library, it was almost noon. Barzini stared at him curiously, but said nothing. Eph settled into the seat opposite – well sagged, really – and propped his elbow on the desk.

"Coffee, dottore?" Eph nodded. Barzini disappeared into his little kitchenette. He emerged a few moments later, carrying two cups of espresso.

"I think you need it very strong this morning, no?"

"Yes. Thank you." His voice sounded a little hoarse. Eph sipped the strong liquid and felt as if a bolt of lightning had been shot through his veins. "Wow."

"It is good?"

"Just what I needed."

"I thought so."

"Please thank Juliana again for her hospitality."

"I will tell her. She will be pleased."

"I have been thinking…"

"Yes?" Barzini perked his ears up.

"I have been thinking, what an extraordinary set of circumstances that brought Matamoro and Mendelsohn together. Almost as if it were fate, don't you think?"

Barzini smiled and took a tentative sip of the espresso. "I am not sure I believe in the fate, but it is unusual, yes."

"But think of it, Francesco; I don't know the end of the story yet, the idea of a commercial industry that flourished in Europe was established in Africa, very likely far earlier than it might have done otherwise. And then there is the notion of weaponry and its uses too. It's as if that society in Bazu took several evolutionary steps in a few months, something that ordinarily takes generations to complete."

"It is a wonderful story, dottore, this much I know."

"But Francesco, it is more than a story. It actually *happened*. These events took place and…" It was at that moment when my father had an epiphany of sorts. Maybe it was the combination of fatigue and the jolting of his senses by the strong espresso, but something happened. His brain began to whirl. The color drained from his face and an electric chill flushed over his frame.

Francesco became alarmed, standing up. "What is it? Are you ill? Do you feel all right?"

Perhaps in that moment, he did look like a madman. "No. I'm fine. Wonderful, in fact."

"You are certain? Your face has gone very pale, signor. I am no physician, but still, I—"

"It's fine, really. I'm A-okay."

Barzini shrugged his wide shoulders, reluctantly. "You don't want to go to the hospital?"

"No. Tell me the rest. What else does Matamoro say?"

"Well, it is very peculiar. As you will remember, the Bazu were becoming very famous because of the loom and the wonderful materials they were making and the costumes – nobody had seen anything like it before. The tribespeople always used natural materials, animal skins or grass, even bark and leaves to make their clothing. And as we know, many often went with little or no clothing because the climate was so hot. So, this was a new thing. Mendelsohn was quite an ingenious man, he wondered about many things. If the material they made from the looms could be dyed, then why not the animal skins too? And so, he made the experiments. At first, he wasn't happy with the results and the Bazu were upset because many fine skins were ruined by Mendelsohn. If you were to find such a skin today, signor, do you have any idea how much it would be worth?" Eph shook his head. "Hundreds of thousands of dollars, perhaps even millions. It would be a very long time before such a thing was discovered and used again, but Mendelsohn told Matamoro that, in his family, they had examined this idea before. The skins were so valuable that it was difficult to use them. They were always sold first and there were many buyers. In Africa, it was a different situation, and no one cared about that so much. It was more of a practical matter and what the Bazu were used to. To change the skin of an animal was, to them, a shocking thing. It disrupted their natural order and Mendelsohn realized that he must be very careful. So he worked quietly on his own and usually very late at night when the others were sleeping. He didn't want the Bazu to become disturbed by these experiments."

"Fascinating," Eph murmured, and it was as if he thought his brain mass would shoot out his ears, so intensely was he thinking.

Barzini looked at him curiously. "You are certain that you are all right, eh? You are looking very strange."

"I am feeling very strange."

"Perhaps you need to lie down. Go back to the hotel and take a little rest."

"The last thing I need is sleep."

"But last night, you do too much. Stay up too late, eating, drinking and…"

"And what?" Eph snapped.

"How do I know what you do? I am just saying, signor, you do not look yourself."

"You're right." Eph jumped up from his chair. "Maybe I do need to take some rest. Thank you, my friend. I will see you later." He half-stumbled, half-ran out of the room leaving Barzini staring at him wide-eyed and shaking his head.

Thus began what eventually became 'The Global View'. The Matamoro story and Barzini's colorful telling of it, helped coalesce swirling strands of information floating around in my father's head. At first, these ideas seemed like a disparate jumble of facts and events, but through the fortunate discovery of Matamoro, his diaries and a willing interpreter, Eph was able to begin to make a series of connections and links. After all, if a semblance of a Renaissance guild could form in an African village, who was to say that other parallel events didn't take place in other parts of the world at different points in time, that it was all part of a continuum much of which was based on inspiration, the coinciding of certain events and plain old luck. Not only that, but ideas and innovation spread around the globe.

"After Matamoro demonstrated the use of the bow and arrow, the Bazu were very enthusiastic. Finally, here was something that would allow them to claim superiority over their rivals, the Arakai, with whom they had fought many battles and never won. Fortunately, very few were killed or even died in these conflicts. It was decided that a great battle would take place. As was the custom, the Bazu sent a runner with a message to the Arakai chief, whose name was M'rumba. The Arakai were formally invited to meet the Baku by the singing stream and fight to the death. The message was also delivered with the appropriate songs and dances, each attesting to the courage and worthiness of the Arakai as opponents of the Bazu. Normally, it took the better part of a day to deliver the message as it was a very formal, even solemn occasion."

My father sat and listened to Barzini carefully, and just as carefully as he had all along, made extensive notes. After his revelation, Eph was careful to tone down his excitement lest he overlook some convention of scholarship. He didn't want to be tripped up on some technical detail over the thesis that was percolating in his brain. Earlier, he had asked Barzini for an English translation of the diaries and Barzini shrugged, and said he'd see what he could do. Barzini continued. "The messenger returned to the Bazu and reported to B'kela that the invitation had been accepted by M'rumba, and the battle would take place during the time of the singing birds, which as it turned out was some two weeks further on. Not only did the tribes have many different gods and rituals, they also had a rather complex way of telling time or making appointments. This did, however, give the Bazu some time to prepare. Immediately, Matamoro set the tribespeople busy at making the bows and the arrows required. He showed them how to choose the wood and how to make the string out of animal guts and to make a notch in the center of the bow so as to sight the arrow properly before it was loosed toward the target. He showed them how to make the arrows and in particular, how to place the feathers so that the arrows would fly far and true. They set up targets and practiced for many hours, first making certain that none of the villagers were in the way because they learned quickly that the arrows, with their flinted tips, were dangerous and painful and could even kill.

The day of the battle dawned and Matamoro felt the Bazu were ready. With B'kela's help, he'd set up a system of commands that would be relayed at his instructions. The two warring sides set up their camps on opposite banks of the Popolimbo River; Popolimbo meaning fast river, full of fish. The spot was chosen because the river narrowed at that point and the water was shallow enough to wade through, rising no deeper than the knees. As with everything the tribespeople did, much music and dancing preceded the battle. The warriors painted their faces and wore ornamental jewelry and masks. The Bazu men also wore elaborate grass skirts and grass bands tied at the knee, ankle, and elbow. With their fierce facepaint, headdresses, ornaments and spears, the Bazu looked quite frightening and when they chanted their war songs in their deep throaty voices and yelled en masse, they sounded frightening too. On the other side, the Arakai matched their looks and temperament. Every time the Bazu yelled, the Arakai responded. Back and forth it went. Matamoro was growing impatient, this was no way to fight a battle.

"How much longer, B'kela?"

B'kela indicated that it would go on for a while yet, so Matamoro sat on a rock to wait and see what happened. There was much drumming and yelling. Finally, one of the Arakai ventured a few steps into the water, yelled, beat his chest, then retreated. One of the Bazu did the same. Then two of the Arakai stepped gingerly into the water and they too, retreated. The Bazu mirrored them. B'kela nudged Matamoro who sat up and watched with interest. They were gathering their courage it seemed, as each time, those who went into the water grew larger in numbers and travelled a little bit farther. As each group stepped forward, there was a great din of rattling and roars from stretched throats, egging the warriors on. Finally, one of the Arakai stood out from the group and launched a spear. It travelled with great velocity and lodged into a tree. There were gasps of surprise and fright from the Bazu. Matamoro stood up from his perch on the rock and nodded to B'kela. The first of the Bazu launched their spears and the wailing chorus went up across the river. Then one of the Arakai, a cheeky fellow, started prancing up and down on the riverbank, wiggling his buttocks at the Bazu – one of the greatest, if not the greatest, insult apparently. Matamoro reached out for his bow which B'kela handed to him. He drew an arrow and lined it up with the notch and drew the string back to his ear. He released the arrow and struck the prancing fellow solidly in the right buttock. The fellow screamed in pain, reaching around to see what had hit him. Hoots of laughter burbled out of the Baku while the Arakai were stunned into silence. Then, Matamoro gave B'kela the signal and fifty archers stepped out of the woods, notched their arrows and let them fly. The air was full of the *zip-zip* sounds of the arrows flying. Many found a target and now the Baku heard screams of pain and howls of surprise. Matamoro nodded again and the archers let loose another round and the lethal *zip-zip* sound hummed in the air like hordes of mosquitoes. The Arakai were dumbfounded. Worse, they were frightened. Some of the Arakai warriors had fallen dead at the feet of their companions. Others were mortally wounded and still others howled in agony. Surprised, frightened, and panic-stricken, the Arakai quickly withdrew leaving their spears behind them as they struggled to retrieve their wounded. A great cry of triumph went up from the Baku and again, there was much singing and dancing. Matamoro was surrounded by a circle of warriors who came to honor him. Afterward, there was the ritual slaughter of a wildebeest and its blood was shared by all. There was much to eat and much to drink as the Bazu brewed their own version of spirits, which was very potent. The chief then offered Matamoro his youngest daughter –who was a pretty girl of some twelve years – according to the custom. All the while, Mendelsohn stayed in the shadows, out of the celebrations. He wanted nothing to do with war and violence. With the women of the tribe, he concentrated on working the looms and turning out materials that could be bartered or sold.

The Baku prospered. They no longer feared the Arakai and under the guidance of Mendelsohn, they gained status with the trading of their materials, the textile business as it was called. Within this small part of the world, there had been a shift in the power balance. For years, the Arakai had been the feared enemy and had terrorized the Baku with their raids and treachery. And now, the Baku had the confidence that the Arakai would not bother them, at least not as much. We do know, dottore, that these conditions do not always last very long. The Arakai, once they had gotten over the shock of their defeat – a defeat which caused them great humiliation and embarrassment – it didn't take long for them to pick up some of these weapons, these arrows and figure out how they were made, how to use them. So, over time, the balance of the power, at least part of it, was made more equal again. But it did take some time, some years actually, for this to happen. As we know, change does not take place quickly and certainly, in that part of the world, the experiences the tribes peoples encountered were highly unusual. The pace of development was very rapid, yes? Due to these outside forces."

"What happened to them? Matamoro and Mendelsohn?" Eph asked.

Barzini rubbed his round face, then smiled. "We don't know what happened to the Jewish merchant, Mendelsohn. Two years after this significant battle, a Spanish ship came to the land of the Baku. Matamoro joined with the crew of this ship, happy to be away from Africa. Mendelsohn, who had many children by this time, elected to stay behind. What became of him, we do not know. Matamoro settled in Spain and eventually became the captain of his own ship. He took part in the Spanish Armada, during which the English sank his vessel. He was taken prisoner and spent many years in an English prison before being released. Having found his captors to be hospitable and his knowledge of sea-faring and indeed, the Spanish navy was useful. Matamoro stayed in England until his death at the age of fifty-seven, signor. Apparently, a carriage ran over him while he was on navy business in London. While in England, he married an Italian woman, a woman of some nobility and they had seven children. Over the generations, the Matamoro name has changed and there have been many different versions, Matamore, Matlock, Montgomery, Matheson and so on."

So, the story had come to an end. Barzini had skipped over the details of Matamoro's later life, details that Eph knew he had to investigate. It was important to discover where Matamoro had been and with whom he'd been in contact. And Mendelsohn; that was a more intriguing story. My father knew he had his work cut out for him, but the prospect was exciting and stimulating. He discovered, subsequently, that Mendelsohn helped spawn a branch of Falasha Jews who eventually settled and prospered in Ethiopia. The Falasha followed their own version of Judaism and the entire community ended up in Israel as part of a massive airlift resulting from a civil war between Eritrea and Ethiopia. The Falasha still resided in Israel today.

Eph's remaining weeks in Florence were productive. He went to the library each day and pored through the archives, often not stopping for lunch. He became aware of how little time he had left. In the evenings, if he didn't dine with the Barzinis, he stopped by their home for coffee and a chat. On his next to last evening, Juliana said: "I wonder what happened to that beautiful lady, that Henny?"

Barzini looked at Eph intently, but drew no reaction. "I don't know," my father admitted. "Went back to the States, I suppose. Planning her future as a teacher."

"Very handsome woman," Barzini murmured, then looked up at his wife. "But she wilted when standing next to you, my darling," he added.

Juliana smiled rather wickedly. "I didn't ask, but I am glad you said so."

"My darling. After having six children together, is there anything I don't know about you?"

"Yes. And I won't tell you now."

Barzini's face clouded. "What? What is it? I demand to know."

Juliana patted his hand. "Ah Francesco, you are such a child."

"You see?" he said, turning to Eph. "She patronizes me. I am no longer a man and a husband, but a boy. This is the true power of women, my friend. How do they do this?"

"I wish I knew but I don't."

"Anyway," Juliana continued. "I hope she is happy now. She seemed very sad, I think."

The other two nodded in agreement, not daring to say anything further.

Less than forty-eight hours later, Eph Goldman drove from Florence back to Rome and boarded an Air Canada flight to Toronto. It was now mid-August and he hungered to see my mother again. He had missed her terribly. There had been a boisterous dinner at the Barzinis the evening before, a farewell for Eph and a promise was made to keep in touch. And this they did, given that many such promises are made with the best of intentions then broken. Eph did keep in touch with Barzini and visited on several occasions. There is even a dedication to him in first edition of The Global View. My mother never went on any of those trips. She never made it to Florence.

23

The Global View was published the year I was born, 1960. My father spent five years researching the book and somehow, during that period of time, managed to get my mother pregnant. Basking in the glow of the book's success some two years later, he did it again and in 1962, my brother, Harry came along.

For the moment, however, there was Egan's art opening to contend with.

I'd arranged Sean and Nathan's favorite sitter, Darcy, a flamboyant fifteen-year-old from across the road. She generally let the boys do whatever they liked. They stayed up later than they should. She smuggled in video games, verboten in our household, and fed them a wide range of snacks guaranteed to elevate their blood sugar to dizzying heights. They played music. They danced. They watched videos. In short, she was perfect.

When we arrived at the Levinsky Gallery, the place was packed. It reminded me of a sock hop twenty years after leaving high school. Music blared. People who should know better jumped around awkwardly. All we needed was some blue-rinsed monitors with plastic handbags to police the floor. The paintings were hung but ignored. I spotted Egan dancing with Bernadette in the middle of the crowd. Her spiked hair stood out like a shark's fin. Sweat poured down Egan's mottled, pink face. His eyes were unfocused. I recognized the song as 'Psycho Killer' by Talking Heads. An art band, at least, was appropriate.

"My God," Sharon exclaimed. "What a scene!"

"It's a happening, all right," I replied. Sharon's other brothers stood by the bar stolidly, surveying the scene with thinly-veiled contempt. They were quaffing ale. Felicity stood between them radiating pride. She held what looked like a tomato juice and sipped at it nervously. "There's the motley crew," I said, nudging Sharon.

"Let's push through," Sharon said. "They'll be glad of a familiar face."

"Right," I said and put my shoulder down. "The bar's there anyway."

Around the perimeter, Levinsky, clad in a black velvet jacket and matching pants, conducted a private tour. The small, earnest group consisted of potential collectors, I assumed. He seemed oblivious to the noise and motion of the bodies. He had stopped before a canvas and pointed vigorously to specific features of the painting. The group nodded collectively, taking it all in. The two couples, stylishly dressed, hung on his every word. After each pronouncement, each couple put their heads together and whispered aggressively. Then, they turned their attention back while Levinsky waited. I gathered Levinsky knew his stuff. I distrusted his appearance instinctively, however. He was a man of fifty with overly long hair and a cultivated beard. He bore a year-round tan and wore clothes obviously too young and tight for him.

Levinsky recognized that Egan had talent, however. I appreciated that. A waiter carrying a tray full of champagne flutes floated by, but I missed him. Sharon and I edged through the ranks toward her mother and brothers. The McCarthy boys had cleared a space around them, just by glowering at anyone who happened by. They'd left their wives at home. Where they belonged. Felicity looked up and waved, spilling a bit of her drink, but she took no notice. Excitement was etched into her face, in the tense way she held herself.

"Hallo!" Felicity cried. "Isn't it grand?" Sharon and her mother embraced awkwardly. I nodded to Kevin and Patrick, which was about the limits of our relationship. We had nothing in common, really, except for Sharon.

"Lads," I said.

Kevin jerked his thumb behind him. "Fancy a quaff, eh, Bern?"

"White wine, Kev," I said.

"Sharon? A drink then?"

Sharon arched an eyebrow. "I can see you're impressed. White wine, then. Thanks, Kev."

Kevin lumbered off. "I don't understand this stuff," Patrick admitted. "I really don't. Do people actually pay money for these things?"

"Quite a lot, actually. It's surprising, isn't it?" I replied.

"It is at that," he said. "Have you seen what they're selling for? I mean, these paintings are Egan's," he declared, diminishing the value automatically.

"No, I haven't had a chance to look around yet," I said.

Kevin returned with the drinks.

"Thanks, Kev," I said. Sharon took hers and blew him a kiss, then turned back to her mother. "Patrick's just telling me about the prices of Egan's paintings."

Kevin took a sip of his fresh beer. "Oh aye," he replied and said nothing more about it.

"Look at that one," Patrick said and pointed. It was the companion to the large red nude Egan had given me. This one was painted in dark green and blue hues. The surface was mottled, as if the canvas wept, dripping tears. The nude had a far-away, dreamy look in her eyes. I liked that painting a great deal. "That's five thousand dollars, that one," he declared.

"Really?" I replied. "Then the one I've got is worth at least that much. If I were you, Patrick, I'd get Egan to paint you a little something. Then put it in the vault."

"That one," Patrick continued, pointing directly over my shoulder, "is twenty-five thousand."

I swiveled and glimpsed 'the wall'. Sharon and I hadn't seen it before as it was placed behind us. To reach her mother and brothers, we headed away from it. But you needed this much distance to take it all in.

"Wow!" I exclaimed. I thought it breathtaking. No wonder Levinsky wanted it at all costs.

It was done as a triptych. The center panel revealed the figure of a young, blond boy, naked. His chest showed a gaping wound, the heart cut out. To either side of the boy were objects of childhood; books, cowboy hat, holster, hobby horse, sled, and teddy bear swirling around. The left panel depicted a dark figure in black on a podium. He held a guitar. This, I took it, was meant to be Rory. The figure on the right was female. The features weren't distinguishable, but she wore a shroud which was partially torn away, revealing her breasts. Deep scratches were visible in the white flesh. The shrouded figure was kneeling, as if suffering or supplicating. Her dark hair was long and wild, looking as if a fierce wind blew it back. The entire painting was trimmed with light. It implied that the emotions were so intense, that the entire thing might ignite in a flash, from the edges in. It was as if it had been painted with phosphorous. God, what a tortured scene. And for a moment, due to the noise, the heat, and my own inner paranoia, I transposed the faces. Under the cowboy hat, I now saw Eph. The virgin-like figure turned into my mother and the little boy became me, wearing a yarmulke, sacrificed on the altar of my bar mitzvah. I stared for a long moment. Then shook my head, bringing the real world back into focus.

"Looks like Eg as a lad," Kevin observed, sipping his beer.

"But twenty-five thousand?" Patrick protested ignoring the subject of symbolism completely. "Nothing is worth that kind of cash, man."

I shrugged, preferring to stay out of the discussion. I thought the painting to be quite disturbing, Egan rutting in despair. Sharon and Felicity were staring at it now.

"My God," said Felicity. "It's something, isn't it?"

"No wonder his landlord wants it back," I said. "Imagine the rent he'd get with that in there?" Then, noticing Sharon's sour expression, I added hastily, "Just kidding."

"Is that me, do you think?" Felicity asked, indicating the shrouded figure.

"I'm not sure," I said. "Why do you ask?"

"Well, it looks like me, you know. And the truth of it is, it brings back thoughts and feelings I've tried to ignore for a long time. Put out of my mind."

"I see."

"You know," she said rather sadly, "I never realized how painful he took his father leaving. Or how my own feelings affected him. I was just afraid, really. Afraid for how we'd live and what we'd do. I didn't have time to consider him then. And now, seeing this, I feel terrible about it."

"Mum, you can't blame yourself," Sharon said. "You did the best you could under the circumstances."

"Did I?" Felicity asked herself, more than anyone else. "Did I indeed?"

"We didn't know that our father would turn out to be a bastard, did we?" Sharon said bitterly. Patrick turned. His ears burned red at the tips.

"You watch it now," Patrick said. He'd been closest to Rory, as the eldest. And we suspected they kept in touch on a regular basis. "He's no bastard, at all."

But Sharon stood up to him. Kevin shrank back a step. He didn't want any part of it. "Any man that'd abandon his family, leave his kids, not pay a penny of support and ignore his grandchildren, is a bastard in my book," she hissed.

Foolishly, I attempted to mediate. "Sharon, calm down, for God's sake."

"Stay out of this, Bernie. I know what I'm doing," she declared. "You were his favorite, Patrick, because you were the oldest. He'd say 'jump', and you'd say, 'how high'.

"What are you arguing for?" Felicity cried. "It's over, anyway. I'm the one who had to deal with it, not you. Besides, I kicked him out, he didn't leave of his own will. Not that he had any to speak of."

Then Patrick muttered something under his breath.

"What was that you said?" Sharon demanded.

"Nothing."

"Say it. Go on, I dare you." I could feel the edge in her.

"All right then, Sharon. I said you were a tight-arsed snob with a head bursting with pride. That's all," Patrick sneered.

Oh my God. I closed my eyes waiting for the explosion. I knew that Sharon, with her temper, wouldn't take that from anyone. Especially from family. She'd probably go for him full out. Like when they were kids.

"Are you having a good time?" piped in a drunken voice, overflowing with good will. It was Egan. He'd appeared before us, his hair matted with sweat and his face filled with happiness.

"Grand," Felicity replied. "Ach, Egan, I'm proud of you son. I'm... I'm... so proud!" And she embraced him, then sobbed into his damp chest.

"Ah, Ma," Egan said. "You know it means a lot. But you're ruining my jacket now. It's not the time for tears, eh? Let's have a drink and enjoy it."

"It's your night, Egan," Sharon said. "Ma's right. We're all proud of you. Seeing your talent on display for all the world."

"You really think you'll get twenty-five thou for that one there?" Patrick asked, nodding to "the wall".

"Christ, I hope so!" Egan roared and threw back his head. "God, wouldn't it be nice, eh?"

Egan's arrival broke the tension between Patrick and Sharon and everyone had stepped back a bit, to let Egan have his due. To their way of thinking, it was only fair.

"Oh my God," I said.

"What is it, Bernie?" asked Sharon.

"There's my dad," I replied.

"Who's that with him?" Egan said, squinting over.

"It's Katherine," Sharon responded, a bit too smugly for my liking.

"Who the hell's Katherine?" Egan asked.

"You met her, you big ape," said Sharon. "Right before you passed out on my living room carpet."

Egan nodded. "Oh, aye," he replied mildly.

I started to make my way over. Katherine was looking about rather nervously. My father tried to look as if he were at home in this milieu. But he wasn't succeeding. I caught his eye and waved. He spoke to Katherine and pointed in my direction. She gave me a brief, unenthusiastic hand flutter. I began to make my way toward them through the crowd, feeling my way through the ebb and flow of bodies.

For a scant moment, I lost sight of Eph and Katherine. They'd been following the current the opposite way. Then, I collided with a man coming from my left. I didn't see him, he blind-sided me.

"Sorry," I said, but he pushed me away and I stumbled. There was something odd about him. He had a square face which was set in its expression, one of determination. Unlike the rest of the well-heeled crowd, this man wore a green canvas overcoat. And it was hot in the room. Very hot. He also wore boots. Construction boots clotted with dried mud. People around him sensed trouble and instinctively shied away. As if they sensed danger.

I was angered at his rudeness. Normally, I was a live-and-let-live sort of guy. Uncharacteristically, I followed him and resolved to say something. But he'd moved ahead quickly and the crowd filled in behind him, blocking my path. I pushed through and realized he was heading for the triptych. I'd lost my father and Katherine, momentarily. Sharon and the others were out of range. I fixated on this guy, on his stiff, broad back. On his shiny, slicked hair. I saw his arms go up above his ahead. He was but five or six feet from the painting now. He held something up. It was dull, metallic, with a long, wooden handle. A bellow of rage came out of him and people shrank back, attempting to scatter. The arms came down in a blur. There was a smack and a sickening crunching sound. Bits of the triptych cracked and shattered. Shards of paint and drywall flew. A piece caught my cheek and I shielded my eyes.

From behind, I heard Egan's scream of anguish and rage. The crowd surged now, on the point of panic. There was a madman in our midst, no telling what he'd do. Some pressed in to get a better look. Others fought to get away, struggling for space. I worked with the movement of the crowd. The hands with the sledgehammer went up again. The wrists, I noticed were exceedingly thick and hairy. They came down. There was another crack and the triptych splintered and flew apart. Egan screamed again. I was close now. The hands went up again. I grabbed hold of the wooden handle and pulled back with all my might.

The madman in the green coat lost his balance and toppled backward. I was on him, pressing him into the floor. I wrenched the sledgehammer free and attempted to pin his arms down with the handle but he fought back. It was pure pandemonium now as the movement of bodies, just legs and feet visible, swayed back and forth. There was a surge, and someone fell across my back. A woman in a tight sheath of a dress, fell across the two of us. Her legs went up in the air, her dress pushed up to her waist, satin pink panties showing.

I wasn't as worried now about the crazy guy as I was about being crushed by the crowd. I could see a look of panic in his face too, as if he were thinking, 'I didn't think this would happen'. A couple of clean smashes and a clear getaway had obviously been the plan. I leaned over him, using my arms to shield my head while trying to force my way up. Then, a pair of hands grabbed my shoulders accompanied by a ripping sound. So much for the good condition of my father's old tuxedo. I found myself being hauled to my feet. When I could focus, I peeked out. Patrick and Kevin had managed to bulldoze their way through and part the crowd. I was standing between them. Kevin helped up the young lady in the tight dress. A bruise was welling up along her jaw line.

"Now, everybody get the hell back," Patrick bellowed, bringing all motion to an instant halt, and I noticed the music had disappeared into the rafters. Then he looked down. "Get up you," he said to the perpetrator in a menacing tone. The fellow, who'd looked so sinister before, nodded meekly.

"Yes sir," he squeaked. Patrick forced an arm behind the fellow's back. The armpit of his overcoat had torn at the seam. Not a good night for clothes, it seemed.

"I'll fetch the blues," Kevin said, going off to phone the police. Within seconds, it seemed, sirens were heard. Sharon forced her way through and embraced me.

"Are you all right?" she cried. "Are you daft, going after him like that? He could have brained you with that thing. Then where'd I be, and the kids?"

"I know where I'd be," I replied. "In a home for the brainless."

"Don't joke," Sharon scolded. "He could have killed you, you know."

"I wasn't thinking. You know I'd never do anything brave or courageous, if I'd had time to think about it," I said.

She smiled and kissed me. "Ach, you would too. But I'd kill you first."

"How's Egan?" I asked. "What's happened to him?"

"I don't know, really," Sharon replied. "Poor bugger. He collapsed. I don't know if it was the shock, the drink or both. Ma's tending to him."

"Well, I wonder who the hell that guy is," I asked.

"I know who he is," Kevin said, after returning from making the call.

"Who is he?" asked Sharon.

"It's Egan's landlord," he replied. "Come to claim his wall, I suppose."

24

The next morning Sharon and I sat in the kitchen looking at the Saturday paper. The 'smashing' incident had made the front page of the Arts section. The photo showed a distraught Egan pointing to the smashed bits of the triptych. Beside him stood a thin-lipped Levinsky, looking outraged. *The perpetrator, whose name was Gerhard Baumann, had been captured by the artist's brother, Patrick McCarthy and is now in police custody. He is being charged with trespassing and willful destruction of private property.*

"What a bloody crock!" Sharon exclaimed. "Trust the media to get it wrong again. You nabbed that guy, not Patrick."

I patted her hand. "That's okay," I replied in mock seriousness. "There are but a few of us who know the whole story. And some day, the truth will come out. But until then…"

"Oh, shut it," Sharon said and swiped the back of my head.

"Well, I guess my dad and Katherine had a great time," I said sarcastically. "What a great first date. Invited to an art gallery opening and it turns into a near riot. Man, you can't beat that for entertainment."

"You'd like to think that an incident like this would kill any chance they'd have, wouldn't you?" Sharon accused me.

"Who? Me?" I replied, feigning innocence.

"Well, I hope they got home all right," she said soberly.

"I'm sure they did." I continued to scan the article for information, thinking it better to leave the subject alone.

She yawned, and stood up to stretch. "I'm going to get dressed. I've got some work to do." She paused, then glanced at the microwave clock. "Isn't it almost time for the boys' lessons?"

Still concentrating on the paper, I didn't look at her. "Yup. I'll see to it." Saturday mornings, Sean and Nathan had swimming, then afterward, guitar lessons. We only had the one guitar, an old one of Rory's that he'd decorated with rhinestones during his country music period.

Over the next week, I went at the book, hammer and tongs. I poured over my dad's old notes. I listened to the tapes. I talked to relatives, friends, and old acquaintances. I began to actually write something. I grappled with this 'spiritual form' business. No matter how much I despised it, that phrase was central to the book and my father's writing. Here's part of what I wrote: *At a relatively early age, Goldman's head began to swim with ideas, his brain seethed with thoughts as if he were on fire. A fever grew in him and raged to burst out... Some early influences were the writings of Spinoza and Montefiori... he was a great admirer of the Americans, Barbara Tuchman and William Shirer and his epic work, The Rise and Fall of the Third Reich. Goldman's ability to see these cataclysmic events in a global context and understand the linkages connecting them, allowed 'The Global View' to deliver its messages with a greater resonance than anything written on the subject before. Growing up in a household that experienced abject poverty, where Goldman struggled to help the family out, earning extra money in any way he could throughout the Depression so he could continue the education he so desperately craved. This put him in touch with and yielded a great sensitivity to the lower-class experience of new emigrants who started at the bottom rung of society and hauled themselves up through hard work, perseverance, and the absolute commitment to a superior education. Oft times, his mother supported the family by playing hands of penny ante poker with women in the inner city neighborhood where he grew up. Those few dollars a week, that Frances – Fanny – managed to scrape together, often meant the difference between eating or not. Goldman, in his early years, turned away from God and religion and like many intellectuals of that period, flirted with leftist thinking, stopping far short of embracing Stalinism as did many of his contemporaries and companions of his youth. In fact, Goldman was one of the few to denounce Stalin shortly after the Second World War, perceiving correctly, that no matter which end of the spectrum, a tyrant was a tyrant, a despot by any other name. He embraced democratic principles wholeheartedly and knowing they were flawed, contended rightly, it was the best thing going until something better came along. Goldman has the ability to see through political artifice and rhetoric, to apprehend the meaning of a leader's words and actions be it Roosevelt or Mussolini..."* Re-reading these words, jerky and flawed perhaps, I have to admit that even I was impressed by what Eph had achieved. And to think it had all began with a charismatic librarian named Francesco Barzini and an obscure Italian explorer, Diego Matamoro. I recalled seeing a photograph of my father taken with Barzini. It was small, square, and badly focused. They had their arms over each other's shoulders and they grinned into the camera. I have looked at that photograph many times and it strikes me each time that there seemed to be a genuine connection between the two of them. That Eph's expression was not just real, but poignantly sincere. Like everyone, my father was a product of his early influences and his upbringing but the breadth of insight he achieved in The Global View, the way he was able to excavate hidden links between achievement and discovery made me shake my head. He had been more than just a historian, in my view, but an archeologist of long ago stories and events. He had the gift of being able to infuse those stories with power and significance. A ruined god, indeed.

I spoke to Egan. He sounded depressed. "How's it going with the show?" I asked him.

"Well," he replied somberly. "Two of the critics slagged me and the rest have been pretty decent, actually."

"That doesn't sound too bad."

"No, not too bad at all," he replied.

"How are the sales going?"

"Quite good, actually. We've sold over half the pieces," he said.

"What does that mean, Egan, dollar wise?" I asked.

"Oh, about a hundred thou so far," he said.

"One hundred! Wow! What's you're cut, if you don't mind me asking?"

"Forty-five percent, Bernie. That's the deal, yeah," he replied sounding like his favorite dog had just died.

"Egan," I said, "that's forty-five thousand dollars! Do you realize that? That's more money than you've made in the past ten years. Hell, more money than I've *made*," I exclaimed. "And you've only sold half so far. That's fantastic. Especially for a first show."

"Oh, it's great. I'm not complainin', you know. Levinsky's going to set me up with a proper studio. No more painting on walls, for me," he said, and I could feel him wince in pain over the phone.

"And that guy, Baumann? What's happening with him? Have you heard anything?" I asked.

"Ah, I don't know really. He's been fined, or released on bail or something like that. I think there's goin' to be a hearing or something but I'm not sure." He paused. "Anyway, Bernie. Thanks for calling and checking up on me, but I've got to go. Levinsky's set up some sort of meeting with a publisher. They want to do a book on my paintings," he said.

"A book?" I repeated.

"Yeah, and I'm not even dead yet, eh?" he laughed.

"Listen, Egan. Have you signed something with Levinsky? You know, like a contract or anything?"

"Ah, well, he's supposed to be acting like my agent. Selling my paintings to collectors and getting a commission like," he said.

"And you've signed something with him?"

"Oh aye. We did that at the very beginning. It seemed to make sense at the time. But then, who knew that bastard was going to destroy my best painting? I mean, I put my soul into it, you know, Bernie? I'll never get that back again. I don't think I'll ever do another quite as good. Everything else'll just be second rate. You understand what I'm saying?" he said glumly. "I think I'm finished even before I got started."

"Egan. Listen, I've got this cousin. He's a collector but he's a lawyer too. I'd like you to talk to him. Just to get an opinion about the deal you've got with Levinsky. It never hurts to get a second opinion, right? Doctors or art dealers, what's the difference?"

"I don't know, Bernie. Look, I've got to go and do this meeting thing, okay?" I insisted. "Will you think about it?"

"Yeah sure. Listen, I appreciate it. I know you're looking after my interests."

"Think about it."

"Yeah, I will. Ta." And he rang off.

25

"…September, 1927. My Dearest Fanny. Dagmar is getting quite large with child now. We have left the Magyars and to be truthful, I fear for my life. Every night I wake up shaking in bed. I dream that Markos is in the room and he is holding a knife to my throat. The very knife he held to my throat when we first met. We are living in a small pension, what they call here a flat, in the Artist's Quarter. I do not yet speak the language well and so must rely on Dagmar to tell me what to do or what people say. I have learned some words and phrases, and each day I am getting better.

"I have written Uncle Herman for your address in Canada. This way I can send my letters to you directly and perhaps you will write me back? This is a confusing time. It is strange to think that, soon, there will be a little one. I don't think I know anything about children or what to do with them. Perhaps it is like having a little brother or sister. It is not something I have ever thought about. Dagmar is calm. She bosses me about and I let her. But she seems to know exactly what to do. Paris is such a big place. If I walk in one direction a hundred meters and then turn and walk in another direction, I am lost. Everything is different but yet looks the same. There is noise and traffic. Never have I seen so many trucks and motorcars.

"Dagmar's plan worked as she said it would. The sleeping potion put everyone into a deep sleep, including the children. I took the lockbox into the woods. When we opened it, we could see it was stuffed with bills and coins and pieces of jewelry. She counted out the bills and coins. There was a mixture from different countries, but Dagmar said it came to about 12,000 francs–a fortune! She counted out half the amount and put it into a leather pouch she kept fastened around her waist and hid it under her skirt.

"Then, we returned the box to its place, gathered our things and left. We made our way to the train station just outside Zagreb. Dagmar had found out the train schedules. We bought our tickets and within two hours came the train to Paris. We'd purchased identity cards on the black market. Two nights and three days later, I was staring down at the Seine. Dagmar also knew people, one Sigmund and his wife, Freda. We stayed with them for a few days until we moved into the flat at 13, rue St-Paul, 3e étage. These people, Dagmar's friends, knew of a small shop for rent. Dagmar wasted no time. Within days it seems, she had it cleaned, stocked and ready for business. Mostly, I stayed in the back and followed her instructions. She showed me how to make objects look older, so they were 'authentic'.

"Some of our neighbors are artists. They are young and very poor. Dagmar looked at their work and talked with them. Those she liked and trusted, she brought in to work with us. There was a fellow named Jean-Guy, who was my age, maybe a few years older. He is a sculptor, but he seemed to understand what Dagmar told him to do. And better, Jean-Guy suggested ways to improve the techniques. There was another fellow too, an American, named Marsh. He was older, nearer thirty, I think. I do not like this fellow. He is loud and arrogant. He dismisses me when he comes in and I take great pleasure in cursing at him in Russian, Polish and Yiddish. He only has eyes for Dagmar.

"This Marsh seems to be a painter with some talent and Dagmar is pleased with his work. In just a few weeks, we have many objects on display. Dagmar has fixed the shop up quite nicely and I must keep it neat for customers when they come in. Dagmar has been busy meeting other dealers in the quarter. Every Sunday afternoon, there is an open market in the square. For five sou, we can set up a table with our wares and sell them to the crowd. Dagmar made up cards with the name of the shop and its address. We have given a great many out to tourists, other dealers and those who live in the city. I am not Isaac or Vlasic any longer but now I am part of an enterprise, my dear sister. I am now Monsieur Redmond, Dealer in Antiquities and Objets d'art. But the truth is, Dagmar is Monsieur Redmond. I am just a stupid boy, I think.

"That is what Dagmar calls me, stupid. She and Jean-Guy and this Marsh talk about me in French. They think I do not understand but I am understanding more than they know. I am quick with languages and every day, these French make more sense. They are no longer clucking like chickens in my face. The words begin to take shape for me. I am learning all the time. When the baby comes, in just a few months, Dagmar will need me to run the business. I must know how to do this. I don't want her to think me a fool. I wish to make these fellows listen to me. We are getting customers and Dagmar was right. They pay for the urns, plates, bowls, pieces of furniture. More than anyone could ever imagine! Who knew such a business was possible? I think it is magic, dear Fanny…"

"…January, 1928. My Dear Fanny. I am the proud father of a baby boy. His name is Armand. I have decided to take my old identity back and the baby is registered as Armand Dubinsky. And I am now Vlasic Isaac Dubinsky. It was hard for Dagmar at the end. We had a midwife to tend her and a doctor who lives in the quarter who is a drunk. But I stayed with him when the time came to make sure he didn't drink. And he stayed sober. When it was all over, I gave him a big drink of brandy and a bottle too. Dagmar worked in the shop right until the day before Armand came along. I have told her she must rest a few days. But she is eager to return, and she will care for our son there. She wishes to keep him with us. And now I must show her I can handle more of the work. She needs to nurse and change Armand. Customers must still be served, yes?

"I have sworn to her I can take care of this for us. My French has improved a great deal. This is my exciting news for you. I am sorry I have not written in such a long time but there is so much to do. I was very happy to receive your letter. The very first!

"I did not know about Mama all this time. I would have said kaddish for her if I had known. To be truthful, Fanny, it was a great shock to me. It is difficult to imagine that she is no more. I suppose Papa took it very hard. My being away could not have been much help. Why does he not come to you in Canada, Fanny? Why does he refuse? What is there for him in the shtetl? I hope you can reason with him. I know he would never listen to me. Not ever. And I didn't do so hot listening to him too.

"I was interested to hear of the child and I hope he is well. Perhaps you will send me a photograph that I may keep of you and your new family. I will put it up in the shop. We have some very nice frames for such things. We buy them for nothing, then work our magic in the back, and sell them for fifteen or twenty francs. It is almost a sin. This fellow Marsh I told you about, has gone back to America. Good riddance. He was a rude fellow and I did not like him. He has a rich family, we hear. They've called him back for some family business. I hope he stays there and we never see him again.

"I still think of Markos and wonder when he will come to Paris. I am convinced he will find us. Dagmar calls me silly and says that I worry needlessly. Perhaps, but the feeling is strong. We do not seem to have much time for each other now. There is so much to do with the shop and Armand keeps Dagmar busy. He seems to eat night and day without stopping even just a little. I wish he would sleep a little more also. Our flat is very small and cramped now. But we cannot afford a larger one. Perhaps in time, if the shop does better. For now, we must carry on, yes, my dear sister? There are days when I feel very old. It is hard to believe that I am not yet twenty…"

"…September, 1928. My Dearest Fanny. Thank you for the photographs. As I said, I have put them into some very nice frames and they are hanging on the wall in the shop. Business has been going well. Since spring, tourists have come and as long as the weather is good, we shall stay busy. We also secure orders from some of the larger dealers too. This will help us when the weather turns colder and fewer tourists come to Paris. We are starting to send goods to other cities and countries. Only on consignment do we allow this.

"Armand has grown tremendously. He is healthy and eats well. But still, I would prefer if he slept more at night. We must watch him carefully in the shop now. He can reach things. Just yesterday, he pulled a vase down, very nearly hitting his head. The loud crash it made caused him to scream. Dagmar thinks we can afford to bring a woman in to look after him during the day. This way, she says, we can look after the business properly. I am not so sure of this. She has proposed her friend Freda, who has a child of her own, a year older than Armand. At least we know her, and she is nearby. I have agreed to try this out for a little while only…"

"…December, 1928. My Dear Fanny. I imagine it is very cold in Canada. We too have snow on the ground here. It seems even colder now that this Marsh fellow has returned. He is hanging around Dagmar again. He is as rude as ever. He has come into some money and this is why he left earlier. Marsh does not need to work for us anymore but still comes by often. Too often. He asks Dagmar to come out with him to dinner. For drinks. To a nightclub. So far, she has refused him. But he is insistent. When he comes into the shop, I must hold my temper, but it is difficult. He tries to insult me. I still get some pleasure out of cursing him in my mother languages. But if he cannot understand, what joy is there? Dagmar enjoys the attention he gives her. She waves off my feelings, calling them 'petty jealousies'.

"I am glad to hear that your husband, Morris, has secured a position with a firm at law, dear sister. I hope you will prosper soon. I do not think that chasing after vehicles in the street is good. It sounds like a dangerous way to live, yes?…"

"…March, 1929. My Dearest Fanny. Much has happened since I last wrote. I now have a record with the flics, the police in Paris. I am sad to write this to you, but I have just been released from prison. The magistrate gave me 30 days for a 'crime of passion'. Do not be afraid, I did not kill anyone. For the first time in my life, I wanted to kill a man, my dear sister.

"You have guessed, I'm sure. This man, Marsh, came into the shop again. I let myself get angry. Armand had been screaming all night. There were many orders to fill. Dagmar had gone out. I told Marsh to get out of the shop and not to come back. He laughed at me and said something in English. Jean Guy was working in the back and came out front. I insisted that Marsh leave immediately. He asked for Dagmar. I told him to leave her alone. He laughed and said he could come for her any time he wanted. He said she enjoyed his company. Again, I ordered him out. Then he laughed at me and said the thing that made me go mad. He told me that he and Dagmar were lovers. Marsh turned to leave. I picked up a vase and smashed it over his head. It knocked him out for a few minutes only. There was some blood. He has a head like a boulder. The vase was of delicate porcelain only.

"Jean Guy ran for the doctor. The drunk doctor who delivered Armand. He was still drunk. The doctor botched the bandaging. I gave Marsh some brandy. A few minutes later, he left. Then the flics came and took me away. In France, much is made of a husband's rights. But only when it comes to the wife. If I had smashed the vase over Dagmar's head, I would have been fined fifty francs and let go. But another man! That is a different story, yes? No fine. Go to the Bastille for thirty days. My dear Fanny, it was miserable there. I do not wish to tell of the horrors I suffered. But I survived.

"Dagmar was very angry with me. I had told her what Marsh said and she denied it. I believed her. And why you may ask? Dagmar is again with child. My child. Marsh seems to have disappeared, he hasn't come around. I asked Dagmar if he came around when I was in the Bastille. She swears he did not. I think that maybe she is a little afraid of me, Fanny. Of what I might do. Of my temper. I think it may not be a bad thing, this fear of hers…"

"...May 1929. My Dearest Fanny. Dagmar grows large in the belly and her irritation grows too. She is in a black mood all the time, even as the air grows lighter here, and the days grow warm and sunny. I can take Armand outside and let him play in the park nearby. I don't think Armand understands what is happening to Dagmar, just that she is getting very fat. We have told him there is a baby inside, but he doesn't believe us. Business is beginning to pick up. There are more tourists now in the city. Dagmar is tired often and must rest. More and more, the business is left to me and I have kept Jean Guy busy. We have done very well with brass goblets and these ceramic plates. People seem to want them and pay well enough too. Still, it could be busier. Last year at the same time, we sold twice as many. I do not know why this is. Perhaps people are just being more careful today. Or they spend their money on clothes and motorcars, in nightclubs and the bistros..."

"...August 1929. My Dearest Fanny. It has been a beautiful summer with little rain and fortunately not too hot. You know that everyone leaves Paris in the summer because of the heat? Except for the tourists, of course, who think it is the best time to travel here. Dagmar has not been well, and this has not helped her disposition. She spends most of the day in bed now and of course, she is always hot. She has grown so large that Armand can't believe it and he pokes her belly thinking he might let all the air out and she will go back to normal. Dagmar snaps at me. I think she blames me for what is happening to her. There is not much I can do. I know she is not herself and I do not fight with her. It is too warm for that. She prays for the baby to be born early. I have told her the baby will come when it is ready and not before and she will feel better as the weather cools down over the next few weeks. It has been slow in the shop and I have Jean Guy working only a few days during the week. I am hopeful it will get better. I am sorry to hear how hard you and your Morris must work to make ends meet. But what else can we do? We are all facing the same difficulties. My best wishes to you, Morris and the boy..."

"...November, 1929. My Dearest Fanny. I now have a daughter. Her name is Gabrielle. I think Armand is very jealous. Children are like this are they not? Were you not very jealous of me? You did not have mama and papa all to yourself, yes? We had quite a fine spring and summer season. There were many tourists, there were many orders. We have hired two more artists from the quarter. We have also taken on two more rooms to the flat. Armand has his own room. And the other is the nursery for little Gabrielle. I think she looks very much like Dagmar, but she is fair. I shall send photographs very soon.

"We have not seen or heard from Marsh. Good riddance. Bah, I spit on him. Our lives are now very full. Very busy. Your Morris still chases the vehicles in the street? He must be careful not to get run down. I have seen such things here. People do not look. They are not careful. And then a lorry runs right over top of them.

"Fanny, I read the newspapers here. A few days ago, I read about this crash. This stock market in America. Do you know of this? People here say it means things are very bad. And when things are bad in America, they are bad every-where else. Is this true? I hear this and I think, that maybe things will be bad here too. Yesterday, I was out seeing a customer. I passed by a branch of an American bank. It is near the American consulate. Many people were milling about. A crowd had gathered in front of this bank. Some pounded on the doors, but no one came. They were not open.

"One man picked up a piece of a brick and he threw it through the front window. Then others did the same. It was raining glass on the street. Many people were cut. Some were women and children, just passing by. Finally, the flics came. There were fights. I hurried away quickly. I did not want to be picked up, I did not want any trouble. I read in the newspaper the next day about this – it was called a riot. The crowd had turned into an angry mob. Many were hurt. Many were arrested.

"I think this trouble has to do with the news from America. Tell me, my dear sister. Do you think this crash of the stock market will make trouble for us here?…"

26

Finally, I received a response from my father to the questions I'd sent to him. The answers came sealed in an envelope delivered by post. I suspected that my father wrote with a touch of facetiousness. I was struck by the irony that he answered me as if I were one of his students. That he was instructing me. About his life. And my own. I sensed too, some impending fear. How do I know this? By my father's reply to the last question: *If you were to write your own epitaph, what would it say?* His reply: *Here lies a man who betrayed his own intellect.* Not, betrayed *by* his own intellect, mind. And the difference I found very curious. He gave no indication as to why he answered in this way. Perhaps I should lower his mark for that. *No apparent understanding of the process.*

It is also clear to me that my father perceived The Global View both as a benediction and an albatross. That he was a victim of its success. At a rather young age, he had hit a plateau. Then, he was stuck there.

My father came to write The Global View after a great deal of thought, correspondence and discussion with his peers and colleagues at home and around the world. A large part of the text concentrated on conflict and how it helped spread ideas and innovation, in addition to terror and destruction. Some of the last chapters were devoted to the Second World War, where he maintained it was a global conflict. And it was his contention that few viewed it in that way. Historians, in fact, he said, explored themes relating to the war as a classic good versus evil scenario. Righteousness on one hand and the devil on the other. There was a tremendous emotional investment on both sides: the Allies and the Axis. For the people, the *volkslander*, this emotion rooted in surging nationalism and patriotic pride. Underlying the ideological surface, however, lay the twin principles of governance and economics.

Using nationalism as a tool, governments – and behind them large corporations – created opportunity. Opportunity to extend their power, extend their reach and capture territory in governance terms or markets, in economic terms. These conditions continued to exist and extended into what we now called the Cold War.

As my father put it in his notes to me, he owed almost everything to The Global View. He would not have had the academic standing, the renown, the financial security or his current position of professor emeritus. He wouldn't have hobnobbed with the famous and wannabe intellectuals otherwise. He would have struggled and we as a family would have suffered without it. The Global View had become a living, breathing entity. No longer just a book. In later years, as reprints found new audiences, there were magazine covers, photo essays, T-shirts, sweatshirts and coffee mugs featuring the trademarked globe with a pair of bifocals stuck on it. Over the years, there has been talk of a syndicated comic strip, a newspaper column and most recently, an animated television series based on my father as a 'nutty professor' type.

Was I bitterly disappointed in his answers because I seemed to play no significant part, except as an afterthought? Were they too pat? Or exactly what his fans wanted to hear despite de Groot's exhortations to 'go for the gusto'? I was troubled, and I told myself that these uneasy feelings went beyond my own eagerness to please and seek attention from him. Something was missing. Something felt wrong. What could it be? My resentment had begun to turn a dark corner. And then there was Florence and Henny Sparshot. How to explain that?

How did I know about Henny Sparshot? My mother had told me during the long periods of inactivity during her illness. She spent a great deal of time in hospital and then at home in bed. I was with her most days. After The Global View was published, Henny had written my father a letter. She had, indeed, gone back to school and earned her teaching certificate. Some seven years after they'd met in Florence, Henny had remarried and had a child with a warm, loving and responsible man. She seemed very content and taught grade four. My mother didn't find out about Henny as a result of the letter. Eph confessed to her that same summer. It had caused her pain, she had said, but in the end, he'd been forgiven. And he had never erred since. She made me swear never to speak of it, never to ask him about it. And I didn't. Only because she asked me.

At the same time, I began to feel Isaac's presence within me. He occupied my thoughts a great deal. Increasingly, in fact. I began to like and appreciate him, almost despite myself. I warmed to Isaac, to the rogue in him. And thought more deeply in and around what I knew. I tried to imagine the connections. Those bridges of events, actions and emotions that occurred between the letters he wrote to his sister. I had labored under the illusion that our family history remained dull and uneventful. That our recent forebears worked hard all their lives, took small pleasures when and where they could and hoped their children would benefit. At least, that's what my father always told me. And he is the historian of the family. So, what better authority?

I watched a bunch of robins pecking at the remains of some toast I'd tossed out after breakfast. The way they used their beaks to eat was very efficient. Admirable, really. Such crisp action. So simple. Perhaps I should write a children's nature book, instead. It'd be easier and less painful. I forced myself to go back upstairs to my office. Otherwise, I'd waste the whole morning staring out the window. Television never distracted me during the day. Same thing with the radio. But pass a window without looking out? Never. There were too many windows in this house.

27

"...September, 1932. My Dearest Fanny. I understand the difficulties that exist everywhere. The past summer and spring were very poor for business. We have a little money saved, but only a little. I fear that we won't be able to keep the shop going much longer. We now have boarders living with us in the two extra rooms. Dagmar and I share our room with the children. Armand has started school and was unhappy at first. He didn't like to be away from his mama. Most little boys are like this, I think. Gabrielle can't wait to go. She will walk out the door without looking back.

"If you could spare even a little bit of money, this would be a big help to us. I know that Morris is working very hard to keep the family going. Things have become very expensive here, Fanny. The cost of everything is climbing and climbing. When the people are trying to put bread in their mouths, it is difficult to sell antiques. You can't eat antiques, yes? Even those who can afford the prices, cheap as they are, refuse because it looks bad to spend money on antiques when many go hungry. It is the appearance, no? Feh! These people are terrible snobs. I think more and more I do not like the French. They cluck. They whine like wounded dogs. They walk about with their noses in the air. Perhaps we should come to Canada, yes? I think about this more and more. But I must convince Dagmar. So far, she is against it. She says that business is bad there. She doesn't want to start over. And it is too cold..."

"...November, 1932. My Dearest Fanny. It is a bleak time in the city now. Many people are losing their lives, their businesses. We have become experts now in setting values on the items in a person's home. Before, this sort of business took place only when a death occurred, yes? But now, we are asked to come and look at things people want to sell so they can eat. They offer them cheaply. But there is little for us. These poor people have no money to pay, so we take something of value for our services, some object perhaps that we can try to sell. A carpet or a lamp, perhaps some silver, but the class of people we deal with usually have plate, not the real thing – no value there. Still, we earn a few francs. And if we can find a buyer for some of these things, we take a small commission. It keeps us going but we are swept up in the misery of it, my dear sister. We feel the pain, see the tears when precious objects filled with memories are taken away rudely. See, someone will cry, there goes Mama's sideboard or they're taking our favorite quilt, the one that was hand-sewn by Aunty. And so on. We take the money, yes. But it is not a good way to make a living. Even I, who have done many things, I feel dirty doing this. I am sorry to sound this way to you, but I feel, these days, there is no one to talk with. Dagmar and I barely speak to each other anymore. I believe that she hates me for what I have done to her. The children. Held her back from her dreams of luxury. She will not forgive me for this. Can you spare us anything? I beg of you, my dear sister. Help us leave this godforsaken place. I know our lives will change if we come to you in Canada. I pray for this every day."

"…January, 1933. My Dearest Fanny. Sometimes, we must laugh at ourselves, yes? Even when it seems things can't get any worse. The days and nights are very cold, and we cannot afford the money to buy coal for the fire. I have no gloves or a warm coat, so I wear two or three sweaters and a jacket. I look like a prizefighter, wearing clothes that are too tight. For the children, it is too cold. Finally, I couldn't stand it any longer and I went to a store and 'borrowed' some mittens. I thought I might be arrested but I was skillful enough to get away with it. At least for now. As I was saying, one evening, I was locking up the shop, but even this seems pointless. There is little to take, almost nothing of value but still we go through the motions. We pretend life is like it always was and we hope the next day we wake up to find out it is true. Do you understand this? Do you feel the same way, my dear sister? It was about eight o'clock in the evening and very dark. There was practically no business that day. I was distracted, not thinking at all. My head was swimming with thoughts but nothing clear. I stepped out into the street without looking. I heard a noise and turned to see a motorcar coming right at me. Before I knew it, I was thrown up into the air and landed on the sidewalk, the breath crushed out of me. Can you believe it? A well-dressed gentleman in evening clothes gets out of the car and comes over. 'My God!' he cries, 'Are you all right?' My breath came back slowly and I nodded. 'Can you stand?' he asked. I nodded again, and he helped me up. 'I am terribly sorry, Monsieur,' he said. 'You stepped right in front of me.' 'You should call the police,' said a man who happened by. 'This fellow almost killed you.' The gentleman looked alarmed. 'The police? Well, I'm sure there is no need for that, eh, my good fellow?' He gave me an encouraging look. 'Get lost,' I said to the busybody, who went away, cursing and muttering under his breath. 'We can settle this between ourselves, can't we? I'm running late for an important dinner engagement.' I said nothing in reply. 'If I give you one hundred francs, will that help?' he asked quietly, looking around to ensure we weren't overheard. Again, I said nothing. 'How about one hundred and fifty francs?' I held my tongue. 'Here's two hundred francs,' he said, and thrust a wad of bills into my hand. I looked at them. I couldn't believe it, Fanny. A small fortune. 'Very well, then sir and I thank you.' The gentleman shook my hand. 'Once again, my dear fellow, my apologies.' Then he hurried off to his motorcar and sped away. I watched it disappear down the darkened road. I tried to clear my head, it was still fuzzy, and my shoulder began to throb. But then I began to think. This was more money than we could make in a month in the shop. Slowly, I walked up the steps to our flat. Wouldn't others be willing to pay as much in similar circumstances?..."

"...February, 1933. My Dearest Fanny. God is laughing at me now. Truly, he is and thinks me the greatest fool. Such silly plans. I tried this trick again with the motorcar. The first time, I didn't handle it quite right and the fellow ran over my foot and kept driving. Can you imagine? And now I must hobble about like a cripple with no money for a doctor. Dagmar told me I deserved it, trying such foolish things. 'You could get killed and where would we be,' she said. And then she slapped me across the face. I tell you, I became so angry I wanted to kill her, but I couldn't let the children see the anger and hatred in me. They were looking with such wide eyes, innocent and fearful at the same time. But I can be stubborn and decided to try again. I chose a busy street and watched the traffic for a while and made sure that I could time my actions properly. I found a fancy motor and followed it, waiting for the right moment. Then I stepped out and it worked perfectly. You would have thought the way I flew into the air and landed that I was a gymnast. The car was driven by some old dowager, a prune-faced shrew who shrieked at me, ignoring my pain. She made such a fuss that the flics were called, and they arrested me. Can you believe it? They took me away. The woman was screaming at me in hysteria and because of her class, her station, I was taken away. It didn't matter really, the flics yelled at me and pushed me around a little bit but after they had taken me several hundred meters away, they let me go and told me to watch out or the next time I would be sent up before the magistrate. And as you know, Fanny, they have me on their files and I could get a harsher punishment this time. So, I am doubly sore and hobbling, running an empty business, fighting with my wife, frightened for my children and God laughs, yes? He is having his joke on me. Bah! I spit in the face of God. He never did me any good. You hear my story and now I beseech you again, let me come to you in Canada and take my family away from this wretched life. Please, my dear sister."

"…March, 1933. My Dear Fanny. It is done now. We let the shop go. Business has been terrible, and we could not afford it any longer. I am pleading with Dagmar now about moving to Canada. But for now, we must go back to the old ways of plying our trade. I do not want to do this. I have become comfortable, perhaps. The money you promised has still not arrived. I beg of you to think of us and our difficulty…"

"…October, 1934. My Dear Fanny. I understand your Morris. After all, who are we to him? Just photographs on a wall. Or names on a letter. That is all. If you could reason with him, I beg you. We still don't have enough for the passage. Go to him one more time my dear sister…"

"…December, 1934. My Dear Fanny. Yesterday, I had the fright of my life. We have returned to our previous life on the streets, dear sister. I have returned to my former life and identity. Isaac is gone, and Vlasic has taken his place. Vlasic can be cruel. He can be heartless. He takes action when necessary. Dagmar and I have worked with the children. We have taught them what needs to be done. We need money to live and to eat. They understand this. Gabrielle has taken to it easily. She is a joy. A treasure. Armand sulks and complains. He does what we ask but must be pushed and prodded all the time. Young boys, I think, are weak. They cling to their mothers. They miss the bosom.

"Tourists still come. Mainly Americans and some English, even when the weather is cold. For the English, it is not too different from their own weather, yes? Something about Paris, dear Fanny, there is a magic to it for those with money. I was working near the Eiffel Tower, because of the tourists. There is a great square nearby and people mill around. It is a meeting place. And there, in the crowd, I saw Markos! Some children were with him, I think. I'd just sent Gabrielle and Armand on ahead. Dagmar had gone home. There is no question he saw me, dear sister. Our eyes met across the crowd. My only thought was to run, run away as fast as I could. Markos shouted. He shook his fist and forced his way through the crowd. I could hear his curses at my back as I slipped between the bodies around me. I heard his cries of anger, his hatred. It made me afraid. He's come to take his revenge, Fanny, I know it. As if we didn't have troubles enough already…"

"…January, 1935. My Dear Fanny. I think I should wish you a happy new year. It is cold and miserable here. We are living like animals. Always hungry, scrabbling for money. At night, I have terrible dreams, nightmares. I dream that I am in a dark laneway and there is no way in or out. Each way I turn, Markos is there, grinning. He is holding a knife. The one with the long blade. He is about to cut my throat. But I can see he is in no hurry. He takes his time. He laughs. I see the metal of the blade shine in the darkness, reflecting the light of the moon in my face. His eyes glow like coals. He is a monster, a golem risen from the grave to devour me. I try to run but cannot. Markos approaches, laughing. I fall backwards into space screaming… and then I wake up, sweating and trembling. I have not yet told Dagmar of seeing him. That he is here in Paris. I do not wish to frighten her. It is difficult enough. It is clear he has not come to make wine. This is not his purpose. He searches for us and soon, I think, he will find what he is looking for. And then, my dear sister, who knows?"

"…March, 1935. My Dear Fanny. Last week, I thought my nightmare had come to be. Markos and I met, face to face. I had put my hands into many pockets that day and was happy, for the moment. I sent the children to school. It was a fine day, cool perhaps, but signs of spring coming. There was no dampness in the air and the sun was out, beautiful and strong. People had removed their coats. Men wiped the inside of their hats with their handkerchiefs. I like the warmer weather. It is better for us because more people come out. There is more business to be done, yes? I didn't want to think about anything for the moment. I wanted to enjoy the sunshine and the growing warmth. I wanted to feel like everything was perfect, just for a little moment, my dearest sister. I wanted to believe that Dagmar and I were deeply in love. That we were prospering. That the children were happy. That we lived well and fully. Just for a little moment, Fanny. That's all I asked. But dreaming takes away things, yes? It leaves us unprotected.

"And when I looked up, I saw the dark eyes of Markos staring back at me. They were angry eyes, yellowed, and shot through with red. He was unkempt and smelled. His hair had turned grey. Deep lines were carved into his face and the skin was loose about his neck. I could see, suddenly, he was a pathetic old man. And when I looked at him, dear Fanny, he must have seen something in me. In the way I looked. And he surprised me. I thought he would raise his fist. I expected to see the blade appear and slide into my belly. Instead, dear Fanny, he wept. Tears rolled down the deep grooves in his face. Markos, the man I had feared. The man who had become my nightmare, wept in my arms like a child. He smelled like the street, the garbage and the sewer. He told me he slept outside. That he had lost everything. So, what could I do? I took him home with me to meet his grandchildren. I took him home to say I was sorry for what we did. I took him home to hear his story. And that is how I will always remember this spring, my dearest sister. Broken dreams and a crushed spirit, yes? But still, I was hopeful. I don't know why. I'd been prepared to kill him you know. I'd also prepared to die…"

At this point, I stopped the tape for a moment, moved by this encounter. Embracing Markos that way. It was taking a chance but at the same time, such a humane gesture that I was surprised. Isaac was a rogue, yet capable of acts of kindness. I took a sip of the rapidly cooling coffee. It was cold and I spat it back in the cup. I knew he was desperate but there is always someone worse off. He could still take pity.

"April, 1935. My Dearest Fanny. We have the story of Markos. And it is sad, indeed. He is very, very ill. It is the lungs. He coughs all the time. It is the consumption. There is much blood. Markos eats but a little. Dry crusts and sometimes, a boiled egg when we have it. It is not often. He stays in bed most days and I think in a few days, he will be gone. In the short time he has been with us, he has wasted down to almost nothing. The family is gone, drifted away. The children went with Dagmar's mother. His brother was arrested and thrown in prison back in Budapest. They have not seen each other now for six years. There is no money for a doctor. Dagmar was surprised and afraid at first. The children were merely curious about this old man. This grandfather who appeared from nowhere. But the years between Dagmar and her father seemed to have dropped away. They were so close once. I know she – I mean, we – wounded him deeply when we ran away. I think the money was almost a small thing at the end. Markos loved his daughter, yes. He missed her, so he said. The old man could see how we lived, dear sister. That our fortunes were low. I think if we had been rich, that might have made Markos insane. But we were no better than him, at the end. Worse perhaps. And very little to hope for..."

"...May, 1935. My Dear Fanny. Two weeks ago, Markos died. It was peaceful, he died in his sleep. It frightened the children and they stayed away. Dagmar wept for him. She wept deeply. It is strange, yes? We do this to him and yet, the bond is there. It is strong. Stronger than we know. Stronger than we think possible. We arranged the funeral ourselves. How else? There was no money to do anything else. To die this way is not such a bad thing, perhaps. In peace, asleep. But not to be remembered by anyone, is sad, I think. I did not care for Markos and even, feared him but still, it made me feel sorry for what had happened.

"I don't know if things can be worse. I fear we may soon be begging in the streets. The children have been good about it, but I can see their pain. Gabrielle has her mother's spirit. She is very clever and learns quickly. Armand has disappeared inside of himself. He is sullen and angry most of the time. Who can blame him? We had a life, a good life. It was taken away. And now he is angry. He doesn't even know who to accuse. He spends much of his time on the street with other ragamuffins and urchins. He's stopped going to school. This causes me great pain. Great pain. Go to the family again, dear sister and ask. I promise you the money will be well spent. Give my regards to the boy. Tell him I hope he is well. From what you say he is very clever, very capable. He will go a long way..."

"...June, 1935. My Dear Fanny. Thank God for the warm weather. It is a relief from the miserable wet and cold. We are to be thrown out of our flat tomorrow. We must gather our things, meager as they are and find another place. I think we shall be living with Dagmar's friend, Freda. She and her husband have managed to hang on. He still has his job working for the city, sweeping up the streets. There is always a need for that, yes? People like us to clean up the garbage left behind by others. There will be eight of us in two rooms. At least, we can pay them a little toward the rent, but it gets harder each day. There are times when I think it would be better to follow after Markos. He is out of pain now."

"...October, 1935. My Dear Fanny. The colder weather is coming, and it brings a chill to my heart. I live to steal, in order to eat. I bare my soul to you my dear, dear sister because you are the only one who knows me so well. I have allowed Vlasic to take me over completely. Sometimes, I think this Vlasic is a monster who is capable of anything, even murder. How did we come to this? Did we have a choice? I dream about our home and life in the shtetl. Perhaps I would have been better off to stay there with you and Mama and Papa. Perhaps I would now be in Canada living a different life. Since my last letter to you, I have been arrested twice by the flics and put in prison. It was sixty days this time. Being there brings out the cunning. Each day, each moment is a fight for survival. If you are weak, you are crushed. The life there is very simple. I beat a man very badly because he stole my blanket. I didn't want to do this, but it was a matter of honor. If I didn't, then it would tell all the others that I was weak. Then they could do anything to me and I would be powerless. I made a friend there. His name is Theodore and he is a thief by trade, a large fellow of good disposition who sees his time in prison merely as an interlude, time that must be paid as part of the demands of his profession. Like a doctor spending time working in a hospital to secure a license. Fortunately, he is well known there, and the others don't bother him. He carries a metal file in his sock that he uses if there is a need. We became friendly and then no one bothered me again. Theodore is serving ninety days for beating up another man and so I left him in prison after my time was completed. We have spoken about working together afterward and who knows? We shall see. I can still make a small living my own way. But I have been miserable thinking about Dagmar and the children. They do not come to see me, and it is lonely without them."

28

"...January, 1936. My Dear Fanny. You do not judge me, do you? I know I can tell you anything, and yet you must feel that my heart is still good, yes? Do not feel that you have abandoned me, my sister. I have made my own choices, good and bad but the world can be heartless, and we lose a little bit of ourselves every day in this life. It is so easy to become swallowed up and forget everything. My prison friend, Theodore came to see me. He needed an extra hand, he said, for something. He asked me if I would be interested and that the pay would be three hundred francs for my trouble. Ah, my dear, if only I had said no. But three hundred francs would feed us for two, possibly three months. What could I say? Two nights later, Theodore came again. He had a car outside and we went down to the street. Some other men were in the car. It was dark and I couldn't see their faces. Nothing was said, no names were mentioned. We drove for some twenty minutes or half an hour until Theodore stopped the car and we waited. After a few minutes, a truck came by. 'There,' said Theodore. 'That's the one.' We followed this truck through the streets until it turned down a laneway. Theodore stopped behind it and got out. We followed. It was only then that I saw the pistols and suddenly, I was frightened. It was dark and cold, and I knew this was not right for me. The truck driver hadn't climbed down yet. Theodore crept alongside of the truck. As the driver opened the door, Theodore struck him on the head and the fellow collapsed. I dragged him out of the way. It was then that it happened. The driver had a companion who saw what had happened. He too, had a pistol. A warning went up and suddenly noises like booms crashed out into the night and I smelled the bitter air and this other fellow fell back against the truck. Theodore had shot him. The others came and dragged him to the side of the lane and dropped him there. The poor fellow! One of the other men climbed into the truck and started the motor. Lights around us had come on and Theodore called to us to hurry but I was rooted, I couldn't make my legs move. Theodore slapped me twice in the face very hard, then growled something at me. I went with him. We got back into the car and followed the truck for another five or six kilometers. I didn't know where we were. They parked the truck in a garage and I was to help unload. Still, no one had spoken but I could see by the worried looks of the others, they too were afraid. Only Theodore appeared calm. The truck was full of spirits, brandy and champagne. Three of us unloaded the truck and piled the wooden crates along the wall, where they were covered with a canvas cloth. Theodore watched us quietly as if we were day laborers, digging in the street. The crates were very heavy, and it took an hour of hard work to complete the task. When it was done, Theodore gave me three hundred francs and another two hundred on top. The others stayed in the garage while he took the motorcar and drove me back to the flat. 'Not a word,' he said to me, 'or you know what can happen to you.' I nodded to him, saying I understood perfectly. Three weeks later, Theodore was arrested and charged. He got ten years for it. One of the others made a deal with the flics. Me, I was lucky, they didn't know my name and I never saw them again. As soon as I heard what happened, we moved out of our flat quickly and quietly without saying where we were going. Without the five hundred francs, I couldn't have done it. The children didn't mind but Dagmar was angry. She didn't speak to me for three days. I think about the poor fellow who was shot and left in the lane like an animal. I decided to stay within my own trade. At least, there was little chance of someone dying because of it. We found two furnished rooms for fifteen francs a week."

"... April, 1936. My Dear Fanny. I am sorry not to have written sooner but it was a matter of wanting to write something that might lift your spirits. I am sad to hear that your Morris still struggles and that little has improved in Canada. Is there anywhere in the world where people are free? I ask myself this question, over and over again. There is a darkness everywhere. I hear things. See things in the papers. There is a new fear. We see fights in the streets between the fascists and the communists. Spain has exploded and with it, the loyalties have come out here too. Sometimes, I am afraid to go out on to the streets, but I must if I am to earn a living. My only pleasure these days is cleaning the pockets of a fascist. Yes, it is very pleasurable. Not that I mind taking from the communists, but they have so little, nothing in their purses at all. God is absent, yes?"

"…August, 1936. My Dear Fanny. You seem so far away from me, even from my thoughts sometimes. I feel like we exist in separate places that have nothing to do with each other. I am dreaming of the day we will meet again. Of the day I can embrace you and your family and know again what it is like to feel whole. Only pieces of me are left. Dagmar and I argue constantly. Sometimes, I go out and get drunk. I don't come home because I can't face it and when I don't come home we argue because I was away. When she goes out, the same thing happens. The children begin to hate us for what we have done to them. Armand barely speaks, just grunts like an animal. Only Gabrielle is cheerful. What a delight. She takes everything in a natural way. She reminds me of you, dear sister. I wish I could give them a better life."

"…December, 1936. My Dear Fanny. Do men still come to your door, looking for work so they can eat? It is the same here, also. The same bleak looks on the faces. The same feelings of helplessness. The same emptiness. I think that even hatred is better than this. At least we feel something, anything. Better than a cistern that has been sucked dry, yes? How do we keep going? I don't have the answer to this, but I think about it all the time."

"…February, 1937. My Dear Fanny. Today, Armand was beaten on the street for his shoes. I admit, I didn't come by these shoes honestly, but to steal like this from a young boy? Even I would not do such a thing. He came home to us crying, his nose bloodied, his toes half-frozen. Such a state he was in. I went to comfort him, and he turned away from me. He went to his mama only, who looked at me as if it was my doing. Gabrielle saw that I was sad and gave me a hug. What a treasure. But for her, I could not go on. So, what did I do about the shoes? Naturally, I 'borrowed' another pair for him."

"…July, 1937. My Dear Fanny. The season has been poor, very poor. Because of the troubles and the war in Spain, many people stay home, I think. There are fewer and fewer pockets to pluck and wouldn't you know it that there are many of us in this business. Fights have broken out, disagreements over the best places to be, even disputes about who saw someone first. It is unbelievable. Last week, a fellow threatened to take me to the magistrate over the spot I had. 'Are you crazy?' I said. 'We are thieves and you want to take me to the magistrate?' I had to laugh in spite of my misery. It shows the world is meshuga I know of no other word that makes sense, yes? We wear this mask and at the same time, fight for the leavings of those above us. I spit on it. I spit on it all. I want to come to Canada so very badly. Life must be better there. I can't believe it isn't. Tell, me please, that I am right. You must tell me, dear sister or I think I will die not knowing."

"…November, 1937. My Dear Fanny. We survive, barely. Dagmar is out from morning to late at night. I don't know where she goes and who is with her. I am looking after the children. There is such a black mood here. There is much darkness. We are still trying to save enough for the passage over, but it is difficult. Please, help us if you can, dear sister…"

"…June, 1938. My Dear Fanny. I haven't heard from you in such a long time. Why have you forgotten me? We need your help very much. Once again, please send us the money for the passage. If it is at all possible. If not for me, then the children. I will send them first. Dagmar and I will come after. There is such despair here. It is everywhere. We hear of terrible things. Whispers of horror, dear sister.

"Dagmar doesn't understand why there is such hatred against the Jews. I think secretly, she is relieved. That the Magyars have been spared. But I have been reading the Yiddish newspapers and they are filled with terror. They cry about the brutality. Good people thrown out of jobs for no reason. Others disappearing without warning. There are whispers, dear sister of camps built by the Germans out in the woods. They send people, Jews, Communists, even Gypsies, and they don't come back. We hear of mass graves and official denials. I tell this to Dagmar, but she doesn't believe me. She calls it 'Jewish propaganda'. I read of the Germans and how strong are their armies. How we cower in fear against them. The government here is weak, yes? They do not care for Jews, dear Fanny. No government ever cared for the Jews. Vlasic can fight this, but Isaac cannot. If there is war and the Germans were to come, I fear for what will happen. Dagmar looks at me now only with contempt. I think she hates me more every day. Blames me for what has happened to us. She is looking for a way out, I think. A way out on her own.

"I heard from Uncle Herman, yesterday. After Kristallnacht, Europe appears to be on fire. No Jew is safe from harm. The Nazis have given any thug or criminal a free pass to steal and kill. This can happen without fear of arrest, you understand? The world, dear sister, has turned over. Uncle Herman has left Budapest. His shop was looted. He was attacked and beaten on the street. He just escaped with anything he could carry with him. It is very frightening. I have a gaping fear within me, my sister. I need your help more than ever, more than ever…"

There was a pause on the tape and then I heard Mrs. Bernstein say the following: "That's it, Bernie. The last letter I record for you. Such a sad story. So many, so many sad stories, Bernie. By the way, you owe me nine hundred dollars," she said.

29

Knowing that it was the last of Isaac's letters, listening to it gave me a chill. I felt my flesh rise in fear. All I wanted to hear was what happened? What happened to them? As a writer, I needed to hear the end of the story. Not knowing, I imagined the worst. This was my family, and this was new information about my own history that had been unknown to me. I thought of Isaac and saw my face in his. I had to come up with the nine hundred to pay Mrs. Bernstein.

Sharon and I perched on the big sofa in the living room, each of us positioned at either end, our feet touching in the middle. Sharon looked tired and overworked. She ran her fingers through her hair. "Even when Egan's successful, he screws it up."

"That hasn't happened. Not yet," I said.

"No, of course not," Sharon said bitterly. "Only millions of people are laughing at him!" Then she yawned hugely and with considerable grace. "Come on you. Let's get to bed. I'm knackered," she said, then pulled herself off the couch with exaggerated effort.

"You want me to carry you?" I asked. "You don't look like you'd make it on your own."

"Hah! I'd like to see you try, Tarzan."

She stood up and readied herself. I think she expected to jump up in my arms like she'd seen in the movies. What I had in mind was more of a fireman's carry across my back. I bent down to pull her over, she brought her legs up to where she thought my arms would be. Her right knee connected with my jaw and I went over backward and pulled her down with me. We fell, Sharon on top, with a thud in the narrow space between the sofa and the coffee table. Momentarily trapped. I'd cracked my head on the floor. Thank God for carpeting. But still, I was a little dazed. We were flat out nose-to-nose.

"That was brilliant," Sharon said. "Thanks for the lift. Is your head okay?"

"What?"

"I said, is your head okay?"

"Nothing that some extra strength painkillers wouldn't fix," I said, trying to reach around to feel for bumps. "You didn't really expect to just leap into my arms, did you?"

"I did," she said.

"What? And destroy my back?"

"Not if you bend your knees to take the weight."

"You've been reading those 5BX brochures again," I said.

"Five B what?" she asked.

"Listen," I said, and wriggled around. "Now that we're down here…?"

"You're so predictable, Bernie, really. But not tonight, okay?" she said.

It was then that it came out of me. Thoughts I'd kept to myself for too long. "Do you like our children?" It wasn't easy asking a question like that when you were millimeters apart.

"What?" Her eyes opened wide and I could see the irises expand and the flecks of gold in them. "What are you asking me?"

I steeled myself, determined to press on now that I'd made the jump. "I'm asking if you like our children. It's a simple enough question, isn't it?"

"Why? Why are you asking me now?"

"Well, you don't spend much time with them."

"That's not fair. You know how things are at work for me."

"And you're not answering my question. Do you like to spend time with them or not?"

"I don't know what you're talking about." I felt her struggle, then push against me. "Let me up, you big lummox, will ya?"

"Not yet." I held her wrists. She was flushed with anger, fully red-faced and beginning to seethe. She shook her hair out of her face. "Do you love our children?"

"Of course I do, you crazed bastard! What the hell are you trying to prove?" She began to buck her hips, struggling to get away from me. But I was adamant.

"And me, Sharon? Do you love me?" I asked her in a quieter tone. She stopped then and lay still, frightened by the softness of my voice. Her face damp with sweat.

"For God's sake," she said. "Why would you think I wouldn't?"

I let her go, rolled over halfway and pushed myself up to my knees, then looked down at her panting on the floor, blouse pulled out of her slacks, long hair tousled. My god, she was beautiful. I could feel acid rising in my chest.

"Sometimes I think I just make things convenient for you, tidying up the messes."

"Ach god," she moaned. "Help me up, will ya?" she asked and held out her hands. I pulled her forward to me. She took my face in her hands. They were very warm, burning almost from the chafing on the carpet. "No," she said and coiled her arms around my neck like a snake. "Of course I love you, Bernie and the children too, snotty blighters though they are." Then she let go and pulled away. "Am I that bad? Really?"

"You're the absentee father," I said. "The one I never had. I don't want our kids to feel the same way about you."

She nodded. "Don't you think I don't know what that's like? Rory, that slippery bastard, was no good to us at all. I don't even think of him as a father." I remembered the row she'd had with Patrick at the gallery, the intensity of it, the threat of coming to blows. Her bitterness ran deep as a gulley. She peered at me intensely, calmed by her own seriousness. "And you? Do you love me still, Bernie? Am I attractive to you?"

I stood up and held out my hand and appraised her. "You're a mess but you'll do, I suppose." I let out a sly grin. "Why don't we go upstairs?"

"Back to that are we?"

"Yes, I suppose we are," I said quietly.

"And if I said no?"

"Then it's no." I held her look and we stared at each other for a long moment and in that instant I hurtled back through time to when I was twenty-two and I could see her, eyes blazing, and cheeks flushed with vigor and youth. "I want you, Sharon. I've never wanted anyone else."

She took my hand then and gave me a half-smile. "You're bloody eloquent when you want to be." Holding hands, we walked up the stairs, staying close, not saying another word.

30

De Groot had summoned me. It was like a royal beckoning, an aristocratic au-dience. I crammed the hundred-odd pages I'd written into my briefcase and sailed down. I found him in his expansive office, languidly smoking a thin cigar, watching the smoke curl to the ceiling. He seemed paler than usual, accentu-ated by the white suit he wore. I noticed yellowish tinges in his lank hair.

"So," he intoned. "What precious cargo are you bearing, hmm? I can't wait to see."

"And hello to you too, Julian. Nice to see you." He reached out his bony hand and I placed the wad of pages in his elongated palm.

"Aha. Good. You've been making progress then?"

"Naturally. What else have I got to occupy my time?"

"You've been solving the riddle that is Ephraim Goldman, I take it?"

I hesitated, then cleared my throat. "That part is coming along. Slowly."

De Groot reclined, having placed the pages before him. "Well don't tarry, the sands of time are shifting, hmm?" He rocked for a moment, then tapped some ash. "You will be ready, won't you? We are working furiously on the marketing campaign, you know. I've set up an appointment to have your portrait taken for the back cover and you've simply got to get me all the family photos as quickly as possible. Here," he said, tossing some boards across the desk. "What do you think of these for the front?"

I looked at the mock-ups. The first was that detested symbol, that of the globe with the graduation cap and glasses. *Too jokey*, I thought. "Too jokey," I said and passed it back. The second featured a line drawing of my father's face and it had been cleverly blended into that of Einstein's. "This one's interesting, but kind of heavy on the psychoanalytical, don't you think?"

De Groot shrugged. "I'm asking you, dear boy."

"Well, that's what I think." The last one was a photograph, one of my father at a young age, in his dreamiest state. "Where did you get this? I asked.

De Groot smiled. "We can be resourceful when we must. What do you think, hmm?"

"Well…"

"Yes, my choice too. That's it. Settled then."

"But…"

De Groot was all business now. He snatched the last mock-up out of my hands and slid his glasses on. "Yes, it will do rather well." He glanced up at me. "And don't forget that Harriet has booked you on a cross-country media tour beginning the last week in September. Fifteen cities, six interviews a day. I tell you, Bernard, people are primed for this. We've been sending the press releases all week. There will be a launch party at Pesto on September 23rd, followed by a book signing at the World's Most Gargantuan Book Store. Rather neat, don't you think? It fits well with your father's book."

"Ah, I should mention…"

"What?" he asked in a sharp tone.

"I've decided to write it in the third person."

"I see." De Groot frowned. "A bit impersonal, isn't it?"

"But I needed the perspective, you see."

De Groot smiled. "Oh, I get it. You've found something, a bit of the naughty stuff, eh? And thus, it's easier for you to tell it this way. Say no more, Bernard, I understand. And I trust, it will be breathtaking. In any case, it's too late to change now. We're all set. The machinery is in gear, eh?" And he permitted himself a slight chuckle. "I shall read this and get back to you shortly, how's that? And looking forward to it too." De Groot stood up then, taking some moments as he unfolded himself. I too, stood, awkwardly and once again found myself outside in the hall as he smoothly closed the door, wriggling his fingers in farewell. He always managed to miss closing the door on them. I drove home feeling despondent. The book was already a disappointment and it hadn't been published yet. Naughty bits. What the hell was he thinking of? I could only guess.

The next morning, I drove down to the Universal Jewish Organization offices on University Avenue. I had an appointment with a Mr. Greenberg. Recently, there was an article in the Toronto Jewish Gazette about the UJO's new genealogical database. It was part of a worldwide network of such databases. Thus, anyone searching for lost family or clues to missing relatives, had the means to find them. This database, I had read, was some fifteen years in the making. Researchers had fanned out across Europe and Eastern Europe and pored through town records, checked gravesites and death charts, examined the millions of Nazi and Allied documents recently released. Then, somehow, the data was compiled and entered into a computer and catalogued in such a way that those looking for information could find it more readily. I managed to jump the queue on the strength of my father's name. Apparently, Greenberg was an admirer, he'd studied The Global View in university. And when I told him who I was and that I was doing research for my father, well, he just put me to the head of the list. I felt a bit guilty, trading on my dad that way. But only just a bit.

The UJO offices were rather spartan. Industrial carpet visibly worn in spots and utilitarian, metal-framed chairs and one magazine rack formed the reception area. Apart from the receptionist's desk. My father would have approved. It felt and looked like an organization that relied on donations to survive. I announced myself to the receptionist and shortly, Mr. Greenberg came out and shook my hand. He was a short man in a dark suit, bristling with energy. He wore a yarmulke pinned to his woolly head. We shook hands.

"Come," he said and beckoned to an open doorway. He settled himself behind a forlorn wooden desk. "Sit," he commanded easily. I sat. An impressive looking computer commandeered most of the space on the desk's surface. "I wish to give my personal attention to this matter," he said crisply. "And incidentally, do you think your father would mind?" he asked and pulled out a copy of The Global View. The book was well-thumbed, I could see. "Sign it, you think?"

I took the copy from him. "I don't think he'd mind a bit," I replied.

Greenberg smiled, briefly, but he did smile. He could have used some orthodontics work, I noticed. Then he went back to business.

"You must fill out this form," he explained, handing it to me. "It will give us details on what you want, the parameters of the search. There is also a twenty-dollar charge," he added and shrugged apologetically. "Before you do that, Mr. Goldman, why don't you give me a little bit of background. It may help."

"Sure," I replied and described to him what I wanted and who I needed to find. Greenberg sat and listened. He was attentive throughout.

When I finished he spoke. "It is a mystery, isn't it? I have heard so many. Each story is very compelling. I never tire of hearing about them. The need to know, the desire, as you say, to finish the story is very strong within us. Come," he said reaching for the form. "Let's see what we shall find."

The next few minutes were taken up by Greenberg's typing. He was not a quick typist and it seemed to take a long time for him to enter all the information. "Sorry," he said. "There are many screens to fill out." Then, he hit a button with a flourish. "Now we shall see what comes back. It will take a few moments only."

I had requested information about my great-grandparents in Poland, as well as, Isaac, in France. While we were waiting, Greenberg offered me some coffee. I shook my head, I was too nervous and coffee would go right to my bladder. I folded my arms across my chest to give me the feeling that I was squeezing my heart. It had begun to jump a bit.

Greenberg peered at the screen. "Ah, here we go," he said. "I will print it for you and then you can take a look." The computer made some clicking noises. Behind the desk, the printer started to hum. I watched as the electronic carriage ran back and forth across the paper. Each pass brought me closer to what I needed to know. After a moment, it was done. Greenberg reached over and ripped the paper out of the carriage. He handed it to me. This is what I read: Mendel Dubinsky had died in 1931 of natural causes. Rachel Dubinsky had died in childbirth in 1922. There had been the registration of a child in the name of E. Dubinsky. Fanny Dubinsky had emigrated to Canada in 1927. That was the Polish part.

The second part of the report covered France. There were three Dubinskys', initial 'I', living in France during the years 1927-1938. Of the three, two died during the war, one in Auschwitz and the other in Bergen-Belsen. The third had survived. He returned to Paris in 1945 and then emigrated to Israel in 1949. And that's where the report ended.

"Did it tell you what you needed to know?" Greenberg asked.

"I don't know," I replied. "Of the three 'I. Dubinsky's', only one survived the War. He emigrated to Israel in 1949. And then, there's the mention of some relative I never even knew existed. An E. Dubinsky, born to my great-grandmother. Apparently, she died in childbirth," I said.

Greenberg nodded. "Ah, interesting. You wish to know about this Dubinsky in Israel, I bet?" I nodded. "Perhaps, I can help you. I will send a message to our office in Jerusalem. They can enquire and send me back information. It is very fast. Within twenty-four hours, we should know if this Dubinsky still lives in Israel. But it will cost an additional five dollars," he added, almost apologetically.

"Fine, thank you," I replied and handed over the fee. Greenberg stood up. He shook my hand.

"The girl will give you a receipt. For tax purposes," he said. "When I get the information back from Israel, I will call you. Will you be home tomorrow?" I nodded. "Good, then we shall see." Then Greenberg added, "You won't forget about my autograph, will you?" I shook my head and Greenberg smiled once again.

I drove home with my head awhirl. This was almost too much information, too quickly. Too much meaning.

31

Early the next day, Greenberg called. He spoke crisply into the phone.

"I have the information you require," he said. "There is an Isaac Dubinsky and he is registered at this address in Jerusalem. Have you got a pencil?"

"Yes," I replied, scarcely able to breathe. I wrote down the information. "Thank you," I said and hung up. I stared at the words on the scrap of paper. Could it be?

Everything started to move but not as quickly as I would have liked. I sent a wire to the address I was given in Jerusalem. I tried to compress all I needed to know and explain in under fifty words, but it was difficult. For a week, I waited nervously. I was agitated.

"Take it easy, Bernie," Sharon said. "You're as jumpy as a cat in heat."

"Sorry."

"It's okay. I understand, really. You're snapping at everyone."

"Sorry," I said again, lamely.

I tried to keep focused on the book.

I wrote: 'During his thesis years, Goldman hit on this phrase, "spiritual form", something that is ambiguous at best, but defines his work, his renown all at once. It is a puzzling phrase because the words don't match ideally. Something that is spiritual doesn't have a physical form in of itself. There is the possibility, however, that what comes out of the spiritual, how it is realized, will then take some sort of physical shape. This is what Goldman meant when he coined the phrase. Little did he know how it would be picked up and added to the modern lexicon as we know it today. Perhaps, only the phrase "Catch-22" has achieved greater use in its permeation of society…' I read those lines back and then thought, what the hell was I trying to say? It sounded more pretentious and uptight than anything my father had ever written. I glanced at the calendar. Barely ten weeks to go. My heart leapfrogged in my chest.

The days passed more slowly as I tried to concentrate, to grapple. *Get the writing done,* I growled to myself in the mirror while shaving. It was like licking cement. Rough and hard. Impenetrable. I found myself pacing more. Up and down the stairs. Along the hall and back. Up and down the stairs again. To the kitchen, down to the basement, up to the living room. I was getting some exercise at least. The few evenings she was home, Sharon watched me with a worried look but said nothing. She knew I was on edge. But her pointing it out wouldn't have helped. And she realized it.

On the eighth day, I received a call from the wire office. The message was short. It said, 'Come at once'.

I called Sharon at the office. "I'm going to Israel," I said.

"When?"

"A week Sunday."

"Okay, then," she said but I could hear the hesitation in her voice. "Look, I know you have to go, but are you sure you have to go?"

"Of course I have to go. What do you mean?"

"I don't know what I mean, Bernie. It'll be strange having you away, that's all. I mean, it's never happened before has it?"

"Well, no," I replied. "It hasn't."

"It's just that—" she began.

"Just that what?" I asked.

Sharon sighed. "I'm afraid of what you might find there, Bernie. I don't want you to get hurt, you know? Family things can be strange. Trust me. I know that much, at least."

I paused.

"Don't worry about me, Sharon. I can handle it. But will you be all right? With the kids I mean?" I asked.

"We'll survive, I suppose. I'll order take out, that's all. The kids will love it," she said.

"And be covered in zits when I get home," I replied.

Sharon said, "How long will you be gone, then?"

I hesitated. "I don't know. Not too long, I don't think. But I've got an open ticket, just in case."

"I know you have to do this, Bernie," she said, sounding more like she was trying to convince herself about it. There was a long sigh, an elongated rush of breath into the receiver. "Anyway, we can talk more when I get home, okay?"

"Okay."

"Love you," she said half-heartedly, and hung up.

That evening she came home late and woke me up.

"What time is it?" I asked groggily.

"Half-past eleven. I want to talk to you." She was perched on the bed. I could smell her perfume, see how her carefully applied make-up was still intact. I heard the rustle of her pantyhose underneath her chic skirt.

"What is it?"

"I've hired Mrs. Diaz. To help us out like."

It took a moment but then I sat straight up. "What? Are you crazy?"

She held her perfectly manicured hand out to stop me. "Don't get your knickers in a twist. That is, if you're wearing any and listen for a second. It makes perfect sense, do you see? You're gallivantin' off to the Middle East and I'm here on me own with the kids. And there's always something on at work. We've got an executive board meeting in two weeks and all the financials for the year have to be done. And when you get back, you'll be busy as a maggot on a dead fish working on the book. She'll be a great help to all of us. She can keep the place spiffy and make meals too, if that's required. I've thought it all through."

"I'll say you have."

"And I know what you're going to say..."

"That I can't stand the woman. She hates me."

"Wherever did you get an idea like that?"

"Listen, Sharon, you weren't here with her before. She never talks, just gives me the silent treatment and that disapproving look. Like I'm some sort of eunuch because I stay home and have a wife who goes out to work."

"Oh bosh, you're making it up."

"I'm not. She's a bloody terror."

Sharon crossed her arms and gave me the look that said there was no further discussion on it. "Well boyo, you've got her and make the best of it. It's a done deal."

"When does she start?"

"Tomorrow morning." I groaned and pulled the covers up over my head. Sharon pulled them off me. "I was lucky to get her. She had to come out of retirement for this."

"I'll just bet she did. And demanded thirty percent more for the privilege."

Sharon shrugged. "Not exactly." She stood up and kicked off her shoes. I watched. I couldn't get enough of seeing her undress. "Besides, it's been six years since she watched the boys when they were little. Maybe she's changed?"

I laughed but it came out more like a corrosive honk. Sharon unbuttoned her blouse and hung it on a hanger. "She's got her own car now. Her hours are seven to six Monday to Friday and nine to three on Saturday. Evenings she's off home and Sundays we have to ourselves."

"Only to prepare for the ogre yet again on Monday."

"Don't be melodramatic."

"I'm not. I'm sober as a padre at mass."

"Hah."

The next day was Saturday and I crept downstairs about eight o'clock. It was very quiet. I poked my head cautiously into the kitchen. Sean and Nathan were sitting silently at the table eating breakfast. They looked up at me and the expressions on their faces could only be described as fearful. Nathan sighed and went back to eating his Lucky Charms. Sean shrugged, gave me a small smile, and left his spoon in the bowl. I spotted her then. The dark hair, now shot with silver, tied in a severe bun. The stocky, powerful figure, the ever-present apron, pristine and unwrinkled, knotted around her thick waist. She turned as I took a cautious step.

"Good morning, Senor," she said. The heavy-lidded eyes appeared half-shut. Her thick, unrouged lips creased in a frown of disapproval. It was the only expression of hers that I'd ever seen. There were more wrinkles now, more lines in the once-smooth forehead but otherwise, she appeared unchanged.

I nodded. "Mrs. Diaz." I sat down.

"Here is your juice, your coffee and your cereal. The milk is there," she said in her deep, mannish way, almost swallowing the sounds as she spoke. "You see, I do not forget."

"I see. Yes, thank you." I poured milk into my cereal. I hated having everything at once. I liked to have it in turn but that's the way she was. I felt afraid to make any noise, not even the spoon clanging against the side of the bowl, lest I disturb her. She created an oppressive atmosphere around her. My spirits sank.

"I'm done, Dad," said Nathan and slid out of his chair.

"Yeah, me too," said Sean and went to follow.

"Uh-huh," said Mrs. Diaz and tilted her head.

Nathan looked sheepish. "Oh yeah, I forgot." He carried his bowl and glass to the sink. Sean followed suit. They stopped and waited. Mrs. Diaz gave a small nod, then they scooted off.

"You see?" she said to me. "They are very easy to handle if you know what to do." Implying, of course, that I didn't. I gritted my teeth and took a slurp of the coffee. It was hot, and it burned my lip but I kept my mouth closed. I wouldn't give her the satisfaction. Just then, Sharon came in, bundled in her robe.

"Mrs. Diaz," she exclaimed. "How good to see you." And Sharon kissed her on both cheeks.

"You too, Misses." And Mrs. Diaz beamed.

"This is going to be wonderful, don't you think, Bernie?" she asked me as she sat down, and Mrs. Diaz placed toast and tea in front of her automatically. Jesus, how did she know when to get it ready, how to time it?

"An absolute thrill, darling," I said, and tried not to make it sound too sarcastic. Sharon paid me no mind, just sighed contentedly.

32

It was a gloomy day and unseasonably cold. I intended to visit my father at the summerhouse. The air felt damp. I knew there'd be clouds of black flies waiting to attack as soon as I left the car. As I drove, I remembered an incident from my childhood. I was about seven at the time, playing in the corridor outside my father's study. On this day, the door to the study remained open. I looked in and saw my father talking on the phone. My father liked to talk and walk so he had an extra long phone cord installed. This way, he could talk into the phone and pace around his study without being impeded. Physically, my father was awkward and had tripped over the cord more than once. On this occasion, he was engaged in some intense discussion. I don't know who was on the other end. But looking back, could it have been Einstein or Russell, perhaps?

I remember standing in the doorway watching him pace to and fro while he spoke. I wasn't even sure he noticed me. I wasn't allowed in the study, so I stood right at the entrance, not daring to step over the line. Just watching. I just wanted to look at him, I suppose. I waited for several moments, standing in my shorts, holding my ball and then finally, my father crossed the room and shut the door in my face. With that act, he'd closed the door to my soul. Didn't even glance my way. Not important enough, I guess. Or something of an unnecessary distraction. He hadn't even paused his conversation. I was so close to the edge that, when the door closed, it actually touched the tip of my nose. I remember feeling really low after that. Terribly insignificant. And hurt in a crushing way, pain pulsating in my shallow chest. I slunk away to my room and hid for the rest of the day. Neither my mother or Harry could find me. I didn't even come down for supper. And I knew too, that my father didn't even realize what he'd done. That he'd squashed the ego of a small boy without a thought. The damage of that act had been almost unconscious. He'd never even considered the consequences. If asked about it, I'm sure he wouldn't even remember. So much the worse.

I parked in the gravel drive and made a dash for it. I was right about the flies, they were vicious. The front door was open, and I went in. The phone was ringing and I heard my father answer it.

"Dad?" I called. I heard him murmur into the phone and then hang up. He came through, dressed in a navy blue sweat suit.

"Hi son," he said. "That was Katherine on the phone. She was thinking of coming up. I told her it wasn't such a good idea right now." *Aha*, I thought. So, it had progressed this far. "Have you eaten?" he asked. I nodded. Mrs. Diaz had packed me a lunch that I ate in the car. "How about some coffee?"

"Okay."

"Come on into the kitchen," he said awkwardly, as if we existed as mere acquaintances. I followed him back. The sliding glass doors stood open a crack, but the screen stayed closed. I shivered and slid the door shut. My dad poured out two cups.

"What's that?" he asked. I'd forgotten that I was holding a copy of the book. I shoved it his way.

"Autograph," I said.

"What?"

"Autograph. Autograph. Just write your bloody autograph in it, will you?"

"Fine. Let me get a pen, all right?" he replied irritably. He got up and rummaged around in one of the kitchen drawers, found a well-chewed pen and sat down. "Who to?" he asked.

"Uh, Greenberg," I said.

"Greenberg," he repeated.

"Right."

"Is there a first name?"

"Uh, uh, mister. Mister Greenberg."

"Funny. Very funny," he muttered as he opened the book and scrawled his name. "There," he said and pushed it back at me.

"Thanks," I replied. We sat for a moment, saying nothing. Boy, was that ever comfortable.

"I'm not staying long," I said. "There's still a lot to do." My father nodded and handed me a steaming cup. We sat at the kitchen table facing the doors. We could look out on to the lake from there.

"You feel the need to go, I suppose," he said.

"Yeah, of course," I said.

The conversation continued to wither. It reminded me of the time just after my mom had died. We hadn't talked about her. Hadn't talked about her dying and what that had meant. "I don't really know why I'm here," I said. "I just felt I had to come. I feel like I should tell you about my will," I added facetiously.

He looked at me and I suddenly thought he'd aged in the past little while. Really aged. My dad didn't notice the humor at all. "I think I understand," he said. "We've never been an emotional family, Bernie."

"That's an understatement," I declared.

"Except for your mother. She was a bundle of emotions. Very much like your Sharon. Maybe that's why I like her so much. It's her honesty and spunk," he said.

"Do you know why I'm going?" I asked him.

He shrugged. "To find some answers, I would guess," he said quietly.

I felt a bit exasperated. "No, I meant, do you know exactly? The circumstances?"

"Not specifically, no," he replied. "If I could read your mind, then maybe I'd give you a better answer."

"You think it has something to do with the book?" I asked.

He considered his coffee mug. "Yes and no," he said. "I think you'll find out when you get there."

"But then again, I may not," I said.

"Well," my father mused. "It's a helluva long way to go for nothing. At least, you can see the country, Bernie. That'd be worth it. I always wanted to go. Your mother and I were planning a trip. But then she got sick."

"I know."

My father got up and took his cup to the sink. He rinsed it out under the tap. "I've made a decision," he said with his back to me, and then turned around.

"What's that?" I asked.

"I'm going to retire. I mean, really retire. No more work. Just enjoying the life I've got left. I've already told the University. They want me to donate all my papers to the library," he said.

I was taken aback, I'll admit. My father always seemed to be working. Work defined him. It made him. "But what will you do with your time? You don't have any hobbies. I mean, you don't whittle or putter about like other dads. You never did."

He nodded. "That's true. I never indulged in those things. But I think I'd like to travel, while I'm still well enough. Your trip to Israel only reinforces it for me. That I should be getting out and doing more. Not sit around and mope."

"Don't think I've ever seen you mope," I replied. "I get the distinct feeling you're not talking about doing this on your own."

My father sighed, and looked at his sneakered feet, then squinted over at me.

"I never said you weren't perceptive, Bernie, did I? You always noticed things, even when you were little. You could tell when your mother and I had argued, or when she was upset about something," he said.

"Are you planning on doing this travelling with Katherine?" I asked.

He gave a snort. "See what I mean? Perceptive. An important trait for a writer," he said, then paused. "Katherine and I have talked about it. She's willing to take a leave of absence from her job."

"Just what kind of trip are we talking about here? A world cruise?" I asked in horror.

My father rubbed his stubbly chin. "Maybe something like that. I don't know. Right now, I'm keeping my options open," he said. "Don't you see, Bernie? I'm keeping my part of the deal."

"What do you mean by that?" I asked harshly.

"Well," he said. "I'm stepping aside. Stepping out of the spotlight. Just like I said I would. It's your turn now, son. And I'd suggest you make the most of it." He waggled his finger at me, the teacher admonishing his student. God, I hated that.

I nodded. "Yeah, thanks. Good advice," I retorted bitterly.

"Katherine can never replace your mother, you know that. I hope you know me better than that too. But I think that maybe, your mother would have approved. That she would have wanted me to seek companionship. To not be alone," he said.

"Well," I replied. "It's a good theory, isn't it?"

"I'm done with theories and theorizing," my father replied. "I think it's time that I actually did something. I've thought too much. I'm sick of it."

"I see," I said. "So now you're going to explore your emotions, is that it? Finally, after all these years, you're going to express your feelings? To who? Not us. Not me and Harry and Sharon and the kids. Well, it's a little late for all that, isn't it?"

"What are you so bitter about?" he asked. "Have you been so deprived? Have you lacked for anything? I thought your mother and I gave you just about everything we could." Suddenly, he looked indignant. He was thinking, how dare I complain or question.

"No," I replied quietly. "I was never deprived. Not in that way." And I paused to think about what I wanted to say. I took a couple of breaths. "You know, when Harry and I were kids, there were times when we just wanted you to be like other dads. That's all. Did it ever occur to you that we would have liked you to come to a soccer game or a swim meet? Christ, you even missed my high school graduation."

"I came when you graduated from university," he retorted.

"Sure," I cried. "Because it was only fifty yards from your office on campus."

"I was working," he said.

"I know. And I think that you enjoyed your work more than being at home. More than being with mom. And us."

"I loved your mother very much."

I slumped back in my seat and squinted at him. "Yeah sure. But you never took her on a world cruise, did you?"

My father came over and placed his palms on the table. I'd gotten to him. He leaned in and glared at me. "Now don't be like that," he said. "You're being unreasonable and unfair. You don't know what it was like then. Or what I had to do. For Christ sake, man! Don't be like that, Bernie," he cried and actually banged his fist down on the table. The crockery jumped. Eph winced and rubbed his knuckles, calming himself. He took a deep breath. "You know, besides being perceptive, you think you know it all too, don't you? Let me tell you, my son, that you don't. Smart guy. You always were a smart guy."

"Not even you know," I said quietly.

He squeezed his hands together, clenching and unclenching. Then we stared at each other for a long moment until I could hear the room sounds, the fridge vibrating, the ticking of the clock, the wind rattling the storm windows. Something was happening, cracking open a little bit. I wasn't prepared. It was unexpected. It scared me off. I backed down.

"Okay," I said. "Okay. Maybe we should talk about this more when I get back. Maybe we need some time to think here."

Eph nodded. "You take all the time you want, Bernie. I've done with it now," he declared.

"What does that mean?"

He sat in the chair opposite and leveled me with a look. Full of meaning. What meaning? "I may have left by the time you get back."

"What!" I said. "What's the rush? I'll only be gone a few days."

"Well, we'll see," he replied. "You may want to stay on a bit. You never know what you may find there."

"You know I can't stay. There's Sharon and the kids." Was he implying that I'd abandon them?

My father folded his arms. "Look, I'm not saying that I'll be gone. I'm just saying I might be, that's all. I'm just looking at a number of options," he said, thinking hard, then, he made his decision and came out with the following pronouncement. "And I may sell the house," he declared.

"What?" I was incredulous now. I loved that house. The thought of it going to strangers made me sick at heart.

"Well," he said quietly, as if he would keep me calm by speaking in a low voice. "You didn't expect me to stay there forever, did you? It's getting too much for me. The upkeep, the maintenance."

"What do you mean? You don't do any of that yourself. You have people do it for you," I said angrily.

"Exactly," he replied. "It's a bother and expensive."

"Oh, for Christ sake," I said, mired in frustration. I stood up. I never got anywhere arguing with him, anyway. He was just too clever. Like me, he had an answer for everything. In that way, I was truly his son. I could see the same traits in Nathan, too. "I've got to go now. But I want you to promise me that you won't do anything before I get back."

Eph shrugged and said, "Probably nothing will happen. You know that I don't move quickly on things."

"You didn't promise," I said and turned. "Thanks for the coffee."

"Sure," he replied. I began to walk away. He called out and I stopped without turning around. "Bernie. You're a good writer," he said. "I wouldn't have agreed to this otherwise. Just be open-minded, that's all I ask."

I stopped, then shrugged, still not looking back. "Yeah, well whatever," I replied. "But no promises, Eph. We don't seem to be very good at keeping promises in this family, do we?" And I kept going. I imagined him sitting there, arm outstretched and grey head bowed.

I got into the car and drove home. Hard and fast. Afterward, I realized I'd forgotten the damn book.

33

That evening, I had a great deal of difficulty getting to sleep. I was excited and overwrought. The brief encounter I'd had with my father worked my nerves further still. Rubbed the edges raw. He'd acted uncharacteristically, changed the pattern. Yet, I felt instinctively I would find out part of the answer in Israel. I squirmed and writhed.

"Hey," Sharon said from out of the darkness. "What's the matter?" And she wrapped herself around me.

"I had a nightmare about Mrs. Diaz." I felt the warmth of her flesh.

"Go on," she said. "You didn't." It didn't matter. The heat of her put me to sleep.

Sunday morning, I was up early. Sharon and the kids were still asleep. I showered deeply, letting the hot water seep into me. I tried to work out the knots in my muscles. The bathroom was filled with steam.

I was sipping my second cup of coffee when the phone rang.

"Bernard, you're up I take it."

"Yes, Julian. I'm up."

"I've read your pages and it does show promise, I must say."

"Thank you," I replied acidly.

"Nothing salacious, so far, is there?" He sounded amused in a dry-witted way.

"Not really."

"Not to worry, Bernard. You're doing a fine job. Keep going. That's what I wanted to say."

I was puzzled. High praise from de Groot. "Well, thank you."

"Not at all."

"I was going to call you."

"Oh yes?"

"I'm going to Israel, a week from today."

"Vacation, is it? Or further research?"

"I'm just following up some family connections."

"Very well, then. Have a lovely time, Bernard. But don't let it hold up our schedule, hmm? After all…"

"Yes, Julian, I know. The machinery is in gear."

He gave a raspy laugh. "Exactly."

"It shouldn't be more than a week I should think."

"Well then. Have a wonderful time, Bernard. Stay out of the desert at high noon. And I shall speak to you upon your return." He rung off. I held the phone to my ear listening to the dial tone as relief flooded my being. De Groot was being generous and understanding. It was the right thing for him to do, I decided. After all, if I didn't finish the book, then what could he do?

I continued working throughout the day. The boys went off to a baseball game with a friend. They were going to be treated to dinner as well and wouldn't be back until about eight. Sharon went off to the gym for the afternoon and then she was meeting Katherine, of all people, for a low-cal meal. I was on my own. I worked steadily away, stopping for a light lunch. Then, I took a thirty-minute nap and started in again. Nearing three o'clock, the phone interrupted me. I was tempted to leave it, but one of the boys might have been taken ill or it could have been my father or who knows?

"Bern?" said a slurred voice.

"Yeah?" I answered, puzzled for a moment. "Egan?"

"Tha's righ' old son, it's me…"

He was in a bad way and to be in a bad way on a Sunday afternoon meant it was serious.

"What's going on?"

"Ah," he hesitated, gathering his thoughts for what seemed an eon. "There's been a bit of bother…"

"Where are you?"

"Em… I don't know, exactly. Hang on a minute," his voice faded into the background as he pulled away from the receiver. "Hey, hey," he called. "Where am I?" I heard some muffled voices going back and forth and Egan attempting to offer some sort of explanation. Then someone came back. A new voice.

"P.C. Burns here, who's speaking?"

"Oh, hello Constable. I'm Egan's brother-in-law."

"Your name sir?" he asked briskly.

"Goldman. Bernard Goldman. Look, what's going on?"

"Your buddy here, has been brought in as a D&D."

"Sorry?"

"Drunk and disorderly."

"Where is that exactly?"

"52 division."

"What can I do?"

"Well, sir, you can come down and bail him out. We'll let him off with a warning, this time. But I've got to release him into someone's custody and you have to sign a surety bond that he'll be in your care and your responsibility."

"I see."

"Are you willing to do that, Mr. Goldman?"

"Uh yes, of course. I'll be right down."

"Do you need directions?"

"No, it's okay. I know where it is, Constable. Thank you."

I parked the car on a side street and walked around the corner of Sorauren on to Dundas and up the wide, concrete steps of 52 Division Headquarters. This was the inner city, a mix of blue collar, hard-working families, sandwiched in with the homeless, drug dealers, hookers and the new class of young professionals buying up cheap real estate, lofts mostly, and doing them over. The glass in one of the swing doors was cracked. Some dried excrement had been smeared on the metal guardrail. Still, it was a lovely day, and this was the worst Toronto had to offer. Its seamy underbelly. I went up to the front desk and made an inquiry, the officer glanced up at me, heard what I had to say and jerked his head to the right, all without saying a word. Egan was slumped on a bench. I touched his shoulder and he started.

"Whaa?" His watery eyes took a moment to focus. "Oh, it's you, Bern. Thanks for comin'. I know I've made a mess out of it."

"What happened? This isn't like you. Well, not exactly. I mean, it's Sunday afternoon."

He squinted up at me. "Is it? Already?"

A thick-wristed hand shoved a cup of coffee in at him. Egan glanced up at the young constable, all six feet three of him, iron-haired and broad-shouldered.

"Burns," he said to me. "We spoke on the phone." I shook his hand. Egan took a tentative sip, then made a face.

"Liquid tar'd taste better."

"I'm not sure you'd know the difference," Burns said, but with a hint of a smile. He motioned me aside.

"What happened?" I asked him.

"Nothing much, really. He was found asleep on a slide in a schoolyard about two blocks from here. Some kids were out playing, and they wanted to slide, you know? And this big guy here, was blocking the way. The kids found it funny, him snoring away but one of the mothers wasn't amused. She called us in. It took a while to wake him up."

"But he didn't resist? There wasn't any trouble was there?"

Burns screwed up his smooth face. "No. Just cranky from sleep really. He's been cooperative. Tell you the truth," and he leaned in closer to keep his voice down, "he seems kind of depressed. Sad, really. Not angry or violent. And looking at his size, he could have caused us real trouble if he'd wanted to, you know?"

"You have some papers for me?"

Burns nodded. "Yeah. Right over here." And he indicated a desk. He went around and sat down and began shuffling through some papers. He reached into his breast pocket and pulled out a pair of wire-rimmed glasses. "Can't read without these damn things," he grinned. "Here we are. If you could just sign these two, we'll give you custody of him. These indicate that you're taking responsibility for him. That's pretty well it. But if he steps out of line again, you might be fined."

"How much?"

Burns shrugged. "It's hard to say. Might be a couple of thou, depending on the circumstances. You willing to do that?"

"Sure."

Burns nodded, then gave me a thoughtful look. "You two must be close."

"Egan is a very talented artist. And like many artists, he has a fragile temperament."

"You mean," said Burns with a smirk, "he has a drinking problem."

"Well that's one way of putting it. We've all got demons. You too, I'm sure."

Burns gave me a wide smile. "Sure, I like to kick puppy dogs. You got ID? Something with your photo on it?" I handed over my driver's license and birth certificate. He wrote down my address and phone number. "Sign here. And here," he indicated on the two forms. I signed. Burns scrutinized the signature, then reached out a hand to me. I shook it. "Mr. Goldman, he's all yours. And good luck to the both of you."

"Thanks," I replied, feeling a bit grim about it. Egan was now my responsibility.

Egan hunched down in the passenger seat. He clutched what was left of the coffee in two hands, like he'd forgotten about it. "What happened?" I asked him.

Egan shook his head, hair hanging down his face, over his forehead and in his eyes. He ran a hand through the tangled mess. "Levinsky dropped me, Bern. Said there was a clause in the contract that allowed him to do it. Said I was too much damn trouble."

I turned to him and caught a good whiff of his sour breath. "And the paintings he sold? Has he paid you yet?"

"Not a bloody penny."

"What about the triptych? The one that was insured?"

"Nothin. Says the insurance company's trying to diddle him."

"Oh boy."

"What can I do, Bern? He's got everythin' I own. Everythin' I've done." Egan squeezed his face tight and tears dripped down his pale face. "I feel like I've had me heart ripped right outa me chest, man."

"We'll think of something, Egan. Right now, we'd better get home." And as I drove I thought of the warm reception we'd receive from Sharon and dreaded it.

"You get yourself cleaned up now," I said. "You know where everything is. I've got to do some thinking here."

"Yeah. Okay." He stood there, looking like a derelict and smelling like one too.

"Is there anyone else you can stay with?"

He shook his head. "Don't think so."

"What about Bernadette?"

"Took off to California last week, with some kid in a van."

"I see. Well off you go then. You're pretty rank, you know?"

Egan ran a hand down his face, pulling at the loose skin. "Ta," he said and shambled off to the bathroom downstairs.

Sharon came in humming a tune. She appeared relaxed and distracted. I was sitting in the living room reading the paper, trying to finish off the crossword I'd started.

"Hello luv," she called. I heard her drop her keys into the glass bowl we kept by the door.

"Hi."

She came in and plopped on to the couch beside me. "Oh Christ, I'm exhausted."

"Good workout?"

"Bloody right it was. That instructor is a sadist, she is."

I smiled. "That's good. You'd complain if she wasn't."

"Boys not back yet?"

"No, but I expect them soon."

"How was your afternoon, then? Did you enjoy the quiet?" she asked, and rubbed my thigh distractedly.

I folded the paper and put it beside me. "Yes. It was very productive. How was lunch?"

"With Katherine?"

"Right."

"She's very taken with your Dad. Smitten, I'd say."

"With him or his aura?"

"Is there a difference?" Sharon looked puzzled and wrinkled her nose as she asked the question.

"I'd say so."

"Then, it's him. She's enchanted with him. They seem to get along famously."

I was tight-lipped. "I see."

She dug her nails into my leg and leaned in. I could smell her perfume and shampoo as her hair swung forward across her face. "I think they make a good couple."

"You don't think she likes him for his reputation, the fact that he's a celebrity or his money? After all, she's a single mother with two children. She has to think of them and their security."

"My," she replied and opened her eyes wide in mock surprise. "You do have a devious mind. No, I don't think that at all, actually. She's a well-paid professional and owns her home. Her finances are in pretty good shape."

"How do you know?"

"I took a look at them and gave her a bit of advice. You know she may be giving up her job for your Dad, don't you?"

"I thought it was just a leave of absence."

"Who knows what it'll turn out to be? But she's willing to make the sacrifice and she worked damn hard to get to where she is. Being director of human resources for a large insurance firm is nothing to sneeze at, don't you know. And she didn't have much in the way of help from her ex, that's for damn sure. Bloody men, have it all their own way, don't they?"

"I do."

She gave me a smirk, and pulled back a bit, settling into the couch. "Damn right you do, boyo and don't forget it."

"They'll do what they want regardless."

"Who?"

"My father and Katherine. He doesn't care what I think or feel about anything."

"Ach, you're wrong there. Why are men so bloody stupid? Why can't you just talk to each other and say how you feel? Get past all of this resentment and bitterness?"

I sighed. "That'd be too easy, I suppose. You know we have a hard time talking about our feelings. It's always been like that."

"Don' I know it just? Answering a question with another bloody question. God, you just go around in circles that way, getting nowhere."

I decided it was time to change direction since talking about my father and Katherine just got me depressed. "Listen, we've got a visitor."

"Who?" And then she glanced up.

Egan stepped in. His hair was combed back, and his face was clean. He'd shaved and put on fresh clothes I'd given him. "Hello, Sharon," he said mildly.

"Now what's the bloody trouble?" she asked, anger rising in her voice.

Egan shrugged. "Now hold on," I said. "Your brother's got some problems and there's no need to get worked up about it. Levinsky has screwed him out of his contract and he hasn't been paid a nickel."

"I can't even pay for me room. I'm completely flat."

"So, you want to sponge off us, I suppose?" Sharon stood up and jammed her hands on to her hips.

"Now hang on, for God's sake. You know I'm leaving in a week, right?"

"So?" she asked defiantly, not pleased about that either.

"Well, I thought that Egan could stay here until then and—"

"And what?" I could see the color rise up into her cheeks, the freckles on her face darkened, almost blood-like.

"...he might come with me to Israel. Get some perspective on what's happening and get out of your hair for a while."

"What?" she cried. "Go with you? Are you taking bloody leave of your senses? You're there to do your work, not nurse this big baby here."

"Now just a minute, Sharon..." Egan began to raise his voice and belligerence crept in.

"No, that's not it," I cut in. "Egan will be pretty much on his own. You're right. I've got things to do there. But it might be good for him too, to get away."

"And you're wanting us to pay his fare too?" she asked.

I shook my head. "No," I replied. "I'll cover it out of my advance. I've got more than enough left."

She looked at me fiercely. Things were not going according to plan. Her lips were tight. "You're daft. The two of ya." Egan and I exchanged sheepish looks. He grinned slyly at her.

"Probably," he said. "Yer on the right track, ye are."

34

The week passed quickly enough. I stuck to my routine; swim, home, then work. The house took on a repressive air. It was the dour countenance of Mrs. Diaz. Sharon took no notice, but the boys were certainly quieter. They kept their rooms cleaner too, and as soon as breakfast was done, they headed off to the bathroom to brush their teeth, then slipped off to school without protest. No cajoling. Somehow, Mrs. Diaz managed to convince Sean to stay still while she applied the sun block. After which, she'd give me a triumphant and superior look. But at least Sharon was right about one thing. It left me time to concentrate on writing and I got a lot done. Magically, Egan managed to charm Mrs. Diaz somehow. I heard them in the kitchen, his voice light and silky, hers edgier and brittle but one morning, the second day Egan stayed on, I heard Mrs. Diaz laugh and then Egan chuckled with her. I pulled myself to a stop. I don't think I'd ever heard her laugh. Didn't think she was capable of it. I shook my head. Perhaps miracles do happen? Later that day, I told Sharon about it.

"Yes, well, she is human you know," she replied, unwilling to concede that Egan had anything to do with it.

"But it seemed so out of character."

"Ach, you know that Egan can charm the scales off a snake if he's a mind to."

"Well, he's worked his magic this time."

"Don't make such a big thing out of it, will ya? It was just a laugh."

"Whatever you say, honey bunch." And I made kissy noises into the phone.

"Ach, you're a fool sometimes, Bernie," she said before hanging up, but I could hear the lightness in her tone and knew she didn't mean it. Saturday evening, we lay in bed. Egan and I were to be picked up by airport limousine around noon on Sunday. We were just holding hands. It was her time of the month, she'd said. Egan was downstairs playing Nintendo with the boys. They were slaughtering him.

"You know I'd rather you didn't go."

"I know."

"And you're to be careful. There's bombings and shootings and all sorts of carry-on."

"Right."

"You've got my permission to use Egan as a shield, if you must," she said in all seriousness.

"For God' sake. He's your brother!"

"Right. And I've got two more just as good. But there's only one of you, Bernie."

"You don't mean that."

"I do. I do mean it," she replied in a fierce tone.

I gulped. "Well, I'll make sure it's safe. For both of us," I added.

"I'd feel the same way if you were traveling to Belfast or Londonderry, you know."

"Sure."

"It's just… I hate what I hear about what goes on over there."

"Exaggerated, I'm sure. Like most things."

She looked over at me and with her face scrubbed clean, she was a young girl again. The girl I first met. "I know I give ya a hard time, sometimes…"

"Who – you?"

She slapped my shoulder. "Oh, shut up, you silly fool, I'm talking. But I don't mean it. I really am trying to do everything for us, Bern. You must believe that. All of us. I think about it constantly. Maybe, I'm obsessed, but that's the only reason I kill myself all day long dealing with those hard-hearted bastards who want to squeeze money out of the ground, you know?"

"I know." She lifted my arm and snuggled closer.

"Let's cuddle for a wee while, eh?" Some time later, I heard and felt her breathing grow deeper and drifted in and out of consciousness myself, on the verge of sleep, when suddenly I sensed a presence.

"What? What is it?"

"Bern," said Egan, putting a finger to his lips.

"What do you want? I was almost asleep."

"I know. Sorry. I was wanting to ask… em, do you think I should pack some toilet paper? Just in case?" He held up the roll.

I smiled grimly in the dark. "I think there'll be a good supply where we're going. Don't worry about it."

He shrugged. "Okay. Just thought I'd better check."

"Right," I whispered. "See you in the morning. Boys okay?"

"Tucked right up," he replied. "Ta." Softly, he tiptoed to the door, shutting it behind him.

35

"Show me what you've got," I said. Egan held up two shopping bags. Their contents were wrapped in plastic. "That won't do. You can't get on a plane with that. You'll look like an immigrant. They might stop you at the check-in. I've got an extra case in the basement. You can use that."

Egan smiled sheepishly. "All right then." It was Sunday morning and we were just about ready to go.

I had one bag to take and it sat on the threshold. At noon on the dot, I heard a car pull into the drive and sound its horn. We'd just finished a light lunch.

I kissed Sharon and the boys goodbye. Sean and Nathan were uncharacteristically mute. They weren't used to this, I'd never left them before. It had always been Sharon going on trips. They made me promise to bring them back something. Something special. I said that I would. Then Sharon and I embraced. She whispered in my ear.

"I hope you find what you're looking for, luv," she said.

"Me too."

"We'll be waiting for you."

"You're sure?"

She opened her eyes wide. "Of course I'm bloody sure. Where do you think we'll be? In the Bahamas?"

I shrugged. "Who knows?" She punched me in the shoulder. "Ow." Egan stood off awkwardly to the side, nervous and stiff. His color was bad but at least his eyes had begun to clear.

"Goodbye Uncle Egan," the boys said simultaneously and gave him a hug each.

"Bye boys. You be good 'uns for yer ma, now." They nodded. Egan looked at Sharon; she was hanging back. "Come on now. Don't be like that." He held out his arms and stepped forward. They embraced but Sharon held herself stiffly. Still, it was a start.

"Take care of my husband, you big ox."

"Aye," he replied. "Ta then." And we were out the door.

Security was very tight on Israeli Airlines. Being in first class or coach didn't really matter. I'd wangled a couple of first class tickets. It took just as long, and they were just as thorough. We waited in the lounge until our names were called. Egan had two quick drinks. But still, our bags were opened. We were sniffed by dogs. Our backgrounds were probed. Everything went through metal detectors not once, but three times. When we boarded the plane, there were guards with automatic weapons carefully watching every move we made.

"Christ," Egan exclaimed. "We couldn't be safer than that, could we?"

I wasn't a happy flyer. Normally, I tried to pretend it wasn't happening. I just prayed the time went quickly. I'd pop motion sickness pills, then drink a double rye on the rocks and try to sleep for as long as I could. During the flight, I got up to go to the bathroom twice, ate when necessary, and drank only when thirsty. I didn't even watch the movie.

"You're great company, you are," Egan complained. But he was content to roam the plane, talk to other passengers, and hear their stories. He gobbled the food, watched the movie, and enjoyed himself thoroughly. He was like a kid on a trip to Disneyland.

We tried to eat the dinner that was served, always awkward on a plane and doubly so for those of above normal size. "Ach, sorry Bern. Didn't mean to knock ya there." And he scooped some mashed potato into his mouth. "You know, I had the feeling that Sharon had this crazy idea that you weren't going to come back. That you were going to find something there. In Israel, I mean," he explained for my benefit.

"Like what?" I asked incredulously, as if she would think I could leave her. Even give it a thought. Apparently, my dad thought so too.

"Some kind of calling, I guess," he replied. "Discovering your roots. Something like that. Maybe your soul, man. Who knows?"

"She thinks that I don't have a soul?"

Egan punched me on the shoulder. Hard. "Now look," he said. "I never said that. And you won't be telling Sharon, neither. Or I'll crack yer head wide open."

"Ow," I said and rubbed the spot. What was it about this family and punching?

"And the other truth, if I may say, is that I feel like I'm in purgatory, myself. What can I do about Levinsky now?" he said.

"We'll get a lawyer and sue him, that's what."

"He's holdin' all the cards. The man's shrewd as a ferret, that's for damn sure. Besides I can't afford a lawyer. I can't afford anythin', especially this trip."

"It's okay," I said in my most unconvincing way. "It'll work out."

With characteristic optimism, he replied, "Like hell it will."

Just then, a stewardess was making her way down the aisle.

"Ah, Miss," Egan called, stopping her. "I'll have a Guiness please. Bernie?"

I shook my head. "Make it two," said Egan, smacking his lips. "Might as well enjoy myself while I can, eh?"

The plane landed at five o'clock in the morning. In Ben-Gurion Airport, the armed presence was striking. Soldiers in full uniform patrolled everywhere, even in the loos. Their expressions were blank. Official military faces. Some gathered in small clumps, talking quietly among themselves. But the eyes were watchful, never stopping to search. Never resting on a single place or individual. God, they seemed so young to bear such a responsibility, I thought. Dark, soulful faces and penetrating eyes. And then, it struck me for the first time – they were all Jews. For the most part that is. *Congratulate yourself on recognizing the obvious,* I thought. But I'd never experienced it before. Surrounded by Jewishness in a land that hosted conflict stretching back across millennia. The land that had given birth to western civilization. The feeling of it. I shook my head. The force of that one thought delivered some bare insight as to why passions ran so high here. Why there was always so much at stake.

"They're really prepared for war, aren't they?" said Egan in a low voice. "Christ, it's like Belfast all over again." He didn't want to be overheard, in case someone's nose got out of joint. Neither of us had any interest in staring down the barrel of an Uzi. Outside the terminal, we found a cab. The driver, a burly Russian Jew, didn't get out to help with the luggage. He merely sat and waited, but he did pop the trunk so we could toss our bags in.

"I'm Sergei," our driver said in slow, thick English.

"Ta," said Egan. Sergei looked at him a bit strangely but nodded.

"Hi," I replied.

"Where you go?" asked Sergei.

"The Four Seasons," I said. "Jerusalem."

"Good. Nice place," Sergei said, and the cab lurched away from the curb. Sergei kept the window open. He chain-smoked, and the ash kept flying into my face. I didn't care though. This was Israel.

The rim of the sun edged up on the horizon casting an expanding ray before it, illuminating the scene. I wasn't prepared for what I saw. The new and the old smooshed together. Sergei leaned on his horn as he came up behind a van hogging the road. I'd been drifting, lack of sleep and the queasy anticipation of what was to come had claimed me.

I turned my attention back to the fertile valleys and the barren hills. The stone walls and famous gates standing adjacent to new condominiums and offices. Even at this early hour, the streets, many of which were made of hand-carved stone, crawled with traffic. The ascent into the city, as we bumped along in Sergei's Toyota which had seen better days, revealed patches of greenery. Public parks which had been added as the city's boundaries expanded after 1967. Hard to believe the old city had been built 4500 years ago and was still inhabited. Still thriving. And not behind a glass case in a museum somewhere.

"My God," said Egan. "It's bloody amazing, isn't it?" He craned his head around. "Bernie, man. I've never seen light like this. Pure gold. Do you see? Give me some brushes and a canvas and I'd be content forever, by God," he exclaimed.

"It's beautiful, all right," I replied.

Sergei bobbed his grizzled head, craned around, flicked some ash and showed some blackened teeth. "You see now what brings the people here? After two days, I tell you, you will never want to leave. Trust me, I know," he said.

"Sergei," I said. "Just watch the road, man."

He put up his hand. "Sure, sure. No problem," he said and turned around. Irate horns screamed in my ear.

June was one of the hottest months and the heat pressed in on us like a blanket. We wore polo shirts and light khaki pants and still, our clothes felt like woollies, itchy and uncomfortable. We got to our hotel and checked in.

"What time do you figure on visiting, then?" Egan asked.

"About ten," I replied.

"Okay. Will you be all right?" he asked.

I smiled weakly. "Sure. I'll be fine, I guess."

Sergei didn't get out of the cab, but he did open the trunk so we could retrieve our luggage. As his cab clattered on into traffic, I heard his voice rise above the accelerating motor. "You will find good fortune, here, my friends!" And was gone.

"Are they all like that here?" asked Egan.

"Probably," I replied.

Egan grinned. "Good," he said, then paused, looking around at the street. Already, black-suited worshippers, their fringes flapping as they walked briskly, headed to services. The young boys moved in packs, speaking excitedly. Older boys, youths, walked more slowly, contemplatively, tugging at their downy beards as they discussed, dissected, and analyzed a portion of the Torah. Secular Jews intermingled, distinguished by the starchiness of their white, cotton shirts, sandals, and shorts, both the men and women. Everyone seemed to be moving quickly, bristling with energy. Looking at them made me feel drained. "It feels good to be here," Egan said suddenly. "I just have a very good feeling, Bernie. I brought my sketch things with me. I can't wait to get to work, you know?"

I looked at him wearily. "That's great. But I'm beat. I need some sleep."

I went up to my room and lay down on the bed. I set the clock radio for eight-thirty which gave me about two hours of rest. Then, I fell into a dreamless sleep.

I awoke feeling extremely fatigued and thick-headed. I took a cool shower and it helped revive me. I called Egan's room to make sure he was awake. He was. He couldn't sleep, he said. He'd ordered breakfast and it was on its way. We'd eat together. Afterwards, Egan said that he was going to explore the area a bit, then maybe sit on the terrace and sketch until lunchtime.

"Don't worry about me," he said. "I'll be okay. Yeah, I'll be fine, Bernie. You don't look so hot, though."

"Jet lag," I replied. And enough angst to cripple a herd of camels.

36

Outside on the bustling street, I hailed a cab. I showed the driver the address. He said it wasn't far, about fifteen minutes drive. It was punishingly hot. A difficult adjustment after the early summer weather I'd left back home. It could be quite cool in Toronto in June. The sun cast a dazzling brilliance everywhere. The streets, consisting of stone and asphalt mixed with white sand, pulsated in the intense light. Colors looked brighter, more vibrant. The gradation of blue in the sky radiated richer, more vivid. Even the air pollution caused by motor traffic couldn't dull the sky's intensity, heightened further by the complete lack of cloud cover. Shadows cut deep, sharp-edged and pitch black. You could hide an elephant in those shadows.

I noticed Arab vendors and laborers swathed in kaftans and headdresses. Bedouin women walked demurely behind the men, who proudly strode ahead. An orange seller here. A window washer there, or a street cleaner. At one intersection, an Arab road crew worked their pickaxes into the tarmac like a chain gang. I saw and heard the roar of camouflage-painted army jeeps and lorries and the diesel engines of the modern buses that stopped to pick up passengers. As we drove on, I saw a group of old men, standing at a bus stop, praying in unison as they waited. It was a blur of images and noise. Most native Israelis wore T-shirts, shorts and sandals, the women carried leather satchels over their shoulders. In contrast, the ultra-orthodox men wore dark suits, broad-brimmed hats, and black leather shoes. Some wore leggings and boxed fur hats, even in that heat. The orthodox women wore shawls over their long-sleeved blouses and ankle-length skirts. Like the Bedouin women, they trailed behind the men, talking among themselves. How the old and the new seemed to coincide so naturally. Israel and Jerusalem, places of contradiction that limped forward.

Somehow, people managed to work things out and got along just enough to keep the country running. I shook my head. I didn't understand it, and I knew it wasn't for me.

Without warning, the cab veered sharply, and the driver braked so hard, the tires squealed. He gestured. I had arrived. I paid the cab off and looked toward my destination. A small apartment building, a quadplex. I walked up to the common entrance, went inside and followed the numbers upstairs to a doorway. I felt very tense. I took a deep breath, then knocked.

I waited a moment, listening to sounds within. I heard someone fumbling with the lock and the door opened.

A young woman stood on the threshold. She was very pretty, striking in fact. She stared at me, then put her hands up to her face in shock. Without saying a word, she backed slowly away, as if I was the carrier of some deadly disease. She disappeared around a corridor and I heard a rapid exchange of voices.

"Nothing like a good first impression," I muttered to myself.

Then, a middle-aged version of the young woman appeared. She looked at me, coolly before she put out her hand.

"I am Gabrielle," she said in perfect English. I took her hand. It was warm and the skin smooth. I started to reply.

"I'm…" But she held up her hand.

"I know exactly who you are," she replied. "Please come, Bernard. Papa is waiting. Come," she said and ushered me in. As we went in, she added, "Forgive my daughter. My daughter, Dagmar. She was just startled to see you."

"Sure." I didn't know what else to say.

The apartment was large and airy. It opened up to reveal high ceilings and broad windows. The floors were made of ceramic tile. Lush plants had been placed in every possible nook. Canvases which had an oriental look and feel hung on every available wall.

"Whose paintings?" I asked. "They're wonderful."

"My daughter's," Gabrielle replied.

"I'm here with my brother-in-law, Egan McCarthy. He's a painter also. Perhaps I might bring him over to see these? At some point, I mean," I stammered. Cripes, could I sound more like a fool?

"Of course, Bernard. I'm sure Dagmar would be happy to see your friend."

"Thank you." I felt ill-at-ease, a fish out of water.

I stopped for a second, feeling as if I couldn't breathe. My heart jumped around like mad.

Gabrielle looked at me with some concern. "Are you all right? Perhaps you're tired. You've come a long way. Would you like to sit for a minute?" she asked.

I shook my head. "No, I'm fine. This is a bit overwhelming, to find family that you didn't even know existed, I'm just excited, I guess."

"Yes, I understand. Papa is anxious to see you too."

I nodded. "Let's go then."

37

Gabrielle led me down a long corridor, the walls of which were covered in what looked like Spanish or Mexican artifacts. Ceramic figurines and delicate vases stood on small shelves at many levels, attached to the walls. The corridor snaked along high walls, leading up to a skylight that lit up the floor but cast part of the area in shadow. It was like being outside on the street and finding yourself in a blind alleyway with a locked door at the end. She knocked on the door, then opened it without waiting. There, in a straight-backed wooden chair, sat an old man. He must have been in his mid-to-late eighties, I guessed. His white hair had been brushed to the side. His full moustache drooped down the sides of his mouth. Light streamed in from a window and he appeared to glow. As we entered, he used a cane to push himself to his feet. One eye had a glazed, opaque look, the iris covered over, marbleized. Its condition reinforced the intensity of the other eye that stared at me. If moments can be frozen in time, then I suppose that's what happened. I stared back through a thin veil beyond the years, trying to put the image of the young man in the photographs I'd found together with the elderly wraith I saw before me. Just a glimpse of the devil in the lopsided smile.

"Ah, Bernard," he said in heavily accented English. "I have been waiting for you."

I clasped his gnarled hand in both of mine. "Isaac? It is you?"

"Yes," he answered slowly and sank into his seat. We stared awkwardly at each other for a long moment.

"Gabrielle," Isaac said. "Bernard and I will have tea."

"I'll bring it, papa," Gabrielle said. After she had left, Isaac gestured.

"Sit, please, sit, young man," he said.

"I can't quite believe I'm here," I said.

"And so?" The old man smiled. "Why not?"

"Everything's happened so fast."

"So it would seem to you, Bernard, yes. But not for me, no. Many things have taken a very long time," Isaac said cryptically.

My brain began to work, slowly. "A moment ago, you said you were waiting for me. Why is that?" I asked.

"Yes. Your father wrote and told me you would be coming," replied Isaac.

"My father? My father wrote you? You know my father? When did this happen? He wrote you when?" I demanded, startled by this news. Isaac looked away. He seemed to drift off somewhere for a moment and I wondered if the old man had lost his marbles. But no, he merely waited as presently, we heard the rattle of spoons in saucers.

"Ah, the tea," he said and smacked his lips. Gabrielle came in with a tray. She set it down on the table. She poured it into tall glasses on saucers, spoons at the side, Russian style with lemon and sugar. With it came slices of lemon cake.

"If you need anything, just call, papa," she said.

"Yes, darling, we will," he replied. "She is a joy, my daughter, a pure joy," he said after she'd left the room.

"I'm sure," I replied impatiently. "Now, about my father?" Isaac nodded slowly. He sipped the tea and smacked his lips again. Then, he helped himself to some lemon cake. He offered it to me and I shook my head.

"Too early in the morning, perhaps," Isaac said. "Ah, you young people always watching what you eat. Worrying about the weight. One thing when you get old, why worry about things like that, yes? What's the point?"

"Of course," I said. "Everyone looks forward to getting old just for that reason."

Isaac laughed. "You have the sharp tongue, Bernard, this I can see. Don't get frustrated. You're here and that's a little miracle. Don't you think so?" he asked.

"I don't know. I guess so."

"Okay, now we get down to the business. I don't want you to get more frustrated. That's no good in this heat. Since coming to Israel in 1949, I figured this out," he said. "You will hear things, Bernard. Things that may surprise you. Yes, I know your father, the famous historian, quite well. We have never met in person. But we are well acquainted. He wrote to me, Bernard. He told me about this book that you are writing. He told me that you found the letters I wrote to Fanny, my dear sister," he said.

"But how could he know I found the letters?" I said.

Isaac sighed and shook his head. It was as if he were saying that the naiveté of youth never ceased to surprise him. "Because he left them for you," Isaac said. "And he knew, that eventually, you would find me. The only problem was time. I am an old man. I have not been well. But in this, we agreed. That you should be allowed to find out in your own way," he said.

I sat back in my chair. I put both hands to my head. Electric shocks coursed through my body. "You planned this? He planned this? But why?" I asked. I leaned in again.

Isaac bobbed his head. "Of course. Of course. You have come a long way. You need to hear the answers to your questions. But where to start? Ah, perhaps, with the letters? The last letter that you read, it was written when, Bernard?" he asked.

"1938, I believe," I said.

Isaac rubbed his chin. "Good. Good," he muttered and thought a moment, gathering his memories. Then, he began. "As you know, this was a very difficult time. War was coming soon. Things were bad and if you were a Jew? Well, we all know the answer to such a thing. I wrote asking my dear sister for money. Money that we needed to get away, but the money never came. And there was no answer. No answer," he repeated and held his palms upward. "I felt, Bernard that my dear sister had abandoned me for good. Then, things began to happen. My beloved Dagmar left me. I was left with the children. This fellow Marsh came back and took her away to America. So, it seems that what Marsh had told me was true. They had been lovers. And he couldn't get her out of his mind.

"Dagmar and I quarreled then. A great deal. There was little money. We couldn't make a living and we closed the shop. Then Marsh showed up and she was gone. This was early in 1939, just before the war. Armand, my son, disappeared. He'd become an unruly boy, you see, Bernard. He'd become like me. He fought with his father and after one big fight, he ran away. I learned later that he joined the Resistance. Imagine, such a young boy, barely old enough for a bar mitzvah, and he is fighting Germans." Isaac paused, and a single tear rolled down his cheek from the one good eye. "Armand died in 1942. Something to do with blowing up a train. They were caught, and the Nazis shot him and others as well," he said and paused to blow his nose with a linen hanky and wipe his good eye.

"I decided to leave Paris. We knew the Germans were coming, sweeping everything in their path. To be a Jew or a Gypsy was like a death warrant. I decided to go home, after all those years. Yes, yes, a crazy decision but the world had gone mad. Everybody was running the other way. At that time, Russia and Germany had signed a truce and our village was now on the Russian side, you see. I wanted to see if any family were left. But there was the Blitzkrieg. The Germans were ahead of us and moved quickly. So many tanks and troops, you wouldn't believe. And still, they moved them very fast. It was a tribute to German efficiency. I couldn't stand seeing them in Paris. It would have been intolerable to me," Isaac paused, then took a slurp of his tea. "Years earlier, when Armand was born, I did a very foolish thing. I registered him as Armand Dubinsky and took back my own identity. This was a serious mistake. I had to get a new identity again. And it cost me much of what little money we had; the black market, you see. Desperation drives the price up and they could smell it on us. The question remained, then, how were we to travel such a distance when the world was in chaos?" Isaac asked and raised his hands in the air. He hesitated, thinking back.

"So, how did you get there?"

"Well, I tell you, I didn't know. Then on the night before Gabrielle and I were to go, there was a knock at our door. It must have been midnight or later. Who could this be? I asked myself. I opened the door and I saw Armand standing there. He was half-way between a boy and a young man now but still, he looked so grown up to me. So different from the little one who held on to his mother's skirt. Who put his small hand in mine.

"'Papa,' he said, just like he used to when he was very little.

"'Armand,' I said to him. 'You've come back to us? You will come with us?' I asked him. And then I noticed an older boy behind him, maybe nineteen or twenty.

"'This is François,' Armand said, introducing his friend. I let them in. They sat down and I could see they were restless, nervous. The two of them filled the room with their restlessness, Bernie.

"'Papa,' Armand said, 'I know we have quarreled, but there is so much going on and we have a job to do. We fight the Germans everywhere and anywhere we can. The movement is growing all the time. I heard you were leaving Paris.'

"'From who did you hear this?' I asked him.

"Armand shrugged. 'I just heard,' he said. His face was dirty and he looked as if he'd been sleeping in the streets.

"'And what else did you hear?'

"Armand blushed. After all, he was still a boy. Still my son. 'I heard you want to go to Poland. I do not think this is a good thing to do, Papa. It is very dangerous. I do not think you can get there on your own. But I know you can be stubborn. I think that I get this from you, perhaps. This is why I bring François with me. He will guide you. Take you where you want to go. We have many friends. Many contacts who can help.'

"I looked at François, who had been silent. 'This is true?' I asked him.

"He nodded. 'Yes, it is true,' François replied simply.

"Gabrielle went and sat by her brother. She put her arms around him and laid her head on his shoulder. 'Come with us, Armand, please,' she said.

"Armand stroked her hair. 'I cannot, Gabrielle. But you will be safe with François. He will take care of you. Papa, there is a church and a priest there who is a friend of ours. You will go to him when you reach Poland. François knows the way. This priest, Father Milsovic, will take care of you.' Armand stood up suddenly. It is late, Papa. I must go. I am expected.'

"I could see he was embarrassed, Bernie. That we'd had arguments and fights was true, but he didn't want to leave this between us.

"'Armand,' I began to say.

"'Papa,' he said and came into my arms. I held him just as I used to when he was little. 'We will see each other after the war, yes? After the Germans have been defeated, Papa. Take care of Gabrielle. Meet me back in Paris. We shall be together again. I promise.'

"I looked at him, Bernie. My handsome young son. My little man. And then, as quickly as he had come, he left me. Left me forever.

"And so François guided us to Poland. And as Armand had said, it was dangerous but along the way, many kind people helped us. Given a bed in homes, in churches; the Underground seemed to be bigger and better organized than I had thought. We went to Father Milsovic and he gave us shelter. Beside the church was a small clinic and I got a job there as an orderly. Gabrielle helped out in the church with the cleaning and did laundry for the clinic too. We seemed to be safe for the time being. Then, after about six months, there was an outbreak of typhoid in the area. By this time, the Germans had overrun everything and effectively, we were under German control.

"Many people died. I was very frightened of getting it too. But the doctors were very careful, and I followed their instructions closely. It was life or death, you see. Everything seemed very bleak. Very dangerous. But after the typhoid outbreak, the Germans seemed to forget about us a little. Eventually, the typhoid subsided, and we had survived it. But many others in the area died.

"You might think this difficult to believe, yes? That the Germans could be distracted so easily? But do not forget, Bernie, other things were occupying their attention. The disaster in Russia on the eastern front, partisans operating in France and Poland. The campaign in North Africa. And they were cleaning out all the ghettos, especially in Cracow and Warsaw. This was a big operation. And then, there was the resistance in the Warsaw ghetto and that delayed their plans, too. Where we were, it was peaceful, more or less. They cooperated. The people gave the Germans no trouble. This allowed them to look at other things. We prayed, of course, that it would last until the liberation.

"I remember one day in May 1942, this priest, Milsovic, called me to him. He asked me to do him a favor. 'Yes,' I said, 'what is it you want me to do?' He wanted me to take the blood samples to the military courier at the perimeter of the town. You see, Bernie, the German military command had ordered their troops to stay outside by a certain distance because of the typhoid, but they demanded that blood be tested constantly to see if there was any danger of it spreading. They were afraid they might get it themselves, you see. God forbid, they should be infected. The radius all around was about thirty kilometers but from this village, perhaps just ten or fifteen kilometers to the boundary. The clinic kept its own ambulance. I don't think that's what you would call it today, mind you. Today, it would be called a piece of junk that started when it felt like it and if you were lucky, would keep going too. The gasoline was rationed, and the ambulance could only be used every so often. But every two or three weeks, the doctors were obliged by the military governor for the area, a fat pig named Herr General Werner Bloch, to deliver the samples. Then, they'd be sent on to Warsaw to the laboratory for the testing.

"On this day, the priest asked me and I said, okay, I will do it. By now, I know my way around a little bit. There's only one road in and one road back, so the command post isn't difficult to find. I wasn't happy about it, but I had been lucky too. The doctor himself normally delivered the samples but many people were sick at this time. The farmers inside the perimeter were still allowed to grow food but the people in the village suspected they were hoarding a lot of it for themselves. There wasn't much money to pay, anyway. As a result, people were hungry, children were getting sick and so on. The doctor was too busy to go.

38

"I got in the ambulance and I was happy to see it started without too much trouble. I took the samples and started to drive out of the village. It was very peaceful. You know, if I didn't know better, I wouldn't have thought there was a war on. The drive took me through the woods which, for about a kilometer, were very thick. You could almost pretend you were somewhere else. Driving from the sunlight into the shade, I got a shiver. The branches were thick with leaves blocking the sun. I am not paying attention too well, in my driving and suddenly, I look up and must stop very quickly. Two men were standing on the road. They pointed rifles at me. They were dressed like peasants with caps and sweaters, even though the weather was warm. I stopped the ambulance and prayed the motor would not stop.

"They motioned to me to get out. I did this slowly, I didn't want to get shot because they were nervous. Fortunately, I was wearing my outfit from the hospital, the white jacket and pants, I mean they would be white if we had proper detergent to clean them. I looked like a medical person. I approached the two men, until one told me to stop.

"'What is it you want of me?' I said. 'I must deliver blood samples to the military command.' One of them lowered his rifle. I could see behind his blond beard that he was young.

"'One of my men is sick,' he said. "He must go to the hospital with you. Turn this ambulance around and go back,' he ordered.

"'But I cannot do this,' I protested.

"'You can if I shoot you and do it myself,' this young one said to me.

"'I must deliver these blood samples. Then I can come back for you and your man and take him to the hospital,' I said.

"For a moment, Bernie, I thought this young fool would shoot me. He was angry but then he hesitated. To shoot would make a great deal of noise, even in this bit of forest. They did not want to draw attention.

"'Why are these samples so important?' he asked.

"'They are for the typhoid,' I said.

"The young man stepped back. 'Typhoid?' he repeated. 'What do you mean?' Now the other fellow with him was looking very scared and began to back away. The young fellow snapped something at him and he stopped.

"'Why do you think no Germans are here?' I asked him. 'Because we are under the quarantine for typhoid. For thirty kilometers around,' I said.

"The two stepped back a bit and talked so I couldn't hear them. I understood that they were partisans and had been using these woods, perhaps, as a hiding place.

"'I must get going,' I said. 'I am expected. If I don't show up, there will be trouble for everyone.' They looked at me like you would look at a piece of dirt. I wasn't a fighting man and so, not worth the respect. The young fellow strode up to me.

"'Very well,' he said. 'But I will come with you. To make sure you come back by yourself, without some Germans for company.'

"I protested to him. "But of course. I will come back. This is the only way. If you come with me and get caught, we will both be shot. Believe me, I'm not in love with the Germans.'

"'My comrade needs help and you will supply it,' he said. 'Or I will shoot you right here.'

"'Then we take a ride, okay, comrade?' I sneered.

"'I will cover myself with the blankets in the back,' he said.

"He climbed into the back. The other fellow disappeared into the woods. This is a brilliant disguise, I said to myself. This fool is going to get us both killed. But I got into the ambulance and then the stupid fellow poked me with the barrel of the rifle to get going. Instead of being afraid, I found myself angry and annoyed. At the stupidity.

"'Don't poke me,' I snapped at the young fool. 'It might go off.'

"'I won't shoot you unless it is for a good reason.'

"I drove on for about three kilometers. We left the woods. The command post was about five kilometers further on.

"'What is your name?' the fool asked me from under the blanket.

"'Vlasic,' I replied.

"'I am Hugo,' he said to me.

"'It is a pleasure, Hugo, having your rifle at my back,' I said.

"'Is it true?' he asked. 'About the typhoid?'

"'Yes, of course, it's true.'

"'You are not afraid? Of catching it?'

"'Of course I am afraid, but what choice is there? It is better to take my chances here than getting my head shot off by the Germans,' I said. 'At least they leave us alone… Now put your head down, we are near the post. Be still and do not move,' I hissed.

"The priest had told me what to do. A German sentry with a machine pistol stood outside the command post. I stopped the ambulance about fifty meters away. I got out and carried the samples, walking slowly until the sentry held up his hand to me. Then I set the tray of samples down on the ground. And backed away. I looked over my shoulder and saw that idiot Hugo had crawled into the front and was peeking out. I stood stiff at attention and hoped the Germans wouldn't notice. The young fool. Another German sentry came out of the command hut and handed the first one a pair of rubber gloves. They were afraid of being infected, you see. The sentry, a big, ugly brute he was, put them on. He came forward to pick up the tray. I could hear the glass vials rattling in their holders. He held the tray as far out from him as he could, like he would catch the typhoid if he even breathed. Almost, I laughed. The big German walked slowly, like a duck, back to the hut. I nodded at the other one and he waved me off. I got back into the ambulance.

"Hugo was laughing.

"'Did you see that idiot?' he said. 'He walks like the duck.'

"'And what the hell are you doing?' I said. 'Keep your head down, or you'll get us both killed.'

"'All right, all right,' growled Hugo. 'Don't forget who's got the gun here, Vlasic, okay?'

"'Don't be stupid, that's all I'm saying.'

"'Yes, yes,' he said. 'I could have picked that German off easy, you know? It would have been a clean shot.'

"I had turned the ambulance around and drove slowly off.

"'I don't want to know your business, Hugo. But I think you're not that stupid. And you wish to help your comrade. We will drive him back to the hospital now. What about your friends?'

"Hugo looked at me suspiciously. 'What about them?'

"'We can't take them too. We have only room for the one who is ill and perhaps one more. That is all,' I said.

"'Don't worry. They will stay behind. I will come with you. To make sure my friend is cared for,' he said.

"'You sound like a man who makes decisions,' I said to him.

"'Yes,' he said. 'And sometimes that decision is to shoot, right?'

"It went as I said. We picked up Hugo's friend and put him in the ambulance. Besides Hugo and the other fellow and the one who was sick, I counted about fifteen others. This worried me, greatly, Bernie. If the partisans were operating in the area, it would draw attention. The Germans would come, and our little haven would be in danger. There was no Russian border anymore. Not to speak of. By then, the Germans had pushed in toward Moscow and almost taken it but got stuck in the wintertime. The border was moving almost every day. Who could keep track? And because we were cut off, we didn't get much news.

"Hugo left his friend at the hospital. The sick fellow had a ruptured appendix and needed an operation. But sadly, it was too late for him. The poison had spread through his body and he died a few days later. There were no drugs to help him. It was quite sad. We buried him in the cemetery. The doctors reported back to the Germans that, he too, had died of the typhoid. So many deaths…" Isaac sighed and drifted off into a type of reverie.

39

My attention was drawn to voices in the hall outside. I heard a man's voice, deep and vigorous. The door opened and a tall man, once broad, came in. His hair was white and cut short. His eyes were blue and his skin lightly bronzed. I put his age at about sixty, but he was in good physical shape. He seemed younger.

"Ah, Bernie, I want you to meet my son-in-law," Isaac said.

I stood up and stuck out my hand. "How do you do?"

He took my hand and crushed most of it. "I am Hugo," he said.

I turned and looked at Isaac in surprise. "Hugo?" And Isaac nodded and smiled. "The same Hugo?" I asked.

Hugo released me and put his hands on his hips. "So, Isaac has been telling you his stories, has he?" he said.

"That's why I came here," I replied.

"Yes, I know," said the son-in-law. "You've come a long way. But it is worth it, I bet."

Isaac gestured. "Sit Hugo, sit for a moment. I was telling Bernie here how we met in the forest so many years ago."

"Hugo," I said. "Do you mind if I ask how old you are?"

Hugo laughed showing a fine set of teeth. "Not at all. I am seventy-two years old."

"Really?"

"Yes," he replied. "Life here has been good to us, eh, Isaac? If not for Isaac, I wouldn't have come. I wouldn't have met Gabrielle. But the first time I saw her, she was just a young girl of twelve or thirteen years. But even then, she was very beautiful. You were talking about Yossi?" asked Hugo.

Isaac nodded. "I just told Bernie how he died."

227

"Yes," Hugo said. "It was sad. Yossi was my childhood friend. We grew up together. We joined the Russian army together. Together, we deserted the Russian
army." He laughed. "We went into the woods and fought the Germans together.
I am proud to say we killed a great many and some lousy Polacks too," he said
with some bitterness.

I was confused. "You are not Polish?" I asked.

"Oh sure," he replied. "I was born in Poland. When the Germans invaded,
Yossi and me crossed the border to the Russian side. We thought we would
be fighting the Germans. I was a mechanic and ended up in a tank crew as
the commander. Yossi was my gunner. But when Stalin signed the peace with
Hitler and we sat around wiping our asses for a year, we left. After the war, I
could not stay in Poland. I would have been shot, you see, for desertion. But I
can tell you, we fought longer and harder than the Russians," he pronounced
with obvious pride.

Something dawned on me, finally. "You. You are Jewish?" I asked.

Hugo slapped me on the shoulder, almost knocking it into my chest. "But of
course, Bernie! What did you think? In those days, we had to fight the Polacks
as much as the Germans. It was madness," he said. "After Yossi died, I went
back to the forest where I had met Isaac. The men were upset. Disturbed by
the typhoid. Afraid they would catch it. I said the area made a perfect base of
operations. We argued for a bit and finally, I convinced them. We stayed there
for about a year, off and on. The Germans were clever and tracked us. I think
too, that the Polacks gave us away. By 1944, the whole area was under siege
and the Russians and the Germans were on the move. Barriers had come down.
One night in August of 1944, we walked into an ambush. Most of the men were
cut down. I was wounded in the shoulder here," and he touched the spot, "and
here," he said, indicating his right thigh. "I managed to roll into a deep ditch
that was covered by bushes and I passed out. When I awoke, it was the next
morning and they had left, whoever they had been. Twelve of my men had been
shot. Their bodies were left for the animals to pick at. I was weak and had lost
much blood. I was not that far from the hospital. Several kilometers perhaps. I
waited until night and walked there. It took almost until the sun came up and
I staggered in, hoping I was not seen. I still had my pistol and would have shot
any attacker and then myself, if necessary. Isaac – Vlasic then – took me in.
He got the priest, Milsovic. He dressed my wounds and then put me to bed. I
was several weeks recovering. It was decided to give me a new identity from

one who died and was buried at the cemetery. If the Germans found me, I'd be shot. And the same for the Russians. The Germans were retreating. There was news of the Americans and British making a big push into France. Isaac and I sat talking late one night and we decided to take our chances and try to get back to Paris," he said and stopped, to remember. Tears welled up in his eyes. "In some ways," he said. "It was a wonderful time, what do you think, Isaac? "

Isaac merely shrugged. "We survived, Hugo. That was the main thing. I didn't know yet about Armand. Still, I had the hope we would find him alive."

Hugo patted Isaac on the arm. "I must go. Gabrielle and I go to do the shopping now." He stood up and stretched. "I get stiff sitting for a short time. It is the old age, I am feeling it." Hugo squeezed my neck affectionately. It felt like a C-clamp ratcheted tight. "We see you again, Bernie, okay? You come back for dinner tomorrow night and we serve you a proper meal."

"Okay," I replied. "Thanks." Isaac and I watched him go.

Then Isaac leaned over and whispered to me. "Hugo killed at least ten men, you know. One with his bare hands."

"Really?" I said, not knowing how else to respond, but having felt his tensile grip, believed it.

Isaac continued his story.

"We stayed with the priest until the big invasion. He had been very kind to us. We had no way of repaying him. Then, we all returned to Paris, but I was not happy there. And that was when I wrote to my sister again. It was now 1946 and I had not heard from her in almost eight years. I was angry and bitter about this. How could she have abandoned me? I wrote and told her of my feelings. Not long after, I received a letter back. But, my sister wrote, we never received any letters from you, dear brother, during that time. We did not know what had happened. And, Bernard, since we had moved several times after closing the shop, my sister didn't have our address. Without my letters, Fanny didn't know where to send letters back.

"So, I ask myself, how could I send letters to Fanny and not have them received by her? This is a puzzle to me. And then I find the answer. Fanny writes me. She is heartbroken and very upset. She tells me what happened. She tells me why they didn't get my letters. In truth, she thought that we had all died during the war. After all, just about everyone else had been sent to the camps, no? When I wrote in 1946, it was a miracle to her," Isaac said.

"But what happened?" I asked. "Why didn't she get your letters?" And a feeling of dread flooded into me.

40

Isaac nodded slowly. "Yes, this is a good question. There was a boy. And this was a very bright boy. A very ambitious boy. At the time when I wrote my sister asking for money, this boy would have been a teenager only. But already, he was making his mark. In school, he was brilliant. The mind was very acute but the heart, my dear Bernard, was hard. This boy. This arrogant, jealous boy, hid the letters from my sister. In truth, my Fanny was not a wealthy woman. Her Morris was barely making ends meet. They too, were suffering. They had sent me money before and I had spent it. About this, I will not lie to you, Bernard. One time, I took Dagmar and the children to the south of France for a week. I felt we needed a little holiday. Our life had grown so difficult, so very difficult," and he sighed at the memory of it.

Isaac continued. "I had been the one to cry wolf, yes? Once too often, perhaps? Perhaps. So, the boy hid the letters when we really needed the money to survive, to make our escape. He didn't want us to have the money. It deprived him, you see," he said and paused. "I had so wanted to come to Canada," he said.

My throat was dry. I sipped a little tea. "And who was this boy?" I croaked.

Isaac held his hands up. "This boy was my brother, you see. The little brother I had never met. He was born to my beloved mama who died in childbirth. Fanny took the baby with her when she went to Canada and raised him like he was her own son," he said solemnly.

"And the boy's name?" I asked in fear. It was almost stark terror now.

"Ephraim," Isaac replied. "Ephraim, my little brother."

I was completely numb. "But how…?"

Isaac smiled sadly. "Of course. How can you understand? Your father is my brother and Fanny was not your grandmother, Bernard but your aunt. But there were many years between them and it seemed to make some sense, that you would think this. Your father was deeply ashamed, this is true. He wanted to forget. To distance himself from what he had done. And so, he took my mother's name, Goldman, for his own. And so, you are now a Goldman, Bernard and not a Dubinsky."

Perhaps I had known it, or guessed. But to hear it out loud, spoken by this old man in this faraway place. It hit me. My heart jumped, creating an up-tempo jazz routine in my chest.

"Yes," Isaac said. "Life, Bernard is strange and wonderful. You started to grow and as you got older, the resemblance between you and me came closer. Your father had the photographs sent to my sister. Every time he looked at you, Bernard, you reminded him of me and what he had done. I think he tortured himself with this," Isaac declared. He raised his forefinger and pointed upward. "I am not a believer, you understand, but God had a hand in this. It was his way of making your father suffer a little bit. I couldn't say I was sorry. But it was a wound that did not heal for anyone. My Fanny died deeply unhappy, unable to make her peace. The family has been scarred, Bernard," he whispered.

"He knew I would find out," I said.

"Yes," Isaac replied. "He knew."

"He never tried to stop me."

"No," Isaac said, "he couldn't. He had to let you find out. This much I give him."

I got up from the table, not even aware that I was standing. Isaac was still speaking. "Perhaps someday, Bernard, you will find it in your heart to forgive? Perhaps, one day," he said.

I could not look up at first. "And you, Isaac? Have you forgiven?"

The old man paused, then gave me a wan smile. "Not yet, Bernard. But I am working on it."

I left the apartment with the promise to return the following evening.

My brain reeled. I went back to the hotel and slept, so I didn't have to think. I really didn't want to think. At all.

41

I returned the next evening with Egan in tow. As soon as we walked in the door and Hugo spotted Egan, his eyes lit up. They hit it off royally. In fact, it was fair to say that Egan hit it off with everyone, royally. We had a fabulous time and I forced myself not to think about my father, but concentrated on enjoying my new family. I supposed this is what Sharon had meant. What she had feared. But it was silly, I thought, nonetheless.

Egan had transformed. While I had been talking to Isaac, he'd walked about the city with his sketchbook. He'd filled it. I'd never seen him so full of energy and enthusiasm. He looked younger. Both he and Sharon had that deep worry crease between their eyebrows. But his skin had grown smooth and lighter. His complexion had ruddied, but in a becoming way. There was much laughter. Egan told his stories. I related the story of when Egan announced the opening of his show and then passed out, dead drunk, on our carpet. That prompted Hugo to bring out the slivovitz. He forced some on me, too. Even Isaac drank a little. By the end of the evening, Hugo and Egan were singing, terribly off-key. Gabrielle smiled indulgently. Dagmar looked embarrassed. Isaac fell asleep. Some time around midnight, we got up to go. But Egan had exacted a promise from Dagmar to act as our guide for the next few days.

We indulged in tourist activities. Dagmar took us to the Wailing Wall and Temple Mount. We rented a car and drove to the Golan Heights. We saw Mount Zion and the Sea of Galilee. We trekked the Sinai and floated in the Dead Sea. Finally, finally, I'd had enough. This revelation about my father weighed on me. I must see to it. And I couldn't wait any longer. I took Egan aside.

"It's time for me to go," I said. "I'm leaving tomorrow."

Egan nodded. "I figured," he said, then hesitated. "I'm going to stay a while, Bernie. I like it here and to tell you the truth of it, I think I'm falling for Dagmar. What do you think of that, eh? Do you think it could work, man?"

It wasn't as if I hadn't noticed. The bumping of their shoulders together in the car. The light touch of her hand on his. The way she looked at him, fleeting glances. I smiled and clapped him around the shoulders. "Why not? I married an Irish lass, didn't I? Why shouldn't you be with an Israeli? Hugo and Gabrielle seem to think you're a swell guy. What will you do for money?" I said.

"Hugo's got some connections and says he can sort something out. Dagmar says I'll fit right in with the artistic community here. Apparently, they're all a wee bit insane. I feel like I've lost everythin' back home, you know?" I nodded and smiled grimly. "Will you be all right? You act like you're balancing a load of bricks on your forehead."

"I'll be fine," I replied. But would I?

Egan and Dagmar drove me to the airport in Hugo's new Land Rover. I gave Egan a big hug and Dagmar a demure kiss on the cheek. I went into the terminal, then stopped and looked behind me. I saw the tall Irishman and the slim Israeli girl standing together, their bodies touching. Egan raised his hand and waved. I waved back, then turned and walked toward the gate.

The return flight seemed like an earlier memory. I'd said goodbye to Isaac, knowing that we'd never see each other again. Perhaps, he was simply waiting to close off this part of his story. He'd told me of his life after he emigrated to Israel in 1949 and it was just as remarkable as the letters. That is, if he could be believed. But as stories and storytellers go, he ranked very high.

As promised, I bought the boys T-shirts and other souvenirs. And for Sharon, I purchased a gold necklace with a Star of David. I hoped she'd like it and would wear it, too.

On the plane, I felt like I was suffocating. I'd sent Sharon a wire letting her know when I was arriving. I couldn't wait for the flight to end, for it to be over, to get home. I missed being away. More than I thought I would. I'm not a traveler, me.

The plane landed after midnight. I had tried to sleep but couldn't. I hadn't slept the night before either, tossing and turning in my hotel bed. My brain, my emotions, my body, raged feverishly.

Several overseas flights landed at the same time. Big jumbos eating up the tarmac. It took eons to get through customs. Despite the late hour, people packed the terminal. Throngs of people milled around as if it were an open market-place. Different tongues jabbered at me. I pushed my way through the crowd. I looked for Sharon. I was desperate to see her. It felt as if I'd been away for an entire year. My head pounded, and I sweated terribly. I felt despondent, staggering from fatigue.

Suddenly, I saw her. A flash of orange as she pushed her way through, her head bobbing amongst the slow-moving travelers. I fought my way toward her. I screamed her name. It seemed like a barrier of flesh and damp clothes and clunky suitcases had been thrown up in our path. Finally, we met. She threw her arms about me. I was very happy. I didn't really focus on what she was saying. I was just so happy to be home. So pleased to see her.

"What?" I said. "What are you saying to me?"

"It's so bloody noisy here," she shouted. "It's your dad, Bernie."

"What about him? Is he okay?" I asked.

Sharon bit her lip and gave me a baleful look. "I don't know how to tell you, so I'm just going to blurt it out, then."

"What? Tell me what for Christ sake!"

"He's getting married, Bernie. To Katherine."

"Whoa…" I felt my knees buckle. I was going down. Right there in the airport terminal. I sat on a piece of luggage. Didn't even know whose. I sat, bowed, head in hands. Then I felt a tap on the shoulder and looked up into an indignant face. Vaguely Mediterranean in appearance. "Sorry," I said and stood up. He gave me a dirty look.

"I didn't want to hit you with it just as you came off the plane," said Sharon, pushing the car to 140 kilometers an hour. "I thought it'd be too much of a shock."

"Well, I'm glad you waited," I said.

"Sorry." And it sounded genuine.

"I'm just… I'm just… I don't know what I am," I said bitterly.

"Well, I don't blame you for feeling that way. But he is an adult, you know. And he asked her, by the way."

Then something occurred to me. Through the haze. "You're happy about this aren't you?" I accused her.

Sharon focused on the road and didn't answer for a moment.

"It doesn't bother me, if that's what you mean," she replied easily. "But don't push the blame on me. I never thought it would come to marriage. I thought your dad needed some companionship, that's all.

I groaned. "When is the blessed event?"

"Saturday. He was just waiting for you come home," Sharon said.

Saturday was two days away.

That night, Sharon and I stayed up talking. It was past three in the morning before we got to bed. I told her about Isaac, Gabrielle, Hugo and Dagmar. I told her about what I'd seen and experienced. I told her about Egan and Dagmar and how I thought this would be it for him. That I wouldn't be surprised if they stayed together as a couple. I didn't tell Sharon about my father and his legacy of shame. Or how he'd led me by the nose these past months. Deceived me from birth.

Early the next morning, Sean and Nathan were on me. Before I was conscious enough to realize it, they were squirming around under the covers. Sharon was in the shower.

"Dad. Dad. Did you have a good time? Did you bring us something? What did you do there? What did you see? Did you go to the desert? Did you bring us some sand? Where is Uncle Egan? Did he come back with you? Where are our presents?" And on and on.

"Boys, give me a minute, will you. I got in late last night. I'm still very tired..."

It didn't seem to matter. Each one took an arm and tugged. Before I knew it, I was on the floor, the covers all around me.

"All right, all right," I conceded. I was too groggy to be angry. "I'll get your things and then we'd better have some breakfast. School soon."

"Aww, Dad," whined Nathan. "Can't we miss it today? We're not doing anything anyway."

"Yeah," screamed Sean. "Let's skip school! Yeah! We can go to the big water slide. Yeah!"

"No way. We can do that after school is finished for the summer. Get off me. I've got to get washed. You two get dressed and I'll meet you downstairs in ten minutes. Hurry up now," I ordered, back into the routine without effort. They scampered off. Sean gave me a look as if saying, *it was worth a try.* I smiled at him. Got to admire his persistence when it came to mischief.

The sober presence of Mrs. Diaz hadn't lifted. She brought me coffee in her taciturn way and acknowledged my thanks with a slight nod. I think she was angry because I didn't bring Egan back with me. I sighed. After breakfast, I presented all the gifts to rounds of appreciation, thank you's, and appropriate hugs. I'd even brought a peace offering for Mrs. Diaz. A silver wristlet. She looked at me, her face pulled back in surprise.

"Thank you very much," she said and went off to admire it. Sharon gave me an appreciative look.

"That was thoughtful," she said.

"Well, if it brings some peace between us."

"A little bending goes a long way," she replied, and I had the feeling she wasn't talking about Mrs. Diaz now. Then I shooed the boys off to school. Sharon got ready to leave for the office. She wore her peach outfit. The skirt was quite short. The heels accentuated her legs. I went and kissed her with meaning. She pushed me away.

"Stop it," she laughed. "I've got to go to work now, you horny dolt."

"I've been away almost ten days," I said. Sharon sighed.

"I know," she said. "And I've missed you too. But I've got to go to work right now." Sharon could be irritatingly stubborn at times.

"All right."

With a hand on her hip, she gave me a look. "When are you going to see your Dad?" she asked.

"I've got to see him this morning, don't I? There isn't much time given the circumstances," I said.

She turned to go, picking up her things. "Are you sure there isn't something you're not telling me?" she asked. Ouch. That sixth sense.

I put on my innocent face. "What do you mean? Like what?"

"I know you, Bernie Goldman. And I can tell when you're not telling me the truth," she said and waited for my answer. None was forthcoming. "Suit yourself then. If you don't think I can be trusted," she said.

"Nothing to tell, Sharon. Really. Nothing to tell. You have a good day at work. And I'll call you later, let you know what happened with my Dad, okay?"

"Okay," she said and went to the door. "You're not going to hit him, are you?"

"Hit him? Why would I do that?" I asked.

"Something about the expression on your face, that's all. Bye," she said and was out the door.

What would I say to my father? I didn't know. I really didn't know.

42

I rang his doorbell around eleven o'clock. He was expecting me. He opened the door wearing the same tracksuit he'd worn at the cottage. He nodded and stepped back. I went in.

"Hi son. Welcome back," he said. "How was the trip?"

"It was swell. Simply grand," I replied. "What are you doing?" I asked, seeing all the boxes with the flaps up and the shelves emptied.

"Packing," he said and went to a box and dropped in a handful of books.

"What's going on? Apart from you running off and getting married, I mean."

"I didn't expect you to be thrilled about it," he said.

"Look," I said, launching into it. "Why do you have to marry her? Why can't you just live together? Try it out for a while. Then, if you're sure that the two of you are compatible, then you can get married."

He frowned. "I don't think I need your permission, you know."

"I see what's happening, here. You waited until I was out of the country. You went behind my back."

Eph gave me a sour look. A sour, prune-faced, old man's look. "I'm selling the house, Bernie. I don't want it anymore. I guess this represents the start of a new phase in my life. I want you to know though that the money is going straight into a trust fund for the boys. I mean that. I want them to have it," he said evenly, as if he'd rehearsed it all week.

"Well, that's very generous of you, Dad. But there's no need really. Sharon and I can take care of Sean and Nathan," I said with an edge in my voice.

He responded in kind, picking up my tone. "They are my grandsons and I'm going to do it anyway and don't be so damned stubborn. It's done and that's the end of it," he declared, then stopped, having run out of steam, breathing hard. "You want some coffee or anything?"

I shook my head. "No, I don't want anything. Look," I said again and hesitated. "I didn't come here to fight with you, you know? I came to try and understand what happened. What's happening. I don't know where to start, really. My thoughts are all jumbled up," I said. "Sharon told me not to hit you," I said by way of a joke.

"She did?" he asked and took a step backward instinctively.

"Let's go and sit in the kitchen," I said. "That is, if you haven't packed away the chairs."

"Not yet," he replied.

We trooped into the kitchen and sat down. A carafe of coffee sat on the table and some cups.

"She's not here, is she?" I asked.

My dad shook his head. "She left an hour ago," he replied, picking up a half-full cup but not drinking from it.

"Ah, good," I said. "That is reassuring." Once again, there was the extended silence. I could have screamed. "When are you leaving?" I asked.

"Sunday morning," he said. "Early."

"And where are you going?"

"London, then Paris. We're going to rent a car and just drive around Europe, down through the south of France to Italy, then Greece and Israel. I told Isaac we'd visit. I want to meet the family, too," he said. "See if we can patch things up before it's too late."

"And how long will you be gone?"

He shrugged. "I don't know. Three, four months."

"And where will you live when you get back?"

"Probably at Katherine's at first. Then we've talked about finding our own place somewhere. I'm not sure. It's too far away to think about right now," he said.

I felt the need to stand up suddenly. Couldn't bear the confines of the chair and the small kitchen. I slapped my palms on the table making the cups and saucers jump, the spoons dance and clatter. I reached out, and out of pure frustration, took a swipe. The cup in my father's hand flew across the room sending a spray of coffee across the floor. It caromed off the edge of the counter, ricocheted up into a cupboard and landed in the sink, smashing into hundreds of pieces. My father was dumbstruck. He stared at me, wild-eyed and frightened. I smirked at him. It felt good to do that. Liberating. "You've gone weird, Eph, you know that? You're getting married to a woman half your age, a stranger no less, you almost destroyed your relatives during the war for purely selfish reasons... who the hell are you, for Christ sake!"

He rose, went to the counter, and ripped off some sheets of paper toweling. Then, he got down on his hands and knees and began to wipe up the spilled coffee. I watched. "If this were some soap opera," he said, scrubbing away, "I could say that I wasn't your father, but your father's evil twin who took his place. Then all could be forgiven, couldn't it? But I can't say that, Bernie. I am your father and yes, yes, I did those things. Unforgivable things. But you must understand how I thought, how I saw what was happening at that time," he said, having completed the wiping up. He stood up slowly. I heard his knees crack. He threw the soggy toweling in the garbage. He turned, leaning up against the counter, watching me, gauging my reactions.

"Go on," I said.

Satisfied that there wasn't anything else to whack about or whip at him, he continued in his lecturer's voice. "During the Depression. We were very poor, barely had two nickels to rub together. We huddled under one roof. My sister Fanny and her husband, Morris, did the best they could, but it was tough. Really tough. And these letters kept on coming from Isaac, pleading for money. Always, he was asking for money. And each time, they'd scrape together what they had and send it. And what happened, I ask you? He blew it, every time. Once, they went on vacation to the south of France. We ate cabbage soup for a week and he takes his family on a vacation! He spent the money on antiques for his shop. Let's face it, my boy, Isaac was a goniff, wasn't he? He lied. He stole, and he cheated. He made his living as a pickpocket, for god sakes. And this was who we were supporting, I ask you? What would you have thought? I was working very hard, Bernie, to do well at school. I worked. I delivered groceries for the market. I went around the neighborhood and did odd jobs, just for some extra cash to help out. You know, I applied for a scholarship from high school. I qualified, you know. My marks were the highest in my level. And do you know what happened?" he asked.

I shook my head. "No, what?"

"I got turned down. You know why? Because I was a Jew, that's why. It was just like that. Not that anybody would admit to it," he said bitterly. "That money we sent to Isaac was supposed to pay for my tuition at university. Instead, Morris managed to get a small loan, at an exorbitant rate of interest, I might add, from the local moneylender, and from the money I made, I managed to make do. But I was angry, Bernie. I was deeply bitter about it, deeply bitter," he said, raising his bushy eyebrows as his voice thickened with emotion. "Bernie, we didn't know what was going to happen. I didn't know about the war and the camps and the Germans. At that time, who could imagine the horror and the savagery? I was only a boy. Barely a teenager. You can't know how I felt. But at least we were safe. After the war when Isaac wrote to us, I can't tell you how relieved I was. I felt it was a reprieve, that it was some sort of sign. And it was encouragement for me to do well. To get on with what I was doing. And any success I may have would be a vindication for my selfish actions. Yes, I was successful. I don't apologize for that. But you can't know how I felt then," he concluded. "You can't judge me," he declared.

I rubbed my chin. Like he would after listening to a dissertation. "Nice thesis," I said. "But on the oral part… fail. I give you a D."

He looked up at me, eyes flashing. "Don't joke about this. I'm telling you the truth."

"I'm not joking," I said. "I'm just being you. Just being your son, that's all."

Eph stood up and looked at me angrily. "All right then. Be my son. And if you're the son, the man I know you to be, then you'll do what I ask. Do what I need you to do," he said harshly.

"And what's that?" I asked.

"I'm not joking, now, Bernie. I'm serious."

"All right. What?"

He came up to me then and seized me fiercely with both hands. The tips of his fingers pressed into the soft flesh of my shoulders. I winced. "Write the damn book. Just do it." He held me like that, my shoulders hunched up, for a long moment, then gradually released his grip. "Sorry." He looked at his gnarled hands like they belonged to somebody else.

I shook my head, then rubbed my left shoulder. "You're placing me in an untenable position. You know that? If I tell the truth, you'll be vilified and so will I. The critics will say that I'm exploiting your shameful past, stepping on you to haul myself up. We'll both be hated or ridiculed. Is that what you want? It will be exactly the type of book de Groot wants."

"I know that."

"And that doesn't bother you?"

My father sat opposite me and moved his chair in until our knees were almost touching. "Not in the way you think. I know you can pull it off. This will be your beginning and I can give it to you. Besides, Bernie, you have an obligation now. How can you pull out of it? The machinery's already in gear, isn't it?"

I was confused for a moment and blinked. "What? What did you say?"

He sputtered. "Just that the whole thing is rolling now. It's like an assembly line, difficult to stop."

"You said the machinery's in gear."

"So?"

"Oh my God."

"What? What is it?"

I think I put my hands to my throat as if I were about to gag. "You. And de Groot."

"What about us?"

"He knew, didn't he? He knew because you told him. Oh my God, how could I be so stupid?"

"What did he know?" my father asked quietly.

I stood up, laughing weakly, or crying, I'm not sure. "That's why he didn't say anything about my going away. He knew about it all. He didn't say anything about the draft I gave him, either. Only gave me compliments. Because he knew what else was to come. And you told him, didn't you? Didn't you?" I yelled the words and my voice echoed obscenely in the small kitchen.

My father covered his face with his hands and held them there. Without taking them away, he nodded ever so slightly. I seized his wrists. "Why? For god's sakes, tell me why?"

He looked away. "I did it for you."

"Ha! That's a good one. Try again, Professor."

"Okay, okay. Maybe I'm not sure why. Maybe it's the guilt, plaguing me all these years. What I did as a boy and then occupying this higher moral plane in my career. The more I thought about it, the more everything else seemed so pointless. It was a weight that just became too heavy, Bernie. I can't explain it any other way."

"I don't know if I can accept that. If it's good enough."

My father nodded. "I know. And in a way, I can't blame you."

"I thought you hated de Groot."

He shrugged. "He's not a bad publisher, really. Maybe I shortchanged him a little."

"It's a mess, isn't it?" I asked of no one in particular.

We were silent for a long moment. Me standing, my father sitting, hands clasped on his knees. "What are you going to do?"

I knew what he meant but I didn't have an answer. The question just hung there. "I don't know. I bloody well don't know."

43

"Are you coming or what?" Sharon asked. "'Cause if you are, you'd better get a move on." It was Saturday morning. My father was getting married in two hours. "You can't miss your dad's wedding, Bernie. It isn't right."

I looked at her. At my wife. Her face filled with indignation. I still hadn't told her and wasn't sure now if I could. She thought it was because of Katherine that I didn't want to go.

"You go," I said.

"This won't help anything. It's not going to change the fact that they're together. What are you going to do, not talk to him again? You don't know how much longer he's going to be around. It's practically a sin." I didn't say anything. "Well, at least help me with the boys. I think I'm going to murder them. I've got to get my face on."

I helped Sean and Nathan tie their ties. I made sure their shirts were tucked in and their shoes weren't dusty, their hands weren't grubby, and their faces were clean. I made Sean comb his hair twice.

"Aw, Dad," he grumbled, but he went back into the bathroom and dragged the comb through it again.

"Won't you come with us, Dad?" Nathan asked. "Please?" I looked at him in all his scrubbed innocence and my heart melted. Sean came out of the bathroom and somehow, his fly had come undone and one shoelace was untied. I looked at him and shook my head.

"Put your jackets on boys, and I'll meet you downstairs." Nathan exchanged looks with his brother and they went out. Slowly, I went and got dressed but it was with a heavy soul.

About thirty people were gathered in the back yard of my father's house. My brother Harry and his wife. They had no children. My Aunt Tsippy, who was eighty nine and had to sit down on a hard-backed chair which dug itself into the lawn under her weight. There were family friends and colleagues of my father's. Katherine's children and her mother were there. And a few of her co-workers. An open-sided tent had been set up and at the top of the lawn was the makeshift altar. They were to be married by a Unitarian minister, a middle-aged woman with long, gray hair who wore a robe and sandals. A hippy gathering, forty years later. The day was cloudless and the air still.

"Isn't this lovely?" Sharon remarked. She had gone to kiss my father who hovered around nervously, chatting to the guests. Katherine was in hiding somewhere in the house. "I'll just go look in on her," Sharon said and walked away. The boys were running about the yard. They were the only kids, but they always had each other. I didn't watch too closely. My thoughts were elsewhere. They could have nose-dived into a muddy ditch and I wouldn't have noticed or cared.

"Hello Bernard."

"My god, what are you doing here?"

"I was invited," said de Groot. "Lovely day, isn't it? Perfect weather."

"Yeah," I replied listlessly.

"Let me introduce you to my wife. Margaret, this is Bernard Goldman. He's going to be on the best seller lists this fall."

A petite blonde woman pumped my hand. "How thrilling for you. So nice to meet you, Mr. Goldman." De Groot sent Margaret off to get some champagne.

"I didn't know you were married, de Groot."

"Hmm? Oh yes. And I have two children. A girl and a boy. They're both away at University. Lars is at Stanford and Emily is studying pre-med in London."

"Ontario?"

"England, dear boy."

"You surprise me."

De Groot's long face lit up. "I do so enjoy that." He paused. "Well then... what about it?"

"What?"

"You know what? The book of course."

"What about the book?"

"Don't play games with me, Bernard. I have a great deal riding on this, you know. You are a little reticent, is that it?"

"Perhaps." Margaret returned with the champagne. De Groot seemed even taller on uneven ground, accentuated by the habitual white suit and now, broad-brimmed straw hat he wore that shaded his face. The dark glasses made him look even more sinister.

"Ah, thank you my dear. Why don't you introduce yourself to Bernard's wife; Sharon, I believe. She's that striking looking redhead over there."

Margaret looked at him knowingly. "Of course, dear." Then she leaned in to me. "Don't worry, Bernard. Julian seems like an ogre but it's really all a big act."

De Groot smiled indulgently. "Run along now." Then he turned to me. "Where were we?"

"The book."

"Yes. Write it. You won't regret it."

"What makes you so sure?"

"Because I am the publisher and it is my job to know these things."

"You colluded with my father."

"You make it sound like a conspiracy."

"Wasn't it?"

"No, of course not. Your father came to me like a penitent. I was sworn to secrecy. He knew you were clever enough to figure it all out by yourself, old boy. And he was right. And that is why I know this book will work and you are the one to do it up right. Only you, Bernard, there is no one else. I get these feelings about things you know, and I have never been wrong. That's why I am a successful publisher, Bernard. Where a multitude of others have failed miserably. And I know one other thing – that you want more than anything to be a successful writer, hmm?" He took a long slurp of the champagne.

"I wish I could share your certitude," I said bitterly.

De Groot patted me on the back. "You will. You will," he said mysteriously, in a light tone. Then he looked over at the dais. "I see the gathering is about to begin. Come Bernard." De Groot put his arm around my shoulders and moved me alongside him. I sniffed and caught the subtle aroma of lavender. "Together Bernard, we shall make miracles, hmm? Have no fears on such a wonderful and joyous day."

I moved stiffly beside him, slightly out of step, but as we drew up to the edge of the group awaiting the beginning of the ceremony, I caught my father's eye and he smiled at me and nodded. He raised two fingers to his lips and I understood suddenly that I was bound to go ahead. The chain had fallen from my heart. That I would produce a book De Groot could ride up the lists. Oh yes, I would make my father into a ruined god. The world would know him as a fully fleshed human being. And now, illuminated in the sunshine, turning to see his new bride coming towards him with a smile that lifted her expression above us and to him only, I saw that he had moved on to a place where he couldn't be touched. De Groot had turned his attention to the dais where the minister had assumed her position. I felt a hand touch mine and Sharon was beside me. She'd been crying, but she smiled through her tears. I looked down. Sean and Nathan were standing in front of us. Nathan glanced up, and gave me a wink. I pulled the two of them closer to me. I was proud of them, I realized. And wanted them to be proud of me. My mind raced. I saw myself opening the New York Times Book Review. I saw my name and the ranking. Bernard Goldman, I read. Spinning Through Time, the title. On the bestseller list for fourteen weeks.

"Ladies and Gentlemen," said the minister in a calm, serene tone. "We are gathered here…"

44

Almost fifteen weeks later to the day, I cradled an advanced copy of the book in my hands. It was a wonderful, pleasurable feeling; almost sensual. But it was tinged with sadness too, even regret. The night before, my father had called from Israel. He and Katherine had made it there. Isaac had died in the night. He didn't wake up when Gabrielle brought his morning tea. The funeral was today. I could look out now and see it all, my family spinning through the generations. I remained satisfied that the story had been told. Yes, the machinery now moved into high gear. Tomorrow, I left on the promotional tour.

Dear reader,

We hope you enjoyed reading *The Global View.* Please take a moment to leave a review in Amazon, even if it's a short one. Your opinion is important to us.

Discover more books by W.L. Liberman at https://www.nextchapter.pub/authors/wl-liberman

Want to know when one of our books is free or discounted for Kindle? Join the newsletter at http://eepurl.com/bqqB3H

Best regards,
W.L. Liberman and the Next Chapter Team

The story continues in :

A Loafer's Guide To Living (The Goldman Trilogy Book 2) by W.L. Liberman

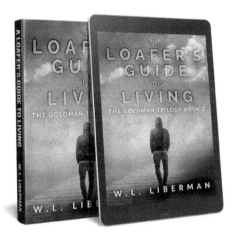

To read first chapter for free, head to:
https://www.nextchapter.pub/book/a-loafers-guide-to-living

About the Author

W.L. Liberman believes in the power of storytelling but is not a fan of the often excruciating psychic pain required to bring stories to life. Truthfully, years of effort and of pure, unadulterated toil is demanded. Not to sugarcoat it, of course, writing is a serious endeavor. It is plain, hard work. If you've slogged away at construction work, at lumberjacking, delivery work, forest rangering, sandwich making, truck driving, house painting, among other things, as I have, writing is far and beyond more rigorous and exhausting. At the end of a long, often tedious, usually mind-cracking process, some individual you don't know pronounces judgment and that judgment is usually a resounding 'No'. This business of writing is about perseverance and stick-to-it-iveness. When you get knocked down and for most of us, this happens frequently, you take a moment to reflect, to self-pity, then get back at it. You need dogged determination and a thick skin to survive. And an alternate source of income.

W.L. Liberman is currently the author of eight novels, two graphic novels and a children's storybook. He is the founding editor and publisher of TEACH Magazine; www.teachmag.com, and has worked as a television producer and on-air commentator.

He holds an Honours BA from the University of Toronto in some subject or other and a Masters in Creative Writing from De Montfort University in the UK. He is married, currently lives in Toronto (although wishes to be elsewhere) and is father to three grown sons.

Also by the Author

- Dasvidaniya

- Looking for Henry Turner

- The Global View (The Goldman Trilogy Book 1)

- A Loafer's Guide To Living (The Goldman Trilogy Book 2)

- Dead Fish Jumping On The Road

9 781034 470618